T0354062

Against the Grain

James Haydock

authorHOUSE®

AuthorHouse™
1663 Liberty Drive
Bloomington, IN 47403
www.authorhouse.com
Phone: 1-800-839-8640

First published by AuthorHouse 08/16/2011

ISBN: 978-1-4634-0641-7 (sc)
ISBN: 978-1-4634-0642-4 (hc)
ISBN: 978-1-4567-9522-1 (ebk)

Library of Congress Control Number: 2011909377

Printed in the United States of America
Bloomington, Indiana

This book is printed on acid-free paper.

Children of the grain toiling in the sun,
Nor was it easy going against the grain.
—John Donne, 1622

Chapter I

He sat before the fireplace and studied the flames. Before supper he had put on three well-seasoned logs, and they had done their job of chasing the chill from the house. Each log had flickered, burst into a blaze of orange and purple, and burned rapidly. Two of them were already falling into red-hot embers, and with iron tongs he added another. The short autumn day was nearly over and a blustery night was fast approaching. A rising wind from the east rustled fallen leaves, whistled around the eaves of the house, and rattled the windows. The fire caught the wind and sprang to life in the iron grate. Tongues of flame cast shifting patterns on the yellow-pine walls, and in the patterns he could see outlines of trees and fields and flowing streams. A young woman brought into the room a kerosene lamp and placed it on a nearby table. Its base was the color of ripe peaches and on it were delicate pink flowers. Instantly the room became brighter and the flickering patterns faded. The time was October in the year 1860. Politicians were crying havoc and prodding the dogs of war. A winter of surmise and cold uncertainty was in the making and sure to come.

The warm luster of the burning lamp settled on Jeremy Heartwood's graying hair and gave it a reddish tint. It reminded his daughter of better days when she was younger and he was stronger. At that time a reddish beard complemented his unruly copper hair, and she was a bouncy little girl in blonde pigtails. Now with winter calling, she was a lively, imaginative, intelligent young woman of twenty-two. In her simple mauve gown with a cambric collar, she embraced her life as she found it but was given to lofty dreams. Her brain rustling with images of a bright future, she wanted conversation with her father but hesitated when he seemed lost in thought. In the kitchen she cleaned the last of the supper dishes and placed them face down on the table for the next meal. She treasured her set of blue-rimmed plates. They had belonged to her mother, who died when she was born.

Catherine was turning from the table in its little alcove off the kitchen to join her father at the fire when they heard a knock on the door. Both of them paused to listen to the sharp tapping on hard wood and did not speak. When darkness came, the door was always locked with a heavy iron bar across it. Even when the weather was warm, especially when home alone, Catherine was careful to lock and bar the door. Painted brown and trimmed in dark green, their farmhouse nestled under a sprawling live oak and blended into the landscape. It was only a mile or so from the larger house of their neighbors but well off the road and isolated. In uncertain and volatile times neither Jeremy nor his daughter could afford to ignore caution.

Beggars sometimes came to their porch and door, even at night, asking for a handout. Scavengers, or grubbers as some people called them, were rapidly increasing in number and came stealthily in darkness but often in broad daylight. Clothed in rags and wearing looks of desperation, they seldom left a house empty-handed. Foragers in groups of half a dozen or more skulked into barns and outlying buildings to steal anything they could carry away on foot. Most of them had once been productive citizens, but unforeseen events had made them rogues of bitter temper. Catherine thought she knew the knock and hoped it meant pleasant company for an hour or so. She wanted to open the door at once, but the times demanded discretion. Glancing at her father, her smooth brow slightly creased, she hesitated.

"No need to worry, Katie" said her father, "but don't take any risks. You can't just fling the door wide open, y'know. It's probably old Harvey here to pick up the soup I promised him. You did save a little from supper I expect. He needs a jug of thick potato soup for his children, and some milk for them too and some corn pone if we have any left."

"I have the food ready for him," Catherine replied, "but I don't think it's Harvey. He has a different knock."

She moved quickly to throw the latch and open the oaken door just wide enough to identify their visitor. The knock of one staccato tap followed by two more had sounded familiar, and the smiling face of the young man in the dusky doorway put her at ease.

"Who is it?" asked Jeremy, rising from his chair.

"It's our good friend Matthew, Papa. Matthew Kingston."

"Ah, hello Matt!" called Jeremy from across the room. "What brings you out on this lusty, gusty autumn night? Come in! Come in and sit a spell. The wind is rattling the rafters, but we have warmth and light here. Katie has soup on the stove and some buttery pone if you'd like a bite."

2

The young man entered, took Catherine's slender hand in his own, clicked his heels together, and bowed from the waist. Quickly catching the tone of his playful behavior, she responded with a smile and a curtsy. It was a game they played for amusement at social gatherings, and now they laughed. His tall, muscular body was plainly clothed in a gray woolen shirt and hard cotton trousers. On his feet were clodhoppers, heavy shoes with thick soles, and yet he moved smoothly with an easy step to the fireside.

"I just came from supper, but knowing how good a cook thy daughter is," he said in Quaker plain speech, "I just might take thee up on that offer of soup and pone before I leave. Right now I have a favor to ask thee."

"Ask away, my boy. Lord knows you and your papa have granted us plenty of favors down through the years. It's about time we repaid a few. What can we do for you?"

"Will you take me in for the night? I know it's short notice, but two traveling Friends came to our house this afternoon and will be there a day or two. Jesse and I gave them our bedroom. Mother put Jesse on a pallet in the kitchen, and I thought you and Catherine might find space for me here. If it's not convenient I can sleep in the shed in spite of that nip in the air."

"It's no inconvenience whatever," replied Jeremy. "Small as it is, you're always welcome in this house. We don't have the luxury of a guest room, as you can see, but we can make a dandy temporary chamber for you. In fact, we can do it now. We'll divide the house like Gaul into three parts. Well, maybe not three parts but three bedrooms when we're done."

Though older than sixty, Jeremy Heartwood was light on his feet. Except for bouts of indigestion that came on without notice, he was glad to tell anyone who would listen that his health was excellent. He was a round and chubby man with sloping shoulders and a thatch of gray hair as thick as in his youth. The copper had faded from each strand of hair, but his weathered face was open and honest with blue-gray eyes that twinkled. His movements were as quick and nimble and nervous as those of the squirrel that scampered among the branches in the live oak outside. In dark trousers and a vest of butternut brown that made him look in the shadowy light somewhat like the squirrel, he was genial and friendly and laughed easily. Though born and bred in England, his speech had a southern twang.

"Katie, bring me that extra quilt from your room."

He went to the one closet in their house and pulled out several two-pronged metal forks larger than common table forks. His daughter brought the old quilt, wondering what he planned to do with it but asking no questions. All her life she had seen her father make something out of nothing. His inventiveness in a time of need always surprised her.

At his feet was a three-legged stool and in his right hand was a hammer. "Now will you lift it up, please, when I get on the stool?"

Briskly he moved to the center of the room where a post supported a roof beam. He mounted the rickety stool, paid no attention to its unsteadiness, and hammered the forks through the quilt into the beam. In minutes they had a thick, opaque curtain to divide the room in half.

"You'll have privacy there," he said, looking into Matthew's smiling face. "All you need do is run the sofa in behind it, and you'll sleep like a stone. My bed is over there near the fire."

"And you'll have warmth too," added Catherine, laughing. "The quilt makes a good wall but doesn't reach to the ceiling or floor."

"It'll do just fine," said Matthew, "and thank you. If you'll hold the curtain up just a little, I'll put the sofa behind it right now."

He rolled up the carpet that covered the wooden floor and began to push the heavy, deerskin couch under the raised quilt. Just as he was passing under, bent over to move the piece, Catherine let the fabric fall on his head and back. In a moment he was enveloped in stifling darkness. The quilt shut out the light and placed him in a prison in which he could barely breathe. In some confusion, after what seemed to him a long time though only seconds, he scrambled to light and freedom.

Both Catherine and her father found her little joke amusing and were laughing at Matthew's reaction. With mock austerity he scolded the young woman, and she laughed all the harder. Her father, sensing a deliberate display of theatrics and thinking it was a happy occasion for the two, smiled broadly. Yet a strange unease had settled on Matthew. Puzzled by what it could mean, he kept the feeling to himself.

Sensing his discomfort, Catherine quietly trained her brown eyes on him to study his face and bearing. As he sat with feet wide apart on the deerskin couch, testing its comfort, she looked him over with that analytical gaze of hers that everyone knew. She had eyes that could see a long way into things. He was tall and strong, healthy and handsome, soft-spoken, gentle of manner, and free of male arrogance. She wanted to believe he was brave as well, but how could she know? Had the quilt suddenly become his shroud? At twenty he was too young to be taken seriously, but she liked him and had known him from the time they were children. He was not yet a man in the eyes of the Quaker elders, nor even the law, but the times would test his mettle as a man as surely as they would test hers as a woman.

3

Jeremy had gone back to the fire to make himself cozy and warm before going to bed. It didn't occur to him that maybe the two young people wanted to sit alone on the couch behind the quilt. So through the barrier that shut them away from him he called out to them.

"Come and sit here, Matt. And you too, Katie. The fire is nearly gone and we have no more logs for tonight. I want to hear about the Friends in your father's house. Have they come to attend the meeting tomorrow?"

"That appears to be their main reason for coming, sir," Matthew replied, ducking under the curtain and taking the chair near the hearth.

"Did they travel by wagon all the way from Philadelphia or from some other place in Pennsylvania?"

"They came from the North. I'm not sure exactly where, but quite a distance I heard. They ran into some difficulty along the way."

"Oh? What kind of difficulty?"

"It appears they got lost on an unfamiliar road and had a problem with unfriendly people. Some thugs demanded to know who they were and where they were going and what they were doing. Two men tried to rob them."

"Oh, I'm hearing about things like that too often now."

"Well, they managed to fend off the robbers somehow—I don't know how—and find their way here without any more trouble."

"Are they young men? Strong men?"

"No, not really. But one of them is a feisty little man and perhaps resisted. The other is tall and thin and not in the best of health. They came in a wagon with a couple of strong horses and plenty of supplies covered by canvas, but both of them were very tired when they got to our house."

"I don't doubt it! Had to be a long, long trip over bad roads."

"And not the best kind of weather for traveling, but they intend to go farther south from here. Father cautioned them not to go deeper in these parts the way things are now, but they are men with a cause and headstrong."

Just as the two began to talk Catherine came and sat on the three-legged stool close to the glowing embers. She told them she wanted to nurse her knees before the fire and warm her feet before bedtime. Mainly she wanted to participate in the conversation but reluctantly held her tongue. She was a wholesome young woman with fine, creamy skin and blonde hair and looked younger than twenty-two. Taller than her round and chubby father, her body was firm and feminine. Her long legs and slender waist gave substance and shape to the dress she was wearing. Its color was a pale and delicate purple, not the ubiquitous Quaker gray worn by most women in their community. As she sat on the stool her flared skirt draped gracefully over her knees and reached almost to her ankles. On her feet, close to the dying fire, she wore dark green slippers made of felt.

Near the neckline of her dress and to one side she had pinned a tiny bunch of red autumn berries. They accented her beauty, and her father saw nothing wrong with that. With each change of season she decorated the walls of their dwelling with scarlet berries, yellow leaves, glistening holly, and sprigs of evergreen. Now in the autumn of 1860 her seasonal decoration glowed with sheaves of golden grain.

Chapter 2

Jeremy Heartwood lived with his daughter not far from the sea in North Carolina. Blue Anchor was the name of the village, and to every child who would listen Jeremy explained how it got that unusual name. An early farmer plowing a field in 1815 snagged a rusty anchor embedded in the soil. No one could explain how the anchor was found miles away from the sea in a field recently cleared of woods. The plowman scraped off the rust, painted the anchor cobalt blue, and displayed it in front of his cabin. In time, as more people decided to live there, the hamlet came to be known as Blue Anchor. By the time it grew into a village, its name had become official. Nearly 400 residents, mainly farmers and tradesmen, lived there. A separate list counted the number of slaves in the community, and by 1860 it was a short list. The charm of Blue Anchor, nestled in the midst of fertile farms near the Great Dismal Swamp, would diminish when the war began but endure. Soldiers in blue and gray would come and go and desecrate the land but do little to mar the natural beauty that changed with the seasons.

The Heartwood farm with soil as flat as a watermelon seed was situated only a few miles from the swamp. On a clear day one could see open fields as far as the eye could reach. In the swamp, however, under its thick canopy of trees, the sharpest eye could penetrate but a few hundred feet. The farm had rich and carefully tilled acres but also boasted a brook of clear water, patches of live oaks, and a stand of tall pines left untouched as thick and natural woods. The neighboring farm, owned by David and Rachel Kingston, had larger fields under cultivation but shared the same meandering brook that flowed lazily toward the swamp. The two families had struggled and prospered in this region longer than two decades.

Jeremy Heartwood and David Kingston came from England as young men in the third decade of the nineteenth century. Kingston met and married a New Englander named Rachel Moore, and within a year they had a little daughter they named Gracie. In the meantime they opened a small grocery store in their neighborhood to eke out a living. It didn't make them rich but kept the wolf from the door and food on the table.

Heartwood came to America from Surrey with a delicate wife who had spent her childhood in London. She loved the streets and squares and bustle of the big city, but with some reluctance went with him to America. On a steamer they crossed the Atlantic in steerage, a voyage of more than three weeks, and in the congestion and confusion below decks she was sick most of the time.

Upon arriving in America, though pale from the ordeal of crossing the sea, she was remarkably pretty. An air of serenity surrounded her and was noticed by all who met her. Her complexion was high and clear with not a single mark to mar it, and her gray-green eyes were large and misty. Looking at her fine form and lovely face, one thought she was in the best of health and in control of any conceivable combination of circumstances. But after one or two years in their new home the roses fled from her cheek, and she seemed to slip into decline. They went to Boston to live, but Martha Higgins Heartwood did not like the bleak winds of New England. For three winters she urged her husband to move to a more gentle climate.

Before that could happen the fragile woman died in childbirth, leaving behind a bereaved husband and a daughter who inherited her beauty. In a brief and poignant ceremony with few people attending, she was buried in a Boston graveyard the first week of May in 1838. The sun was shining when the casket was lowered into the ground, but an hour later a heavy rain turned the gravesite muddy. Heartwood went back the next day to make it tidy, and later he put loam on the bare mound to make it green with grass. Also he erected a slab of stone at the head of her grave and paid a mason to engrave it. One may read even today the terse inscription: *Martha Higgins Heartwood, Wife of Jeremy, Died Too Soon.* Her husband would not marry again.

2

Jeremy Heartwood liked Boston and thought he could make a good living there. In the Irish neighborhood where they lived in cramped quarters not far from the tenderloin district, people on the brink of poverty were sometimes drunk and disorderly but often friendly and generous. The city's business district, not far from the big houses of the rich, boasted broad and airy streets lined with shops that seemed to be flourishing. Finding work was not a big problem, and for a time Jeremy was an apprentice printer for a local newspaper. It was a dirty job that stained his hands with ink and blackened his fingernails, but lifted his spirits as he came to believe it promised something better. A well-trained printer with sound credentials had a future. However, when she was alive, Martha had wanted a milder climate. So Jeremy decided he would move southward to honor her memory and make a living by farming. He found an old map of the eastern United States, closed his eyes, moved his hand in a circle, and put his finger on the state of North Carolina.

"I will go there," he said to his friend, "and raise my daughter there."

"If you must go," David Kingston asserted after talking the matter over with his wife Rachel, "we will go with you. If we go, and of course we shall, my wife will look after your daughter."

In the middle of summer, with scant hopes for earning money and with little more than he was able to carry in an old wagon, Heartwood began the long and uncertain journey southward. In a larger wagon, his wife caring for the child, Kingston followed. Their odyssey took them to the coastal plain of North Carolina, close to the Virginia border and not far from the busy seaports nearby. There they found land that could be bought on easy terms. The lush acres were suitable for farming but covered with trees and tangled undergrowth which had to be cleared. It was labor that broke the strong backs of many good men, but Heartwood and Kingston endured. The timber they cleared from the land they sold to help pay off the mortgage.

The winters were mild compared to those of New England, and so temporary cabins on semi-cleared land met their need for shelter. Food was often scarce though wildlife was plentiful, and they learned to shoot well. Also they planted vegetables that could be preserved for use in winter. When the first crops came in, they were able to make steady payments on the land until they owned it. In time they built simple but comfortable homes, cleared more land, brought it under cultivation, and began to reap abundant harvests. Slowly they established two prosperous farms adjacent to one another. The days of incessant struggle were good, they agreed years later in calm and comfortable reminiscence, but not always good.

As they trudged southward through the heat of summer and the chill of autumn, Rachel Kingston cared for the motherless infant with warm integrity. She had an infant of her own a few months older than Heartwood's daughter. The care and feeding of another child placed a burden on the young woman, but she did it without a murmur. As infants

Catherine Heartwood and Gracie Kingston were often thought to be sisters. With fair skin and wispy blonde hair, they even looked alike. As children in rural North Carolina, growing up in a world that was never easy, the little girls were inseparable. Then one dark day in November, Gracie died of pneumonia in her ninth year and the bond was broken.

Losing her first-born child, Rachel Kingston lost the self-control her Quakerism had taught her and cried out like a stricken animal. Wringing her hands in deep despair, she prayed for deliverance; she wanted to die. The surviving playmate was inconsolable as well. The men of the two families were helpless to do anything, knowing only that time would heal the wound. They agonized over the loss of the child but felt that all who loved her would be stronger for it. They went on working, sharing a dream and struggling to make it real. Not a day passed when they didn't assert their determination to make a good life for their families in spite of Gracie's tragic death. Rachel Kingston, bereft and grief-stricken, came to love Catherine as though she were Gracie and went on with her daily life.

3

They were strong and capable in those years and not easily defeated by adversity. But losing Gracie made the Kingstons value their son Matthew even more. He was two years younger than Catherine Heartwood, called Katie by her doting father. Some years later another son was born to Rachel and David, and they called him Jesse. The boy would quickly become a sturdy, bright-eyed little fellow with a quick intelligence that triggered a sense of mischief. Then to their amazement a bright little girl came to them four years after Jesse, and they called her Anna. Because she was the youngest and arrived by accident, the whole family received her as a rare and special gift from a loving God.

In the fall of 1860 Jesse was ten years old and big for his age. Anna was six and growing like a weed. She was a bossy little girl at times but blessed with a flower-like purity of personality. Her classmates in her first year at school were neither plain nor pretty, and neither was Anna, but she was winsome and different. Her finely chiseled face was like pale ivory, its delicate sheen accented by vivid blue eyes and a perpetual smile. Her body was thin and supple and full of energy. Absurd little things made her happy, and the pleasure she found in little things made others love her.

She lived every day in faultless and innocent joy, and often she revealed an intense curiosity beyond that of other children. Once in summer she sat for an hour cross-legged in the sun, watching an ant struggle with a leaf many times its size. What did she see in that little drama? Others saw only the leaf and the ant and the hot yellow ground on which it toiled. Anna saw more.

Jesse with flaxen hair and the broad shoulders of his father was becoming handsome. His wind-blown mane was the color of wheat in sunshine, and in summer his face was always tan. As a growing spirit of revolt stirred within him, his favorite activity, so to speak, was running barefoot with the hare. But as a well-taught child of Quakers his instinct rode with the hounds. He knew he would never be walloped for misbehavior, but he dreaded the kind of scolding his mother was fully capable of delivering. Also he knew the limits of his freedom and so managed to stay out of trouble most of the time. For both of the children a stern lecture from their dignified father was as good as a whipping. Many parents in the middle of the nineteenth century believed that sparing the rod spoiled the child. These Quakers, going against the grain, reared their children with discipline but also with kindness and a generous dollop of patience.

The Kingston family by 1860 was as complete as it would ever be. Gracie had been taken from them, but other children had filled the void, and they looked forward to many years of productive, happy lives. If Rachel had been a few years younger, she would have had more children. Also, if Jeremy Heartwood had been able to meet and marry a healthy young woman in those days, his family would have grown too. Even so, he thanked his God and his lucky saints for the daughter who graced his life, for she had brought him steady and reliable happiness. Together in the little house under the sprawling live oak the two of them reaped the rewards of hard work and sober living and were loved by all who knew them.

Working together, the men honed their skills on hardship, facing their problems with persistence and solving them one at a time. Though both avowed they were resolute pragmatists, they were also dreamers. Chatting at twilight when their work was done, they saw themselves in contest with unrelenting forces stronger than they but never smarter. They were men with brain as well as brawn, and they were determined to wrest a good living from nature even when nature resisted. To boost his confidence, Jeremy often quoted a line from Wordsworth: *Nature never did betray the heart that loved her.* He knew the line was not in touch with reality, and so did his friend Kingston, but it became nonetheless a mantra for the two of them, a Vedic verse of wishful thinking. Both of them knew that nature is merely there, doing her thing whether man likes it or not, and doing it without knowing that man exists. And yet in time perhaps those natural forces personified would show their tender side and treat them kindly. Now more than two decades later, they found themselves in harmony with nature, but living in a man-made social order that thrived on forced labor. Trained in Quaker principles of equality, they believed the system was evil to the core and would eventually die of attrition. It would not.

4

Heartwood had left England not to obtain greater freedom to exercise a simple faith, but to find economic opportunity and a better life. A dissenter in sympathy with the Quakers but not in full agreement with their doctrine until later, he had fashioned for himself in a family of Puritans a personal religion based on a love of nature after reading Wordsworth. That religion he could practice at any time in any place without fear of reprisal. In later years, devouring the works of Thomas Carlyle, he had stitched into his philosophical tapestry the value of work to bring one closer to God. *There is endless salvation in work,* the Scotsman had asserted in thirty-nine volumes praising silence. Reading those words, it seemed to Jeremy they were penned for his benefit alone. In his youth, badgered by poverty and hardship, he had found his salvation in work. In a long conversation he aired his views before David Kingston who dissected them as they talked to find they were similar to his own. Chatting into the wee hours of the night, Kingston explained the tenets of his faith as he knew them, and Heartwood in time became a Quaker.

Subscribing to Quaker beliefs that worked well for him, David Kingston placed high value on the worth and dignity of all human beings. At quarterly meetings he argued that even the lowest beggar has fundamental rights, and no government should have the power to seize those rights. Perhaps the most important of all human rights, he asserted whenever he had the chance, was the right to human freedom. As a young man, when he settled in the South, the institution of slavery had struck him as peculiar and oppressive, but at the time he was too busy making a living to oppose it and had in fact yielded to it. As the years passed, however, he had second thoughts and worked diligently with the Society of Friends to abolish it. The moral wrong of slavery was to him as ugly as the moral wrong of war. Both were evil. In the glare of disturbing social and political events filtering southward from Lincoln's Washington, both weighed heavily upon him.

For several years David had worked hard with willing blacks whom he treated well. With their help he built a prosperous and satisfying rural life in a pleasant place. In time he freed his slaves, declaring he would never again be the owner of another human being. They were free to leave or to work (if they chose) for a reasonable income. Most of them remained on the Kingston farm, but some with an itch to see the larger world drifted away. Heartwood and other Quakers in the community had followed David's example, and in their common cause had become a close-knit group. However, some of their neighbors, God-fearing Bible thumpers who accepted slavery as an economic necessity, cried out against them. Heaping stigma and opprobrium upon them and vilifying them in some of their churches, southern Protestants and a few Catholics called the Quakers misguided abolitionists.

Later the peace-loving Quakers would be called pacifists, not an inaccurate term, but also dirty names not worth repeating here. When the Civil War began to batter their lives, Quakers in both the North and South would attempt to resist its ulcerous violence and inhumanity, and for going against the grain some would be ostracized and spat upon. A small group in eastern North Carolina, citizens of a village with a distinctive name, would endure consistent, almost daily outrage but manage to survive. Armies in conflict with a mission to destroy each other would also hurt the ground itself and anyone in their path. For the duration of the war, they would tramp through Blue Anchor and its fertile farms again and again.

The story went that a young man more foolish than brave stood in the path of advancing soldiers with a pitchfork. For them the pitchfork was a weapon. He was slain before he knew what hit him. Later it was said that while making hay the man went on the road with the implement in his hands merely to look at the soldiers. Whatever his reason for being there, the result was the same. Any person, accidentally or otherwise, who dared oppose the raw power of troops on the move was shot and tossed into a ditch. It mattered not who he was, nor what force he stood against. Both armies were deadly and primed to kill anything or anyone standing in their way.

All the Quakers in eastern North Carolina were taught to be courteous and careful in the presence of troops. But the North viewed them as enemies because they were Southerners and the South despised them as stubborn pariahs. Consistently they refused to bear arms in defense of the Southern way of life, and for that they were persecuted. In the fall of 1860, the Quakers of Blue Anchor knew that swift, irrevocable change was producing uncertain and dangerous times. Prudent and calm and disposed to wait, not one of them cared to predict the course of future events.

Chapter 3

At the Heartwood farm those inside the snug little house paid little attention to the unquiet evening outside. The wind whistled around the stone chimney and a branch of the towering live oak brushed the roof. Twigs flying in the wind struck the window panes with force, and the windows rattled.

"It seems we're in for a storm," Matthew observed, quietly speaking to Catherine. "That wind is picking up, sounds like a cat fight on the roof."

"It always blows like that during this time of year," said Jeremy, reassuring his guest. "We needn't worry. This little house is like its owner, old and creaky and weathered but durable."

"And it's warm too, Papa. You mustn't forget that!" joked Catherine. "It's strong and well-built and warm! And it has gables with wooden-lace trim in dark green. Not every dwelling has that."

"Exactly!" said Matthew, laughing "It's a fancy house, well-built and comfortable, and smells good too!"

"Oh, then it's surely not like me!" Jeremy retorted. "You're smelling the herbs and spices that Katie brings into the house."

In the midst of the banter they heard another sound, sharper and more pronounced than the wind or brushing branch, a knock on the door.

"Wonder who that could be," Catherine mused.

And then she remembered. Harvey was there for the soup and was late. She recognized his knock: two hollow taps, a pause, and two more taps. At the stove she poured the simmering soup into an ample earthen jug. Beside it lay several pieces of cornbread wrapped in a cloth. With the food in hand, she opened the door to greet a thin black man who had once been their slave. Later he became a free worker for wages, but had to leave work when tuberculosis afflicted him. The father of four children, he was rapidly aging and looked older than his years.

Harvey cherished his liberty and often spoke of it as the most valuable commodity any person could own. But now in grievous times he worried about the safety of his family. If they remained in the South, all of them could be taken captive and resold. He had been resold only once in his life.

His original master, a German immigrant named Herman Heckrodt, had sold him to Jeremy who eventually freed him. Now he lived with his wife and children in a cabin on Jeremy's land. Once he asked if he could be called Harvey Heartwood because he didn't like the German name. Jeremy thought it over and concluded that Heckrodt was his legal name, and he should keep it. Besides, Jeremy told him, Harvey Heartwood sounded a bit comical. Harvey Heckrodt was a somber name and dignified.

"I would of been here earlier," he said by way of apology, "but my ol' lady, ain't feelin' too good, and I didn't want no chillen coming out on a night like this. It's chilly, y'know, and windy and real dark too."

"We don't mind you're late," said Catherine. "And those are good reasons. I hope your wife will be feeling much better when morning comes. Give her a bowl of this soup with corn pone and bacon."

"Oh we don't have no bacon, Miz Catherine. That got et up a long time ago, but I sure do thank you and yore daddy for all you doing for us."

"We can spare a few slices of bacon," Catherine assured him. "Just put them in a skillet and fry them nice and crisp and pour the grease into the soup. There's nothing like bacon grease to flavor a good potato soup."

In a moment she was back at the door with the bacon. Jeremy was aware of what she was doing but didn't protest. His generous and loving daughter was charitable to a fault, and he liked her all the more for that.

"I'm awfully glad to have this," Harvey said, taking the food with a nod of his graying head. "I'm more than glad to have it. I know it's gonna make my Susan feel a whole lot better."

"And what about you?" asked Catherine. "Is that cough any better?"

"Well, it ain't no worse, Miz Catherine. But it's bothersome. Don't have no medicine for it, but Molly Danmar done said she gonna bring me some."

"Oh, I hope she does. Is there something we can do? I can throw on a shawl and go to your place. Matthew can come along too."

"Oh, no, Miz Catherine. That ain't necessary. We gonna be jus' fine."

Jeremy was standing beside his daughter with milk from the cellar. It was rich with yellow specks of fat and thick. He had poured almost a gallon into a pewter container and placed it in a box to make it easier to carry.

"This milk is fresh and good-tasting and will make Susan feel better I think. You take some too, Harvey, and be sure to give some to your children. If you need any help from us, anything at all, just let us know."

"I will," replied the visitor, placing the soup and rolls in the box and turning to leave. "Thank you, Mistah Heartwood, and you too Miz Catherine. We gonna be all right, I jus' know it. The good Lord ain't forgot us yet."

Shivering in his threadbare coat and raising the collar to his chin, he strode quickly to the road and disappeared behind the hedge. The night was cloudy, but the autumn moon edged into view and threw a daub of dappled light upon his path. He walked along as fast as he could, singing in a deep baritone an old spiritual he had learned as a child: *I got wings, you got wings, all God's chillen got wings. All God's chillen got wings.* Even though his voice was thin and husky, the haunting melody of the old song soared upward to the moon.

2

Catherine closed the door, put the iron bar across it, and came back to the fireplace. In the grate were smoldering embers red as blood. As Jeremy went to check on the livestock and bar the rear door, she stooped to cover them with ashes. Only in coldest weather did the fire burn at night.

"Let me do that for you," Matthew insisted, his shoulder touching hers. "Did I tell you that father's traveling friends brought along two big boxes of clothes? Tomorrow at our house they will go to people who need them."

"My papa needs a new hat. The last time it rained in the night he jumped out of bed and stuffed his good one in a broken window pane. He was too sleepy to know what he was doing."

Her musical voice was lilting and light of tone and her story funny, but she didn't laugh and neither did he.

"Jacob Darboy was supposed to come from his store with new glass but never did. We heard later there's no glass to be found anywhere."

"Everything is scarce these days. Darboy said in August we would have new metal hinges for the barn doors in a week. It's October and we're still waiting, and I think we'll have to settle for leather. Even leather isn't so easy to find anymore and forget about new boots. Oh, the boxes from the North! What needest thou, my lady," he asked playfully, "a new dress?"

"Well, this old one," she muttered with some embarrassment, fingering the dress and smoothing a wrinkle, "is . . . well . . . old."

She was laughing now, and Matthew shared her laughter. He picked up the berries that had fallen from her bodice to the floor as she rose from the hearth. They lay warm between his fingers and he looked at them.

"Would this color do?"

"Bright red?" exclaimed Catherine with mock horror. "Do you really see me as that kind of woman? I surely hope not! I must have something gray to honor a long tradition, something plain and simple."

"Thy hair is not gray," he replied in traditional Quaker speech, "and thy looks are not plain."

He was smiling as he spoke, and she could see a twinkle in his eye.

"My hair is surely not gray but not red either!" she retorted. "Anyway, how would thee know if I'm plain or not? Do you really look at my looks?"

Before he could answer she withdrew to her bedroom and shut the door. Behind it, quickly donning her night clothes, she stifled a desire to laugh. Afterwards she was puzzled by a feeling of excitement that came over her. In her comfortable feather bed with its smoke-colored eiderdown, she nestled her blonde head on a fat pillow and listened to the wind rattling the roof. She thought of Harvey, remembering his infirmity, and hoped he got home safely. Her father, snug and warm in the large oaken bed he once shared with his wife in New England, was drifting into sleep. Matthew in the little room created by the quilt lay wide awake on the hard deerskin couch. A blanket covered the couch, and yet its smooth and tough leather felt cold. He would lie awake for an hour.

In changing times these three shared a common cause: to weather any storm that came their way. Each of them, falling slowly into slumber, wondered what tomorrow would bring. Outside, perched high on a limb of the sprawling oak and oblivious to human concern, a blinking horned owl heard a rustling of leaves. A sleek nocturnal rodent scurried along the base of the house. The bird raised its feathers on either side of its large eyes, hooted twice as if to give warning, and swept downward on its prey.

3

Catherine Heartwood with abundant energy had been a light sleeper all her life. When others complained of a poor night's rest and spoke of hearing nocturnal sounds, she could relate in detail all that went on through the night. It seemed to those close to her that she never slept through the slumber part of any night, even when she was a child, and yet when morning came she arose well rested and eager to face the day. On some occasions when half awake, she once confessed, she heard celestial melodies riding the air around her. Though Blue Anchor could boast only one or two old men who sawed on fiddles and one or two prepubescent girls learning to play the piano, Catherine loved music. Particularly she liked the intricate music of a full orchestra, but in a pinch even a barrel organ would do. Once in a larger community she went eagerly to a concert and sat as close to the orchestra as she could get. The first sigh of the instruments seemed to free a pent-up bird beating with fluttering wings against her rib cage, a living thing wanting release. The oboes and clarinets of Schubert's *Unfinished Symphony*, and the stringed instruments responding in counterpoint, lifted her to blue skies, gentle breezes, and pristine beaches bathed in sunshine.

This night on going to bed, she had listened to the wind as familiar music and soon fell asleep. Later as the howling wind diminished and ceased to blow, she found herself wide awake and listening to the clock strike three. Sitting up in bed, she thought she heard footsteps near the house. In the barn the livestock seemed restive and not at peace. She had heard that foragers were in the area, creeping from farm to farm and stealing anything they could get their hands on. The thought that strangers could be lurking near the house, even those with no intent to do harm, frightened her. Rumor had it that a woman her age was molested by night prowlers when she grabbed a broom and threatened to strike them. Instead of running away, they stripped her to the waist and danced around her cackling and gesticulating. In minutes they closed the circle tighter, pounced upon her, and pinned her to the ground. When two men with rifles came running from the house, they let the woman go and dissolved like swamp phantoms into the night.

Catherine huddled deeper in her blankets, visions of violence running through her head, her rich imagination overly active. Her cozy bed was no longer warm, for something strange and cold and stark had barged into the room and was hovering nearby. Shivering in her blankets and her double-knit nightgown, she waited for a beefy fist to pound on the front door. Tense and alert for any sound she might identify, she waited. It never came. Reassured by the silence, she composed herself and slept.

The night passed without incident. Dawn came with a scarlet sky, and then the sun. She was up with the sun, smiling and pleasant and ready to make breakfast.

Through the double window that flooded her kitchen with sunlight she saw a man coming toward the house. Her instinct was to call her father, but then she recognized the form and gait of Matthew Kingston. To her surprise, he had arisen an hour before and had milked the cows. In each hand he was carrying a large pail of milk. His broad, handsome face seemed at peace with the world and he was whistling a familiar tune. She opened the back door for him, and he put the milk on the side bar without spilling a drop.

"What a beautiful morning!" he exclaimed, taking a deep breath and flashing a smile that revealed white and even teeth. "I can't remember seeing the fall colors so bright, so glorious. Believe me, every leaf is a miracle! Every lingering flower is pearly with dew. And the sun is already warm."

"I was surprised to see you coming from the barn so early. I thought you and Papa were still asleep. I heard gentle snoring from Papa all night and thought I would let you both sleep until I had breakfast ready."

"Oh, I've been up at least an hour. I milked the cows and fed the stock and groomed the horses. Found a brush and curry-comb in the harness room with collars, tugs, and traces on the wall. Thought I'd give your father a little more sleep, you know. I hope you don't mind."

"Why should we mind?" asked Jeremy appearing suddenly behind his daughter and stuffing his shirttail inside his trousers. "Before winter comes you can split a couple cords of wood, slaughter a hog and dress it, salt the pork, and stow it in the cellar. Come spring you can plow and sow the back forty. Nope, we don't mind at all, do we Katie?"

With a mischievous wink, impressed by his own wit, he kissed his daughter on the cheek and sat down to eat. She placed on the table hot, yellow cornbread fresh from the oven, scrambled eggs from a black-iron skillet, sausages simmering in their own heat, and fresh-brewed coffee. Butter and cream in whimsical ceramic dishes adorned the table, and so did the blue-rimmed plates with their matching cups.

"Sit down, Matt, and dig in while this good food is hot. I'm hungry as a horse. You must be too."

He passed the platter of eggs and sausage to his guest. Holding the pot's handle with a dishcloth, Catherine poured the coffee.

"We don't have any sugar," she said apologetically, "but there's a bit of honey in the cupboard if you need to sweeten your coffee."

"I take mine black and bitter," said Matthew with a hint of masculine pride, scooping the eggs to his plate and forking three sausages. "I have to eat and run, you know, have to be home to help the folks with the meeting."

They ate breakfast with a hearty appreciation of Catherine's cooking and talked about the meeting. Weighty matters would be discussed that day, but for now they would keep the business of the morning light. In half an hour their breakfast was over. Jeremy was telling a good story and Matthew was laughing. Catherine was wearing a smile and clearing the dishes. Her blonde hair, rimming her face and shining in the morning sunlight, resembled fine autumn gossamer.

"I really must go," said Matthew, "and thank you for that delicious breakfast and your generous hospitality."

"You're welcome," replied Catherine, washing the dishes.

"Don't mention it, my boy," chorused Jeremy. "I'm glad we could be of service. We'll be seeing you again at the meeting."

As they stood in the doorway, Matthew glanced at the tall clock in the corner, its shining brass pendulum swinging back and forth. The clock was very old but kept perfect time with a comforting tick-tock, tick-tock. He recalled hearing the pleasant sound of the old clock all through the night and waking up with a start when it clanged at midnight. It had come in Jeremy's wagon from New England to North Carolina and was now regarded as an heirloom. It struck on the hour every hour. At noon and midnight it set forth such a clamor as to make the little house tremble.

On the porch Matthew leveled his eyes on Catherine's pretty face and wished her good day. They would see each other again at the Meeting House and maybe have lunch together. After the meeting he would help her mount her pony, and they would ride home together. A gallant little bow signaled his departure. He strode briskly down the path, crossed behind the hedge to reach the white-washed fence that marked the boundary line between the two farms, vaulted over it, and made his way home using the shortcut.

"Our friend seemed quite chipper this morning," observed Catherine. "He said he actually slept well on the old couch."

"Yes, I think he did," said her father, sitting down at the small desk near the window. "We need to watch the time, Katie, and not be late. I need to review some of the points I hope to make at the meeting."

It was Catherine's cue to prepare for the day as quietly as she could. "Ready for more coffee?" she asked.

Chapter 4

As late as the middle of the nineteenth century, in the rural regions of North Carolina, residents owned few wheeled vehicles that could be used for comfortable travel. The unpaved roads were rocky and dusty in dry weather and muddy quagmires in rainy weather. Near the coast in the outlying districts of Blue Anchor, the shifting sand and gravel were almost as troublesome as the mud. Every homestead had at least one all-purpose wagon, but the vehicle bounced with some violence over sturdy roots in the road and often got stuck in wet sand. At least once a year harried citizens petitioned the bureaucrats in Raleigh to improve the poor roads, complaining of the gride of wheels in sand, but they claimed lack of funds and did nothing.

David Kingston hoped to solve the problem when he bought a coach for his family. For centuries a symbol of prosperity and good fortune, the coach was a practical solution and vastly more comfortable than a wagon. Even though David placed little value on material things and didn't cultivate pride of place, travelers on the road saw the owner of a coach as a person who had risen in society and was due respect because he had earned it. The driver on the high seat bellowed with laughter as anyone passing gave the vehicle plenty of room. When Matthew vaulted over the fence and came to the house, the handsome old coach was in the backyard ready for two broad and strong horses to pull it. Jesse and Anna, standing by the carriage in their special go-to-meeting clothes, wanted to watch the harnessing.

Visitors had come to the house, and that meant a change of routine for the children. It was the change that delighted them. On this day, instead of remaining home to do chores, they would sit side by side with adults at the Quarterly Meeting. When the break came at noon they would have good things to eat, tasty food prepared by many hands, and freedom to run and play with their friends. They had heard tales of how long and boring a meeting could be, but all their lives they had been carefully taught the virtue of patience. They assured their parents they would not squirm with boredom or whisper to each other, but practice firm self-control.

An ancient servant who had been on the farm many years brought the horses over to the carriage, and Matthew helped with the harnessing. Moses was now the family coachman. Though religious in his own way, he had no problem with pride as a deadly sin. He was proud of his job and amused by the envy it created among those less fortunate. His shoulders rounded by toil and moil when he was young, he sat proudly on the high front seat. His head touched the clouds as he drove spirited horses and waved to persons he passed on the road. Roots in the road were a bother, but in time he learned how to cross them without violent jarring. When at times a wheel of the carriage sank into the sand, he found youthful help to extricate the vehicle. His age gave him certain rights.

Jesse wanted to sit on the high seat and ride beside Moses. He asked Matthew if it would be all right.

"It's not dangerous at all," he said defensively.

"You will have to ask Papa about that," replied his brother. "Anna will sit behind me on Caesar. I'll strap on the pillion for her."

"Will he go slow?" asked Anna apprehensively.

She had once been on the powerful black horse when he broke into a canter and dashed through a grove of trees and careened across a stony creek and galloped through a corn field. The stalks of corn whipped her legs and made them bleed, but the stallion stopped as soon as they were out of the corn. It was a joy for her to ride with her brother, but the remembrance of that event was fearful. She was a sensitive child with an awesome memory and a wholesome love of colorful objects, soft things, and fresh flowers. Her favorite toy was a smiling rubber doll in a pink dress, and she liked very much her stuffed wooly lamb with button eyes.

"I will keep him quiet," assured Matthew, smiling at the small figure in a large sunbonnet. "Don't let him see that head rigging, though. He might take it for a barn door and run for it. Now you run to the house."

"I will skip instead," she retorted, already showing independence. "Running is something boys do. They always run. I like to skip."

Matthew put the saddle on Caesar, attached the pillion, and walked the horse behind the carriage to the front porch. On the verandah the two visitors from the North were talking casually with David Kingston and his wife Rachel. The woman stood under a lattice which supported a dormant rose bush. The tentacles of the roaming bush almost touched the soft grays of her bonnet and shawl. They lacked the brilliance of summer but displayed a few clusters of yellow in the midst of deep green.

Stepping onto the porch, Matthew reached up and snapped off a small faded rose. With exaggerated gallantry he presented the rose to his mother.

"With this rose I honor thee and thy good works!" he announced with a theatrical flourish.

She smiled graciously and thanked him with mocking good humor.

"Well now! Aren't you the gentleman! I do declare!"

She held the rose gingerly between slim fingers and fondly looked at it. The petals were dusty now and no longer vibrant. She remembered a verse she had read about roses fading as summer fades. But this rose would no longer be exposed to the elements and would fade no more. She would keep it close to her heart and care for it. Years later someone found its petals pressed and preserved between the pages of a thick book.

2

A tall, angular, taciturn man known to Matthew as Mifflin, was leaning against the wall looking on. His face was clean of line but sallow and made of leather. His deep-set eyes were like glassy marbles in the leather. Nodding approval as he shifted his position, he seemed embarrassed by the sentimentality of the scene. David Kingston, stepping away and moving toward the coach, chuckled with satisfaction. The quiet man nodded only, and his companion went on talking. In his middle forties and growing stout, Jacob Pembroke wore a scraggly beard accented by fair skin. Though square and short and becoming florid of face, he was powerfully built. He spoke with a cadence more rapid than Matthew was accustomed to hearing, for he had lived most of his life in Pennsylvania. He seemed more energetic than the tall man and more alive. He was earnest when he spoke.

David Kingston stood beside the coach to help his guests enter. With a signal to Moses to climb to the driver's seat, he assisted them as they placed a foot on the high step to move inside.

"This step is ungainly and higher than it ought to be," he remarked. "Some later models had fold-down steps that almost touched the ground but not this one. I could never understand how women in heavy skirts manage these things. As you can see, it's hard enough for a man in trousers."

It was a genial comment intended to entertain, but unwittingly David had mentioned a social problem that irritated his wife. Rachel had spoken at a Monthly Meeting on the cumbersome costume of women and how it impeded their daily lives. Now she could have made spirited reply to her husband's comment but chose to remain silent. She had once seen a young man strip off his clothes and dive into a pond to rescue a drowning child. It was a valiant act that moved her deeply but also set her to thinking.

"Why can't women do that?" she asked her companion. "We're not lacking in courage, and we could be taught to swim."

"Yes, we could be taught to do anything a man can do," her friend replied, "but I doubt it will happen soon. Do you really think a woman in the clothing we must wear could do what he did?"

Rachel was a willowy girl at that time, a member of the weaker sex, but already in rebellion against the way a stiff and stultified society viewed the activities and abilities of women.

"Women could do that if given the chance," she insisted.

"Well, maybe. But would you strip down to almost nothing as he did?"

As Rachel asserted her independence and pleaded for equal rights, she could feel her warm blood rushing to her neck and face. A young woman in her underwear, springing into action and emerging wet and revealing like the sirens of old, was an image yet to be accepted even by her.

In the heavy coach the conversation continued, monopolized by the man with the florid face. John Mifflin, nodding in acquiescence some of the time and looking at objects flashing past the window most of the time, said nothing. David interjected a comment now and then and so did Rachel, but Pembroke with eyes flashing did most of the talking. Jesse sat with Moses on the high seat, and Matthew followed on Caesar with Anna clinging to his waist. The road had ruts from a recent rain but was covered with pine-needles which softened the ride and muted the sound of wheels and hoofs. They were on their way to the Meeting House and to a meeting viewed by their fellow Quakers as one of considerable gravity. The matters to be discussed would affect not only those present, but future generations as well.

They would be talking about slavery and the dire necessity to abolish an institution they viewed from all accounts as evil and oppressive. At least one among them would remind the others of the first protest issued against slavery in 1688. It came from the Quakers of Germantown, a village near Philadelphia. From that year onward, at regular intervals, the Society of Friends issued appeals urging slaveholders everywhere to release their fellow men from bondage. They were pioneers in the movement against slavery, and they maintained as well a steadfast position against war. They argued that no war is ever justified, not even as a last resort. No war can claim even one shred of glory, for no war ever fought was ever won by anyone. It was an allegation very difficult to refute.

3

Before the beginning of the Civil War in 1861, Quakers in the North had already emancipated their slaves. In the South that option was more difficult and more complicated. If a family found a way to free its slaves, invariably they incurred the wrath of slaveholding neighbors. Their children were bullied at school. Their barns were sometimes burnt with livestock inside. The people who supplied them with seed in the springtime often refused to do business with them. The slaves they had freed, despite their certificates of freedom, were sometimes rounded up and sold farther south. The cases of Quakers who still held slaves near Blue Anchor were to be carefully examined at the Quarterly Meeting in the hope of finding solutions.

As the Kingston coach approached the Meeting House, an animated conversation continued inside with Pembroke doing most of the talking. When he paused to take a breath, David spoke to explain the protocol and procedure to be followed as the meeting got underway. Pembroke and Mifflin nodded with knowing smiles. In Pennsylvania they had attended many such meetings soundly based on Quaker tradition. This meeting, however, would be different for them. In this community many miles from Pennsylvania they would be appearing as honored guests.

Astride Caesar with his little sister on the pillion, Matthew Kingston paced slowly along behind the stately old coach. Clinging to his waist, Anna was chanting a nursery rhyme from one of her books. Then suddenly and without preamble she began to recite the Greek alphabet. She had learned it all—*alpha, beta, gamma, delta, epsilon, zeta, eta, theta*—and she would use it years later as a medical student. Her chirpy voice emphasized each letter, moving faster near the end. Detecting the rhythm and rhyme and laughing with wonder, she made a song of words without meaning. Though close to David's ear, her chanting did not disturb his thoughts.

They centered on the slavery question in a practical way. A man once owned by his father and lately given his freedom had been seen at high risk near the extensive Bolton farm. Dan Becker had gone there hoping somehow to get his wife Edna away from Thomas Bolton. Living apart from her and worried about her welfare, he was not truly free. All outdoors was for him a prison in which he paced like a caged tiger. The slave owner had refused to sell the young woman to David Kingston and had threatened to send her farther south. The thought that he might lose his lawful wife to persons who saw her only as a piece of property was driving Dan to recklessness. He was known to be impulsive in his actions, and Matthew couldn't be certain the man would not resort to desperate, even violent measures. Even worse, if Dan were to come on the plantation and cause a scene, Bolton would not hesitate to have him shot.

On more than one occasion the wealthy planter had meted out harsh punishment to those who crossed him. He had little patience for anyone whose views or way of life differed from his own, and he stood in stern opposition to Quaker doctrine. Particularly he disliked abolitionists who happened to be Quakers. They wanted to abolish slavery, but if he were to lose his slaves the life he had worked so hard to achieve would go with them. With no laborers to work his land, his entire estate would fall into ruin and be sold by the state to recoup taxes. Bolton knew that his neighbor had offered to purchase Edna at a good price, but for only one reason. He wanted to certify the young woman as a free person and allow her to run north with her husband. That proposal Bolton could not and would not condone.

Just thinking about it made the man more resolute than ever. Anyone trying to persuade him to let Edna go free would be throwing snowballs into a lava pit to lower the temperature. So what could he do, Matthew asked himself. Dan had said he wanted to get to the coast with his wife and take a sailing vessel to the North. Was it possible? Matthew knew that his father would never help him with such an enterprise. The man opposed slavery, but to help a slave run away was equivalent to stealing and unthinkable. *Thou shalt not steal* was a commandment not to be broken.

Mulling over Dan's plight, and carefully weighing the pros and cons, Matthew could see no immediate solution. In the meantime an explosive and destructive event might develop. He would have to intervene without delay to steer Dan away from the Bolton place and try to calm him. Tomorrow he would have to find Dan Becker and work something out with him. That could be difficult, for the former slave was in hiding and not to be found on any terms other than his own. It was well known that he was capable of melting into the night or the mists to appear again only when he himself decided the time was right. Even so, the two of them would have to talk and try to find a way to secure Edna's freedom. Then and only then could husband and wife be together, but at what cost?

Chapter 5

"Hello!" called Catherine as she and her father caught up with the Kingston coach. She was riding full saddle a brown pony trotting beside her father's mare. As a little girl learning how to ride, she scorned the sidesaddle as a device for sissies and never used it. Matthew thought her greeting was lilting and musical. It came to him on the still air like mellow notes from a stringed instrument. He turned to look at her. She cut a fine figure on horseback, aristocratic in a manly sort of way but feminine. Graceful in the saddle and skilled as a rider, she liked horses more spirited than her pony.

"You seem to be lost in reverie," she laughed. "I had to call your name twice. For a moment I thought you had become hard of hearing."

"Hey, Catherine! Hey!" yelled Anna. "Your hair is braided!"

"Hello, Anna! Yes, braided! I like that bonnet you're wearing!"

"Oh, I really didn't hear," interposed Matthew, his horse coming alongside her pony. "The rattling of the coach maybe."

"That old coach has seen better days, and so have the horses. I strongly suggest your father buy a new deluxe coach and some fine horses to pull it. Moses wouldn't object to a sumptuous new coach!"

"You're right about that," bantered Matthew, "he's a bit too proud even of this one. And the old coach certainly has seen better days. A new one and fresh horses to pull it? Ah, Catherine, you're dreaming! These days people have to make do with what they have and hope to keep it."

"You said it, my boy!" said Jeremy riding in closer. "Make do and hope a roving band of scavengers don't seize it all."

Fortunately neither he nor his friends had been troubled by foragers or scavengers, but he had heard that stealing food and livestock was on the rise. Also the scavengers were increasing in number and ready to run off with anything they could lay their hands on, even a live pig. He knew of one farmer with a small spread who had lost his one and only plow to night prowlers. He wondered how anyone on foot could run off with a plow. Of premium value to the hapless farmer, the grubby grubber probably grew tired of its weight and dropped it. Or maybe he sold it for a dollar.

Anna was tugging at Matthew's coat and waving to someone. Her brother turned his head to glance at people on their way to the meeting. Behind him in a phaeton drawn by a splendid white horse was grave-faced Josiah Bosh, owner of the village mill. Farther back and moving faster, a cart on two wheels jolted precariously over roots in the sandy road. Harnessed to the uneasy cart was a young steer that carried James Baxendale's family at a frisky trot. He had an old mule at home he used for plowing, but the mule was too stubborn to pull the cart faster than a slow walk. The overloaded and rickety cart groaned as it clattered along and seemed on the brink of upset, but the giggling children seemed oblivious to any danger. The whole family waved merrily as they passed.

Catherine's brown eyes danced as she waved back. The father drove the cart from his spring-supported seat while his wife and four children jostled one another on the straw-covered boards behind him. The baby didn't seem to fasten anywhere and bounced up and down like an apple in water. Mother and children were too busy easing themselves over obstacles in the road to take a firm grip on the little one. The cart went on at good speed and turned without incident into the yard of the Meeting House. It was a broad expanse of ground bordered with sheds built to protect the animals in bad weather. Baxendale tied the reins of the steer to a fence post.

2

"What will you do with the baby, Amy?" asked Catherine as she rode into the yard, dismounted, and came over to chat. "I'm thinking she must be two years old by now."

Amy Baxendale and her toddler were out of the cart and standing in the yard. The other children were gathered round her.

"I reckon she'll sit quietly with me. And yes, the littlest one turned two last month. She's a handful all right, but I think she'll behave."

"She's growing so fast and looks so healthy!"

"Oh, she eats like a pig! She has a griddlecake in her pocket to nibble on, and I think she's kind of tired. All that bouncing, you know."

"Yes, I know! I saw her bouncing like a rubber ball as you passed."

"Well, she is sort of rubbery, y'know, and at her age bouncing is fun."

Amy was busy smoothing the wrinkles out of her calico frock and inspecting her children. All were scrubbed squeaky clean and shining. As the women exchanged good-natured comments, Matthew came up and walked Catherine's pony to a nearby shed.

The Kingston coach rolled in, and the couple with their two guests from the North entered the Meeting House. Adjusting her riding habit and letting her braids hang forward across her shoulders, Catherine entered the building with Anna and Jesse. She had always felt a special serenity in this quiet and spacious room where the Quakers worshipped their God, and where in secular meetings they tried to solve the problems of their daily lives. She looked around, casting her eyes in all directions, and saw many friends. Breathing deeply the woody fragrance of the room, she felt at peace.

The sun, producing a soft and special autumn light, filtered through the unstained windows and painted the pine walls a warm and pleasant richness. The hard brown benches, shiny in other seasons, now wore a delicate iridescence. On some of the benches were tan cushions, but the Meeting House was as plain and simple as the doctrine set forth in it. The room had no altar, no lighted tapers, no cross, and no statuary. At its front was a clay pot with ferns from the swamp but no baptismal font, no mural tablets, and no flowers. Sitting on the foremost bench, one could see no organ, no choir, and no collection plates for tithing as in the churches of the day. It was a Quaker invention, this Meeting House, elegant in order, simplicity, and efficiency. It served them well.

The men strode into the building in double file and quietly took their accustomed seats apart from the women. David Kingston led his visitors to a platform in front of the congregation, the elevated gallery reserved for dignitaries, and sat next to them. The women in voluminous silk, woolen, and calico skirts created a muffled flurry as they took their seats. They gathered on their side of the house with their children beside them. The little boys and girls had been carefully taught to be silent in the Meeting House, but they were not required to remain as still as statues. Their legs dangled and swung back and forth. They propped their heads against the rail of the bench in front of them, or the one that formed the back of their own. With curious eyes as big as saucers, they gawked at the gathering crowd, their excitement mounting but under control. Mischievous boys made ugly faces at each other when no adult was looking. High spirited

Jesse was in the mood for horseplay, but a stern look from his mother calmed him down.

Catherine sat with Rachel Kingston and the children on a bench that seemed to grow harder by the minute. Matthew wanted to speak with her about Dan and Edna, but was expected to sit with the men. On the platform, holding the position of elder in the assembly, sat Jeremy Heartwood. David Kingston, Josiah Bosh, Jacob Darboy and other elders were also there and waiting. In time the last step on the wood of the uncarpeted aisle was lost in calm talk reduced to a murmur. When all were seated, the room became very quiet. Then absolute silence prevailed.

Outside the hush was no less profound. The sun had absorbed the early autumn haze and now lay hot on the bare ground and scant grass. A green and brown lizard scampered across the yard and scuttled into a pile of rocks. No breeze jostled the gray moss hanging from every limb of the live oaks, and no birds sang. A fat, gray-brown squirrel with a bushy tail bigger than its body scurried from tree to tree but made no detectable sound. Sitting beside a closed window, Catherine could hear only the muted stamp of a horse's hoof on the sandy soil.

3

Tall and trim with broad shoulders, David Kingston stood behind the lectern and read the formal letters of introduction describing Jacob Pembroke and John Mifflin. He emphasized phrases of compliment and praise and paused to see the effect on those listening. He asked whether anyone objected to the presence of the two men at the meeting and was met with stony silence. Interpreting the silence as full approval, David signaled the elders to stand up and welcome the traveling Friends. In spare language their spokesman, Josiah Bosh, indicated the willingness of all present to accept the visitors and listen to any message they felt called upon to deliver.

It was the cue John Mifflin had been waiting for, and after a brief pause demanded by tradition he was on his feet. He was taller, thinner, more reserved than his companion, and gave the appearance of being tired. Together they had come many miles in their wagon to visit this community, and both hoped they would be able to accomplish something memorable. At the Kingston homestead Mifflin had said little, preferring to let Pembroke do the talking. Now in this interval of silence and wonder, dressed for the occasion in a Prince Albert coat showing signs of wear, he stood on the lofty platform to speak. Slowly, with a show of feebleness that was hard to define, he laid his hat on his seat and moved to the lectern. He faced his waiting audience, turning his head to view them all, and paused to cough softly into a handkerchief. Then he thanked them for attending the meeting and hoped they would listen to what he had to say. A movement among the faces, but not a sound (not even from the children), expressed their readiness to listen.

In a full, deep voice he read a passage from his Bible: *This is the word unto Jeremiah from the Lord. Every man should let his man servant, and every man his maid servant, go free.* He was not there to sermonize, he said with somber sincerity, but to talk about a very important subject, make salient points about it, and perhaps open the door to a viable solution. The biblical injunction would be the text of his prepared speech, but no one at the meeting would have to sit through a dull sermon as though in a church. He paused to allow a flutter of laughter here. His text or thesis was the main point he wished to make, and he supported it with eloquent argument. He delivered detail and example and moved skillfully from premise to premise, forgetting all sense of time, to expound heartfelt beliefs. Though he spoke with animation, it sapped his energy and he began to speak in a monotone. The children and some adults lost interest.

The morning sun with its splash of light slowly moved from the wall to the floor. The heads of little girls in sunbonnets began to nod. Mothers removed the hoods and laps became pillows. Girls and boys alike were allowed to rest, even to sleep, until the speaker finished his lengthy appeal. Afterwards drowsy adults and sleepy children bowed their heads in a prayer for guidance. Rachel Kingston, kneeling on the hard floor, led the gathering in fervent though reasoned supplication. A silence of two full minutes, broken only by the whimper of a small child, followed the end of the prayer.

Then Mifflin and Pembroke shook hands with members of the gallery and moved among the assembly. The first meeting with men and women and children all together was now over. Several men on the floor rose from their seats and began to close the shutters that divided the Meeting House into two large rooms. The versatile shutters allowed men and women on either side to transact their business in separate chambers. Although the Quakers were among the first to preach that women should have full equality with men, custom dating from the seventeenth century dictated they address important matters apart. Known for her feminist views and often outspoken, Rachel Kingston supported the practicality of this arrangement. Experience had taught her that the concerns of women in a world shared by the sexes often differed from those of men.

As the women prepared for their meeting in a separate chamber of the Meeting House, they allowed their restless children to run outside and play, cautioning them not to get their clothes dirty. Jesse went to the coach, retrieved the piece of rope Moses had been holding for him, and within minutes had a tug of war going. Anna sat on a rustic bench built around the trunk of a large tree and read her new book, but the activity of the other children distracted her. She put the book inside the coach, asking Moses to keep an eye on it, and joined the other girls in their effort to out-tug the boys. She hoped the adults would soon finish their business inside, for the clock had already moved past the noon hour and she was hungry. Each family had brought along food that would be set on the long table at one end of the yard and shared. For Anna and the other children, the picnic with tasty food and sweet desserts would be the highlight of the Quarterly Meeting.

4

Matthew Kingston waited for the meeting in the men's chamber to get under way. He was thinking of Harvey Heckrodt but also of Dan and Edna and their problem. Thomas Bolton had a reputation for brutalizing a slave now and then when he lost his temper. In conversation at Darboy's store, when asked about how he operated as a slave-owner, he had answered the question with a stern analogy. "How can a barking sheep dog work a flock of sheep," he asked, "if he can't bite a rump occasionally?"

That was his position regarding his slaves, but he had never mistreated Edna. A good-looking and capable young woman, she had become a valuable cook in the big kitchen away from the house. She began her work in the scullery, a room set apart for washing pots and pans, but soon became a cook in the kitchen. It was located in a separate building with a sturdy chimney, a tile floor easily washed down, a ponderous iron stove with an oven, and utensils for cooking. The building was a hundred feet away to divest the big house of noise, odors, smoke, and the danger of burning if a kitchen fire got out of hand. For the southern climate it was a good arrangement.

Edna was second only to the main cook who was becoming infirm and would have to leave. She was in training to take over that job in a month or two. It was a position other workers envied. She wanted to earn the job and have it for a long time, but Bolton had warned her to keep away from Dan. If he should find them together, he told her, on the first offense she would be sent to the fields. There she would work in all weather from dawn to dusk and lose any chance to become chief cook. On the second offense, he would make an example of her and have her whipped. Beyond that he would sell her down river to anyone willing to buy her. The laws governing private property were on his side; she was his property.

From Dan and Edna's predicament Matthew shifted his thinking to ailing Harvey. For sometime, after becoming free citizens, he and his family had lived quietly in a cabin on the Heartwood farm. But now it seemed to Matthew, as well as to Harvey himself, that in grievous times they were no longer safe. They could be seized by unscrupulous men who specialized in such activity and taken farther south. The entire family could be sold again to the highest bidder. The children would be separated from their parents and from each other, and Harvey could lose his wife. Added to all that was a dread disease that was sapping the man's energy by slow degrees and destroying his will to live. So what could be done? The Quaker elders at this meeting could help Harvey in a small way perhaps, but not Dan. Persuasion had never worked with Bolton, and they had no power to wrest Edna forcibly away from the man who owned her. Matthew hoped that some inspired solution would come to him, and soon. Then without preamble a thought lurking in some hidden recess, unspoken and unrecognized, suddenly leaped into life. Perhaps the traveling Friends could be of service. Maybe the wandering abolitionists from Philadelphia could help in some way. He would have to ferret out their thinking on the matter. Would it differ from that of his father? He didn't know.

Chapter 6

In the divided Meeting House the time had come for Jacob Pembroke to speak. He hoped he could speak with eloquence and passion to persuade a selective male audience to embrace his cause. The man had dedicated his life to the abolitionist movement, and while he could be reasonable and just regarding other matters, on this one issue he was uncompromising: slavery had to be abolished, particularly among Quakers. After a brief pause demanded by tradition, he rose and stood as tall as he could, stretching his pudgy frame to its fullest height. Tightly grasping the lectern and glaring at the earnest faces in front of him, he leaned forward as he spoke. His raspy but fluent voice rose in pitch.

"I wish to speak on a subject that has weighed heavily on my mind for a long time. Many slaves on this continent are oppressed, and their cries have entered into the ears of the Most High. With infinite love the Almighty has spelled out our duty in regard to these wretched people. No longer must we delay to exercise that duty."

"Amen!" came a voice from the back of the room.

Pembroke appeared not to notice and went on with his speech. Moved by his own words, he mounted in eloquence and volume until it seemed he was preaching a sermon. Then realizing he was not in a church, nor in a pulpit, he tempered his tone and his rhetoric and began to lecture.

"We should now be sensible of what God requires of us. We must accept the personal sacrifices thrust upon us from the beginning, from the time of our leader George Fox. That perspicacious gentleman founded our Society of Friends during a civil war in another time and place. We know he suffered for his beliefs, as you and I have suffered for ours, but he endured and so did generations coming after him. So must we."

"Hear! Hear!" sounded the same voice in back.

When the stout speaker eventually sat down, his face damp with sweat and red with exertion, the traditional silence prevailed.

Then a murmur running through the audience settled upon an elderly man with a cane. Owing to infirmity, he rose with some difficulty but spoke his thoughts in a strong voice for all to hear.

"Over a period of several years I have supported eleven slaves. For their work I gave them food when they were hungry, shelter when they were cold, and clothing when they were naked. When any of them fell sick, my wife and daughter at some risk to themselves nursed them back to health. Now I feel they must work to support me in my old age. It seems only fair."

To strengthen his argument he tapped his cane twice on the floor. Then with a frown of expectation creasing his bearded face, he looked around the room to see if anyone would respond. Grasping his cane and stiffly sitting down again, he waited. A full minute of silence ensued before anyone spoke. Then Jacob Pembroke himself, standing to be heard, reminded the man that the time had come when slaveholders would have to free all their slaves and pay them a wage if they chose to stay on and work.

Another man, heavy of jowl and with the mute and patient look of an overdriven mule, acknowledged he was the owner of fifty slaves. He was not boasting, he said, because he knew it was wrong to own even one human being. It was wrong to buy and sell people. It was wrong to strip persons of dignity—black or white, brown or red or yellow. It was wrong, short of rapists and murderers, to deprive anyone of basic human freedom. But what could he do in times like these? To free his slaves would not only bring economic ruin upon him and his family, but would surely unleash the fury of his non-Quaker neighbors. And for all he knew, half or more of his freed workers would be sold back into slavery within a month.

Hardly had he seated himself when a brisk little man stood up to speak but waited for a moment to observe the obligatory silence that punctuated the meeting. Its purpose was to allow each speaker time to sit down and compose himself and to let the audience absorb what the speaker had said before listening to another. This man insisted that hardship, not a bad thing, had always been the lot of Quakers. Through the years it sharpened intelligence and vigor and brought strength. Under hardship the strong survive while the weaker fall by the wayside. It was an echo of Darwin's theory recently published for the world to digest.

"Wealth and ease do not wear well with us," he went on. "My friend should examine his situation more closely. Men and women of the world, those who surround us, have never liked us. But we must live by what we hold dear, despite persecution. Otherwise we are nothing. The word to remember, gentlemen, is *sacrifice*. My slave-holding friend, like the rest of us, will have to endure sacrifice and accept his reduced lot with patience. Ah, now we have two words, but why stop with two? Why not three? *Hardship, sacrifice, patience.*"

A surge of quiet laughter rose and fell in the room. They were serious, hard-working men in sober discussion of a wrenching social condition, but they were not lacking in humor.

2

Another pause ensued, each man observing the silence. Ideas were being exchanged and carefully considered in a dynamic atmosphere of give and take. They were honestly attempting to reach workable solutions for difficult problems. They were there not to argue for the sake of argument, but to help one another. Not one person in the room had forensic training. They had come together to do more than merely argue.

A younger man, his narrow face pale and drawn, now took the floor. He spoke clearly but nervously, shaken by emotion.

"I own but two slaves. All the rest were given their freedom. My wife is now in feeble health. We have a family of young children and a large farm. I am not able to hire free workers. Even if I had the means, I wouldn't be able to find reliable workers. If I free the people we now depend on, my family will go under. I cannot farm my land and produce a harvest without help. I cannot survive as a farmer without help. Will the Friends kindly tell me what is the right thing for me to do?"

This was a difficult case but not uncommon, and it generated much discussion. Elmer Alston was known as a kind and constant man but in recent years had fallen on hard times. His wife Hannah had suffered miscarriages in two successive years, and had lost another child at birth. She was not a woman strong in body, and this "female trouble" had exacted a severe toll upon her. Afterwards she was always tired and could never seem to rest. In time she became a semi-invalid, which interfered with her domestic duties and the care she felt obligated to give her five children. Often on returning from the fields her husband found the house in disarray and his wife in bed. Their servant was a well-meaning woman but had to be supervised in just about everything she did, and Hannah was incapable of supervision.

With some reluctance Elmer pitched in and helped with the housework when it became overwhelming. More and more he found it necessary to rely upon his two remaining slaves, a married couple, for domestic work as well as labor in the fields. The wife worked mainly in the house, except at harvest time, and the husband did the farm work with Elmer. One of the Alston children, a healthy boy of twelve named Nathaniel, worked long hours beside his father. However, as in past years, they had lost a good portion of their harvest even in good weather. To bring it in on time required more labor than two men and a boy could summon.

Now authoritative elders in the community were asking Alston to make the supreme sacrifice, release the last remnant of help on his farm even as the health of his wife declined. It would mean certain economic disaster, for the four younger children were too young to assist either Elmer or Hannah. They would lose their farm and their source of income. The struggle and uncertainty would bring resignation and defeat. The family would be separated, divided among friends and relatives. Hannah's fragile health would break and she would die. Alone and homeless, Elmer would shift for himself.

Thinking over what Alston had said, and taking their time to reply, most of the men in the room agreed that as a Quaker and a Christian, he had little choice. Sooner or later he would have to free his remaining slaves. The injunction demanded that all slaves be given their freedom with no exception, however justified. Then when it seemed no just solution was possible, his judges tempered this hard requirement with mercy. It would be right to free these two if they were to agree in a written document to remain as paid servants for a given number of years. Living in a comfortable cabin, they had their own welfare to consider. But if they wanted to leave at the end of a given time, they would be free to go. In the meantime, an effort would be made in the community to hire the necessary help to run the farm. The demand for additional workers might in time bring ample supply. They closed the meeting with two minutes of silence.

3

When the door of the men's chamber opened and the occupants issued forth, noon had become afternoon. Under ubiquitous broad-brimmed hats and a fading sun, their earnest faces wore varying expressions of concern. No man was laughing or joking and few were smiling. Yet they seemed at ease and comfortably sharing a sense of accomplishment. Even though her imagination sometimes worked overtime and threw facts out of focus, Catherine thought she could detect a spiritual struggle that some had passed through, a decision reached and a peace granted. Elmer Alston in particular seemed to walk with a lighter step. The men moved quickly to the laden picnic table, and their wives joined them.

The women had already concluded their meeting and had spread on the long table a wholesome variety of food and drink. The children, unable to wait, had eaten with parental supervision as much as their stomachs would hold. As a courtesy to their men, the wives had not eaten. Though hungry, they had stood guard by the food to protect it from errant flies, the occasional bee, and a breeze coming up from the southeast. Hidden behind wispy clouds, the autumn sun moved lower in the sky and the day was cooler. As the men filed past the table to fill their plates, the women greeted them, made small talk, and sat with them at smaller tables. They ate their food with a good appetite and talked about the events of the day.

Catherine sat with Elmer and Hannah Alston, hoping to learn whether any solution to their problem had been found.

"Well, I think it's good news," said Elmer after some hesitation. "I can't be certain, of course, but with the help of our friends maybe we can reach a satisfactory settlement of our situation after all."

"What did they tell you?" asked Hannah.

"We have to free our help but keep them as paid servants until we're back on our feet. Then if Hattie and Bill decide to move on, I'll look for workers to take their place. It will all be in writing, they said."

"Oh, that's good news. Well, if not good news at least not bad."

"I expect to find someone willing to farm with us for a share of the crop. The elders said they'll make an effort to scare up a supply of labor in these parts to meet the demand. It's the supply and demand thing the economists keep talking about."

"It seems a workable solution," said Catherine. "I just hope your problems will be solved quickly and your farm turns prosperous again."

"Yes," Elmer replied thoughtfully. "They tried to help us and I do believe they will help us. They are good men and will keep their word."

Then abruptly he rose from the table and walked toward the shed where they had stabled their horse, leaving the two women to clear the table and pack. Within a few minutes his wife followed slowly, and Catherine caught up with her to speak comforting words.

"I'm coming to see thee tomorrow, Hannah," she said with tenderness, using the traditional form. "We must take care of one another. In perilous times we have always looked after our own."

The woman nodded and a smile of gratitude chased the pallor from her face. With Catherine's help she mounted the horse behind her husband. The autumn sun had emerged from streaks of cloud, and the long shadows of late afternoon quickly engulfed the couple as they rode away. Catherine walked to her pony in a shed nearby. She was thinking about the hard times and how they seemed harder on families like the Alstons.

Her good-humored father was conversing with the abolitionists and the Kingstons. She wondered why Matthew did not come as usual to assist her in mounting. But the young man had been caught up in the day's events and was eagerly listening to Jacob Pembroke, who had gathered an audience. Matthew knew that John Mifflin was the man with deeper thoughts, but Mifflin was a formal speaker and not one to chat. Also it seemed to him that Mifflin was somehow lacking in energy, defying a serious ailment perhaps to travel south and complete a mission. For Mifflin, or so it seemed to Matthew, the cause had become more important than his own health.

Now he was listening to Pembroke, who grew more expansive and more eloquent as he talked. Marveling at the man's silver tongue and wondering where he learned to speak so forcefully, Matthew lost track of time and forgot to look after Catherine. Provoked by his neglect and with a trace of petulance, Catherine went over to her father and touched his arm.

"Papa, the sun is nearly down. It's getting chilly. Shall we go?"

"Of course, my dear, of course! What a day it's been!"

"It's time for all of us to go," said David Kingston, "and you are welcome to my house for supper this evening. Sarah will surely have it ready by the time you get there."

"Well, we did eat a lot of that picnic food, but you can count on us to do justice to Sarah's cooking," said Jeremy, laughing. "No doubt about that!"

David placed his family in the carriage. Then, shifting his weight from one foot to the other to get the blood flowing after much sitting, he waited for the steward to close the Meeting House and deliver to him the key.

4

An old man, thin and stooped but with an air of great dignity, arranged the tan cushions on the brown benches in the Meeting House. It was not a job for which he was paid. The job allowed him to serve the community and ask for nothing in return. To be elected Meeting House steward was an honor. Methodically he set the carpeted footstools in order, looked down the long aisle, and locked the heavy door. In former times the Meeting House had been left unlocked so that it might shelter weary travelers on the road. Now because the times had changed it was prudent to lock it. The closed door shut away the outside from the now-empty building, and all was quiet. The man gave the key to Kingston who made ready to enter the family coach.

"Isaac," asked David, his right foot on the high step, "do you still have the old black man that's been in your family for years and years? If I'm not mistaken, his name is Seth?"

"He's still with me," answered Isaac Brandimore. "I doubt if he could go anywhere else. I should feel shame without end if I allowed anyone but myself to care for him in his old age. He served me well in my prime. Now I must serve him. The roles have been reversed, you might say."

"Everyone knows you have been a good and kind master," said David as he climbed to his seat in the coach. "But maybe it's time to free Seth even if he stays with you to the end."

"We can talk I suppose," came the laconic reply.

"Drive on, Moses," David called, "and go easy on the roots."

The creaky old coach rolled slowly from the yard into the sandy road. Isaac Brandimore, an old man on an old horse, followed. Others on horseback had moved into the road earlier and had ridden on ahead. Isaac had no thoughts of trying to catch up with any of them. He would let his horse walk at her own pace even if it took more than an hour to get home. To require her to move any faster was unthinkable, and besides he liked the slow pace. It gave him time to reminisce, to remember the books he had read, and to quote passages from them committed to memory. His man Seth, as a gesture of friendship, had broken the animal for him when she was young. He could not remember when Seth was not a part of his life. Now they were advancing in years together. Their day of frost and sun was nearly over.

The sun of this day was now well behind the trees, and the sandy yard of the Meeting House was in deep shadow. A young rabbit sprinted from the underbrush and crouched in the clearing. Ears alert and eyes missing nothing, he carefully surveyed his surroundings. Satisfied that he was alone, he nibbled the spare grass and its roots at ease. The breeze from the southeast was rising stronger. It stirred the streaming moss, making it swing back and forth, and a large bird settled on a tree limb. The rabbit loped toward the silent and deserted Meeting House, paused for a moment near the steps, scuttled to the edge of the yard, and leaped into the brush.

Chapter 7

Moses sat on the high seat of the lumbering old coach, smiling broadly and tipping his hat in salute to riders on horseback who quickly passed him. He flicked the flanks of the horses to make them move faster, but they resisted. It was just as well for the faster the coach went, the more uncomfortable the ride became. Passengers inside were known to bounce to the roof when the heavy wheels hit on occasion a rotund root or a sturdy rock.

As Matthew came alongside, Rachel called out to Anna to come sit in the warmth of the coach on her lap.

"It's getting chilly, dear. You'll be more comfortable with me."

"I'm with my big brother!" the little girl cried. "I'm just fine."

Her mother understood that Anna was already seeking independence of a sort. To be on her mother's lap meant she was only a baby. To be with her big brother on a big horse meant she was big. And she knew with the pure faith of children that Matthew would protect her against ghosts and goblins and hellfire itself, not even to mention the chill of an autumn evening.

Tightly grasping her brother's waist as Caesar broke into a trot, she bounced rapidly up and down on the thin cushion but squealed with delight. Soon they were riding up the avenue of live oaks well ahead of the coach. The stallion knew he was going home and was chomping at the bit, his nostrils flaring, when Matthew required him to pace sedately. It seemed almost like a prearranged signal, for at that moment Dan Becker stepped out of hiding and laid a hand on the bridle.

"Mistah Matthew!" he said excitedly in a hoarse whisper.

"Hello, Hambone!" Anna sang out.

"Hey, Miss Anna. How you doin'?"

"Don't call him that, sweetie. The man's name is Dan."

"You and me gotta talk!" Dan urged. "That no-good Bolton done said he gonna sell Edna down river nex' week. I saw her jus' a couple hours ago. I never seen her so upset. We jus' gotta get off to the swamp, or somewheres, fas' as possible. Is Mistah Pembroke and Mistah Mifflin still around? They ain't gone yet, have they?"

The horse was impatiently shaking his head under the tightened rein, stomping the ground with one metal shoe, and beginning to snort.

"He'll stand calmly," said Matthew, "if you remove your hand."

Dan dropped the rein and stood away from Caesar but close enough to hear every word spoken by the rider.

"Listen to me, Dan. Don't even go near Bolton's house tomorrow. Stay away from that place and keep out of sight. See me toward evening by the barn. I think I can help, but I can't make any promises."

The inquiry concerning the traveling Friends revived and strengthened the idea that perhaps they could help. If Dan and Edna could somehow secure permission, they could travel with Pembroke and Mifflin as servants without attracting attention. Eventually the men would make their way to the North again, and then the couple could choose to go wherever they wanted. But would the Quaker blood of the travelers accept the subterfuge? Both men were older and more severe than himself and would possibly object on principle alone. He would have to be aggressive enough to find out.

"I know a peddler that's goin' north on the east side of the swamp come Thursday," Dan confided. "He gonna cut over to the seacoast, he say, and gonna be at Blackwater on Cypress Road near ten. He kind of half Quaker I think. Never did believe in holding slaves, he told me."

"Can he be trusted?" asked Matthew.

"I dunno. The way things are, I dunno. But I can't stand it no longer, Mistah Matthew. I jus' gotta do somethin' to get Edna away from harm."

The dense and caustic misery Dan was feeling made his utterance unsteady. He couldn't remember a time when he was free of dread, and now the dread coupled with a fearsome uncertainty was worse than ever. Something odd crept into his voice. It sounded as though some invisible hand was choking him. Grinding his heel deep into the sand, he began to moan with a croaking, guttural sound. And then a cry like a stricken animal escaped his throat: "I will not see my wife sold south! No, suh! NO!"

A moment later he was gone, lost in the deep shade of the oaks as the coach came up the avenue. Aware of the squeaking coach close behind him, Matthew's stallion cantered gracefully with his double burden to the house and stopped at the back door.

"I won't tell," said Anna as her brother lifted her from the horse. "I know how to keep a secret. I won't tell."

"Mind that you don't, sweetie. Now gallop inside and get ready for supper. I'm coming too, just as soon as I put up Caesar. And remember, Anna, not a word, not a single word to anybody."

"I won't tell," he heard her say as she skipped away. "I know how to keep a secret. You don't have to worry about me."

She was a child, only six years old. He did have to worry about her. He believed she would try to keep her word, but the odds were fifty-fifty.

2

Matthew was undecided whether he should ask the traveling Friends to take Dan and Edna under their wing or trust the peddler. He supposed the hawker was on his way to Norfolk and had chosen the coastal route as easier. The man could possibly get the fugitives to the coast, but what could he do after that? The Friends might be the better choice. They were known to have freed their slaves but often traveled with servants. No one would be likely to question them. But when it came to assisting any neighbor's slave to escape, it seemed reasonable they would certainly object. He would mull over the matter and hope to find a solution. In the meantime he was hungry.

Entering the dining room, he eyed with pleasure the well-spread table. The oil lamps were already lit and threw a soft radiance over the intricate, satin-like finish of the damask tablecloth. Crystal glasses and bright silver caught the light and threw points of color on wall and ceiling. The table groaned with spiced ham, wild game, and fried chicken as only Southern cooks can prepare it. Mashed potatoes and gravy were near the meats as were deep dishes of vegetables. Yams, black-eyed peas, and turnip greens flavored with vinegar and bacon were ready for the tasting. Sweet corn, green beans, butter beans, okra, asparagus in a creamy sauce, fat biscuits, and fluffy rolls graced the table. An alabaster tureen with an ornate lid sat like a grand lord in the middle. The soup was real turtle. At one end was a steaming rice pudding with raisins, pecan pie fresh from the oven, and a four-layer cake. Nearby was a carved glass dish with its segments filled with pieces of cantaloupe, slices of apple, grapes, and bits of cheese. Beside each plate was a salad of spinach, onions, and autumn radishes.

The clear crimson of sweet barberry jelly caught Anna's eyes as she bounced into the room. The piquant treat on savory, buttered bread was a favorite. She had to be coaxed to eat her vegetables but not when it came to sweets. Even though at the picnic she had nibbled on many snacks, she was ready to eat again. But according to custom, it was necessary for her to wait until the adults finished eating. She sat in a little straight-backed chair beside the freshly kindled fire and waited with wide eyes, absorbing and recording all that went on in the room. The color, the warmth, the scents, and all those smiling faces heightened her sense of fun. Then Jesse with disheveled hair and muffled laughter ran to take his place before the fire. The children knew they would have to wait with a show of good manners until invited to eat. That required at times an abundance of patience.

"Mother," asked Matthew as Rachel came in with a basket of hot rolls, "may I use your room to wash my face and comb my hair? Our guests, the Friends from the North, are still using mine."

"By all means," she replied, "and take Jesse with you after he fills the wood-box. He needs to wash his hands and look a lot more tidy! I must cut his hair before long, it's scraggly."

"Mama is so persnickety!" the boy complained when he and his brother were alone. "Any time people show up at this house she wants me as clean and starchy as a girl! I'm not untidy at all, just comfortable. But not in the loft. I hate sleeping in that cold loft."

His brother, pouring water from the porcelain pitcher into the wash basin to freshen his face and hair, let him talk. The boy had plenty of prattle in him and was encouraged to explain whatever was uppermost in his mind. The men who had usurped his room were uppermost.

"I wish them good Friends from up north would pack up now and go. I reckon it's time for them to mosey outta here, don't you?"

"I thought you were sleeping in the kitchen on a pallet near the stove. It's warmer there and more comfortable."

"No, Mama made me a bed in the loft. More comfortable in the loft she said. But the strings of onions swing right over my head, almost touching my nose. And the squirrels dash around chomping on hickory nuts. It's a sound repeated all night—chirk, chirk, chirk! I believe when not eating they dance with the rats. And I'm sure we have a ghost up there too. I heard him moan and groan when the wind wasn't shrieking."

"Ah, you heard a branch brushing against the roof," Matthew laughed. "As for dancing, what do you know about dancing?"

"Saw it once at Bolton's," said the boy. "Know all about it."

Before his brother could respond, he urged in mock alarm: "C'mon, you gotta go! Them hungry Friends are ready to hunker down at the table, and if you want any meat and potatoes you can't be last!"

3

All the adults, including Matthew, drew round the bountifully spread table and sat down. They bowed their heads in silent prayer and didn't pick up their knives and forks until David said "Amen." That was the signal to begin polite conversation punctuated by passing the dishes and eating. From casual small talk the conversation eventually turned to Isaac Brandimore and Seth, his ancient companion. The man was happy and well cared for and would remain in a comfortable home until the end of his days. He was too old to work and was treated as a valued companion, never as a pet or a piece of property. It seemed a harmless case that might well be left alone.

John Mifflin listened keenly to the arguments without commenting. He sat in silence throughout the meal, eating steadily. For a man suffering from tuberculosis, as he revealed later, he ate with a ravenous appetite. Catherine with impish good humor and not aware of his condition, was thinking he said nothing at dinner because his mouth and throat were constantly full. Afterwards, warming himself before the fire, he announced he ought to pay Isaac and Seth a visit. He would be remiss in his duty should he go on to other places without talking to Isaac about Seth. He would have to go that very evening, for time was running short.

David Kingston, as host and guide, offered to go with him. He had wanted to relax after dinner and enjoy the company and conversation of his friends, particularly his oldest friend Jeremy Heartwood. They had not met socially for more than a month and had much to talk about. But Jeremy put David at ease by declaring he had to get home to care for the livestock.

"I don't like to eat and run," said the round little man as he put on his coat, "but I do have to get home. We can clatter-chatter later, old friend, at my place or yours. I'll have a big mug of hot cider waiting for you."

David could tell he wanted to stay longer but appreciated his tact in a fairly awkward situation. Matthew went to the barn and asked Moses to saddle two horses for his father and John Mifflin.

Moses was good with horses and told him when he was a boy no older than Jesse that horses love conversation almost as much as eating.

"Always talk to 'em," Matthew remembered. "Talk in a nice an' easy way and let 'em know what you doin'. And don't make no sudden moves. That gets 'em upset. Also never step on a pony's foot, he's most peculiar 'bout his feet. And he talks with his ears, y'know. If you wanna know what a horse is feelin', maybe even what he's thinkin', jus' look at the way he points his ears. I'll tell you about that when we have more time."

Matthew offered to help with the harnessing, but the old servant declined the offer, insisting he could do it himself with no problem whatever. He liked to be alone with horses.

"Them two gonna be ridin' tonight?" he asked. "If they is, you oughta tell 'em take a lantern on a night like this. It's gonna be real dark."

"Yes, an evening ride of some importance," answered Matthew. "And that's good advice, Moses. The round harvest moon is the best lantern, but where is it? The night is already black as coal."

4

In the gloom and chill of evening the two men rode side by side, exchanging few words, on the road to Brandimore's house. Mifflin was mulling the task before him and seeking divine guidance. David was beginning to question the necessity of what the earnest Quaker from the North was planning. Isaac Brandimore could be emotional and unpredictable at times. This attempt to reason with the old man could take a negative turn and cause more harm than good. They turned off the main road, David holding the lantern forward, and followed a narrow lane through trees to the small house. The October moon, full and mellow when shining, was hidden behind low-hanging clouds. The night was dark and the lane with its canopy of trees even darker. David was glad Moses had reminded them to take a lantern. Its beam threw patches of light on the gently swaying trees and on the ground in front of them. Then suddenly before them stood the house. They hitched their horses to a nearby tree and knocked on the door.

Brandimore opened the heavy door, squeaking on its hinges, and with no show of surprise politely received his visitors. His manner was not effusive; it seldom was. But warmly he invited them inside. Like all snug little houses, Brandimore's had its own peculiar scent. The smell of leather, of cured calfskin, struck David's nostrils as soon as he entered. It went well with the man's vaunted learning. He was known to have many old books bound in leather and spent most of his time reading them.

"It's chilly out," he said, as they moved into his living room and sat down. "It's chilly and windy but not half so windy as last night. I wouldn't want to be at sea in that kind of wind."

Isaac had never been to sea, had been a farmer all his life though at times a carpenter, a tinsmith, and a toolmaker. He had only seen the sea, but he was something of a dreamer and a reader of books with an eagerness unequaled by anyone he knew. Though his eyesight was failing and the small print brought headaches, he read about sailing ships on the high seas and imagined himself a mariner. Richard Dana's *Two Years Before the Mast* he read more than once and Coleridge's *Rime of the Ancient Mariner* a dozen times. Often he quoted from the narrative poem and mumbled lines from it in his sleep. On awaking he felt he had been on the mariner's ship, scuttling across milky seas unknown all through the night.

Now he was called upon to do business of a sort with a man he liked and respected, but also with a stranger. It was another inconvenience offered by life but seldom found in books. As a little joke he often contrasted his books with his friends. None of his authors were sullen or petulant, and none came uninvited to stay longer than necessary. His books spoke only when he allowed them to speak and never tramped dirt into his house. Surely he got along better with books than with people, though he had to admit he liked having visitors. He invited his guests to sit by the fire and went for a book he wanted to show them. It was not a sea-faring book and not one containing poetry though he had several. His current favorite was Carlyle's *Past and Present*, and he thought it one of the most powerful books he had ever read.

"We need a man like him, with a voice like his, to tackle the problems we have in this country today. We need him right now. He urges his readers to examine the past as a way to find solutions for the present."

"He certainly has identified serious problems in England," said David, "but as I understand it, even though many people have read his books, not a lot is being done to solve the problems there."

Isaac became animated and began to explain why, but David steered the discussion away from the book and asked about Seth. John Mifflin in characteristic silence peered into the fire, his eyelids drooping. He was tired and bored. Isaac's mental gymnastics did nothing for him and Thomas Carlyle was an insubstantial ghost haunting a distant shore across the sea.

Chapter 8

During an awkward pause Brandimore's restless blue eyes, set deep in a leathery rugose face with a tuft of beard on the sharp chin, interrogated the visitors. With empathetic patience they settled on the crusader from the North, offering him the podium as it were. Shifting his angular frame in a chair too small for him, Mifflin caught the drift of his host and fellow Quaker and began to speak. In a resonant voice rendered hoarse by a fit of coughing when riding in the night air, he spoke tersely but with all the kindness he could muster.

"We must look to the freedom of Seth," he said simply.

Old Isaac cupped his head in his hands and gazed at a crack in the floor.

"I'm aware that's your reason for coming here," he replied, speaking slowly and breathing deeply. "For more than a year I've been thinking about it, thinking about what to do."

"And now we must act."

"I always concluded, why bother. Seth is old and feeble but comfortable and content. To change his situation now could affect his health, his state of mind. Good intentions, you know, don't always give us good results."

"Have you talked with Seth?"

"Well, yes. And he says he wants to die a free man."

"This piece of paper," said Mifflin, drawing a document from his coat, "will allow him to do that, will prove you have granted him his freedom."

It was the official emancipation form, drawn up years before by the Society of Friends in Philadelphia and printed with blank spaces for names, dates, and signatures. Placing his reading spectacles on the tip of his nose, in flickering candlelight Isaac perused the document as carefully as he could. With some misgiving, after several minutes of silent hesitation, he signed the form, saying as he did so that it would change nothing. His signature was neat and legible but wobbly on the stiff paper.

David stepped to a nearby room and asked Seth to come into the sitting room. He stood behind a graceful chair with a caned bottom and asked the old man to sit. Seth had once been strong as an ox, but now the weight of eighty years was becoming intolerable. He took the seat with a heavy sigh, his frail old body bent nearly double. He propped his thin hands on his knees and thrust his white head forward. His restless, inquiring eyes, once so keen he could hunt a possum without a torch, fell on each person in the room. He waited for his friend and caretaker to explain the summons.

"Seth," asked Isaac quietly. "Do you know what this is?" He held up the paper close to the old man's face.

"I never learned to read," mumbled Seth.

"You are no longer a slave. This is the proof. It belongs to you. It's proof in writing that you are free. I signed it a moment ago."

He added quickly, lest the old man become alarmed, that Seth would not be required to make any changes whatever in his life. He would continue to occupy his room in this house. His position as companion and friend would not change. He would not have to work for a living; he had done that already. His service entitled him to live in comfort, and this piece of paper gave him the right to enjoy full human freedom. It meant he could make his own decisions, asking permission of no one. On any day he could choose to do whatever came to mind, or nothing.

Seth listened in wonder, his inquisitive eyes darting about the room, his lips beginning to quiver. A bead of moisture formed at the corner of one eye and ran slowly down the old face. He flicked the tear away and raised his hands high above his head. Slowly and reverently, paraphrasing verses from the prophet Isaiah, he thanked his Maker for his good fortune.

"Holy, holy, holy, is the Lord Almighty. The whole earth is full of His glory. Thank ye, Lord, thank ye!"

"Amen, friend Seth," intoned John Mifflin, "Amen."

And then as if inspired, the old man quoted another verse from one of the psalms, "How long, O Lord, how long? How long shall I cry?"

As though it were a line in a poem composed by angels, he repeated the query with slow and measured rhythm: "How long, O Lord, how long?" And then pausing for a moment he added in a full and throaty voice: "I was old to the marrow of my bones, but now I feel young again! I was in the Valley of the Shadow but now I'm whole. The good Lord done brought the light!"

Looking to heaven, he put his hands on either side of the chair and stood up. Without struggle he rose to his fullest height, reaching upward.

The thin old hands almost touched a beam that supported the ceiling. Ghosts of old and thorny things crept through his brain, and he banished them all. He had known all his life that he was the equal of any man, but the world didn't know it. Now the world would know. Now anyone he met would know.

"Almighty God," he cried. "Almighty God and a miracle! Slavery chain done broke at last. Gonna praise God till I die!"

His face was wet with tears and he made no attempt to wipe them away. He had a habit of talking aloud to himself, but now he spoke for all to hear. "All my life I thought I would die a slave. Now I will die a man, a free man. But now hear this, good people. I will not shuffle off to some dark little room and wait for death to take me. I will live free as a bird in sunlight! The good Lord done granted me the dream of a lifetime."

They sat together in the flickering firelight. The four men talked quietly as men are wont to do at the end of a busy day. Even John Mifflin participated. Then Seth rose from his chair and walked with a show of manliness, though with tottering steps, toward the hallway. His face was alight with a genuine joy, a devout thanksgiving.

He turned and said in a voice that he himself scarcely recognized, his casual tone underscoring the new equality, his rights as a free man.

"Good night, gentlemen. Bless you!"

When the bright morning came he was dead. The village midwife heard the news first and walked to the Kingston house to tell David. The old man had died in his sleep and would be buried among the chinaberry trees in back of the house. Seth had planted the trees as a young man to provide cool and shade in summer. As they matured he was fond of using the fruit of the trees to make beads for necklaces that he gave to the children. In season he would crush the hard, greenish-yellow berries to make a crude insecticide that actually worked. His spirit had always been with the trees that grew from his hand, and the grove now seemed a fitting place for him to rest.

Chapter 9

The time had come for the traveling Friends to move southward, and with some degree of worry David and Rachel bade them Godspeed. Elizabeth City near the coast would be their next stop. From there the men would travel to New Bern, an old and charming little town founded in 1710, but destined to fall victim to hostile forces. They would stay there for a week or two on their way into South Carolina and Georgia. It was common knowledge that some people in those states were not willing to tolerate with any show of patience a person who dared criticize their way of life. Pembroke and Mifflin, adamant abolitionists, would be telling them that an economic system they had known all their lives and depended on for their livelihood, one that had brought wealth and a graceful way of life to some people, had to be abolished. How would they take it?

The two men were fully aware that the farther south they went, the more dangerous their journey. They would find fewer Quaker communities, fewer people in sympathy with their cause, and many people opposed to it. On the road, or in any town they came to, they knew they could be ambushed by angry citizens. But their Quaker resolve was as strong as their mission was risky. Knowing they would meet opposition, they embraced their cause as sacred and plodded onward. They were dedicated men unfazed by perils of the flesh, and they would persevere as long as their Maker gave them breath. In Blue Anchor, both David and Rachel questioned the wisdom of two aging abolitionists traveling deeper into the South in volatile times, but they were determined. Nothing anyone could say to them had the power to dissuade.

Pembroke and Mifflin had heard about the fate of John Brown, had heard the cruel little song some children were beginning to sing—"Hang John Brown to the sour apple tree." But they reasoned the abolitionist leader, who was executed in 1859, had been a violent man. By contrast they practiced at all times the passive resistance of Henry David Thoreau, himself an abolitionist. And they followed the teachings of their leader George Fox, who abhorred violence. Fox was persecuted and imprisoned several times for spreading the word, and yet went on missionary journeys through Ireland, Scotland, the West Indies, North America, and the Netherlands. These two were travelers as well, and children of light. As with all good Quakers, they looked to an inner light and felt their God would protect them.

Matthew had spoken to Pembroke in a moment when they were alone about Dan and Edna. Unable to introduce the subject at the dinner table or in front of the fire, he met with the man on the porch and blurted his concern.

"I have a question I need to ask of thee," he said respectfully. "It's an ethical question but also a practical one. Should any person, for whatever reason, help a slave run away from his master?"

He had not intended the question to be so blunt, but now that it was out he waited patiently for an answer.

Pembroke reflected for a moment and replied, "God's laws are higher than man's laws. We all know that. But if I were to help a slave run, I should try to pay the owner for his loss."

There was no time for further discussion, for Jesse was tugging at Matthew's arm. With disappointment the boy announced that since the Friends would be at their house for another night, he and his brother would again be deprived of their warm beds.

"You are going to spend the night with me in the cold loft," he declared with theatrical melancholy, "with me and the onions and the rats and the scampering squirrels and that ol' moaning ghost."

"And what if the rats go dancing with the squirrels, Jay-boy? Will you join in the merriment too? Maybe you could dance with the ghost!"

"Hahah!" hooted the boy, "you won't like sleeping on them hard boards and them smelly onions hanging in your face! That I know!"

"Maybe not any more than you do," laughed Matthew. "But remember, little brother, sacrifice will make you strong. It's a Quaker principle."

Having spoken with Dan before his meeting with Pembroke, and having devised a rudimentary plan to get Edna away from Bolton and to freedom, he didn't object to sleeping in the loft even if the onions did hang in his face. Sleeping there would place him close to the action of the big adventure he expected to get underway when morning came.

2

Her face and blonde hair aglow in the morning light, Catherine Heartwood chatted with Matthew in the Kingston yard as he erected posts for a new clothesline. Her thoughts were centered upon the irony of Seth's death. She was sad and wondering and full of questions. Had the old man lived long enough to know he was truly free? Had his God taken him too soon, perhaps before he could really know? What exactly did he say when told he was a free man? She wanted to know his reaction on hearing the news, the emotion that ran through him whether displayed or not.

"Some people say old people like Seth don't feel much," she said, "but I can't believe that. I think he felt keenly all the time he was growing old. That politician was wrong when he said the old die without ever having known they were young."

"Oh, I think you're absolutely correct on both counts. Old Seth could feel and think as good as anyone. He was at least eighty by the time he died, and some say even older. He frequently talked about the times when he was young and strong. Any person who says the old don't know they were ever young is speaking nonsense."

"I'm glad to hear we can agree on things like that," Catherine asserted. "Isaac Brandimore always chuckled when he said his companion had a heart as big as all outdoors and a mind as sharp as a hunting knife."

"Well, that's a good way to put it. Seth knew what it's like to grow old, and I don't believe he ever forgot what it was like when he was young and sweating in the fields. You never forget hardship."

Matthew went on to repeat what he had heard from his father. He described the joy the old man had felt on going to bed, and how he walked proudly from the room. That evening Seth was given his freedom but also his youth. He was young again and free. He sat by the fire and chatted, a man among men. Feeling young and ready to live another eighty years, he knew with deep satisfaction that he was the equal of any man.

"He lived to enjoy his new status," Matthew quietly declared, "and I wish I could say the same for Dan Becker."

He had wanted to talk about Dan's dilemma, and now was the time. He could work and talk at the same time, and he hoped Catherine would listen with sympathy. He didn't want to draw her into a situation that could backfire and harm them both, but he needed to talk.

"Is Dan in trouble?" Catherine asked, her face showing concern.

"You could say that. He's a free man, you know, but deeply troubled. He's married to Edna, Bolton's kitchen girl, and wants to live with her. Bolton out of spite, or for whatever reason in that hard head, has said they can't be together. He's threatened to sell Edna down river."

"Maybe your father can intervene, maybe reason with him."

"Oh, no. Papa can't do anything. Bolton won't listen. My father would buy Edna if he could, and make her free, but he won't help her run away."

"I can understand why, but I feel so sorry for Dan. He's a free man and has the right to live with his wife even if she has no right to live with him."

"Dan's anger is barely under control. He's nearly wild with the thought of losing her. Now he wants me to help them get to Norfolk. From there he believes they could take a sailing vessel northward."

"Where is Edna now?"

"As far as I know, she's down at the far end of Bolton's plantation. He put her there to work in the fields to keep her out of Dan's way and perhaps to punish her for causing him trouble. I'm afraid Dan could show up there and get into deep trouble."

"Slaveholders do not send cooks to the fields unless to punish them. Did Edna do something wrong? Something to make Mr. Bolton angry?"

"I'm told she begged him to let her live with her husband, that's all. I want to see her and talk to her, but if I tried to do that the overseer would almost certainly be suspicious and chase me away."

"Maybe I can talk to her. No one would suspect a thing."

"No, I can't let you become involved, Catherine. I could never forgive myself if I got you in trouble."

"I want to help them as much as you do. I'll find the woman and tell her to scamper away from that farm as fast as she can."

"Now that really might do it. You're known to ride far and wide in the countryside, and no one would even think twice if you showed up there."

"But where would she go? Where would she meet Dan?"

"Dan will be waiting near the bay tree at the entrance to the swamp."

"Will the woman have to walk all that distance? What if she's seen on the road? Couldn't we help them somehow, maybe hide them in a cart?"

"I don't think so. We can't be seen near the Bolton plantation."

"I will certainly do what I can. What exactly do I tell her?"

"Dan knows a peddler who offered to help. The man is going through to Norfolk tomorrow night with all his goods in a big wagon. He said he would be at a logging station called Blackwater near ten. It's about eleven miles from our side of the swamp. If Edna can run for it when the hands go to supper, Dan will meet her under the big bay tree where the swamp begins. It gets dark early now, and I doubt anyone will notice her. Bolton's overseers are shrewd and crafty men, but they like to drink a few beers after supper. They won't be very alert and won't be counting heads till later."

"I can think of no better time to do this. Even the weather is good for it."

"Yes, the time is ripe. I plan to ride over to the swamp late tomorrow to see if all is going as planned. You may come along if you wish."

He spoke curtly and with decision. A subtle inflection in his voice, not there in former days, alerted Catherine. He seemed invested with greater maturity now, with a readiness and resolve for action she had never seen before. She couldn't define the change that had come over her friend of many years, but she rather liked it.

"I will leave Papa a note and go look for Edna now."

"Your father isn't home?"

"He went to visit the Alstons. I had planned to go over today, but Papa went instead. He left quite early this morning."

"Perhaps he'll be home by noon. Mama wants you and your papa to come to our house this evening for a light supper, good conversation, and perhaps something from one of the boxes."

"But we had supper at your house only yesterday."

"I know, but you won't wear out your welcome. We'll be opening the boxes from Philadelphia, and all the neighbors are coming."

"Those big boxes are mysterious," she called, turning her head as she strolled briskly homeward to saddle her pony for riding. "And the neighbors are fun. We'll be there! And I hope I find Edna!"

"Come early!" he shouted, "and good luck with that!"

By tradition and habit Quakers did not shout. Matthew knew that. But he was young, and the girl was pretty. His mother, standing on the back porch in a peach-colored apron, was shaking her head.

"The posts are up and sturdy," he called out. "You'll have your clothesline tomorrow. It's a promise!"

With the post-hole digger on his shoulder, he walked with long strides toward the barn. There he found Dan Becker waiting for him.

3

The man had draped himself comfortably against a bundle of hay and Scout, the family's rangy deerhound, was close beside him. Dan had a way with dogs and Scout had taken a liking to him. At times when days were slow and languid, he ran his fingers through the dog's coat to find and remove swollen fleas and ticks. The dog seemed to understand exactly what he was doing, and what he was saying, and soon began to lick the man's face whenever they met. Dan sprang to his feet and spit out the straw he was chewing when Matthew appeared in the doorway. For privacy the two went deeper into the barn, the dog trotting at their heels.

"I been thinkin', that's all I can do these days. I been thinkin' 'bout Edna and what she been doin' and when we gonna be together again. I hear Bolton done put her out in some ol' far field a-busting clods, and Lawd knows she ain't fit for that kinda work."

"I've heard she's in the field too," Matthew answered. "But that's a bit of good fortune, Dan. The field is some distance from the house. We would never be able to spirit her away from Bolton's kitchen."

"I know, but how you gonna get her away from a work crew? Them overseers on them big tall horses have eyes in the back o' their heads, and wit' them squinty eyes they can see you a mile away."

"That's why Catherine went to see what she could do. They would never suspect her of anything even if she approached Edna right in front of them. They've seen her riding all over and will take it for granted she went for a good gallop and just stopped to say hello."

"Miz Catherine is doin' that? But s'pose ol' Bolton done already caught Edna," Dan mused, wringing his felt hat like a wet rag. "S'pose she couldn't steal away nohow. S'pose you and Miz Catherine get caught helpin'."

"Listen, Dan, let's have no more supposing," said Matthew quietly but firmly. "Don't think of the danger."

"Well, I can't help worryin' my pore ol' head 'bout the danger. It's my wife we talkin' 'bout, and you know I loves her and wanna be wit' her."

"I do know, Dan, and that's why we're trying to help. We will do all we can to put you and Edna together, but you will have to help yourselves. Just see clearly what you have to do and do it."

"Yessuh, I knows I gonna try hard to do my best. If I don' try hard enough, jus' let me know. Please jus' let me know."

"I see no reason why things shouldn't work out for us," Matthew asserted. "And the peddler turning up at Blackwater soon seems providential. Gather anything you'll need for the trip but don't make it a big bundle. Hiking a dozen miles and more won't be easy and you'll need your strength. I'll give you some money tomorrow."

As Dan thanked him and melted into the shadows, Matthew left the barn to walk toward the house. Anna in a bright little dress not quite in keeping with Quaker or Victorian sobriety romped up to him and caught his hand.

"I didn't tell," she boasted. "I know it's a secret 'tween you and Hambone, but I know how to keep a secret!"

"You sure do, sweetie, and for that you get a treat! Take a deep breath, set your teeth, and hold on tight!"

He swept the little girl from the ground and placed her lightly on his shoulders. As she clung to his head and neck, he galloped like a horse. He ran with a galloping gait, slapping his rump to go faster, all the way to the house and around the house to the front door. The child's cries of delight split the still air and echoed across the fields. He put her down gently, and she skipped into the house overflowing with joy. Her big brother knew exactly how to make her happy. She was certain he was more fun and more funny than anyone else in the whole world. And he was the most wonderfully clever person that ever was born, except of course for Papa. Magically he could make her heart sing even when skies were cloudy.

Chapter 10

"Matthew," came his mother's voice from the parlor as he entered the house. "I want you to saddle Caesar and go ask the people on this list to come and help us open the Philadelphia boxes. I know it's short notice, but I hope everybody will want to see what our friends in the North put in the boxes."

As she spoke she gave her son a list of names. Rachel Kingston was not the conventional housewife of the time, finding her soul in the soul of the house. A public figure with more sentimentality than sense had said that of women, but Rachel laughed when she heard it. Everyone knew she was involved with issues outside the home. Of particular importance were those that affected her community, and now she was hearing rumors of war. She wanted to live in peace. Any talk of war disturbed her.

On the slavery question she was uncompromising. All the arguments she had heard in favor of owning and holding slaves she dismissed with an impatient wave of the hand. Though a very old institution dating back to ancient times and beyond, she insisted it was wrong from the beginning. Its long history did not make it right. She was certain the time would come when the South would have to get along without slavery. The English had found a way to erase it throughout a vast empire, and Americans would have to follow their example. Already in the North a movement was underway to abolish slavery by force if necessary. If those in the South didn't listen to reason, a terrible war would surely follow.

Rachel prayed for a brilliant light to show authorities the way as they wrestled with the problem. The leaders of any nation must show insight and wisdom and perseverance. They must isolate serious problems, study them, and find workable solutions. Let them use intellect to find answers. *More brain, O Lord, more brain! Or we shall mar utterly this fair garden we have won.* She was recalling something she had read and it seemed to fit. She believed people of all creeds, with proper guidance, could maintain the garden harmoniously. It was not written in any book that black people and white people could not live together in peace. But if old, outmoded notions were allowed to fester, they would destroy that fair garden civilization had won. And so she prayed. On her knees on the bare floor she prayed: *Open their eyes, O Lord, and let them see. Let all people live together, respect one another, and work in freedom for a better world. All living creatures, even the beasts that roam the jungle, were born to be free.*

Everyone in Blue Anchor knew that Rachel Kingston was a visionary and passionate. However, if she had known about the enterprise her son was hatching, she would have done all she could to dissuade him. Her Quaker convictions, in tandem with those of her husband, would not allow her to condone such behavior, particularly in her own son. Had she been apprised of the new thoughts that motivated Matthew, she would have called them rebellious and foolhardy, for she was not ready to believe that mentally and emotionally her little boy had come of age. Though twenty years old, he was still her boy frozen in time, not a man at all. She knew that Matthew and Catherine were attracted to each other, but they were only good friends. Any talk of romance was ridiculous. They were too young for that.

The pretty girl her son was spending too much time with had been almost a member of the family when she was a child, especially after the loss of Gracie. But as she grew older and the two families struggled separately to prosper and build a future for themselves, they gradually drifted apart even while living nearby. Rachel went on to have other children even when she was thought to be too old. Jeremy, who lost his wife when Catherine was born and never remarried, at one time was known to have amorous feelings for a widow in the village. He went to her house on several successive Sundays. After a while he began to feel at home at the table of his new friend, and he loved her cooking. She laughed at his jokes and let him know she viewed him as a sensitive man of good humor and high intelligence, and he believed every word she said. He was not the ideal she had dreamed of when as a girl she read Byron with her sister, but he was real and within the realm of possibility. For a time it seemed all was going very well with them, but for reasons unknown they ceased to see one another.

Jeremy Heartwood worked hard to give his daughter a comfortable home, though he never prospered as bountifully as his friend David Kingston. For a number of years David had gathered more wealth than he cared to have and had put much of it in Northern banks. But in recent years, because of the prevailing mood of the times, his good fortune had taken a downward turn. Though willing to pay them well, he had not been able to hire enough hard-working farmhands, and so the abundant harvests of the past were now a memory. The once-splendid coach had already become a sign of better times, and the impressive house at the end of a lane with live oaks on either side needed refurbishing and a coat of paint. The narrow lane, smelling in springtime of young leaves, was known to everyone in the district, farmers and tradesmen alike, as "the avenue of oaks."

2

Growing up in a more humble house, Catherine Heartwood roamed the woods, fields, and rural lanes to be close to nature. When she was but a child, all natural things sang to her a ditty she could take as her own: *This is a new world for you. Explore, adore! Spread your wings to see new things. Learn more, learn more!* Consistently called Katie by her doting father, she learned the names of wild flowers, trees, shrubs, grasses and which berry on a bush could make a piquant jam. In the schoolhouse at Blue Anchor she eagerly sought the knowledge of books. She could point to the constellations in the night sky and identify them by name. She was good at arithmetic and often helped her father with accounts. She liked poetry and liked to quote in sing-song fashion her favorite lines. In particular she was drawn to Wordsworth's melodic praise of nature. Also she liked Keats, who wrote his great odes when young, and John Greenleaf Whittier. Younger than her father by four years, even his name was poetic. He was a rural Quaker with views similar to her own, and his manly voice was influential in the cause to abolish slavery in America. At the same time Elizabeth Barrett Browning was condemning slavery, but the English poet seemed frail when compared to Whittier.

Political issues never kindled Catherine's fire, nor did the stern religion her father had chosen, but like the woman who had become her surrogate mother, she worried about the prospect of war. The Quakers were known far and wide as doves living in peace. Those with different views they would have to resist, especially the hawks calling for war. But what would happen to them if they refused to bear arms? Would they not be severely punished? She believed in the rightness of Quaker doctrine and was moralistic but not zealous. She could see that some Quaker beliefs were perhaps too inflexible for the changing times, and often she felt that some of their neighbors, God-fearing Protestants too, had a low regard for Quakers. That was a painful discovery for a person who believed in essential human dignity, and yet she knew if she didn't stand firm her faith and beliefs meant nothing.

Though older than Matthew, Catherine was intensely alive and blooming. She looked forward to a long and happy life with a good husband who would give her many children. She wanted all the good things life had to offer, all that made life worth living. But she worried that the larger world, given the times, might not be able to grant her the power to exercise her right to pursue happiness? She had loved Matthew Kingston a long time but had always denied it even to herself, for as a rule Quaker women didn't marry younger men. Now the boy she had grown up with was moving into manhood, showing maturity of feeling and thought. She had seen the change that had come over him, and she liked it.

As for Matthew, he felt a strong desire for Catherine which he interpreted as love. He had always enjoyed her company, but in the past year had come to realize that something more than friendship was developing between them. He had not revealed his feelings to anyone, not even to her, and not in much detail to himself. Her mind was given to analysis, to dissecting whatever lay before her to look into its parts, but Matthew shied away from that kind of thinking. He viewed himself as a pragmatic farm boy accepting an imperfect world and hoping in the course of his lifetime to make it just a little better. He didn't see himself as a dreamer or a lover. Romancing a girl was something foreign to him. But keen little Anna, observant beyond her years and with a penchant for mischief, had recently teased him.

"Are you setting your cap for Catherine?" she asked abruptly one afternoon as they completed their chores.

She wanted to be first in his heart but sensed the special fondness he had for Catherine and was a bit jealous. At the same time she was happy to know her brother had tender feelings for one of her favorite persons.

"Setting my cap?" he replied, laughing. "Setting my cap?" He wondered where she had heard that expression.

She was laughing too and loving her little joke. "I hear a lot of things! I'm not deaf and dumb, y'know!"

"Certainly not! You talk too much to be dumb! But c'mon, sweetie, you know I don't wear a cap. Quaker men wear broad-brimmed hats from the olden days. You ever see me in a cap?"

"I know, Mattie, but Quaker men like the girls too! Mama said so! And she said you like Catherine too much for your own good. I heard her talking in the kitchen. She said maybe Catherine is setting her cap for you!"

"Ah, you little eavesdropper!" he cried, lunging at her playfully as she skipped away. "You know you shouldn't be listening to other people's conversations. You're a naughty, naughty girl!"

The little girl was laughing heartily but keeping her distance, alert for any sudden movement. They were both laughing as they entered the house for supper. He dismissed the teasing as behavior expected of a child, but had he been a little too obvious in his own behavior?

3

He said no more about it, but now as he rode on Caesar to deliver invitations his thoughts centered on Catherine. She was healthy and happy. She was silky and sensuous, perhaps even sensual. Her lively personality, her little mannerisms and melodious voice, thrilled him. Now he could admit without hesitation that her warm and feminine presence delighted his senses. In the close-knit community several eligible men had noticed her, but not one had sought her out for special attention. Perhaps they knew from casual observation that she preferred him to them, but he and she would have to talk.

He spent the morning delivering the invitations. The ride was a long one. In a rural setting neighbors lived far apart. At each house he left happy faces behind him. Supper at Rachel Kingston's was always a pleasant event, but tonight they would enjoy the added attraction of opening the boxes from Philadelphia and sharing whatever they contained. Matthew would be in the middle of the group but would try to get close to Catherine and talk to her. Entertaining these thoughts, he patted Caesar on the neck as the signal to trot a little faster. He was on his way homeward when suddenly two people on horseback rode swiftly past him.

They had come along the road with scarcely any clatter of hoofs to warn him, and he was surprised to see Catherine and Richard Bolton riding together. Both yelled a greeting as they flew by, and it seemed to him that Catherine's face was flushed with excitement. Did it come from the exercise and the rapid movement, or from the company of young Bolton? He was the haughty and handsome son of Edna's master. He was known to be proud of his father's wealth and position, aloof among those less fortunate, but courteous and engaging in a manly sort of way and aggressive. For the first time in his life Matthew knew what it was like to be jealous.

At that moment he couldn't know that Catherine had accomplished her mission. She had found Edna in a distant field, sweating from the hard labor of busting clods, tilling the soil, and cleansing it of rubble. Though working with a dozen field hands, in brighter clothing she was easy to identify. Catherine had managed to speak to the woman and had gotten back on the road just before Richard Bolton came riding up. His father had selected him to supervise Edna and her coworkers. Bolton had said he was not able to trust the regular overseers in so delicate a matter and wanted Richard to do it, but the young man had cavalierly gone away for half an hour just before Catherine came on the scene. Now returning, he caught a glimpse of her on her piebald pony and rode over to speak to her.

"You don't often ride in these parts," he said in a friendly tone of voice as he came alongside. "I couldn't be sure it was even you. Did the fine fall weather bring you this far?"

"Isn't it gorgeous?" she responded with a musical laugh. She couldn't be sure he had not seen her with Edna, but she would soon find out. His stallion fell in step with her pony, and they chatted about the weather and the harvest and whether the winter would come with cold wind and rain. Then suddenly, pricking the belly of her pony, she challenged him to a race.

"Years ago we often saw you ride like the wind!" he exclaimed, easily pacing his horse to stay beside her. "I've often thought it would be fun to ride through the countryside with you, but you need a faster animal than that if you expect to outrun me. The poor thing can barely muster a canter!"

He was casting aspersion upon the animal she loved dearly, but she smiled her most endearing smile and laughed at his remarks. She knew he was speaking simply to entertain her but speaking truth. Peg was too old to maintain a canter for long and quickly eased into a trot that withered to a walk. Catherine could see that young Bolton found her attractive, and with pleasant conversation she took advantage of that. With a flutter of trepidation, she became aware that she had entered upon a game she knew very little about, and yet she could tell her ruse was working. Richard Bolton had not seen her with Edna, nor anyone else of consequence in that locale. Of that she was certain.

Chapter 11

Near four in the afternoon most of the families on Rachel's list began to gather at the Kingston house. They greeted one another in the yard, on the wide porch, and in the rooms of the hospitable dwelling. A few animals the spacious stable could not accommodate were tethered to the fence and trees. Guests with carts and wagons parked them on the edge of the yard away from the porch and entrance. The older folk found themselves settling into small groups inside. Shrill and noisy children played happily in the yard. Those in between gathered on the porch in two groups according to gender. They talked about common interests before merging and mingling. The days were now short, but they would have daylight for almost two hours.

A young man near Matthew's age had been away at college for a year and was the center of attention as he told humorous stories about students and their professors. A student reciting a paper he had written said he didn't like the pilgrims of Chaucer's *Canterbury Tales* because even on pilgrimage they broke their vowels. The storyteller did not return when the new school year began because he was needed at home. His situation was fairly typical and not uncommon. Matthew could name several of his friends who had fallen into the same predicament. He himself had planned to matriculate at a Quaker college either in Greensboro or Pennsylvania, but the times were dictating a different course for young men thinking of college.

Catherine was late. Matthew went into the yard and looked down the long avenue of oaks expecting to see her. Just as he was turning away to go back to the group on the porch, he saw her riding toward the house and waited to meet and greet her.

"Sorry I'm tardy," she said as he helped her dismount, "but I had to look after Papa. He sprained his ankle and won't be here tonight,".

"Oh, that's too bad. I hope it isn't serious."

"Any sprain is serious at his age, but it will heal with no problem if he stays off the foot and gets some rest. I made him comfortable."

Matthew took the pony's reins and tied them to a tree. He wanted to put the animal in the barn as a special favor to Catherine, but she had come late and there was no room. For the Quakers in most matters, as they practiced their principle of equality, the rule was first come-first served.

"I was able to see Edna," Catherine happily announced as they walked toward the porch. "It was a close call. Richard Bolton came up just as I got on the road to go home. I'm fairly certain he didn't suspect a thing."

"That's good news! I knew all along you could do it!"

"He thought I was out riding for pleasure and rode with me a short distance. Then he quickly returned to his place as overseer."

"I'm surprised he would leave the job to ride with you. His father must have put him there just to keep an eye on Edna."

"He didn't seem to be taking it seriously, and I think he likes me."

"Of course he likes you! What young man wouldn't?"

"Oh my!" she replied with exaggerated modesty. "You embarrass me!"

"I shouldn't have said it, forgive me."

"Edna is sure she can make it to the swamp, but I'm not sure at all. I do hope nothing goes wrong. It's risky, you know. If something should happen we didn't count on, we could be in real trouble."

"We have to do what we can and hope for the best."

"I suppose. Let's talk later, Matthew. Right now I'm needed in the kitchen. Your mother and Sarah can't do it all, you know."

Removing her riding coat to reveal a fresh and feminine dress of twilled cotton, the young woman was soon busy in the kitchen and among the guests. Rachel had set up a buffet. Each person came with a large plate and loaded it with food. According to custom, the older men went first and then the mature women. After that the younger people of both sexes had their turn, and then the children. Most of the men found a place at table, but the other guests sat with their plates on their knees in the parlor and on the porch. Some of the children ate in the alcove off the kitchen.

The hosts, David and Rachel, hoped that every guest would have plenty of time to eat before darkness came. But before the supper was over Jesse brought in kindling to start a fire, and the lamps in the big living room were lit. Plain and hard-working people relaxed among their kind and enjoyed themselves. It was a festive occasion with plenty of good talk and laughter. It was also a time for sharing, and that would come when the boxes brought by the traveling Friends were carefully opened.

2

When everyone had eaten and the dishes taken to the kitchen, David Kingston brought to the center of the room a large wooden box. He made a little speech to identify the object and to thank the people in the North who had sent it. As he began to pry off the lid, eager faces gathered round the box. Rachel was the first to look inside. It contained a farraginous assortment of hats, coats, trousers, skirts, dresses, and even shoes. She found the container tightly packed with well-made clothing in shades of gray and other muted colors. Gingerly she sorted the top layers and picked up several pieces. Her silken dress rustled softly as she stooped and rose with various items in her hands. Jovial conversation had now become subdued for all to hear.

"Hannah Alston," she called, looking around for the person addressed. "I'm told you would like something for the little ones. Well, these garments from our Friends in the North will save you a world of sewing."

Hannah rose from her seat against the wall and came forward. She took in her thin hands several pieces of children's clothing and examined them to see if they would fit. Nodding her head self-consciously, she expressed her gratitude and stepped back into the crowd.

Then Matthew, digging into the box, found a pair of dark-green trousers that seemed to have Leo Mack's name on them.

"I can sure use them," said the angular man, who earned his living as a traveling tinker. "These old trousers I got on will now become my working gear. Do you mind if I try on the new ones and see if they fit?" He asked the question shyly, awkward and blinking, as if it were somehow out of line

"Of course you may," replied Rachel, pointing toward a bedroom.

Whatever the weather, one could see Mack on the roads early in the morning every morning. Every tool he owned, his entire shop, he carried in his wagon under canvas made from hemp. A mongrel dog named Sparky trotted always beside the wheels. He sprawled under the wagon whenever the tinker stopped at a farmhouse but never seemed to sleep. His tail never stopped wagging, and Mack while mending a pot never stopped talking. The tinker was a purveyor of news as well as a mender of pots and pans.

He rented a single room in a tall boarding house of many rooms. His landlady, Ida Crabtree, told him he would have to get rid of his dog. Later she relented and let him keep Sparky near his horse and wagon in the stable. In winter when the nights were particularly cold, Sparky was allowed to sleep under Mack's bed. Mrs. Crabtree was past middle age, hard of hearing, and the widow of Waldo Crabtree, a scrivener who had come into money before he died. She had good silver and china and kept an orderly house, but visitors were surprised (in good times when food was plentiful) to see pantry items on the bookshelves of her living room. Beside the jars of jam and pickled apples was a farrago of trinkets, doodads, gimcracks, and books.

An inquisitive and talkative woman, she knew all about the lives of her boarders. On the second floor lived a tailor named Holt. His wife complained daily of headaches and nausea. They had no children and were often at sixes and sevens. She called him a blackguard, a blockhead, and a scoundrel but never gave him the satisfaction of explaining why. When that happened he would meekly shuffle out of the room, saying "I'm off for a walk, my dear." His walk usually ended at the rear of the house. Also on that floor lived a bellows-mender and a draper. Though neither had steady work, they had only themselves to support and managed to get by.

A dressmaker named Edith Shawe lived in the rear of the house. It was rumored that Holt and Shawe had more in common than making clothes, but Mrs. Crabtree took little stock in the rumor and tried to squelch it. As long as her boarders paid their dues and caused no trouble, she was willing to overlook an occasional indiscretion. She cared about her guests and was known to be a fair-minded woman. For the evening meal all the lodgers ate at the same large table and talked about the day's events. Most of them were Methodists and given to drink but seldom noisy. Even Mr. Holt and his wife quarreled in undertones. Leo could not abide noise and once threatened to leave when a lodger disturbed the whole house tooting a trumpet late at night. The man protested, claiming he needed to practice to improve his playing, but Mrs. Crabtree turned him out the next day. Now as Mack tried on his new trousers, he was pleased to learn they were tough, a good fit, warm in winter, and comfortable.

3

In the Kingston living room the guests gathered in a circle to see the items that came from the box. Drawing a bolt of fine-looking cloth from near the bottom, Rachel called out: "Catherine Heartwood, I devoutly believe this is right for you!" Catherine graciously accepted the cloth and turned away to inspect her treasure. It was an ample roll of blue merino, enough to make a handsome skirt or even a dress. Before she could examine the soft but tightly woven fabric, Matthew was suddenly there to drape over her shapely shoulders a fleecy white shawl.

"Look at thyself!" he murmured, using the plain speech to honor her and please her. "Look at thyself. Thine eyes have seen the glory!"

She raised her head and saw the upper portion of her body reflected in a fine old mirror. Her face and neck and shapely shoulders were accented by the shawl, and the firelight added to its white a soft amber. In an instant her image a healthy farm girl had become a portrait of splendid young womanhood. Flushed, laughing, aware of her altered appearance and annoyed by too much attention, she removed the shawl.

The portrait in the mirror displayed a faint shift of color but remained as beautiful as ever. Resplendent in simple attire, her neck and face gleaming above her plain but pretty dress, she had become the woman Matthew knew he must claim as his own. Having known her all his life, he could tell the world she was independent, intelligent, and strong, but also gentle, sensitive, and caring. In his longing for her even the air she breathed seemed warm and sweet. He gazed at her reflection in the mirror as one entranced.

"I cannot accept this shawl," she said quietly but with a show of sternness. "It was sent to be worn by an old lady suffering from rheumatism."

"Will it not prevent rheumatism as well as cure it?"

Unable to invent an answer, she turned from him to join the others. But even as she moved away into the crowd, she knew at last that the man she loved dearly was returning her love.

When the first box was empty, the guests began to examine the contents of the second. It was just as large as the first and contained many items of practical use. Jesse and Anna, ten and six years old, had dived into the box to explore its contents before it was brought officially to the middle of the room. It contained men's clothing, another bolt of woolen cloth, broad-brimmed hats, plain Quaker bonnets, and perky little caps.

Glancing at the latter, Matthew chuckled as he remembered what Anna had said about setting his cap for Catherine. Women wore the caps, and so maybe the girl he was hoping to make his own had set her cap for him after all.

Anna had donned a bonnet and enveloped her small figure in a huge white shawl which trailed behind her. Jesse struggled through the maze of a voluminous black coat, finding the armholes with difficulty. He resembled an inert heap of clothing topped with a large hat. When the heap began to move mysteriously across the room, a ripple of laughter from Catherine attracted the attention of David Kingston.

The trim man with broad shoulders had been moving among his guests, practicing his usual diplomacy with kind words and gentle, clever jokes. To be among people deserving respect was a bracing tonic for him. He was saddened by the absence of his old comrade, Jeremy Heartwood, but delighted to see his friends and neighbors enjoying themselves. He turned and beheld in the dancing light of the oil lamps a transformation, indeed a transmogrification, of his children. They had seized the occasion to dress up in costume and achieve something magical and different in their lives. As with children everywhere, it was a temptation they found hard to resist. The boy and the little girl claimed the moment and mounted joyously with it.

They were not looking forward to Halloween, when they could dress up like a banshee or bogeyman, for that celebration of the dark side of Christianity was denied Quaker children. So they contrived to have fun with different identities in odd and outlandish clothing whenever they could. And of course if adults were there to appreciate their effort, the fun was sweeter. Acting on impulse was not one of David Kingston's foibles, but now he joined the children, placed them in a single file with Anna in front, and marched them around the room. The spectacle of two strange little imps from another reality, tramping around in a circle with the dignified Kingston marching behind them, produced irrepressible laughter.

4

The second box was soon empty, and Matthew brought in the third and last. Rachel was again in charge, passing clothing to the particular person who seemed to need it most, and finishing with the garments in which Jesse and Anna had paraded. She held in her hands the hat that Jesse had worn to cause laughter among their guests.

"Jeremy," she called, "Jeremy Heartwood. I do believe that old hat of yours is stuffing a window pane at the moment. This well-made, nearly new hat will surely look good on thee."

A roar of laughter came from the guests. Rachel's sense of humor combined with perfect delivery and showmanship delighted them. But even as she called Jeremy's name she remembered with some embarrassment that he was laid up with a sprained ankle and had not been able to attend the party. His daughter came forward to receive the hat.

"He will thank thee for this, dear Rachel, and I thank thee."

"Give my regards to thy father. Tell him I so felt his presence with us here tonight that I mistakenly called out his name."

When the boxes were empty and the guests had placed their treasure in burlap bags bought from home for that purpose, a large bowl of punch appeared on the sideboard. Beside it were sparkling glasses, crisp linen napkins, and savory walnut bread on little saucers. It was the signal to enjoy the Kingston hospitality before departure. An hour later, pleased with the evening's events and offering their thanks, Rachel's guests left for home.

Matthew accompanied Catherine home, her chestnut pony with varying shades of brown walking behind them and snorting for lack of attention. Under his arm he carried the bolt of merino cloth and on his head he wore the hat given to her father. It was too small for a head covered with a thatch of tousled, reddish-brown hair and Catherine found it funny.

"You clown!" she chided. "Making fun of my papa's new hat!"

"This way I can carry the hat and cloth at the same time!" he retorted.

Becoming serious, they discussed their plan to help Dan and Edna escape to freedom the following night. They would participate in the adventure together. Any danger would be shared. Any excitement, any feelings of a job well done would be shared. Matthew asked about her father.

"Papa will be pampered with tender care until he's up and about," she replied. "Then as a first duty and wearing his new hat, he will thank Rachel for her kindness and generosity."

They reached the house, nestled in shadow among the trees, and stood for a moment in the sandy yard. Gathering her skirt, Catherine made ready to climb the steps, but a hand on her arm arrested her movement. Suddenly—too suddenly it seemed to her—he embraced her eagerly and warmly. Then quickly he brought his lips to hers. As far back as she could remember, no person in all her life had ever placed a kiss on her lips. Except for her father, who sometimes kissed one cheek and then the other, like a French general bestowing a decoration, no male human being had ever touched her. It was a new and strange sensation but pleasant. Again they kissed but only for a moment, and then she was gone.

As if walking on air he led her pony to the barn, put the animal in a stall, and gave her a bundle of hay and some water. Then whistling a popular tune, he took the long way home. He felt happy and triumphant, and shivers of delight reminded him of his masculinity. The new feelings told him he was supremely fortunate. His heart, speaking with a persistent thump, told him it was all a miracle. Within minutes the lyrics of a dreamy old song were assaulting the cool, still air. With gusto but alarmingly off-key, he sang the verse he liked best—

Beautiful dreamer, wake unto me,
Starlight and dewdrops are waiting for thee;
List while I woo thee with soft melody,
Beautiful dreamer, awake unto me!

A mockingbird in a tree nearby, as if in answer to the raucous human heart, trilled a perfect and pristine night song.

Chapter 12

Morning broke with a thick haze that dissipated when the sun was higher. The day was uncommonly warm, a reminder that summer was not yet dead and winter powerless to be born. The trees were losing their foliage, and the fair-weather birds were loudly chirping as if in protest. In the sprawling oak sweeping over the Heartwood farmhouse, a fussy blue jay flitted nimbly from branch to branch. Near the barn a mourning dove softly cooed its familiar and plaintive call. A fat squirrel, perched on a post near the house, gnawed on a nut and chattered as if annoyed. The rising sun was low in the sky and a breeze was coming up from the south. Matthew Kingston knocked on Jeremy Heartwood's door and waited for an answer.

Catherine recognized his knock and stepped outside to greet him. After an exchange of pleasantries Matthew revealed his reason for the early visit.

"Mother would like you to spend the night at our house. She and Papa plan to visit friends some distance from here and won't be getting back until tomorrow. Anna asked if you would come to keep her company, and of course Sarah will be there."

The young woman did not accept the invitation immediately. Taking her time to think it over, she inspected his broad, handsome face, his intense brown eyes beneath an unruly tuft of copper hair, his chin and neck and powerful shoulders, and the way he stood confidently before her. She was thinking it might not be prudent to accept the invitation even with the Kingston cook as chaperone. Only the night before they had entered into a formal courtship, and both knew they were strongly attracted to one another. They also knew that without the self-discipline taught by their Quaker heritage they might pay for their pleasure with pain. As Catherine hesitated, her father called out from inside.

"Come in, Matt, and say hello. I'm laid up a few days, have to stay off this foot. But if Katie wants to go to your house, I can't stop her. I can get along without her. Oh, yes, almost forgot! Tell your mother I'm grateful for the new broad hat. Please thank her for me."

Jeremy was fond of Matthew and encouraged with calm satisfaction the affection the young man had for his daughter. He could not be certain the relationship had become more than a warm friendship, but he suspected as much. He had cared for Catherine all her life and would go on caring for her. But he was getting on in years and had to look to her welfare should he be taken from her. He believed Katie could live quite happily as a member of the Kingston clan, facing with them whatever uncertainty the future might bring. He hoped Matthew would eventually do the right thing and propose to her. He couldn't do better for everyone knew she was meant for him, and she would like to be known as Mrs. Matthew Kingston.

More than once Jeremy had assured himself he would not be meeting his Maker for a long time. He expected to be spry and active well into his eighties. Then as he thought about it he knew that a plan for the unexpected was always a good thing to have. Matthew would be at the center of that plan, and perhaps it was unfolding already. He stood on the porch and waved to the couple as they rode away on Caesar and Peg in the direction of the Kingston house. When they were out of sight, he hobbled from the porch back to the breakfast table. To be left alone in his comfortable little house was a condition he did not mind at all. He looked forward to a good day. The sun had burned away the mist and was slowly climbing up the sky, but an hour later it was shrouded in gathering clouds.

2

At the Kingston house Catherine entertained the children until late afternoon. Then she fed them an early supper, assured them she would return shortly, and left with Matthew for the swamp. Within minutes they were down the avenue of oaks and on the main road. The faithful deerhound Scout, sleek and powerful and a valued member of the Kingston family, trotted beside them. The people they met on the road had often seen them riding together, the dog running at the heels of the horses, and this latest outing would cause little comment. For almost an hour, as they rode on and on, they said little. Both were dealing with nervous thoughts of what lay ahead. Then Catherine, observing a threatening sky, was the first to break silence.

"Matthew, look how dark it's getting. Look at that sky to the west. Oh my, I think we're in for a storm—a bad one."

"If we get a storm it's all the better for Dan and Edna. In storm and dark they'll get to the peddler without being noticed. By now they should be well on their way to meet him, but I want to know if they connect all right."

"I hope they do, but it seems to me their chances are slim."

"Well, it's their only chance to reach Norfolk safely. The hawker and now the storm seem providential. Nobody in rain and storm will be outside the logging station to see them."

"The skies are becoming brighter toward the west," said Catherine, looking behind her. "Maybe we won't get hit by anything after all."

"Maybe. If a storm is brewing in that sky, it just might pass on to the south of us and miss us. But we need to be cautious."

They went on down the road, a sharp breeze rising behind them, and soon came to the swamp. The big bay tree marking the entrance shuddered in the wind. The live oaks gave way to a thicker growth of bay and cypress. Tree trunks of pale gray rose from still pools of black water. Their glassy surface weakly reflected the faint light struggling through the trees. Catherine could remember passing these same pools as a girl and believing that water demons lived in them. A long black snake slithered between the hoofs of her pony and into the water, breaking the sullen surface and churning the water to ripples. It lifted its narrow head to look backward, and Catherine felt a chill sweeping over her. Then she laughed, assuring herself she was no longer a child.

"Are we really going to ride through here?" she asked. "All the way until we find Dan and Edna?"

"We'll turn back if you want," her companion replied. "I didn't think it would be so dark, but the days are short now and it's dark outside too."

"No, we can't go back after coming this far." She was trying to sound brave and determined. "The horses know the way and the road is good."

Heavy storm clouds overhead were about to burst into rain. A flash of lightning, followed by thunder that sounded like a cannon blast, told them wild weather was near. A jagged streak of lightning struck a tree, ran at blazing speed down its trunk, and sizzled in the water. For a moment the gloomy swamp was flooded with a brilliant light that startled the horses. Catherine shivered perceptibly, but quickly remarked that the rain beating against her back was stinging her with cold.

Matthew was alarmed and did not try to hide it. He knew that storms in this region were often violent. The wind could topple huge trees like match sticks, pushing them over as the sodden roots gave way. They were on a narrow road in a murky swamp surrounded by tall trees in muck. He knew they were in danger, but turning back seemed an unwise option. It was just as dangerous to go back as to go forward. Then he remembered an old, dilapidated house he had seen on the road sometime ago.

"There's a logging shack not far from here," he shouted over the wind. "If we can reach it, if the wind doesn't blow it down, we can find it and be sheltered from the rain."

He hoped his voice sounded calm, and he hoped his memory was not playing tricks on him. Maybe the shack was really farther down the road. Maybe it was not on the road any more at all. Swamp denizens could have carted it away for firewood.

They hurried forward under a canopy of trees. The lightning penetrated the canopy to reveal the road for an instant, the horses side by side and the hound flashing red in the eerie light. They went on for half a mile. The heavy shadows lifted as the road came to an open space. Off the road in a tangle of undergrowth stood a deserted cabin built by workmen cutting timber in the swamp. On either side were heaps of old logs covered with rare mosses and almost hidden by nettles and brambles. A thicket of bracken had sprung up around the crude steps to blot all but a corner from view. The door was neither open nor closed but ajar. The wind by now was howling and the forest creaked under the gusts. The horses picked their way across the clutter to the shanty which seemed to shiver in the wind. Springing to the ground, soft and wet underfoot, Matthew lifted Catherine from her saddle.

"Go inside, hurry! The dog will go with you. I'll put the horses on the lee side of the shack and hitch them to something. They'll be protected there and won't run away and you'll be dry and safe."

3

In all the years she was growing up Catherine had never lacked courage, but now she hesitated. She was surrounded by a tangle of thorny vegetation, her companion was leading the horses to the rear of the building, and she was expected to go alone up the rickety steps into a dark unknown. For a minute or two, her shoulders and back shivering under the rain, she hesitated but soon climbed the steps and went inside. The clammy enclosure was not to her liking. She felt it was a room that had always been empty, a room that had never heard laughter. And yet it offered more comfort, even in darkness, than the wind and rain outside. The hound crouched near her and seemed uneasy. He peered into the gloom, venting a barely audible whimper, and moved his tense body closer to Catherine. She moved to a wall, stretching out her hands to find it in darkness black as ink. Distinctly she felt that she was not alone in that ruined abode. Her senses told her that another presence, alive and breathing and dangerous, was there. The behavior of the dog underscored her apprehension, and she was thankful to feel the rotting floor tremble beneath her as Matthew came up the steps.

He stood beside her, so close she could feel the warmth of his body. She stared into the darkness, imagined she saw something move, but said nothing. He was looking at the gathering storm, the torrent of rain.

"It's good we found this place," he murmured, "and just in time. The full brunt of the storm is yet to come. Look at that rain."

A sheet of water descended from the sky, and he drew Catherine closer to the wall. In the flashes of lightning, they could see through the heavy rain dim shapes plainly moving. The thunder and howling wind were softened by the downpour, but the cabin seemed to quake in the gusts. They huddled against the wall for warmth and tried to relax. Matthew was thinking that Scout would settle down and sleep, but his hackles were up and bristling and he was growling softly.

Catherine thought she heard a rustle and something breathing in the far corner of the room. She shuddered and pressed closer to Matthew. He put his arm around her shoulders and exclaimed sharply, "Who's there? Speak out!"

They waited for an answer, for some sort of response. Both were convinced now that something alive was lurking in the darkness close to them. They knew they were not alone. Then through a shuffling sound, a scraping on the floor, came a voice they thought they recognized.

"Is that you, Mistah Matthew?"

The hoarse, low-pitched voice was difficult to hear over the storm. After a few words, peals of thunder drowned it out.

"This Hambone, suh. We here in the corner. We wasn't sure who was wit' you. We had to lay low till we know."

Dan was talking, and Edna was nestled against him. He struck a match to show himself and her. The deerhound, recognizing the voice, sprang forward to paw his old friend and lick his face.

"Git off me, you mangy sack o' bones!" muttered Dan with a burst of laughter. "Ol' Hambone don't wanna be licked by no hound dog!"

"What made you stop here?" asked Matthew, amused by the mutual affection between dog and man but disappointed. He now believed the flight to freedom had failed.

"Why didn't you go on, Dan? You've run out of time!"

"Edna done sprained her foot and can't walk," he explained. "And the peddler is gonna be goin' by, and we gonna miss him, and I jus' don' know what to do no more." A stifled sound of weeping, a steady and prolonged ululation, came from Edna beside him.

"We have to think of something," said Catherine, withdrawing gently from the arm that encircled her. "It seems terrible to give up the whole business after getting this far. Together we must think of something."

"I can ride," Edna mumbled in monosyllables, barely audible, "I can ride but can't walk. If we get to 'im, he can put me in his cart?"

Matthew struck a match on the rough floor and looked at his big pocket watch, a present from his father. They were running out of time, but as yet the peddler had not reached the crossroads and perhaps he would wait.

"Here's a pine knot I took notice of 'fore it got so dark," said Dan.

Soon a little heap of wood was blazing in the decrepit chimney, the pine knot sputtering. By its uneven light they were able to see one another.

"If Edna can ride," said Matthew slowly, shaping the plan as he spoke, "we could put her on the pony and Dan could run beside us to the logging station. All of us but you, Catherine, would get soaking wet, but that's the least of it. The worst of it is leaving you behind."

"You mean I'm to stay here?" she asked, incredulously.

"That's the worst of it," he repeated. "I don't want to leave you alone here, but is there another solution?"

"I wanted to help," she answered quietly and steadily. "Now I can. I'm not saying it won't be scary, but Scout will stay with me. You've said it won't be long. It's a matter of doing what has to be done."

"Not more than two hours at best," said Matthew, admiring her fortitude. "The rain has let up a little. Let's move. I'll get the horses. Gather your bundle, Dan, and be ready to put Edna on the pony."

Within minutes the horses were ready. In the rain and howling wind and darkness Dan lifted Edna easily and placed her on the brown pony.

"God Almighty must of sent you, Miss Catherine," Edna cried. "I'm so grateful!" She uttered the words prayerfully as if in a church.

From the cabin's doorway, Catherine called out to her.

"I came because I wanted to help you, Edna. I came because I couldn't stand the thought of you and Dan living apart. Now go!"

Matthew was hesitant but only for a moment. He knew they could linger no longer. "Scout will keep you company. I'll return as soon as I can. Soon!"

He was already in the saddle. Both horses quickly broke into a canter. Known to be a good runner, Dan clung to Caesar's stirrup to help himself run faster. The woman turned from the doorway to seek shelter in the cabin. In a corner and away from the rain, she listened closely as the rattle of hoofs grew fainter and fainter and ceased.

Chapter 13

Except for the big dog, Catherine was alone in a rickety cabin at night in a swamp darker than any night she had ever seen, and she would be alone for at least two hours. When the streaks of jagged lightning ceased stabbing the sky, darkness pressed upon her with the weight of a blanket that smelled of damp moss. The air was so thick with moisture she could hardly breathe, but Dan's pine knot flickered in the old fireplace and she was no longer cold. She would have to find a way to pass the time and keep her thoughts off her predicament. Her rich imagination could serve her now. She could review the peaks and valleys of her life, beginning with the deepest valley, the loss of Gracie, her closest friend and playmate. But no, that was too long ago and too painful to remember, and beyond that were only shallow valleys with green grass. She would have to focus on the peaks, yes the peaks to bring light and warmth to this dark and dreary place.

She would begin with the tallest and most recent, Matthew's revelation that he loved her and wanted her. "Look at thee!" he had said. And viewing herself in the mirror, she could see him adoring her. She was feminine and pretty, and he was manly, witty, and funny. At that instant she knew beyond a doubt that he loved her dearly, and she remembered that awesome feeling when her soul and heart went out to him. She had loved him for so long, so long. And he was now returning her love! The height of that peak took her breath away. And their first kiss, ah the first kiss! What a strange sensation but so pleasant. Standing on the top of that little mountain, she could view all 360 degrees of the entire world, a sunlit world with flowers and fruits and days of wonder. But no more, no more reminiscence, no more attempt to escape the present. She must focus on the swamp and all she knew about it. She closed her eyes and leaned against the wall to collect her thoughts. Scout lay quietly beside her, she was safe.

2

"The Great Dismal Swamp," she mumbled disjointedly, "the Great Dismal Swamp. Sounds impressive, wonder who came up with the name. Well, the swamp is great all right, in size anyway, and dismal too. More than a thousand square miles in size, they say, and partly surveyed by George Washington. Did he use a new-fangled surveying instrument with a telescope, a theodolite? Theodolite, what a funny word! Did he name the swamp? Probably yes for the first question, no for the second. But the swamp, what about the swamp? The Great Dismal Swamp is a massive tangle of vines and brush and bay trees and bald cypress. It has tupelo yielding timber and flowers for making honey. Slender pine trees and white cedar trees. Wildlife of bear, deer, gray fox, possum, raccoon, muskrat, otters, rabbits, beavers, birds, squirrels, and several kinds of snakes. Whew, so much life!"

She had never liked snakes and shivered at the thought. Her teacher in grade school, Miss Alma Beatonboy, had poured into her head many facts about the swamp, and now with gratitude she remembered them. Miss Alma was a tall, assertive, square-shouldered woman with ample breasts tightly controlled. She lived alone in a yellow house with three dogs and four cats. She flourished a baton when she taught, rapped it on her desk for emphasis, but never used it on a child. No parent dared cross Miss Alma and none had cause to do so, for they knew she was their treasure and cared about her charges. She was skillful as a teacher and patient, but not a woman of ideas. In fact, she had little interest in art, literature, science, or the dreary meanderings of intellectuals. She gave the children facts, and now the facts were proving their worth.

Quickly Catherine went on cataloguing in her imagination all the wonders of the swamp. Wild turkeys all over, an abundance of them, and buzzards on black and rotting trees soon to become peat. Screeching hawks in the trees, snowy egrets, and geese stopping over on their way southward. Swamp flies, delicate antlike creatures with shining gossamer wings, but no sting and no mouth for eating. So fragile they were they fell apart when touched. William Byrd of Virginia led a surveying team over many square miles of dense swamp way back in 1728. When they couldn't penetrate the watery terrain on horseback, they moved in shallow-draft boats they called skiffs. The skiff is still in use by swampers, people who get their living from the swamp. And yes, the mosquitoes. In summer they feast on all persons entering the place, even those who stay on the road. Even the swampers, born and bred here and tough, are not immune. But maybe for a frog the mosquito is a delicacy.

Thomas Moore, believe it or not, wrote a poem about the Great Dismal Swamp. Maybe the name inspired him. The absurdity of an Irish poet across the sea writing a poem about a faraway swamp he had never seen made her chuckle. Then she recalled that strident Harriet Beecher Stowe had published an antislavery tale set in the swamp. The woman, like Moore, had never seen the Great Dismal Swamp. She was living safely somewhere in New England as she mounted her attacks against the South. Moore had visited America and may have seen the Virginia part of the swamp. He could have penetrated deeper too, for the poem was mainly about Lake Drummond in the heart of the muskeg, the word the Indians used. She had never been to that shallow lake, nourishing hordes of fish in its acid-stained water resembling tea, but she had heard people talk about it. George Washington had seen it, and also he had seen this dismal swamp and knew it well.

"George Washington liked this place?" she asked aloud. The ears of the sleeping hound twitched. "Well, he survived it and so did aristocratic William Byrd when it was more wilderness than now, and so will I."

She was sitting on the floor leaning against the wall, snuggled as far as she could get into the angle of the corner, and for half an hour she closed her eyes and dozed. Later she rested her blonde head on warm and faithful Scout and felt herself falling asleep again. She wanted to be awake when Matthew returned, and she felt it wise to be observant. She sat up and looked at the dying fire. When it sputtered out she would be in heavy darkness, but Scout would know of any lurking danger. He pounded the bare floor with his tail. She knew he would do all he could to comfort and protect her, but her imagination translated every sound into something bigger. Raindrops seeped through the leaky roof and fell to the damp wooden floor, and the pat, pat, pat became as loud as a drumbeat.

Then the rain ceased as suddenly as it had come. Through the silence she could hear water dripping on wooden roof slats from drooping tree branches. The fire, casting eerie shadows, dwindled and died and left the hovel in palpable and oppressive darkness. At the moment the fire went out, a bat with moldy leathery wings and the smell of mildew darted from the rafters and vanished. The night quickly became cold and the rough floor hard and uncomfortable. The dog huddled warm against her right leg, his muzzle nudging her hand. She leaned against the wall, her eyes closed, and tried to think of what tomorrow would bring. As she waited in darkness, the mother of fear and mystery, time moved slower than she had ever known.

3

Opening her eyes, she saw a silver light near the doorway. A gleaming steel-blue moon was breaking through the clouds and bathing the boles of cypress trees with steady illumination. They glowed in the eerie light all white against the dark water. The bay leaves glistened like wet leather, and a whippoorwill called from a tree top. Am amorphous will-o'-the-wisp, eerily blue, floated in the distance among the dead trees. Foolish swamp fire, she remembered, *ignis fatuus*, a sprite with a handful of burning hay. It was only a legend, nothing to be afraid of, no cause for worry. She moved her leg and the big hound raised his head. He was very quiet but awake and alert. A shadow crept over a log close to the door of the hut and made her heart beat faster. From the nearby brushwood came a soft, crackling movement.

She held her breath and listened for a sound. The shadow was a passing cloud and the sound in the brush, she told herself, was nothing more than a small animal making its nocturnal rounds after the rain. But could she be sure of that? What if the animal were big and dangerous? What if the sound she heard was not that of an animal but maybe a swamper? The intense stillness, a silence she had never experienced before, oppressed her. The sense of aloneness in spite of the hound for company disturbed her. She strained her ears, hoping to hear the clang of hoofs on the hard road, but heard nothing. She whispered a little prayer, asking for safety.

Scout stood up, shook himself, perked up his floppy ears, and trotted with a soft padding sound to the doorway. He stood as still as a statue, sniffing the scent of the night. His ears were spread wide. Then Catherine herself heard the horses returning, a faint metallic staccato that quickly grew louder. The dog bounded outside to greet his master, and she clambered after him. No longer alone in the dark, she mumbled thankful words of relief. When Matthew on his black stallion seemed to materialize in front of the hovel, leading her tired pony with an extended bridle, she ran eagerly to meet them.

"Matthew! Oh, Matthew!" she exclaimed, her voice ringing through the night air like a birdsong in winter. The pony bobbed her head in recognition and nickered a soft, low whinny.

"I'm so glad you're back!" she said, speaking to Matthew but gently stroking her pony's neck. She was trying hard to remain calm. "The time was longer than you estimated, Mister, much longer."

"No, not really, my love," he replied, chuckling. "We made pretty good time, and not a thing went wrong. Was it lonely here? I would keep loneliness away from thee forever if I could."

Because the words he had spoken sounded like a vague and premature marriage proposal, he quickly added: "Dan and Edna are on their way! Believe me, dear Catherine, they are on their way!"

4

She nestled in his arms for warmth and shelter and leaned her head on his shoulder. His arms were strong and comforting and his body pulsated with life. She thought she could almost hear the pounding of the young man's heart. So close to him she felt calm and secure and not afraid of anything. He kissed her forehead, looked into her smiling face, and kissed her lips. She did not resist, but when he greedily went for a third kiss she ducked beneath his wavering arms and went to her pony.

"The horses look exhausted," she remarked.

"I'm sure they are. Both have done a good night's work. As for me, I shall never feel tired again, not ever, not ever again."

As if to prove his contention, he lifted her easily into the saddle. He was flushed with excitement. She knew his rapid heartbeat was triggered by the events he had planned and carried out with dispatch, but she hoped it had something to do with her as well.

"You must tell me everything," she said as they moved into the road and set their mounts to a slow trot. "I have a thousand questions for you. Did you find the peddler where you hoped to find him?"

"We did. He was coming down the road just as we got there. Fifteen minutes later and we would have missed him. He had a team of good horses pulling a large wagon. Both Edna and Dan climbed inside."

"Oh, that's so good to hear!"

"They slipped under the big tarpaulin that keeps his goods dry. He said they would be safe as a bug in a rug."

"Well, sometimes bugs in rugs get stepped on, you know! I hope he meant snug as a bug in a rug!"

"That too!" Matthew laughed. "He'll look after them, no doubt about it. When the man comes this way again, I'll find a way to reward him."

"Did you get the peddler's name?" asked Catherine.

"I did, and it's easy to remember. Quentin Sadeye. He's a stern, quiet man marked by sorrow but brave and bold. Told us he was part Cherokee."

They were soon at the front door of the Kingston dwelling, silent and shadowy in blue and silver light. Sarah had put the children to bed and gone to bed herself, locking the door but leaving the key in its customary hiding place. Matthew found it and ushered Catherine inside. A candle burned before the mirror. Together they had planned and executed a risky adventure with excellent results. He wanted to hold her close in shared triumph, but when he turned from closing the door she was gone. Quickly on cat's feet she went to Anna's room where she had promised to spend the night.

After stabling the horses he entered the spacious parlor. The hound lay sleeping on the mat near the fireplace. Matthew locked the front door and went to his room to find Jesse fast asleep. Anna greeted Catherine with a sleepy hello. He thought he heard a warm and girlish whisper in reply, but couldn't be sure. Within minutes, his body aching from all the exertion, he slept. The storm had passed on to the east and the night was calm.

Chapter 14

An uncertain October morning came with cloudy skies and falling temperatures but no rain. At the Kingston house Catherine rose early to help Sarah prepare breakfast. The exertion and excitement of getting Dan and Edna off to a new life exacted a toll on Matthew and caused him to sleep later than usual. He woke up to loud and shrill laughter in the kitchen. Catherine was having fun with the children, enjoying their antics. She liked the comical interplay between Anna and Jesse, and they liked nothing better than to gain her attention and entertain her.

Jesse had a riddle for Catherine, "Why do lions eat raw meat?"

"Oh! Because they live wild and close to nature?"

"Nope! It's because they never learned to cook!"

"I have one for you!" said Anna. "Why was the baby ant confused?"

"Because he was just a baby, like you!" cried the boy, making a face.

"No, dummy. Because all his uncles were ants!"

"Hah! Now that's real funny! It's enough to make a mule laugh! Haw, haw, hee-haw! Now I have one for you, smarty pants. What has three heads, is ugly as all git-out, and smells bad?"

"I dunno," Anna replied after thinking hard. "What?"

"Oops, my mistake, you don't have three heads!" He was grinning from ear to ear, delighted by his coup de maitre perfectly delivered.

"Now, Jesse, be nice," cautioned Catherine.

"He's mean," whimpered Anna, "he spoils everything. He's a box of rocks and knows it! But let him answer this riddle. Horses walk on its head all day long but don't hurt it, what is it?"

Jesse didn't know. Anna whispered the answered to Catherine. "I made that one up just then!" she said proudly.

"I give up," Jesse reluctantly admitted, "what is it?"

"It's the nail in a horseshoe! I made it up!"

"Well, horses wear out them nail heads pretty fast," grumped Jesse.

Matthew paused to listen to the chatter, got dressed, and went to the pump in the back yard to wash his face. Then he came into the kitchen and tried to have a private word with Catherine but in vain. Her dewy brown eyes, like those of a doe in flight, darted in his direction but seemed to avoid his own. She was busy, she said, helping with breakfast and had no time to talk just now. She moved from the kitchen to the breakfast room, helping Sarah set the table and carry in the food even as she joked with the children.

"Come and get it!" she called, placing stacks of pancakes on the table. "We have milk and syrup and plenty of butter."

"I want strawberry jam on mine!" yelled Jesse.

"And me too!" squealed his little sister.

"Sorry, but Sarah says only the syrup this morning."

"Sarah ain't my mama," groused Jesse, pretending to pout.

"Settle down, Jesse. And you too, Anna."

Both children noted the edge of command in Matthew's voice and said nothing more about the jam. But they kept up a lively chatter about all sorts of things during the entire meal. Laughing and giggling and making jokes, they slathered gobs of butter on their hot pancakes and soaked them in maple syrup. Then they ate with ravenous appetites, washing down the food in their overfilled mouths with thick milk from the cellar.

2

After helping Sarah clear away the table and clean the dishes, Catherine announced her intention to return home.

"Papa was complaining of indigestion and is still a little lame with that sprained ankle. I can't abide his being there alone much longer. He claims he can shift for himself, but I know he often ignores basic needs. I'm obliged to go home as soon as you bring Peg around."

Jesse in a burst of generosity offered to come with her.

"Well, I guess you could," she replied, "but it isn't necessary."

"Jesse has something else to do," said Matthew. "I will see you home."

Glancing at him and reading his demeanor, Catherine knew she had in this lover of hers a different person. He was no longer the easy-going and compromising companion of only a month ago, he was tougher. She rather liked the change, though he seemed propelled by forces foreign to her.

She could see that his behavior was more volatile than hers, more unpredictable. He was too eager to be alone with her. His newly awakened masculinity puzzled her, bothered her. She made up her mind to be equal in his presence, to assert herself, and yet she could not bring herself to quarrel with him. Though now a woman of twenty-two, she had never been in a close relationship with a man. This falling in love with the conventional and necessary courtship was a first-time experience for both of them. It was like crossing the stepping stones of a whitewater creek in the dark. Either one could slip and fall, and then what?

Older than Matthew by two years, she no longer felt older. In the past, always aware that he was her junior, she had no trouble rejecting any decision he made. Any time she had found herself in disagreement with him she made her position adamant and unwavering. She could remember arguments with him that she had won. More than once she had required him to say with hangdog looks, "You are right, Catherine. You are right and I was wrong." And she would bask in triumph on hearing those words. Until recently she had found it fairly easy to defy him, even to best him. Now she was finding it difficult. He acted decisively now and spoke with authority. He rode home with her. Jesse had something else to do.

They exchanged few words during the brief ride between the two farms. Skies were clearing and the day becoming warmer. When they neared her father's house the young man tightened the bridle and slowed the pace of his horse. In a more innocent time she would have flicked her pony with her riding wand to dash forward and require him to catch her. Now she made no effort to urge the pony onward.

"Will you tell me what's wrong?" he asked, his handsome face showing deep concern. "Have I done something to displease you?"

"No, of course not," she replied lightly, trying to dispel the seriousness she could sense. "Don't be silly, nothing's wrong!"

"Am I being too forward? Am I making a pest of myself?"

She hesitated before answering. For an instant she thought of making a joke of his remark: "Yes, you're a pest! You're worse than a boll weevil in cotton!" Instead she calmly answered, "No, of course not."

"Well, I hope not. I feel good about what we did last night, the Dan and Edna thing. We accomplished what we set out to do."

"Yes, we did! It was a scary thing, for me at least, but you did wonderfully well, Matthew. You did exactly what had to be done."

"Well, you did all right yourself, y'know. You showed plenty of courage staying alone in that place in the dark until I got back."

"I wasn't entirely alone. Scout was with me. I thought he might run after the horses and leave me there alone. I was grateful when he didn't."

"Scout knows how to behave, and I'm glad we had him with us. We shared a risk, you and I, as sharp as a razor's edge. We shared a feeling of triumph too, and we changed the lives of two people in love. It was good."

"It was, Matthew. It's something I shall always remember."

"I'm glad to hear that, and yet today you seem to despise me."

"What can I say?" answered Catherine. "I don't despise you, Matthew. In fact, I . . . I . . ." She stopped. It was as if her tongue had tripped on something. She couldn't say the words he wanted to hear.

3

They rode into the yard and dismounted in front of her house. In the early morning glimmer her shining beauty was like a beacon flashing across a murky sea. And he was a desperate sailor struggling to reach safe haven in a storm, unable to turn his gaze away from her. He wanted to look at her, to absorb her beauty until he felt safe and comfortable, but now was the time to speak words to her.

"You know beyond a doubt that I love you, Catherine. I have said it and will say it again. I love you, my love. Tell me now that you love me."

"Why should I?" she asked, smiling, meeting his gaze.

"Because I want thee to complete me. I want thee to be my wife. I want thee to live a long and happy life with me."

She was on the porch now and he was standing on the bottom step. He was looking upward to her as if to heaven and proposing in Quaker plain speech charged with emotion. She had opened her heart to him like a flower to springtime, but what could she say? Didn't she need time to think it over?

"I won't say no," she replied, speaking without shyness in a soft, crisp voice. "But I can't listen to this any longer. I must see to Papa."

He could tell she was flustered and did not press his case.

"Say hello to your father for me," he called as he led Peg to the barn.

She had not spoken what he wanted to hear, but her look had said it all. That expressive vibrant face spoke volumes. He felt like a hawk lifted up and gliding on gentle currents of air, or maybe like an eagle riding the wind.

Jeremy Heartwood was writing at his little desk when his daughter came into the house. He paused, looked up, and greeted her.

"The ankle, Katie, is much better today, I'm glad to report. Is Matthew with you? I have a favor to ask of him."

"He has just taken my Peg to the stable before returning home."

Some time ago, disregarding gender, she had named the pony Pegasus because the little horse seemed to sprout wings and fly. But soon afterwards she shortened the name to Peg, and the name stuck. For a female it seemed to fit better than the original. And Peg did not look at all like Pegasus.

"Please ask him if he will put my mare in the gig. I want to visit Isaac Brandimore this morning. The indigestion is no bother now, but the ankle could give me a little trouble if I tried to go on horseback."

For a moment his daughter seemed unwilling to act. On the surface there seemed to be no reason whatever to hesitate, but something within her made her cautious. The barn was warm and dark and isolated. It smelled of animals and the life that coursed through them, and her lover was there. She was not ready to meet him in a situation so compromising. In an instant in fervent embrace, both of them could lose the restraint that kept their lives on even keel. A Quaker courtship did not permit lax behavior of any sort. Without exception Quaker doctrine demanded the woman remain pure and clear throughout courtship. Amorous hanky-panky beyond a hug and a kiss was strictly forbidden. Before marriage two older women would question her closely on that, and she would have to give honest answers. Pausing for a moment, she put these thoughts out of her mind, gathered her skirt over her arm, and walked in that direction.

The mist had given way to a sunny but chilly fall day with blue skies and gentle wind. The morning sun warmed her face and dazzled her eyes. Passing the carefully laid woodpile, she felt the crunch of chips under her feet and breathed their woody fragrance. The red barn was the color of rich burgundy wine. Fat chickens and a billy goat loitered in the yard about the door, clucking and bleating and eyeing her every move. A lone bee with black and yellow stripes bumbled in the honeysuckle and spiraled upward in chilly air. Wild geese in a V formation winged their way southward, silhouetted against an autumn sky and honking. Matthew stood in the shade, cinching the saddle of his own horse after removing Peg's. He was not in the barn after all, and she was pleased.

Hearing the sound of Catherine approaching, he looked over the horse's withers and smiled a greeting. Had she come to chat with him for just a few minutes more, maybe to tell him something? In the sunlight her face was golden and her blonde hair caught the sunlight and glistened. A scented freshness surrounded her and seemed to stroke his face as she came closer. He wanted to run to her, sweep her off her feet, and make love to her. But natural reserve bolstered by stern Quaker teaching put lead in his shoes. He went on working with Caesar's saddle, not daring to move as she spoke to him but quickly moving when she finished.

"If you please, Matthew, Papa has a favor to ask. He wants to visit Isaac Brandimore in the gig. His ankle makes him lame, and . . ."

He was already walking through the barn's wide doors to the gray horse and the harness room and the two-wheeled cart. In ten minutes the gig was ready, and Jeremy thanked him as he flicked the reins and drove off.

Catherine had retreated to her room. He could walk into the house, and they would be alone together. He knew that lovers needed to be alone, and yet until she consented they would have to remain apart. He was a needle drawn to a magnet, but unlike the needle he could resist the force that drew him to her. Quaker doctrine had always taught purity, self-respect, and self-control for both male and female. Resisting animal instinct made a person stronger and the prize more precious. As he rode away he called out to let her know he was on his way home.

4

In the damp sand as Matthew came into the yard, he could see the tracks of the old coach leading to the front door and away to the barnyard. That told him at a glance that his parents had returned from their overnight visit. Hitching Caesar to a post, he climbed the steps to the rear entrance of the house. The air smelled of wood-smoke from the kitchen fire. Acknowledging a nod from Sarah, he passed through the kitchen and entered the parlor to greet his parents. They seemed more somber than usual.

"Hello, Travelers! Welcome home! Did you have a pleasant trip, a good time at the Hammond place? Catherine was here and all went well."

"We had a wonderful time, and thank you for asking," Rachel replied. "The children have told us everything. They always become so excitable when Catherine pays attention to them."

"They had a whopping breakfast made by Catherine and Sarah, and all the time they were eating they were having fun."

"Did you get the news?" asked David abruptly. "We heard on the road that Isaac Brandimore has fallen sick. Your mother and I were talking about him, and I don't have to tell you we are worried."

"No, I didn't hear a word. I sure hope it's nothing serious."

"Well, it could be. You never know with a person his age. Most of the night he was delirious and talking about Seth, his housekeeper reported. He told the woman that Seth came and stood before him in a flowing white gown. Hovering above the fuzzy old head was a golden halo that glistened fiercely, and he beckoned Isaac to come with him."

"Oh, that sounds exactly like Isaac, Papa. His imagination often gets the better of him. Maybe he wasn't delirious, after all. Maybe he was running a fever that triggered a fantasy. He's always dreaming, y'know."

"The housekeeper said Isaac laughed and prayed and sweated profusely. Said he was very glad old Seth went to heaven as a free man and wanted his companionship there. A place in heaven was waiting for him, Seth told him. Then the fever broke and he was finally able to rest."

"Oh that means he's better. At this very moment Jeremy Heartwood is on his way to visit Isaac. The man has a sprained ankle and a stomach problem but ignored his ailments to go to Brandimore's house."

"He must have had a premonition he was needed there."

"I wonder if I shouldn't let Catherine know about this. Her father may be away from home longer than expected. She'd worry."

"Jeremy can decide when to come home. He'll have a good story to tell and will want to deliver the news himself."

"What will happen to his place if Isaac Brandimore should pass on?" Rachel asked. "He has no living relatives and only temporary help."

"Tom Bolton will try to buy it. He increases his property holdings at every opportunity. Some of his acres already border Isaac's. I wouldn't be a bit surprised to see Bolton owing half the county in a few years."

"But what if war comes?" Rachel persisted. "A terrible, agonizing war on this ground could hit Thomas Bolton hard, and he could lose everything. It could hit us hard too. All the money we have in that Northern bank, all our savings, could evaporate."

Chapter 15

The autumn afternoon went by quickly. David and his son worked with farm hands until suppertime. His wife assigned chores to the children and baked in the kitchen. After supper he sat looking over some letters in the small alcove off the living room. Matthew near the window was reading a novel by Wilkie Collins, a recent addition to the family library. Rachel and the children were in the kitchen with Sarah. Suddenly a hard knock jolted the front door of the house, and then a second knock. Without waiting for permission to enter, indeed before anyone could respond, Thomas Bolton barged into the parlor and approached David.

"Good evening, Mr. Kingston," said Bolton, removing his hat and trying as best he could to control his anger. He was an abrupt man with a big voice and accustomed to issuing orders that were quickly obeyed. A note of command, of authority, rang out in his speech even on social occasions, but this was no sociable visit. He had come loaded for bear to inquire about Edna. He wanted to remain civil if he could, for he hoped to garner facts to prove his hunch. If he got what he hoped to find, perhaps an open admission, he would legally charge the Kingstons with stealing his property.

"Have a seat, Neighbor Bolton," said David, affably offering his chair to the man and taking another. "I welcome thee to my home. Let me take thy hat and coat, and please have a mug of hot cider. Sarah will serve it."

David received the coat, made of fine wool with visible bands of astrakhan on the front and sleeves, and placed it on the coat rack. Taking a seat opposite, he saw at a glance that Bolton's boots were trimmed at the tops with rich brown fur. Coat, boots, and hat all suggested opulence.

"No, Mr. Kingston, no cider for me. This is not a social visit."

Matthew, who had stood when Bolton entered, nodded to the uninvited guest, sat down again and resumed his reading. David waited for his visitor to explain. Was he there perhaps to name a price for Edna?

"Mr. Kingston, I am here to get to the bottom of a very serious matter. I don't know that you are responsible, but I have reason to believe you had a hand in it. I have lost a girl you once tried to buy from me. We believe she ran off with your boy Dan."

"I doubt that, Mr. Bolton. I've heard she has a good job in your kitchen, and the woman is too smart to jeopardize it. As for Dan, I can tell thee nothing. I saw him last when he helped with the harvest, and we spoke only of the work to be done. I paid him, of course, for the work he did."

"I haven't seen him either, but I know Edna was on the plantation yesterday. Trouble is she didn't come to supper with the rest of the field hands. This morning she was nowhere to be found. So I'm thinking who could have helped her run away and why, and then I thought of you."

He was trying to cover his sense of outrage with a veil of politeness, but the veil was quickly wearing thin.

"I'm sorry to hear that, Neighbor Bolton," replied David with characteristic sincerity. "But truly I can shed no light on thy problem. My wife and I were away all day yesterday and last night. We posted in the carriage thirty miles to visit old friends. We didn't return until this morning."

"Exactly," Bolton snorted, unable to contain his anger. "You went away yesterday morning, and most probably you made arrangements to take my girl Edna with you. Her rascal of a husband, as he calls himself, was probably waiting somewhere on the road and joined your party. You claim you would never steal a neighbor's property, but I don't believe you. I am certain you know more than you are telling me!"

Interpreting these remarks as an insult and not willing to sit in docile submission while his father was being abused, Matthew rose and stood.

"Easy, Matthew," cautioned the older man. "Sit down, please. You have no say in this and no reason to be concerned."

"Will you swear you had nothing to do with my girl running off?" asked Bolton, glancing nervously at Matthew.

"I am not one to swear, Mr. Bolton. Surely you must know that. I speak the truth unvarnished with no need to swear. I have told you all that I know. I cannot abide thievery of any kind, and helping another person's slaves run away is just that. You and I have talked about slavery more than once. We could never agree on much, but on this one thing we do agree. The principles by which I live would never allow the behavior you describe."

"You are telling me you had nothing to do with it?" Bolton demanded.

He was in a rage but half believed this man of good will. He despised David for his abolitionist views but rather liked him as a man.

"I know nothing. I have not seen Dan. I have not seen Edna. For all I know Edna is back in your kitchen right now."

"No, not back in the kitchen. I put her out to work. That's how she got away. My son told me he saw Catherine Heartwood in the vicinity. I can't believe that pretty young woman would conspire to steal Edna."

Matthew could feel the hair on the back of his neck bristle as he heard this reference to Catherine. He fought to control himself. Could he sit by and allow her name to be sullied by the spittle of an angry man charging her with complicity and thievery? He was about to rise and confront Bolton, but something within him said no. He turned his back and went on reading.

The angry slaveholder stared in his direction, his face dark with disapproval. He pointed a wagging finger at Matthew.

"I venture to say that misguided fellow right there knows all about it. My son never liked him, and I don't have much regard for him either. He's an impudent scoundrel!"

"Matthew?" asked Kingston, "Matthew? I really don't think he would be likely to know anything. On the face of it your accusations appear to be unfounded, Mr. Bolton, and your anger does not become you."

He picked up a silver letter opener, turned it over and over in his hands, and quietly regarded his visitor. Bolton's insults had pricked his pride and warmed his blood, but Quaker tradition had taught him to put down anger and especially pride. His frank and open face was calm. He placed the tips of his ten fingers together to make a little tent, waiting for Bolton to reply. In emulation of his father, the more volatile Matthew remained calm.

2

Bolton was baffled. His charges had fallen on deft ears. His fierce denunciation of father and son had achieved nothing, and he had learned nothing. He had not been able to find adequate cause to suppose his visit was in any way worthwhile. His suspicions were as strong as ever but unconfirmed. For a moment his gray eyes burned like hot coals. A surge of volcanic rage ran like a hot current through him. He would have to veer off and attack from another direction.

"You are ruining this country," he cried, his voice hoarse with emotion. "Ruining the country with your damnable antislavery notions. Because of your kind North and South are going to split. A man will not be able to call his soul his own before long, much less his property! The politicians are looking to crush the South, take away our livelihood, make us beggars. And you with your accursed views are helping them!"

"Neighbor Bolton," replied David Kingston quietly, knitting his brows. "I can understand your turmoil, and I sympathize with your loss, but I think you will agree with me that you've said enough."

He rose and stood erect, his broad, impregnable shoulders blocking the lamplight and casting Bolton into shadow. Matthew stood beside his father, more lithe and ready for action than the older man but not more imposing.

"I can tell you this," said the angry slave owner, rising from his seat. "If war comes, you will be indicted as traitors and dealt with accordingly."

The man's furious accusations had now become threats.

"Mr. Bolton, let me show you to the road," urged Matthew. "It's growing dark, and you could lose your way. Let us say goodnight, sir."

The young man's eyes were blazing. His air of quiet command could not be easily resisted. Bolton put on his coat and hat without a word.

Fuming, but deliberately putting down all show of anger, Matthew ushered the agitated man outside and to the avenue of oaks.

"Take a right at the end of the lane, Mr. Bolton. Did you walk all the way from your house? Would you like a ride home?"

In no mood to answer either question, the planter buttoned his coat and hurried away. The night air was becoming chilly, even cold. Matthew went inside to find Jesse lighting the fire. His father was pacing the floor, hands clasped behind him, a woeful look of displeasure on his rugged face.

"He's right, you know. The man is right. The South cannot abolish slavery without crippling its economy. It will not do that willingly. Force will surely be necessary. A terrible, ugly war seems inevitable. It will pit neighbor against neighbor, brother against brother. And the Quakers? Where in the world, with ideas and beliefs peculiar only to us, will we stand? Right in the middle, my son, right in the middle."

In the big fireplace flames of many colors leaped and danced. A knot of pine burned rapidly and brightly to ignite a log. Jesse had built a good fire and now crouched in front of the swirling flames, delighted by the glint they made. The men stood with hands behind their backs and warmed themselves. They had learned long ago that fire provides heat and light. And they had learned that fire can destroy whatever it touches. In the warm glow of the crackling fire, respecting its power, they spoke quietly of troubled times. In another part of the house Rachel was reading a story to Anna.

"And I'll huff and puff and blow your house down," she intoned.

"Can a wolf really do that?" asked Anna.

3

Nothing more was said in the Kingston household concerning Bolton's visit. As a rule, all Quakers tried to learn from unpleasant events but quickly let them merge with daily activity to be rendered inactive if not forgotten. When life became unpleasant, as it often does for anybody living anywhere, they set their minds to solving the problems of the present rather than brooding on the past. And so in time the confrontation was remembered by David only in his prayers.

The days passed and the loss of Edna was reported to the district sheriff, who looked into the incident but could do nothing about it. He made inquiries and found out that no one had seen Edna since the day she did not show up for supper. As for Dan, he had not be seen by anyone for weeks. The sheriff knew that when he wanted to drop out of sight, he had the uncanny ability to evaporate in thin air. He was able to go into hiding for as long as he wished and then suddenly appear as if no time at all had passed and nothing had happened. Bolton was convinced that Edna, his valued cook, was now with the free man who called himself her husband. She would run with him wherever he chose to go. The sheriff insisted he could find no evidence that Edna ran off with Dan.

Fiercely determined to regain his property, Thomas Bolton sent a message to Raleigh, asking the governor to intervene. When the office of the governor didn't bother to reply, he hired a peculiar breed of man, a slave hunter, to pick up her scent and bring her back. On finding her, the man had the authority to arrest her and bring her home by force. He traced her through the swamp and to the crossroads at the logging station and all the way to the coast, but there he lost her scent. Returning to Bolton to collect his fee, he reported that someone had seen a black couple boarding a sailing vessel in Newport News. No one could remember the name of the ship, nor any details concerning the couple. Lacking that basic information, the hunter was powerless to trace the couple farther.

As Christmas was coming on, Matthew Kingston received a soiled and tattered letter from Baltimore. On a sheet of lined writing paper someone, perhaps a harried clerk, had scrawled with a scratchy pen a cryptic message that when deciphered carried a great deal of meaning: *Your pair care of Sadeye now in Canada. On record as Kg & E Saddleoak. Citshp pending.* Sadeye, the name of the Cherokee peddler, was understandable but Saddleoak was puzzling. Then Matthew saw its logic. From Sadeye, the brave man who helped them escape, came Saddle. From Heartwood, Catherine's last name, came hardwood and then an imaginative leap to oak—Saddleoak—an appropriate name to honor Edna's liberators.

But what about Matthew and the role he had played? Of course! The letter K could mean anything, but Kg had only one meaning—King—and that came from Kingston. They were now legally known as King and Edna Saddleoak, their citizenship in Canada pending. The man who had called himself Dan Becker when he married Edna, and Hambone before he was free, would now have a future and a new name. As a free man discovering his ego, he had every right to honor Matthew by calling himself King. He could have used Matthew with the same effect, but he liked King better. In Canada he found work and fathered many children. He grew in dignity as the years passed and ceased to call himself Hambone.

Chapter 16

In the shadowy moonlight, seething with frustration and anger, Thomas Bolton strode briskly homeward. He could have gone to the Kingston house in a carriage or on his favorite stallion, but decided to go on foot the better to think about his problems. He wanted to run through what he would say to David Kingston and how he would say it. He expected to accuse the man directly but hoped he would not lose his temper or precipitate a confrontation. He wanted to get an open confession, or at least a faint hint, that Edna's escape had been engineered by his Quaker neighbor. That would be the proof he needed to indict the man. But he had lost his temper and spoken in anger. He had blasted father and son with insults that seemed not to reach their target. When the ugly scene was over, he knew less than when it began.

He had tried to vent his rage on David Kingston, but was met with that Quaker calmness which provoked him even more. That imperturbable calm, that unbelievable calm he was thinking, had undermined his plans and left him baffled. He had lost a valuable piece of property and had every right to be upset and angry. Not only must he endure the loss, but his only son had been lax in his duties and his neighbors were suspects. Taking Edna from her kitchen and placing her in a distant field was a big mistake. For that he himself must bear the blame. His son had warned him it was not a good idea. Why didn't he listen? He was mumbling these thoughts to himself just as the moon rose above the treetops to throw more light on the road. Marching sullenly in a breeze rising chilly from the east, he lashed the bushes with his heavy, loaded cane for emotional release.

If David Kingston had been able to examine Bolton's walking stick, he would have seen engraved in the polished wood a Latin motto suggesting or even summarizing Bolton's view of the world. *Sine Labore Nihil* read the Latin, "Nothing Without Work." On the silver head of the cane was more Latin, *Per Ardua ad Astra*—"Through Struggle to the Stars." On the metal tip of the cane was this motto, *Cum Grano Salis*—"All With a Grain of Salt." That too was intended to sum up Bolton's philosophy, and yet when it came to losing Edna he did not take it with a grain of salt. Hard, incessant work had made him a wealthy man, but also a man who prized his possessions. And yet as he looked at the larger picture, he understood that gain had to be balanced with loss, and all of it in the final analysis, even life itself, had to be taken with a grain of salt. That was the philosophy he tried to live by, but now events over which he had no control were threatening to take everything from him. It seemed to him that all the fruits of his labor . . .

Then suddenly without notice, from somewhere in the dark, came a peal of derisive laughter. Stopping to listen and look, Bolton fastened his eyes on a vine-clad sweet gum tree thirty feet off the road. In the shadowy moonlight he could see a naked figure standing on a limb of the tree, wearing only a loincloth and grasping a vine. Glistening in the moonlight, he seemed not quite of this world and startled the planter. Bolton was not a timid man, but having never seen a sight such as this, he didn't know what to make of it.

He stared at the scene and finally identified in the half-light the changeling son of a former slave named Bupee Mwewa Search. A free woman, she had once been called Sally Search but now went by her African name. She lived with her son in a rent-free cabin on the Kingston property. Her owner had set her free when her son was an infant. Later he sold his land to the Kingstons, and they allowed her to remain in her home. The wayward boy was known to everyone in the community. Bolton knew him by sight, for often in colder weather the boy brought small game to the planter's kitchen to be dressed and cooked. When offered money for his presents, invariably he shook his head, assumed a rubbery frown, and mumbled guttural sounds. A brightly colored toy or trinket he eagerly accepted.

2

Ethan Search was known far and wide as a strange but harmless boy who took great delight in being close to mother earth. Bupee Mwewa called him Nature's Boy, but he had in fact many names. Isaac Brandimore once said he was a polyonymous person inspiring nicknames. Some of the blacks called him "Thunder Child" because he often emerged from the swamp in crashing thunder and pelting rain just as a storm was breaking. Others in the community fondly called him "Wonder Boy" or "Bupee's

Boy" or "that Changeling Child." He was one with nature, in harmony with the dictates of natural law, and perpetually joyous when not upset. He was rarely less than happy but at times, for reasons no one understood, he would sink into a dark mood and become explosive. At that moment he would find his voice and cry out. Often it was a cackling laugh, or a call, that grated on the nerves.

He could run like an animal and had learned to swing from tree to tree on wild grape vines. In the sweltering swamp he displayed amazing agility, observers reported, swinging from tree to tree and never touching the ground. He was thin as a rail but strong as a bear, and he often displayed an uncanny knowledge of the swamp. Though judged by some as mentally disabled, many believed he could identify on sight all the plants that flourished deep in the swamp and name every animal living there. Legend had it that Ethan could swing across the Great Dismal Swamp without stopping to rest. If he did rest, it was always on a limb high in a tall tree.

In the labyrinth of the dark and mysterious swamp he never got lost, people said, but who was there to see him? A few swampers eking out a living by gigging frogs lived in or near the swamp, but they seldom talked to outsiders. They often spoke to Ethan, however, and the word got around that he was much admired by the swampers. Though known to everyone, the boy had no friends unless he named creatures of the wild as friends. His mother reported that bears seemed to recognize him but gave him no trouble, bees refused to sting him, and mosquitoes never bit. Snakes sunning themselves on tree limbs coiled in readiness when they heard him coming, but never harmed him. The deer stood and watched as he came and went, nodding their heads as if they knew him, and never ran from him.

He had a special understanding of all wild things, of birdsongs for example, and some believed that with a shrill whistle and cackling sounds he talked with the birds. The animals in the thickly wooded swamp had no fear of him, nor he of them. The heat of summer made his bronze skin glisten, but the cold of winter never seemed to touch him. In the chill autumn air Bolton shivered in his woolen coat, but Ethan's bare skin seemed not to feel the cold. Except for the whistling and cackling and high-pitched laughter, the boy seldom spoke. Though his laughter was his trademark and signature, most of the time he was known to be mute. Yet on rare occasions when unhappy, he spoke with ringing tones as clearly as a classical orator. On this night he was shaken, unstrung, and talkative.

3

"Thomas Bolton be an angry man. Thomas Bolton be a sly man. Thomas Bolton try to beat the clock! Hickory dickory dock! He try to beat the clock! But that ol' clock keeps on ticking, Mon, keeps on ticking!"

He laughed with that special cackle of his and swung in a half circle on the vine, his feet coming close to the planter's head.

"Thomas Bolton try to beat the clock. Try to make the time stand still. Don't believe a cold, cold wind's gonna blow 'im over duh hill!"

The wealthy planter stood transfixed, listening intently to every word. He was not afraid but suddenly felt heavy and cold. The visitant rattled on and on, squatting on the limb and laughing. He uttered a piercing cry as if in pain and broke into a mocking singsong. He sat like a monkey on the limb and pressed the palms of his hands over his ears, released them, and pressed again. Then of a sudden he became eerily and ominously serious, his voice curt and crisp in the autumn air. There was no breeze now, and the sounds he made penetrated the stillness like a knife plunged into jelly or human flesh.

"You won't never see Edna Becker again," he taunted. "You done lost her, and Becker ain't her name! Edna done gone to Canaan's happy shore, to Canaan's happy shore! You done lost her, Mars Bolton, and none too soon. People gonna run from you, 'cept a stranger 'side the doh! And Massa gonna sleep in the cold, cold ground! Massa gonna sleep in the ground!"

His words rang and sang in the still night. Catching their cadence and dancing to their rhythm, he repeated them over and over.

"A stranger beside the door?" mused Bolton. "What on earth could that mean? And me sleep on the cold ground when I have a warm bed waiting for me? The little ape's an idiot and babbling nonsense."

The boy clutched the vine with one hand, swung in a wide arc, and dropped nimbly in front of Bolton. His burnished face just inches away, he stared into the startled man's eyes. With perfect enunciation, he repeated his bizarre diatribe almost in a whisper.

"Edna's gone, my dear fellow, gone! Gone to Canaan's happy shore. And a pale stranger waits beside the door. A stranger, a pale stranger, waiting! And you will sleep, Thomas Bolton, you will sleep!"

A moment later he turned to swing away. At that instant Bolton aimed his heavy cane at the vine. He brought it down with all his strength, intending to thwart the boy's escape and thrash him. He didn't intend to injure Bupee's son, only to punish him. But the cane smashed into the back of the boy's skull and laid him senseless at Bolton's feet. Surprised but snorting contempt, the man stooped to examine the limp form. Blood trickled from the back of his head, but the boy seemed alive and breathing. As calm and still as the silence that surrounded him, he lay there as if asleep.

"It's a good thing his head is hard as a rock," Bolton said aloud. "He'll be all right. He'll wake up and find his way home."

The struggling moon yielded and went behind a cloud. The countryside was dark and quiet, but the breeze had come up again and the dying leaves were falling. Except for Ethan Search, clothed only in a loincloth and lying peacefully on the damp ground, Bolton was alone. For an instant he thought of covering the boy against the cold but had only the coat he was wearing, and that he couldn't spare.

"He won't feel the cold," Bolton was thinking as he walked onward. "The leaves will cover him like a blanket. He'll be all right. He'll wake up and go home even before morning comes." And so a nebulous doubt concerning the boy was galvanized into firm belief.

4

The next morning Leo Mack found the body, half covered with dewy leaves, lying near a vine dangling from a tree. The mother had sat in her cabin all night long, waiting for the son who gave her reason to live to return. Though he was wayward and capricious and unpredictable, she loved the boy dearly. Bupee had chosen to remain in the region when her former master moved away because she knew her son loved the swamp and hated change. The Kingstons saw that she and Ethan didn't suffer for want of necessities. The cabin she had lived in for years had a plot for a vegetable garden and a spring in back. It was a good cabin, tightly built with two rooms and a loft.

On occasion, when fancy moved him, Ethan would do half a day's work as some sort of game he was playing. Always he worked skillfully and methodically, following the rules of the game. He liked doing chores at the Kingston farm and felt comfortable around Moses. He was drawn to Matthew but always observed him from a distance. The Kingston animals, Caesar and Scout, had a mystical understanding of his special qualities and befriended him. With Jesse and Anna he was wary and undecided, staring at them from a distance. Even though on more than one occasion they tried to win his trust, he didn't make friends with the children. He had a deep respect for David and Rachel and liked to be in their presence, but would never talk. Sometimes at first light, long before the family was awake, he would furtively slip into Sarah's kitchen for scraps of food. Should the food displease him, he would croak in a loud and hollow voice. That invariably caused Sarah to chase him away for fear of waking the family.

People marveled at how much the changeling knew and wondered how he acquired his knowledge. He knew exactly when the holidays would be coming around, and like clockwork he brought wild game for the table. In that respect he was generous to a fault, often showing up at break of day with a heavy bag full of small game. Matthew asked him once how he was able to catch and kill the rabbits, raccoons, wild turkeys, and squirrels but could get no answer. Once he came with a live turtle and wanted Sarah to dress it and make soup of its meat. She often fussed when he came to her kitchen but fed him anyway. He could describe in great detail, in a rare talkative mood, exactly what people had given him or his mother over several years. He amazed the Kingstons with his knowledge of dates, the calendar, and numbers. His talk was always about the little events of daily life, never about the swamp or its denizens. The Kingston family coach with its large, heavy wheels turning and turning delighted him.

He knew every name of every person, black and white, for miles around and seemed to know when anyone came into the community, moved away, or died. He knew where each person lived and how many people were in the household. But anyone who asked their ages was disappointed, for to him all people were the same age. He knew all the roads and where they intersected and where they went. He had never gone to school, not even for a day, but could read signs on the road. He knew when the creek would run low and when a well would run dry and when a storm would hit. He had never been out of Prudock County but spoke of faraway places, even lands across the sea. His unusual name was eerily appropriate, for wherever he went he seemed to be searching for something, looking beyond the limits of the human eye. He was a chef without a kitchen, a scholar without books, a scientist without a petri dish, and a prophet without a pulpit. He was known to possess a curious assortment of special gifts and was not always pleasant, but all who knew him seemed better for it.

Chapter 17

In the middle of the afternoon Matthew was helping Moses repair the worn hinges on the barn door. He had wanted to replace them with new ones, but Jacob Darboy had not been able to get them. His supplier had told Darboy that anything made of metal was becoming scarce because the South was preparing for war. The journalists were saying that was no longer a rumor but a fact. Matthew hoped they were wrong. Just as the hinges seemed to be working again, he looked away and saw Bupee Mwewa Search in a sweater and blue cotton dress coming across the potato field.

"Bupee is moving like she's older than you," he said to Moses. "Looks like the clods in that field are getting the best of her."

"Yessuh, I reckon her Ethan wears her out. He's an independent critter. Comes and goes like some ol' shadow, is full o' constant surprises. Bupee don't never know what he gonna do nex'. And he don't pay no mind to her. Nothin' more wearin' on a fond mama."

"Well, she's lucky to have him. What would she do without him?"

"I dunno but he sho is a handful, that I know."

"Good afternoon!" called Matthew as the woman approached, stepping slowly over clods made hard by the sun. "Are you all right, Bupee?"

He could tell by the way she carried herself that something in her life had gone wrong and had thrust a heavy burden upon her.

"No, I'm not all right Mistah Matthew. Ethan's been called to glory in a twinklin' of an eye, and the news done upset me somethin' awful. I'm not all right, Mistah Matthew, not all right at all."

He dropped his tools and turned on his heel to face her. "You mean to tell me Ethan's dead? How can that be? Here, sit down on this stump. You look exhausted, Bupee. Are you thirsty? Are you hungry?"

She sat there in a funk, lost in woolgathering, staring across the field at nothing, her thin and drawn face wracked by agony. The nervous, dark eyes were dull and swollen but without tears. Hours of sobbing had broken the mechanism for making tears.

"They found him this mornin'," she mumbled, rocking back and forth and speaking as though reading from a book. "Found him a-layin' side the road near Mistah Bolton's place. Under the grapevine twists he's so fond o' swingin' on. They say he must of swung too hard and just fell and broke his neck. Landed on his shiny bald head, big knot on the back and cut open."

She went on rocking and moaning like a stricken animal. "Why, oh why did he go befo' the golden chariot done come for me?" she wailed.

Matthew's heart went out to her. She had tried to keep her ignorance of the world at bay by loving deeply and living simply. Then through no fault of her own the world came crashing down upon her. Slipping off the stump, she lay face down on the cold ground, pounded it with her fists, and broke into unrestrained sobbing. He tried to comfort her, tried lifting her from the ground, and saw that her face was dry. His mother's cook, observing from the kitchen, came running to help.

Brushing the dirt from her dress, Sarah took the frail woman by the hand and shoulders and led her weeping into the kitchen. Rachel Kingston tried to soothe her with comforting words, but could say little to assuage her pain. The woman sat on a kitchen chair rocking her tiny body back and forth and wailing softly. Sarah gave her a cup of tea, but her hands couldn't hold it. Rachel brought the cup to the woman's lips and urged her to sip. The children romped into the kitchen and got an inkling of what had happened.

"What's it like to die?" asked Anna, wide-eyed.

"You get all cold and clammy and can't talk no more," yelled Jesse, "and they put you in the ground so you don't stink, and they throw dirt on top of you! It's called a burial, dummy, and the hole is a grave."

"Out!" commanded Rachel, swinging a handy broom to wallop Jesse on the buttocks. Summoning the energy that coursed through him, he skipped easily out of the way. She swung again and just as easily he danced away to evade the broom, but quickly the children made themselves scarce.

An hour later Bupee slowly made her way back to her cabin, trundling over clods in the potato field and treading carefully through a cabbage patch. Matthew had Moses walk with her and make certain she would be all right. He said not a word to her as they walked, knowing she wanted silence in her suffering. Weak and shaken, she was grateful for the help he gave her but said nothing either. The woman was not old in years, and yet her burden of woe had bent her double. Her loss was more than she could bear.

2

In his comfortable home, sitting alone in firelight on a chilly night and sipping brandy from an oversized snifter, Thomas Bolton brooded on what had happened the night before. Carefully he ran through his mind and memory the details of his meeting with the changeling boy who had mocked him so forcefully. All that he remembered convinced him that he was as much a victim of circumstance as Ethan Search.

"It was an accident," he said to himself. "I didn't mean to hit the lad so hard, I was trying to strike the vine. As God is my witness, it was an accident. All I wanted to do was make him understand he couldn't be insolent with a man of my stature. He had no right to taunt me like that."

He reached for the bottle, filled the empty glass half full, and swirled the brandy before sniffing its fragrance. Then he drank deeply and went on to defend his innocence before a somber conscience sitting in judgment.

"It was an accident," he repeated, "and all I did was knock him out. He must have died during the night from exposure. His mother will grieve like any other mother, of course she will. But in time maybe she'll realize it's better without him. He was a burden on her, and some people in these parts were afraid of his antics, thought he was crazy."

Bolton regarded blacks as strong human beings, but strong primarily in the physical sense. He believed their strength could be gauged by the amount of work they could do in a day. The value of his workers lay in the labor they did, and he viewed them as lacking in value if they could not or would not work. The changeling, he reasoned, with his babbling and monkeyshines and refusal to work, was of little worth to anybody. He lived in a world of his own and gave little to the world recognized by others. He was always alone and performing risky stunts, and so his death would never be seen as anything but an accident. Already people were saying, the boy's own mother included, that he fell from a vine and landed on his head. "Let them go on thinking that," he said aloud, "for it really was an accident."

The day after it happened Bolton had gone to Darboy's store to hear what people were saying. He spoke to several people who were eager to talk about it, and listened carefully to what they had to say. He was pleased when everyone in the store pointedly stated that Ethan's death was an accident. Without revealing anything he knew about it, with full assurance he agreed. The boy got in the way of his cane just as he swung to hit the vine. It was an accident without a discernible cause, an unfortunate accident, and that he believed until the day he died.

3

The next day, when Matthew came in for supper, his father had a job for him. At table they spoke only of the day's events, but when the meal was over and the children out of the way, David made his wishes clear.

"I want you to be present at Ethan Search's funeral service. Bupee wants the service performed in the Meeting House. That little church she goes to every Sunday can accommodate only a few people. The Meeting House is much larger and more convenient and not far from the burial site. We can do that for her as a special favor if you are willing to help."

"Well, of course I'm willing to help, Papa. What can I do?"

"I want you to be there to keep an eye on the ceremony and see that it goes smoothly. It will be a great comfort to Bupee."

"I have no problem with that, but the boy was found dead only yesterday morning. Wouldn't tomorrow night be a better time for the ceremony? The weather is cool enough."

"I'm in agreement, but she wants the service performed tonight."

"Leo Mack is telling the whole community he discovered the body. But how many people will know Ethan is to be buried so soon?"

"Bupee believes the service must take place as soon as possible to let the soul into heaven before it wanders. She is certain every person who loved the boy will come to the ceremony and attend the burial."

He fished in his pocket, found the key to the Meeting-House door, and handed it to his son. "It's the only key we have. Take care not to lose it."

"I think I'll take Catherine with me on Caesar, if she will go. The horse can handle her weight, and she'll be good company."

Matthew had asked Jeremy for permission to marry Catherine, and her father had quickly given his approval and informed David and Rachel Kingston. They shared Jeremy's deep satisfaction and were vastly pleased. They looked forward to a gala wedding event in the spring, even though the newspapers were darkly declaring a possible conflict between North and South by then. To marry when the fields were misty with bluebells and when the crab apple trees were bursting into bloom would give the couple time to know each other better. Now in October his father had entrusted him with an important mission, and he wanted her with him.

4

The sun was sinking behind the trees when Matthew rode up to the Heartwood porch. Catherine heard his approach and came to the door. Her father stood behind her. His sprain had healed and he was no longer limping. Matthew informed them of Ethan's untimely death, Bupee's unlimited grief, and her ardent wish to have her son's soul move into heaven as soon as possible. The funeral, according to her wishes, would be held at the Meeting House that very evening with interment in the graveyard reserved for free blacks. Already scores of people were on their way there.

"I feel just miserable about this but would like to go," said Catherine. "It will take only minutes to saddle Peg."

"I brought along the pillion," Matthew replied. "Caesar is used to going double. He likes it when Anna rides behind me."

"I weigh a bit more than Anna, and Caesar may not like the extra weight on his back, but I'm willing to give it a try. If we can't afford a carriage after marriage, we may have to ride double quite often."

"After we marry, my love, we must work as a team. We'll be going into harness, you and I, and pulling together."

"Yes! Pulling together! I like that."

In the afterglow of sundown, the big stallion trotted contentedly along the road, Catherine bouncing on the pillion and clinging to Matthew's waist. It was dark as they approached the Meeting House. In the gloom they could see torches burning red and yellow as slaves from nearby plantations converged for the ceremony. The news had spread with curious rapidity, and the slaveholders were allowing their workers to pay last respects to the half-witted boy. They had heard that when he was alive many blacks viewed this strange wild child as gifted with mysterious powers and sitting in the lap of God. He was an innocent, they believed, and walked with the angels even before death. Now they were saying he would live forever in the bosom of God. No slaveholder was willing in the light of such passion to risk refusing any person's request to attend the service.

Thomas Bolton permitted his blacks to join the throng of people who would honor the memory of Ethan Search. He even supplied wagons for the gangs to ride in, but under the watchful eyes of overseers on horseback. He knew it would be an emotional ceremony punctuated by rhythmic weeping, clapping, and song but worth the trouble to him if it soothed the agitation of the black community. His overseers would look after his people—no worry there—and have them back on the plantation to begin work at the break of day. Not a single person in the community suspected he had anything to do with Ethan's death. Of that he was certain.

Matthew and Catherine, riding together on Caesar, arrived to find the Meeting-House yard filled with flickering and sputtering torches. Phantom-like faces darted and bobbed behind them. Dusty forms gyrated in the glare and smoke and seemed to be dancing to unheard music. They hitched Caesar to a post, slowly made their way through the crowd, and opened the door of the big white building. Six young men stood near the door ready to carry Ethan Search's feather-weight coffin inside.

In double file the mourners followed the coffin-bearers to the head of the middle aisle. The men rested their burden on sturdy sawhorses in front of the gallery. In the spacious room people fanned out to find seats. Some of them sat as close to the coffin as they could get. Others sought the darker corners. The torches had been stacked in brightly burning pyramids in the yard. Their fluttering, uneven fire threw eerie shadows upon the building and painted the interior with geometric patterns of reddish light. Apart from the sconces high on the walls, the illumination at the front of the room came mainly from two candelabra at the head and foot of the open coffin.

A steady flow of silent figures filed past to take a last look at Ethan's young face. Often screwed to a grimace when alive, it was now relaxed and almost pretty. The boy who could fly like a bird on a grape vine seemed now at peace. The mourners passed in front of the coffin, looked inside, mumbled a few words, and took their seats on the brown benches with tan cushions. The sound of their shoes on the bare wooden floor blended with a low murmuring that ceased when the service began. Bupee and the tall preacher remained near the coffin. As she stood beside him she seemed almost childlike in her grown-up black dress, like a little girl craving solace and protection. Above them were the unoccupied benches of the gallery. Except for a cough here and there, silence dominated the room. The service was about to begin.

Chapter 18

From her seat farther back, Catherine could see diaphanous shades jostling one another in the gallery. As the lean and stringy preacher rose to speak, they floated upward from their seats, looming from the ceiling but not threatening. When a cold chill ran down her back, she remembered something her father had said when she was just a little girl: *There's some folks that see things, daughter, and there's some that never see even the stars. It's all right to see things, it's all right.* That remembrance brought a cozy feeling of comfort. Most of the time her eyes were open to see the thing as in itself it really was, but sometimes she looked beyond the thing to see the marvelous and unexplained. And that was happening now.

When the preacher turned, while sermonizing, to stare at the space above him, she caught her breath with surprise and wonder. She was certain that he too had seen and recognized the visitants and was acknowledging their presence. As he stared at the gallery benches, seats that everyone else saw as empty, he must have seen the dream-people too. Surely he saw blue and purple apparitions meld into a smoky mass, rise to the ceiling, hover there for a moment, break from one another, and sink back into separate seats. With knowing eyes she had seen them, and it pleased her to know this man had seen them too, but when she looked again they were gone.

A nocturnal wind was rising, soughing in the moss of the live oaks, and blowing the pungent smoke of the torches through the half-closed door and down the aisle. In the blue haze the baritone voice of the gangly preacher rose and fell in measured cadence. The sweet chariot, he said, had swung low to take one of God's most innocent children to and through them pearly gates, leaving the sorrowful mother behind. He spoke with his thin arms outstretched until he could sermonize no more. Then a large man with a large voice began a hymn. One by one the others picked it up, accompanying the swelling chorus with a muffled tapping of feet. Their bodies swayed back and forth as the old hymn grew louder and more animated, bouncing off the ceiling and walls. When it ceased, the angular preacher rose again. His voice was soft now, curiously at peace as he spoke of the grave and the eternal life beyond. Again looking into the gallery,

Catherine saw only a wisp of smoke hovering above the benches. Resin in the pine torches made them sputter.

2

With the preacher's last word the ceremony ended. The men in charge of the coffin stepped forward to close it and nail it shut. They paused for a moment to allow Bupee Mwewa, resting her head on the pine box, to move aside. They waited with a show of courtesy, but the woman did not stir. The preacher gently touched her arm and took her elbow to lead her away. Again she didn't move, her head remaining on the coffin close to Ethan's face. He nudged her shoulder to encourage her to move away, but she began to slip downward to the floor. At that moment the preacher saw the truth. He looked to the ceiling, raising his hands to the rafters, and cried out.

"Oh my! Oh my, good folks! Look here! The good Lord done took Bupee too! She done gone to glory with her Ethan here and now!"

A movement like a wave in water told Matthew that unless something were done fast, there would be a wild rush to look at Bupee's face. It could turn into a stampede, injure people, and make a mockery of the ceremony. If the mounting excitement were not controlled, pandemonium would surely occur. Something had to be done to calm the mourners and keep them in their seats. Quickly Matthew left his seat and went to the coffin.

"Start a hymn," he said to the thin preacher with the big voice.

"But we got to look to Bupee," said the man of God. "She done gone to her heavenly reward and we got to respect her remains."

"Start a hymn at once," Matthew repeated. "Please do it now!"

Sensing the urgency in the young man's words, the preacher asked the congregation to sing about sweet Canaan's happy shore. For the length of the hymn, the rising feeling to move to the coffin to view a miracle up close was kept in check. As it ended Matthew hesitated, unsure what had to be done next. To ask the good preacher to start another hymn would impede the progress of the ceremony and frustrate the audience. A delaying tactic was indefensible. The ceremony had to continue.

Then came an idea, in outline so simple and so beautiful he wondered why he had not thought of it earlier.

"Can we bury them together?" he asked a pallbearer.

The man looked at him with wide eyes and shifted his weight, moving his large feet on the wooden floor, taking time to absorb the question.

"I think we can," he answered. "Bupee is small and this box is uncommonly wide. It was built for a man, not a boy the size of Ethan."

Matthew asked the preacher for his opinion. The man could think of no similar event ever occurring in his ministry, but was certain no person in attendance would object. Bupee had wanted desperately to remain close to her son, and she would now have her wish. He was delighted that he could help her in this small way. Just as the assembly was becoming restive, two men lifted the tiny woman gently and placed her beside her son.

A little girl in her Sunday best, one who had known them both all her life, placed two small handkerchiefs over their faces. In her mind the pieces of white fabric, glowing against the dark faces, were the gowns the two were already wearing as glorified angels in heaven. The baritone preacher, smiling approval, now led the gathering in prayer. Then standing and swaying and lifting their voices to the heavens, the friends of Bupee and Ethan Search sang a wild resurrection hymn. When that was over, the coffin was closed and carried out and placed in a cart.

In double file the mourners followed the pallbearers to the gravesite, singing in sorrowful rhythm and harmonizing on happier notes. They picked up their torches and carried them in procession as they followed the cart in the narrow road to a corner of the graveyard not far from the Meeting-House. The singing rose to a crescendo as they walked and ended with harmonic humming when they stopped. The pallbearers gently placed the coffin in the newly dug grave. The preacher in symbolic gesture tossed some loamy earth on the coffin. Others, including Matthew, shoveled dirt into the grave and made a mound that would hold a stone. The mourners paced around the grave, retreated to form a circle, and bowed their heads in prayer.

3

When the prayer ended, Matthew was asked to say a few words. Taken by surprise, he paused for a moment before stepping forward to stand on a vegetable crate that served as a low platform. With head uncovered, his hat in his hand, he looked into the shadowy faces of those around him. Knowing he had their attention, he spoke of Ethan Search and his mother as integral parts of the community now diminished by their departure. A power like a great wind came rushing into his voice, and he spoke with an eloquence altogether new to him.

"No man is an island entire of itself," he said, paraphrasing John Donne. "Every man is a piece of the continent, a part of the main. Any man's death, any woman's death, and that of a boy like Ethan Search, diminishes you and me. Each of us is a thread woven into the fabric of mankind, and when one thread breaks the fabric tears. When two threads break, and that's what we have here, we have a rip in the fabric. Ethan is gone from us. Bupee Mwewa is gone from us. Neither will return. Now therefore, send not to know for whom the bell tolls—it tolls for thee."

He explained that God's ways to man often seem puzzling but cannot be questioned. We must accept the sorrow visited upon us by a person's untimely and grievous death even when we cannot understand why. From the circle of mourners rose a many-throated moan, then louder cries. Pausing for silence, he asserted that mother and son were together again, traveling to a new, eternal life. Standing side by side, hand in hand, they would meet and greet St. Peter and walk in triumph through the pearly gates.

"Be joyous for them," he said as cries of *hallelujah* grew louder and louder, "Be joyous for them and remember them."

Another hymn rose spontaneously and weeping could be heard above it. The mourners began to clap their hands in time with the music and to stamp on the sandy ground. The chorus swelled to an echo and died away. Another hymn, one that called for rejoicing, rose again from the mourners. Ethan was now at rest and so was Bupee. Both were in a better place. The circle then broke into smaller groups that went on singing as they made ready to leave. Their flaming torches vanquished the darkness and illuminated the road homeward. As they came to their cabins, overseers on horseback carefully observing, they extinguished the firebrands in the sand to reveal a sparkling canopy of stars in the night sky.

Once more at the Meeting House, in the glow of torchlight, Matthew locked the heavy door. Then extinguishing the torch, he lifted Catherine to the pillion as though she were Anna. A lone bird, white and shining in the gloom, glided across the yard. They rode home through darkness alleviated but a little by faint stars. Wild grapes, chilled now and dying, invested the damp air with perfume. A few crickets, defying the lateness of the season, chirped in the bushes near the roadside, their song a plaintive and high-pitched *tweet-tweet-tweet.* The music of the mourners came and went and receded into silence in the distance.

In a window at the Heartwood house Jeremy had left a candle. It glowed against the floral chintz curtain, and its flame allowed Catherine to make her way inside. Matthew kissed her quickly, and bidding her goodnight, rode off on Caesar. Inside a tiny fire danced in the grate, and she huddled over it for comfort. Her father was already in bed, and she would be snug in her bed soon. The season of harvest store was almost over, and the winter with all its uncertainty would soon be upon them. But if winter comes, mused Catherine, thinking of Shelley who also died too young, can spring be far behind?

It was a fleeting thought that centered on a new season and a new beginning. Fall had come with death. Spring would come when winter slipped away to bring the miracle of restoration and new life. Young and hopeful and looking forward to her wedding day, Catherine Heartwood thrilled to the thought of vibrant new life in springtime. She often looked to the future but found little time to think of the present. The larger world beyond Blue Anchor was demanding attention, but maybe the problems peopled discussed would be solved soon. She couldn't know that in the spring of 1861, the very time she hoped to shine on her special day, social and political events would spark other events that would turn the entire nation into a tinderbox.

Chapter 19

In the fall of 1860, people in and near the hamlet of Blue Anchor lived from day to day without a steady flow of news from the outside world. They knew about contentious political factions becoming each day more vocal and belligerent, but they were not privy to hidden influences that seemed ready to ignite horrendous events. The Quakers in particular knew that abolitionists of every stripe were petitioning Washington to abolish slavery, and their efforts were causing much unrest in the South. If war came, Quakers near the coast in North Carolina would find themselves between the combatants and harassed by both. They would attempt to resist outside interference in the daily round of their lives, but resisting they would quickly discover that forces stronger than they were in command. Because the principles by which they lived dictated passive resistance in unsettled times, and particularly in wartime, they would have to go against the grain and take the consequences.

For those who wanted to see an end to slavery, and the Quakers were part of that group, the 1850's proved to be an ugly decade of violence and turmoil. Its culminating event was John Brown's raid on the federal armory at Harpers Ferry, Virginia. The fiery abolitionist assembled a force of sixteen whites and five blacks a few miles north of the village, armed them, and gave them rudimentary training. On a Sunday night in the middle of October in 1859, the ragtag insurgents seized and occupied the government arsenal in Harpers Ferry, killing seven people and wounding ten or more. Brown's intention was to arm as many as five hundred slaves with weapons from the armory, establish a military base in the mountains, and terrorize slaveholders in Virginia. Although all went well at first, the assault failed.

Federal troops under Colonel Robert E. Lee arrived the next day and decimated the abolitionists. Ten were killed, seven were captured, and four escaped to be hunted like animals. Brown was indicted on charges of conspiracy, murder, and treason. He was executed by hanging before the year was out. Northern abolitionists, admiring his fortitude and purpose, viewed the man as a fiery but misunderstood martyr. Lincoln accurately called him a misguided fanatic. Jefferson Davis, given to robust exaggeration, called the raid with its abrupt and deadly ending: "the invasion of a State by a murderous gang of abolitionists bent on inciting slaves to murder helpless women and children." It was drivel, silly nonsense, but drivel many Southerners devoutly believed. The Quakers of Blue Anchor, all of whom despised slavery and wanted to see it shrivel and die, shook their heads in disbelief. Rhetoric that ignored the truth would never work, nor would violence.

They had heard the stories of earlier revolts dating all the way back to 1712—those of Prosser, Turner, Vesey, and others—and they knew all of them had failed. In the summer of 1800 Gabriel Prosser, born in 1776, rose up against the city of Richmond to protest the brutality and inhumanity of enslavement. James Monroe, Governor of Virginia, called out the militia to put down the insurrection scarcely before it started. Prosser and thirty-five of his followers were summarily hanged.

Nat Turner, a preacher who could read and write, hoped to achieve freedom for his race by citing biblical scripture. When that did not work, he resorted to violence. Interpreting a solar eclipse as the signal for action, he launched his insurrection on August 21, 1831 in Virginia. Though many lives were lost, it too was suppressed. When the insurrection failed four days later, fifty-seven whites were dead. In the aftermath, angry survivors went on a rampage and killed more than one hundred blacks. Turner and sixteen of his followers were quickly executed.

Less than a decade earlier Denmark Vesey, who had planned an abortive slave rebellion in Charleston, South Carolina, was executed in public with thirty-five followers. Vesey had come to the United States from the Caribbean as a slave but later bought his freedom. He planned what would have been the largest slave rebellion ever, but Charleston authorities got wind of the plot and arrested its leaders before the uprising could begin.

These slave revolts against a cherished way of life, coming at regular intervals, alarmed most Southerners. Except among the Quakers, they wiped out every vestige of Southern sympathy for abolitionism. In the North, however, the abolitionist cause was gathering steam. William Lloyd Garrison condoned violent resistance to the Fugitive Slave Law and hailed John Brown's abortive raid on Harpers Ferry as an act of supreme courage. Harriet Beecher Stowe had given the cause a boost with *Uncle Tom's Cabin*, published in 1852. The antislavery tale was enormously popular, and was called by some in the North "the greatest book of the age." Enraged Southerners denounced it as a hideous distortion of the truth. Rachel Kingston read the book in the summer of 1855 and pronounced it powerful propaganda but lacking in art. At a Quarterly Meeting she spoke of the book with rising but rational fervor, insisting that alone the melodramatic story could never become a catalyst for violence. However, along with other protests rapidly increasing in number it could possibly trigger a conflict between North and South to be long remembered.

2

A devout Quaker, Rachel despised war and hoped the eradication of slavery could be accomplished without violence. The process would take a long time and perhaps cause social upheaval, but it would certainly be a better course than war. It seemed to her that people of influence and power in the North were not willing to wait for a peaceful solution. And powerful people in the South seemed equally headstrong. An institution so vital to the economic health of the South would not on its own fade into the light of common day. Privileged Southerners would have to work with powerful and patient Northerners to reach a solution. But instead, in stern defense of slavery, they were developing a militant philosophy. Thomas Bolton and thousands like him had already proclaimed they would fiercely resist any threat to their way of life, fighting with their bare fists if necessary. Except for the marriage of her son in the spring, Rachel Kingston dreaded to think of the future.

Abraham Lincoln had received in the spring of 1860 the nomination of the newly formed Republican party, and before the year was out he was elected President. Leo Mack, making his rounds as a tinker in a biting wintry wind, drove through Blue Anchor with the news. In a logical though inconclusive way he thought about the events of the day and was eager to report them. Few people seemed to know where the man got his facts, but most of the time they were accurate. Running against a splintered and contentious Democratic party, Lincoln had captured the election with 180 electoral votes against 123 for all of his opponents combined. In speeches and debates, he had made it clear that as President of the United States he would view slavery as an evil institution to be abolished by slow degree within a given period of time. And once gone, it would not raise its hoary head in some other place. On no condition would he allow slavery to gain a foothold in any territory becoming a new state.

Lincoln's election immediately threw the South into uproar. Southern Democrats branded him the leader of the abolitionists and denounced him as an unabashed demon bent on subjugating their region, destroying their economy, and abolishing their way of life. Within days they were talking of secession. The loudest outcries came from South Carolina, but voices were lifted also in North Carolina. From the capital, the day after Lincoln's election, came the following dispatch from a zealous reporter: "Raleigh, N. C., Nov. 7, 1860. The Governor and Council are in session. The people are very much excited. North Carolina is ready to secede." The Quakers of Blue Anchor received the news with alarm and foreboding. Some of their neighbors, fearing the future, were stoking fires of secession.

3

On a frosty day in late November, Leo Mack approached an isolated farmhouse, his aging mare struggling against the weight of his wagon and his mongrel dog Sparky trotting alongside. A cold breeze was coming from the southeast, and a stinging mist was in the air. The day before had seen abundant snow, and the muddy road was frozen and smooth. In some places snow and ice lay deep in the gullies beside the road. Fall had become winter.

"Hello, Leo!" called Isaac Brandimore as the tinker pulled into the yard. "I have some pots that need mending, and you can tell an old recluse about the events of the world. You look like you might enjoy a little warmth, and that dog looks like he could use a rest."

"Well, I'll tell you this, Isaac. My feet are as cold as a well digger's ass. That raw wind gets to the bone. And that dog? Oh, that dog has miles in him yet! But he won't object to resting a spell, not him."

"He sure is thin," countered Isaac, "I can count his ribs."

"Oh, them ain't ribs! What you see is muscle from all the exercise he gets trotting over creation at the wheels of that wagon. He's good company but can be kind of ornery if you cross him."

"Oh, I won't cross him, Leo. That's a promise!"

"His tongue is hanging just a little, so I guess he's warm enough. He'll rest under the wagon and be still. If you happen to have a bone he can gnaw on, he'll be even more content."

"No bones, but I'll find a couple pieces of zwieback for him. It's almost like a bone, you know, and good for his teeth."

"Well, that's mighty kind of you, Isaac. But don't go giving him stuff you can eat yourself 'cause I know you ain't rich like some folks."

Gathering his tools to take inside, Mack waited for Brandimore to come back with the twice-baked biscuits. Then as Sparky settled under the wagon and gnawed on his treat, the traveling tinker spoke with an air of concern.

"I guess it gets lonely out here, with your man Seth passing away. I heard you were sick a while back. Nothing serious I hope."

He expected to get a reply he could carry to a neighbor as one of the tidbits he used to promote his business. The dog sniffed at Brandimore's roomy shoes, circled behind him, and walked back to the wagon for more hardtack. Finding none, he shook himself vigorously and lay down beneath it.

"Oh, I was a bit under the weather," Isaac said, as they went into the kitchen, "but my friend and housekeeper brought me around handsomely. She's a fine woman and I'm lucky to have her. Not here at present though, went home for a few days. Now what about you, Leo? Any problems with your health or with making ends meet? It's not easy growing old, is it?"

Leo Mack had lived in the midst of hardship so long it had come to be his element. Poverty he took for granted like day and night or the sun and moon. His struggle with penury, biting at times and unceasing—a condition that might have crippled another man—he accepted without complaint. If he had been a weaker person, he would have entered a plea of indigence at a Quarterly Meeting and received assistance from the community. But to ask for help had never entered his mind, not even when his trade brought him so little revenue he worried about paying his landlady. Ida Crabtree really cared about the welfare of her boarders, and he felt as long as he could live in her house he would never go all-out hungry.

Leo was a gregarious man but eccentric in behavior and deeply private. He was not about to reveal his troubles to Brandimore or anyone else. And so he replied only to Isaac's last question.

"Easy growing old? Guess not, but I'm gonna work till I drop. Can't do nothing else. Getting a bit creaky in cold weather but gotta work to make a living. What's more, there's many a good tune played on an old fiddle."

"Yes! The music is plaintive and sweet in the autumn of our lives," said Isaac with a chuckle. "Keats called it the season of mists and mellow fruitfulness. Pretty words, I think, but I'm finding more mists than fruit."

"Misty outside right now. Been that way all morning."

4

Mack grinned wide enough to show his yellow teeth. A glittering gold tooth seemed to mock the others. Often when talking with customers he covered his mouth to hide his teeth and to block any lingering bad breath. He seldom talked about himself, and he disliked metaphorical observation made by others. So he asked about current events.

"Have you heard the election results and all the talk of secession? A lot of people hereabouts are worried."

"And they have good reason to be," said Isaac, pulling up a chair as the tinker set up his equipment on the kitchen table. "Only a couple years ago Lincoln insisted that Pierce and Buchanan had conspired to nationalize slavery, bring it from the South to the North and the whole country. Abe Lincoln thought even the prospect of such a thing was scandalous. You remember his most provocative remarks in that speech, I guess."

Mack hesitated. "I don't go in much for politics with these pots and all. You mean what he said about a house split down the middle falling in half like a chunk of wood?"

"That's a good analogy, my friend, a very good analogy. But I think he said a house divided against itself cannot stand."

"What do you think he meant by that?" asked the tinker.

"Well he meant these United States will have to become either all slave or all free. We can't have it both ways. And that's why the house, this nation, is gonna be split right down the middle, to use your phrasing, like a chunk of wood. I'm afraid we're in for some hard times."

The tinker stopped his work on the pot and looked surprised. "You say the times ain't hard already? I beg to differ."

"Well, you can say hard times getting harder."

Mack was eyeing a pot of soup simmering on the stove. The steam rose from it and filled the kitchen with a fragrance of spicy potatoes. His empty stomach wanted him to ask about the soup, but a natural delicacy made him ask about the pot.

"Is that a good, sound pot? Sure wouldn't want it to spring a leak and have that soup spill on the stove and floor."

Isaac took the hint and filled a deep bowl for him when his work was done. He ate the potato soup with a good appetite, talking about his trade. Leo lived alone and didn't look after himself well enough to maintain good health. His liver sometimes got out of whack, but he would make his rounds nonetheless, yellow about the eyes. Although Mrs. Crabtree fed him as best she could, his stomach often growled for good food.

"I don't charge as much as some others I know, and so I don't eat as well they do. But I do good work."

"That you do," Isaac assured him, "but what else do you know about all that's happening on the political scene?"

This man who read books with wavering eyesight in a solitude thrust upon him was eager to learn from any source. He was always glad to have a visitor, and he liked chatting with the tinker.

"Can't talk no more now," said Mack. "Have to get on over to the Alston place and pay them a visit. Hannah is not well, you know, and Elmer is overworked and don't know what to do."

"I know and it's sad. I certainly hope Hannah gets better. And I did hear something about Elmer not having enough help to bring in his crop."

"They had a couple of younger folk, man and wife, but let them go. Jeremy Heartwood gave the couple money to buy their freedom. They gave it all to Elmer and got a signed certificate, and he hired them at fair pay, I hear, but that means they could leave any time they feel like it."

"I suppose the couple will stay on as free laborers."

"Well, yeah, but they could leave any time they get a sudden hankering. Who knows what's gonna happen? If the Alstons have any work for me, I'm not gonna ask for cash."

Leo would barter with the Alston family, and with others strapped financially, but he expected cash payment from the scholarly Brandimore. If the man had money to buy books, he could pay to have a pot mended. He mentioned a fee which he said was lower than usual.

"That's because recently you lost your man Seth," he said with a show of concern, "and had to go out looking for part-time help. I'm glad you found a good housekeeper. What did you say her name was?"

Isaac was thinking about South Carolina's threat of secession and didn't seem to hear the question. He paid the sum Mack named without hesitation and helped the tinker carry his equipment outside.

Flicking the reins as the signal to move, the tinker drove off without a word. He felt he had talked enough for one little job even when rewarded with the tasty soup. His customer stood on the porch and watched the wagon wind its way out of the yard and down the road, Sparky following behind.

"What does South Carolina hope to gain by that?" Brandimore asked himself, speaking softly to the cold air. "And my state too? Maybe the good people in Raleigh will display cooler heads. But if this secessionist fever mounts, I don't see how any one state can hold out for long against the others. Oh, nothing good will come of this, nothing good at all."

Chapter 20

A few weeks later, with Christmas only five days away, South Carolina seceded. In a flurry of redundant verbiage, the union between South Carolina and other states was dissolved, and the state became "a free and independent country." Intent on sending a message to Washington, those in favor of secession had overwhelmed the moderates and temporizers, and the vote was 169 to nothing. On Christmas Eve delegates at the convention crafted a *Declaration of the Immediate Causes Which Induce and Justify the Secession of South Carolina from the Federal Union*. It noted "an increasing hostility on the part of the non-slaveholding States to the institution of slavery," and it chastised Northern states for not returning fugitive slaves to bondage. Slavery, abolitionism, and Lincoln's vaunted stance against slavery had lit the fuse of this incendiary event, not states' rights or some other cause.

Mississippi seceded in the second week of 1861, followed a few days later by Florida, Alabama, Georgia, Louisiana, and Texas. In February delegates from these states met in Montgomery, Alabama where they drafted a constitution for the Confederate States of America. Before the end of February, Jefferson Davis of Mississippi, a soldier and Indian fighter turned statesman, was inaugurated president of the new breakaway nation. Its first official flag boasted an eye-catching design and was called the Stars and Bars. At the outset the flag had seven stars arranged in a circle to denote the first seven states to secede. By the end of 1861 it had thirteen on crossed bars, denoting four additional states and the Confederacy's claims to the dual states of Kentucky and Missouri. The new flag was still on the drawing board after the Christmas season ended and well into the new year, but it would soon be flown in the midst of jubilant cheering.

For the Quakers of Blue Anchor, Christmas of 1860 was a time of great uncertainty. Accustomed to calm and peace and the freedom to practice a simple faith, they found themselves in an atmosphere of fiery excitement and suspicion. Secessionist news spread rapidly to and through the settlement and to surrounding farms. South Carolina had taken the lead. That meant other states would follow, including North Carolina.

Even those villagers in sympathy with the North knew it was inevitable. At the Quarterly Meeting the Quaker elders discussed these developments and their possible effects, allowing anyone in attendance to join the discussion. While no one could agree on the exact causes of so drastic an action as seceding from the Union, most were aware that slavery in the South and the rumblings in the North to abolish it was a key issue.

In the meantime the daily round of life in Blue Anchor—working, eating, and sleeping—went on as usual. The Kingston family was busy making plans to entertain their neighbors at their customary Christmas feast. In the chestnut suit that made him look like a saucy squirrel, Jeremy Heartwood visited the general store, where some had gathered to discuss the events of the day, and told a good joke. It generated laughter and for a moment chased away the somber mood of the place. Isaac Brandimore asked the library committee to purchase a book he wanted to read. After a week of indecision, the committee declined his request for lack of funds. Leo Mack, looking forward to the Christmas party, put his old wagon with its tools and his old dog Sparky in temporary storage. Already he was assembling the news he would bring with him, news of national events as well as juicy gossip gleaned from his customers. A spirit of peace and harmony would prevail at the seasonal party in spite of troubling events rapidly developing in both North and South.

Even as Christmas came and went, a daily dose of heated propaganda fueling secession fever was turning neighbor against neighbor and brother against brother. Thomas Bolton, with the support of Calvin Swope and others, had made reckless statements about abolitionists in general and Quakers in particular. His position on that issue did not make a lot of sense to some of the more thoughtful who heard him, but the majority nodded their heads in agreement. The fancy word, abolitionist, had become a dirty word.

"We can tolerate these people and their devious behavior no longer," he ranted before a small group near Jacob Darboy's general store. "They have stolen our property in the past, they will continue to do it in the present, and they will not fight when war comes. We need to send them packing to the North where they belong! Everybody knows they prefer the North to the South, so why not send them there?"

Inside the store, only a few feet away, the targets of his furious rhetoric went about their daily business. Young Quaker men and women coming out of the store heard every word and shook their heads in disbelief. In the aftermath of Ethan Search's murder, which he now saw as the perfect accidental crime, Bolton had become a rabble rouser. With the specter of war haunting a confused nation, he had become divisive in speechifying, dissembling, and dangerous. He made it clear to all who would listen that he would do all he could, sacrificing his fortune if necessary, to maintain "our cherished way of life." Anyone opposing his views would be in trouble.

The Quaker community decided something would have to be done to show appropriate reaction to that kind of conduct. Before the planter could cause irreparable harm, someone would have to find a way to defuse him.

"But how?" Oliver Hatcher asked.

"We'll find a way," Matthew Kingston asserted.

The elders at the Quarterly Meeting cast stern glances at both young men and cautioned patience. Jeremy Heartwood, wearing a frown that seemed out of place on his genial face, offered a bit of advice.

"Easy now, you two. Don't let that young blood make thee reckless. We can't do anything extreme—can't do a thing we might regret later."

2

At dinner on Christmas Day of 1860 the Kingston guests were keenly aware of the swirling, fast-moving events that would soon change their lives. They spoke of South Carolina's bold act and speculated as to what would happen next. They discussed Bolton's bitter antagonism, weighing divergent opinions but reaching no consensus on what to do about it. All agreed that little could be done to placate the man until he openly tried to make good on his threats. Jacob Darboy doubted that Bolton would do anything rash: "He's a talker, not a doer. He just likes to hear himself talk. Pay him no mind." Others proposed a long-standing Quaker principle: *When in doubt, wait.*

It was a somber discussion for a party intended to celebrate the joy of the season, but there was light conversation too and good things to eat. After dinner as the guests went into the parlor to be near the fire and a large window looking out on new-fallen snow, Isaac Brandimore drew Rachel Kingston aside to ask her a question.

"Have you seen Elizabeth Barrett Browning's new poem? She calls it—audaciously I think—'A Curse for a Nation.'"

Before Rachel could gather her thoughts to answer, he offered details.

"A remarkable piece, though I can't say I've read it yet, only snippets. Published this year and reviewed by a Richmond paper just recently. The reviewer quoted liberally from it. Called it 'passionate propaganda from the pen of a frail poet who aspires to move mountains.' An obvious echo of hostility there, and no wonder. The poem condemns our country, both North and South, for allowing the institution of slavery to become so entrenched."

When Rachel expressed interest, this solitary man who hungered to exchange ideas with anyone who would listen, eagerly continued.

"An angel appears before the poet and tells her to write a curse for a nation dishonored by an evil institution and in need of coming to its senses. She falters, but the angel commands her to 'weep and write! A curse from the depths of womanhood is very salt and bitter and good.' Oh, I wish I had the whole thing. The little I've seen is passionate and powerful."

As Isaac was quoting from the poem Catherine and Matthew paused to listen and moved in closer.

"The little you quoted does indeed sound interesting," Rachel was saying. "Mrs. Browning, as you know, is a great champion of freedom. For her to write against slavery seems fitting, I suppose, but also ironical. She is certainly closer to her subject than Harriet Stowe in New England. Her family, you know, built its wealth on the labor of slaves in the Caribbean."

This unassuming, intelligent, and compact woman of forty-two, a dozen years younger than the famous poet, was not a great reader and did not view herself as an intellectual. Yet frequently in conversation relating to the arts she brought forward little-known facts that surprised her listeners.

"Her family is wealthy?" asked Brandimore. "It's my understanding that she and her husband live in a modest villa in Italy, and Robert—a great poet in his own right—shops for their food in open-air markets."

"They do live modestly, but her papa, who views her as an invalid and didn't want her to marry Robert, lives very comfortably in England."

"I read *Aurora Leigh* a couple years ago," interjected Catherine, steering the conversation back to the poet's work. "It took me forever. She had some good things to say about women and womanhood, but I really believe she could have said them better in forty pages instead of four hundred."

Rachel nodded in agreement. She had tried to read that lengthy novel in verse too but soon gave it up as a lost cause.

"Sometimes I begin to yawn when a poem exceeds the length of a sonnet," she laughed. "Anything longer quickly becomes unbearable. And yes, I couldn't find myself in sympathy with Aurora. I don't really like bluestockings, you know. They seem so stuffy, but I do like Elizabeth. The woman has talent and courage and believes as we do."

"I have a copy of *Sonnets from the Portuguese*. Do you know those poems?" asked Brandimore, speaking to Catherine. "You and your betrothed would do well to read them once a year. 'How do I love thee? Let me count the ways.' That sort of thing—powerful poetry. Meant for young people in love, just right for you and Matthew."

"Oh, I don't know," chuckled David Kingston who had joined the group to stand beside his wife. "I'm no spring chicken but I like that poem and know it almost by heart."

"Yes, and he recites it very well," laughed Rachel. "It's one of his favorite verses, and he quotes it sometimes at table by candlelight. Children in bed, you know, and just the two of us enjoying a late supper."

Catherine smiled broadly and gave David a look of mock adoration. "You must teach Matthew how to behave like that!"

As laughing faces turned to observe his response, Matthew was the first to move away into the general company. The others soon followed.

Isaac Brandimore, left alone by the window, gazed into the half-tones of purple shadows on snow. It seemed to him that his point about slavery and help from across the seas may have been missed. In that relaxed after-dinner atmosphere, precise thought among the guests roamed free of restraint. Oh, well, no matter. He longed to meet that remarkable woman, and also her famous husband, and perhaps learn from them. In six months, however, Elizabeth Barrett Browning would lie dead.

3

At the Christmas celebration, the Kingston guests spoke also of Matthew and Catherine and their impending marriage in the spring. From the time of their engagement they had planned to marry when the fields were green with new life, the trees in tiny leaf, and the lilacs in bloom. But as they made their plans they didn't know the season of new beginnings would see their troubled nation pulled apart by civil war. Brother would fight against brother in the deadliest conflict of modern times. It was beyond imagination, even Catherine's, that before the carnage ended more than 620,000 young men in their prime would perish. The Civil War would claim more American lives than any other war in our country's history and would be the most savage. At Christmas the Quakers of Blue Anchor suspected terrible events were in the making, but they could not believe those events would move so fast. As 1861 began, a new nation was being formed. Jefferson Davis as president quickly set up a cabinet and sought peaceful relations with Lincoln's government. At the same time he prepared for war, paying particular attention to federal military installations in the South. Fort Sumter in South Carolina, at the entrance to Charleston harbor, was of paramount importance. Southern forces had to be in control of the fort to control the harbor. Davis and his cabinet knew that without a key international port to call their own, the Confederacy would have difficulty claiming sovereignty on the global scene.

As David Kingston discussed these issues with the elders of the community, he insisted that only seven states would never be recognized by the rest of the world as a sovereign nation. Furthermore, if war came, that paltry number pitted against twenty-three Northern states would be crushed within a month. Kingston's son believed with his father that war was inevitable, but asserted the original seven states would soon become a dozen. Matthew had now become interested in all that was going on, for he had heard that South Carolina was mobilizing an army and calling for volunteers. Young men by the thousands, his age and younger, were answering the call. Boys as young as fourteen, seeking high adventure and willing to lie about their age, were eager to enlist. Of the horror of war they knew nothing.

If and when North Carolina seceded (and just about everyone knew It was only a matter of time), the authorities would expect every young man to volunteer. Any able-bodied person who chose not to do so could find himself in deep trouble. Traditionally the Quakers had spoken out against armed conflict, and Matthew was certain he would never be able to participate in a military campaign that required him to carry a weapon and use it. He hoped this dilemma of mind and heart could be resolved quickly and peacefully.

And yet he doubted sincerely that would happen. There was talk that when war began certain groups of people would be exempted from military duty, or would be able to buy exemption. In Raleigh some legislators were already drafting an exemption act that would become law should war begin. Because of their religious beliefs, Quakers would be able to buy exemption, it was thought, but that seemed hardly fair to others. For now it was something Matthew was not willing to consider. Perhaps farmers who brought in food crops would be quickly exempted, and was he not a farmer?

Chapter 21

In Blue Anchor, March came in like a tiger. February had been a cold and snowy month, and March gave promise of more cold and high winds. The weather was not good, but Leo Mack's old wagon was on the road. He had said to Isaac Brandimore that he would work as long as he could because he could do nothing else. In hard times he had to make a living, and he was also a traveler. It was in his blood, and so he urged his old horse to trudge from farmhouse to farmhouse even in bad weather. The dog Sparky was becoming thinner and thinner but trotted beside the wheels wherever the wagon went and lay under it even when the ground was frozen. No one ever saw the dog riding beside his master.

In the first week of March in 1861, Leo visited Brandimore again. When he was there in November he ate a piping hot bowl of thick soup, and he hoped he might be just as lucky again. While eating or mending a pot, he would tell the solitary man the latest political news from the North as well as from Raleigh and points southward. It would be a fair trade.

"Hello, Leo! Come in, old friend!" cried Brandimore as Mack pulled into his yard. "Come in out of the cold and bring that dog with you."

"Oh, I can't do that," Mack replied. "That dog is trained to guard my stuff. You wouldn't believe how fierce he can be when riled."

"Yes, I know," Isaac chuckled. "You've told me more than once that he's all muscle and fit as a fiddle and ornery when crossed. But I still say he's welcome to a little warmth if you want to bring him inside."

"No, he'll be just fine layin' under the wagon. No wind there and not too cold, and besides he's used to it."

By now the tinker was on the porch of Brandimore's quaint little house and heading for the kitchen. Always, in any house he visited, he went directly to the kitchen more out of habit than professional duty. As he walked through the sitting-room, he caught the scent of old leathery books and his nose twitched. He preferred the scent of something cooking.

"I don't guess you have any mending for me to do. I was here not long ago. Still remember that potato soup you gave me."

"Oh, the last time you were here I had some work for you, but don't seem to have any now. I do have a rabbit slowly boiling on the stove, and I hope you'll stay long enough to eat a few bites."

"I like my rabbit fried," Leo confided, "but I won't object to a boiled rabbit if it's tender and tasty. Old folks like us shouldn't be eating fried rabbit anyway. My teeth ain't as good as they used to be."

Removing his coat and broad hat and sitting down in a straight Quaker chair, he flashed his bad teeth in a wide grin and chuckled. At the stove Isaac stirred the boiling pot and added more salt.

"I boil my meat most of the time these days. My digestive system won't take fried foods any more, but tell me the latest news and then we eat."

"Well, I guess you know all about Lincoln's inauguration yesterday in Washington. 'Twas a big event. Hundreds standing in the cold to hear him speak. Gave a rousing good speech some are saying."

Mack was fairly certain that Brandimore, living in isolation and not leaving the house very often, had heard little. It was a ploy to stir interest, to get the conversation started.

"Well, I did hear that Jeff Davis was inaugurated as President of the Confederacy only two weeks ago. And I heard Lincoln would have to move into Washington protected by soldiers for his ceremony because of the upheaval we're going through. Looks like secession is creating a firestorm."

"Yup, he took the oath of office on the East Portico of the Capitol. Soldiers all over the place, but he went there with President Buchanan in an open carriage. The building was covered with scaffolding, I heard, 'cause they're replacing the dome."

"What did Lincoln say in his speech? I'm eager to know. These are truly the times that try men's souls, Leo. Lincoln is walking on a bed of fire!"

"Well, it was a long speech and I didn't read it all but the main point he made, as far as I can recollect, is he will preserve the Union at any cost. He said the states must remain united 'cause we live in the United States. And he emphasized *united* and said no individual state has any legal right to leave the group, the United States, and go on its own."

"What did he say about slavery? Anything about that?"

"Oh, he said he wouldn't even try to abolish slavery in the South, but he wouldn't let it get a foothold in other states or territories."

"In earlier speeches I think he said he would not rest until he saw slavery abolished. I think we are getting mixed signals here."

"In this speech they say he was calling for some sort of compromise. Said he wouldn't use force to interfere with slavery as we have it now, but wouldn't let it move into territories that wanna become states."

"Preserving the Union at any cost means war, of course. I can't tell you how much I dread the future. Oh, this rabbit's done, old friend. Pull your chair up to the table and let's eat. We have some tough bread to go with it."

"Well, Isaac, I don't mind if I do, but I can't stay much longer. Have my rounds to make, y'know. Have to make a living even in bad times. Me and the horse and that dog have to be on the road. We're travelers, y'know, from way back. And what about that housekeeper of yours? She doing right by you? Name's Olga? Don't recollect her last name."

Isaac didn't answer the tinker's questions. His mind was on politics and the pressing issues of the day, and he stammered that he had tried to examine them carefully to reach cogent conclusions but without a favorable outcome. Digesting the fancy language, Leo couldn't resist a rejoinder.

"You think you have," he said, "you scholars with brains think you have examined everything, every visible part of everything, but maybe it just ain't so. I've examined very little myself, except the bottoms of old kettles and saucepans, but people say I have a good head on my stringy shoulders and a good store of commonsense too."

"Indeed you do have that," Brandimore assured him, not in the least upset by Leo's view of the scholarly life. "You have a vast store of commonsense and the gift of gab too. I sometimes envy you, my friend."

2

Half an hour later Leo Mack was on his wagon again and steering his old horse in the direction of Darboy's General Store. He would not be going there to buy anything, for goods in the store were becoming scarce. Mainly he had a hankering to chat with men more like himself and share with them the news of the day. Also he expected to pick up more news and some scraps of gossip he could pass on to others as he made his rounds. He pulled his wagon into the yard, tipping his hat to the driver of another wagon trundling past the store on his way to the mill.

For decades Darboy's General Store had been a magnet to draw the people in the settlement to spend their money on a wide assortment of goods at reasonable prices. The store was located on the main road and clustered about it were twelve to fifteen houses. They would grow in number in the years after the war, and the store would struggle to stay open facing tough competition. Later a consortium remodeled the old building to house a new and more expansive store which kept the old name. Darboy's had become a landmark in Blue Anchor, and no one wanted to see it go. In the first and second decades of the new century the struggling little village became an active and prosperous town with shops, offices, churches, restaurants, businesses, a water works, a larger school, and a mayor elected by the citizens. Soon afterwards the townspeople built a centrally located park where young and old alike could sit on benches and review the day's events. Just before sunset and after supper it became a custom to walk there in the calm of a southern evening to see and be seen.

Entering the store, Leo Mach smiled and shook his head as he glanced at the colorful posters on the south wall. They advertised remedies for upset stomach, sore throat, fatigue, scrapes and cuts, grippe and pneumonia, diarrhea, constipation, joint pain, and poor eyesight. Other posters praised in flowery terms ingenious farm implements and items for the home. On another was the portrait of a lady in a hat offering a medicated snuff that would relieve headaches, dispel melancholy moods, and shrink hemorrhoids. Mack knew the placards were old and fading and full of lies. He knew also the general store for some time had ceased to carry the wondrous potions and grand machinery they advertised, for as soon as the war began most of those things dropped out of sight. A yellowing broadsheet advertised in fat letters, hand-printed by the seller, a well-built open carriage with good wheels. That was the wagon Mack had bought on easy terms to use in his business.

The wagon had been consigned to Darboy who would take a share of the profits when sold. As a favor to Mack, for he knew the man was struggling to make a living, he sold the wagon without taking a commission and even helped the tinker get it at a lower price. From that time onward Mack went to the store for leisurely chatting whenever he had the time. The store owner was a congenial man and made his customers feel at home even when they didn't buy anything. Mack had seen the similarity between Darboy and the founder of Quakerism and wanted to let others see it. In the farmhouse of one of his customers he had come across an old painting of the man. He traded some work for it and soon afterwards gave it to Darboy to hang in his store. All who saw the portrait agreed that venerable George Fox in 1681 was remarkably similar in appearance to Jacob Darboy in 1861.

It depicts the founder of the Society of Friends as a corpulent man of late middle age in natty black with round shoulders and broad arms. On his large head is a squat, black, broad-brimmed hat. His long hair, falling well below the nape of the neck, glows white against the dark tones of his clothing. Below his ample double chin and clean-shaven face, a neck cloth of white complements the white hair. The pale-gray eyebrows, bushy and beetling, stand under a smooth forehead and over large remote gray eyes. The round and fleshy cheeks show a set of wrinkles near the mouth. The lips curve upward in a sly, restrained, sardonic smile. A Roman nose, slightly to one side, separates the genial eyes that fasten on the observer. The portly, well-fed man looks outward upon the world with full acceptance but with the caution of a clever person who sees danger there.

3

Darboy had discovered how closely he resembled Fox and made the most of it. In the Meeting House, he accepted the capable leadership of David Kingston, but in his store in Blue Anchor he was the leader and master of ceremonies of any group that congregated there. He was in his element in that identity and looked forward to playing the role whenever he could. One blustery day in April of 1861, as a motley group of men gathered to discuss the events of the day, he led the discussion. They had work to do, for spring planting was just around the corner, but each had a craving to know how recent events would affect their lives. Darboy had said no one should worry. "Just keep low and don't make a fuss. Our village is too small for anyone to notice, and the non-Quakers will tire of trying to give us trouble."

Blue Anchor, however, was part of the South and close to Virginia. If the Rebel army, already forming in South Carolina, were to move northward to Virginia, the Quaker settlement with its surrounding farms would likely be in its path. On the other hand, if Lincoln (now seen as a fiery abolitionist by most Southerners) were to send troops to Charleston to defend the Federal fort there, the village of Blue Anchor would be in their path. Entire regiments of armed soldiers, professed enemies of the region and living off the land, could tramp through with an impetus to kill and destroy. Even if they were so disposed, the people could never hide in the swamp or the towns to the east. An exodus seemed unlikely even when propelled by furious events, and many citizens of the village could suffer injury or even death. So reasonable persons had cause to worry.

The talk in Darboy's store was mainly about secession. Notwithstanding what he had said in his inauguration speech, after South Carolina seceded Lincoln seemed unwilling to compromise. He was adamant and unyielding even when Virginia, Tennessee, and North Carolina indicated a willingness to discuss issues around a conference table. If Lincoln called up troops to punish the states that had already seceded, surely all three of these states and two or three more would break away from the Union. Jacob Darboy predicted that Arkansas and perhaps Maryland would secede, and so the original seven could become twelve. The Confederate States of America could grow even to fifteen if certain border states went along.

"What about Fort Pickens in Pensacola and Fort Sumter in Charleston?" Peter Whitehurst asked. "As we all know, they're Federal forts. Will the Union let the South take them?"

"Jeff Davis wants all the military installations in the South to be under his control," Darboy answered. "But Lincoln is opposed to that. He has said no pocket of military power will be delivered willingly to the Rebs."

"That means the South will have to take the forts by force."

"Well, Lincoln has made it clear he will use force against force. According to what I've heard, he's already building an army. Thousands of volunteers are streaming into Washington."

Darboy's hearsay information was accurate. Incendiary activity was occurring in Washington, and the air was filled with cries of war. At the same time, as a precautionary measure, Jefferson Davis was instructing General Pierre Beauregard to move toward Charleston. The sovereignty of the new nation depended on controlling that key international harbor. Fort Sumter at the entrance to the harbor had become a symbol of the South's independence. To have the fort remain in enemy hands was unthinkable.

"Sooner or later the talking is gonna turn to fighting," said Whitehurst.

"If war comes," advised Darboy, "we Quakers will follow the inner light and do God's bidding as we see it without shirking."

"Amen," someone said.

"In the meantime we must husband our strength, be guided by our convictions, and be ready to resist any action not sanctioned by our faith."

4

Jacob Darboy was pleased to see the group listening intently to his words and showing themselves in full agreement. He wanted to say more, but at that moment Richard Bolton with Calvin Swope entered the store. He was there to buy hardware to fix a bridle. The men sitting around the cast-iron stove with its round heated paunch glanced in his direction. They saw a handsome, well-dressed young man of personal force and confidence. At the counter he turned his back on Jacob Darboy and addressed the group of young Quakers, speaking just loud enough to be heard.

"You are thinking war will break out soon. Well, I'm looking forward to service as a Confederate officer," he said proudly. "It's my opinion that a War of Northern Aggression is inevitable, and we must fight to defend the Southern way of life, our heritage."

His stooge was digging his hand into a candy jar, finding a peppermint stick, and asking the cost. Darboy paid no attention to him.

"I am no extremist on the slave issue," said Bolton, "but I will fight to preserve what is mine and the only life I know."

"Hear! Hear!" Swope called out, licking his candy and glowering at the young men in Bolton's audience.

He was a stupid man but strong as a bull and intensely loyal to the Boltons. He would in time go off to war and catch a bullet in the spine.

"Our slaves will have to go," Richard continued. "That much I grant you. Changing times will take them. But no meddlers from within or without will wrest them from us by force."

Raised in the midst of wealth and schooled in the art of command, he was haughty and arrogant but intelligent and capable of reason. A year or two older than Matthew Kingston, his opinions were more liberal than his father's and more flexible. Yet father and son alike despised all opponents of slavery as misguided or ignorant. Pacifist religious groups, such as the Society of Friends who called themselves "conscientious objectors" and refused to bear arms, they condemned as cowardly.

"When war comes," Richard Bolton asserted as he took his package of hardware and laid some coins on the counter, "it will swallow you and your kind. Oh, yes, you smirk as I say this, but you will lose everything if you refuse to participate—your land, your freedom, even your lives."

"How much are the chocolates?" asked Swope, his lips wet and brown from chewing chocolate-flavored taffy. Again Darboy ignored him.

The group near the stove, willfully refusing to demonstrate even one spark of anger, protested Richard's comments with a surge of laughter. Their spokesman at the counter, requiring Bolton to look at him, made answer to the young man quietly and calmly.

"We're made of sterner stuff than that, young man. You'll see."

"Yes," rejoined Richard, paying for the candy and striding with just a hint of a swagger to the doorway. "Yes, Mr. Darboy, we shall certainly see. And not in some distant future, mind you, but soon."

Chapter 22

A week later at four-thirty in the morning—on Friday, April 12, 1861—the first shots of the American Civil War were fired. When dawn came Fort Sumter at the entrance to Charleston harbor was in flames and crumbling. The bombardment continued through the day and into the next day. General Pierre Gustave Toutant Beauregard, a native of Louisiana and a wealthy railroad executive after the war, had demanded evacuation of all troops a day earlier. The Union commander, Major Robert Anderson, refused to comply and attempted to bargain. Succinctly, but with an air of compromise, he assured the messenger that his men would abandon the fort if supplies did not reach them by noon on Monday. Interpreting that remark as an attempt to buy time to secure reinforcements, Beauregard decided to strike before dawn with all the force he could muster. The maneuver worked. On Saturday the surrender was signed in the fort hospital, and a ceremony outside accorded full military honors to the defenders of the fort. On Sunday, April 14, 1861, with colors flying and drums beating, Anderson and the soldiers of his garrison marched out of the rubble to board vessels that would take them north.

The shelling of the fort, with cannons firing every few minutes, was fierce and unrelenting. The pounding rattled windows in downtown Charleston, and residents stood on rooftops or went on boats into the harbor to view the bombardment and surrender ceremony. Except for one Union soldier, who died by accident when Anderson was permitted a fifty-gun salute to his flag, neither side suffered fatal casualties. On April 15, Lincoln called on 75,000 volunteers to suppress the rebellion in the South. He didn't recognize the Confederate States of America as a nation, and so a declaration of war to preserve the Union was unnecessary. Two days later Virginia voted to enter the Confederacy, and in North Carolina the sentiment against secession was rapidly changing. The country was teetering on the brink of a precipice. A savage, bloody war was in the making.

As these events unfolded, Matthew Kingston was ready and eager to marry Catherine Heartwood. All winter long they had planned to marry in the spring. However, in conference with their parents they agreed that a day in June of 1861 would serve them better than April or May. By the end of May, North Carolina had seceded from the Union—after Virginia, Arkansas and Tennessee—to give the Confederate States of America eleven states. The slaveholding state of Maryland had gone with the Union, and so Matthew's prediction of twelve fell short by one. North Carolina, his native state, was now as fervent in rebellion as neighboring South Carolina and was raising an army to fight any Northern army bent on invasion.

Even though Quakers in the Southern states had many friends in the North, particularly in Philadelphia where the sect began in this country, they were viewed by the Lincoln government and by the North in general as the enemy. On the other hand, because they were seen as abolitionists, pacifists, and perhaps sympathizers, throughout the South they were held in distrust and often despised. And so they found themselves squeezed between opposing hostile forces with a threat of persecution from both. With good reason, as war drums began to beat, they were apprehensive and uncomfortable. A change in the weather, however, improved their mood.

A new season had begun, the miraculous season of spring. The unrelenting winter had loosened its grip, and the ground was warm and mother earth was coming alive again. Under a pale blue sky the grass was green and lush, and the live oaks were in budding leaf. The flowering dogwoods were ablaze with a grand show of white and pink, graceful pines swayed in the breeze, and blooming lilacs filled the sweet air with fragrance. The robins were back and seeking secure places to build their nests. A hungry nuthatch moved up and down the trunk of a tall pine tree, searching for insects. Nature was alive and pulsating, and there was a rustle in the earth. From a distance, as field workers tilled the soil, children on the playground at the village school could hear an old slave song drifting and breathing on the wind. *Chilly water is dark and cold. Chills my body but not my soul. Let's wade in de water, chillen. God's gonna trouble de water.*

2

Rachel Kingston was saddened by reports that her Southern neighbors distrusted Quakers, but on this day in early June she was angry. Born Rachel Moore, and only a few years out of Ireland when she met David, her Irish temper sometimes erupted despite Quaker teachings that urged calm. Before noon little Anna had run into the house crying as if her heart would break. She had gone to the local mill in Blue Anchor with her father, who was there with grain to do business. As she waited in the cart for him to return with cornmeal and flour, an unwashed boy aged nine or ten ran up to her, clung to the cart, and looked her squarely in the face. Barefoot, earthy, and skinny, his clothing was soiled and ragged. A trouser leg was split open, and his right knee was skinned and bleeding. His freckled young face was screwed into fierce animosity. Grimacing, he glared at her and confronted her in a nasal, high-pitched voice.

"Yo're one of them Quakers, ain't you? Yo're one of them dirty Quakers! You shore have yore nerve to be seen in public!"

Anna looked at him curiously, thinking he was surely trying to play some kind of game with her. He went on jabbering louder and louder.

"My papa says dirty Quakers ain't no good, oughta be run outta these parts. If you was a boy, I'd drag you off that cart and bash yore brains in, I would. So whut do you say to that, huh?"

The little girl understood every word Timothy Swope spat out in his back-country dialect, but she was too young to grasp the cruelty implicit in the words. At first she thought he was joking, for no one had ever spoken to her like that, and she had never been told that she was different. But when he picked up a rock and began to dance around the cart, chanting "bash yore brains in," she sensed a developing danger and asked the boy to stop.

He responded by hurling a rock at the cart. It struck the rear wheel and broke into little pieces. Then he picked up a larger stone and threw it, hitting the side of the cart just below the seat. Anna heard the blow, felt only a tremor, but was instantly afraid. The boy was dancing around the scared little girl and yelling, "bash yore brains in!" He went looking for another rock. The noise alerted a man in the mill who kindly went to David Kingston.

"Your little daughter," he said, "she's out there crying. Some bully is picking on her. I think you'd better go and see what's happening."

Kingston rushed outside to encounter the bully, thinking he was some overgrown oaf who had nothing more to do than frighten little girls. He saw only a scraggy, skinny boy with a pale and pinched face not much older than Anna. The boy turned and ran, yelling obscenities, and the man knew that something ugly had penetrated his world and he was vulnerable.

On the way home he tried to comfort Anna, tried to cheer her with a humorous repetition of the nursery rhymes she loved, but the lesson in cruelty had moved from head to heart, and she was beyond comforting. She had learned that another child wanted to bash her brains in, and when he called her dirty Quaker it sounded dirty and made her feel dirty. Surrounded by loving people all her life, she was not prepared to come face to face with persecution born of prejudice handed down from father to son.

"It's Bolton again," thought David, sadly shaking his head. "Swope is Bolton's stooge. The man can't think on his own. Bolton's venom went through him to the boy."

At home he explained what had happened at the mill and urged Rachel to make as little of the incident as possible. Reluctantly she agreed to keep it to herself, but as late as supper that day she was fuming.

"I will not have my children treated in that manner, not by anyone!"

Her Irish temper was up and active. For a moment she had forgotten that some people are carefully taught to hate anyone unlike themselves and manage to pass on their hatreds to their children. For a moment she had forgotten that she and her family were living in dangerous, explosive times. Her North Carolina was preparing for war, and its citizens were being conditioned to hate. In the midst of endless chatter, people of every persuasion were taking sides—fire-eaters against pacifists, slaveholders against abolitionists, the southern part of a unified nation against the northern. Soldiers were marching off to war, tramping through green meadows to kill and be killed.

Young men with the same language, the same culture, the same background, even the same physical appearance would fight each other in bloody warfare and die. Men who had the same life experience, the same heritage, and even the same last name would become bitter enemies. A newspaper headline said it best: "My Brother, My Enemy!" Under the broad and black headline was a sensational story about two brothers who just happened to live in different parts of the country when the war began. Simple location on a map, the states in which they lived, had made them sacrificial enemies to fight and die in a bizarre and bloody dance of destiny.

3

Virginia would be the unhappy ground for most of the battles. A strong man in good weather or bad could walk there from Blue Anchor. Military brigades farther south were already moving in that direction. In the third week of July, at Bull Run near a town called Manassas, the dogs of war would slip their leashes to bark and bite. Thousands of young men in their prime, seeking nothing more than adventure, would die. In that context one could view the emotional wounds of a little girl in a forgotten village as relatively insignificant. But for Rachel Kingston a child used as an instrument to bruise the heart of another child was not insignificant at all. It cried out to be corrected, but how? She would try to forget the incident and hope it would never happen again. If it did, she would find a way to act.

That evening Rachel calmed herself by letting her thoughts center upon the impending marriage of her son and a young woman whom she already loved as a daughter. No adjustment whatever would be necessary, for the girl had always been a nominal member of the family. The marriage in that sense was merely a formality to make it legal. The date was set for the third week in June, and she hoped the weather would be cool and pleasant. The couple would marry in the Meeting House, with friends and relatives attending, and later they would return to her house for the customary reception. Afterwards perhaps just the two of them would go on a trip together, for the honeymoon as a custom was then coming into favor, but of that she was uncertain. Where could they go in wartime?

"There is so much to be done," she told herself, "so many details to be worked out. So much to do to insure their happiness."

If Brandimore had argued as an intellectual exercise that hap or circumstance, fate or destiny or whatever you wish to call it, often prescribes the limits of human happiness, her rebuttal would have been simple and direct. If such a force does indeed exist in the civilized world, it is a force for human will to resist, put down, or change.

"No marriage can be entered into lightly," she had said to her son, "and particularly your marriage to that good woman."

She wanted to be certain their vows were taken reverently with a full understanding of mutual responsibility for each other. She felt duty bound to establish and cultivate on the wedding day a supreme happiness for the two that would resonate far into the future.

"But so much to do in so little time," she mumbled, tossing in her bed and jolting her husband half awake.

As with any Quaker marriage, Rachel was thinking of important procedures that had to be met before the ceremony could take place. The Monthly Meeting would have jurisdiction over the marriage and would eventually sanction it. In the meantime, Matthew and Catherine would submit their intention to marry in writing. The written consent of surviving parents would also be required. When that information was in hand, Rachel would appoint a committee of two older women to interview Catherine in private. With time-tested queries, they would determine that the young woman was pure and chaste, in good health, and unencumbered by any previous relationship. Matthew would also be required to certify "clearness of body and soul" before a Quaker elder. The man would question him in detail to affirm good character, moral and mental soundness, and robust health. At two Monthly Meetings the elders would examine all the documents relating to the candidates. If they were deemed satisfactory, a committee of chosen women would publish its formal consent. If any document proved unsatisfactory, there would be no wedding. Not one person, not even the oldest among them, could remember a negative report.

In due time the couple would announce the date and place of the event, though everyone knew the wedding would take place in the Meeting House. Four people not of the immediate families, two men and two women, would be appointed to attend and judge the ceremony as impartial observers. Later in formal meetings open to all they would report their findings. The report would say in essence that the marriage of Matthew David Kingston to Catherine Martha Heartwood on the date and place as shown had been accomplished legally with simplicity, efficiency, dignity, and good taste.

After all procedures were met, the wedding invitations, plainly written in a good hand, would be delivered. The Meeting House would bulge at the seams with a hundred people or more, or the ceremony could be quite small. The size was dependent on the bride and groom and their families. The marriage Rachel Kingston was planning would have many guests, but no extravagant expenditure, no conspicuous display of wealth, no music of any kind, no rings as in traditional marriages, and no minister presiding. A typical Quaker wedding, as this one would surely be, aimed for a spare and simple elegance in a setting close to God. Friends and relatives would bask in the warmth and joy of the occasion and remember it for years.

Chapter 23

Near the middle of June, a bright and balmy day with fresh breezes and blue skies, Catherine went to the Kingston house to ask important questions about her wedding dress. Having lost her mother in infancy, she could bring such matters only to her future mother-in-law. Her father, attempting to help her as best he could, had measured the bolt of merino that came from the Philadelphia boxes and reported good news. He felt it would be enough for a dress that would flow gracefully from her shoulders and waist to cover all but the tips of her shoes. She hoped the thin woolen fabric would not be too warm for a day in June. To find out more, Catherine sought Rachel's advice.

"What do you think?" she asked, placing the cloth on the kitchen table as the older woman prepared a pot of tea.

"I think it's pretty," said Anna, who had skipped into the room with Jesse close behind her. "I think it's soft and pretty."

"I think it's pretty awful!" bellowed mischievous Jesse. Catherine made as if she would grab the boy, but he ran away hooting and laughing.

Rachel was about to order the children outside when Catherine put her arm around little Anna and drew her close. The child nestled against the young woman, smiling happily though whimpering softly. Of all the people she knew in the world, Matthew was her favorite and Catherine her second favorite. Parents and animals didn't count. And that mean old Jesse didn't count either. But Sarah and Moses were favorites too.

She wanted to watch as a paper pattern was placed on the cloth and sharp scissors brought from a drawer. She said not a word about Timothy Swope, and the women hoped she had forgotten all about him. As she studied what they were doing she chatted easily and happily. The cutting of the cloth was a precise and time-consuming step in the making of what they hoped would be a stunning dress. However, one snip of the scissors in the wrong place could ruin everything. The operation was not entirely complete when Catherine made ready to return home.

She went into the yard where Moses stood with Peg and was about to speak with him. Then of a sudden, looking down the long avenue of oaks, she saw her father's gig approaching.

"That's odd," she said. "Why would Papa be coming here at this time of day? I thought he wouldn't be back until late afternoon."

"Maybe he forgot somethin'," said Moses. "Some old folks is ver' forgetful, I should know."

She waited for the light two-wheeled carriage to reach the house and pull into the yard. Moses stayed with the pony as she ran to Jeremy's old horse, grasped the reins, and stroked the mare's neck and ears while speaking to her father.

"Is something the matter, Papa? I thought you would have visited Harvey and his family by now and gone on to spend some time with the Alstons. I didn't expect you back so soon."

Jeremy sat stiffly in the cart, beads of sweat on his forehead and his round body hunched forward. The smile that lived perpetually on his open, honest face had disappeared. He took off his new hat, the one from the Philadelphia boxes, and with a large handkerchief mopped his brow. Then slowly, as though he himself were as tired as she had been, he reported that Hannah Alston was dead.

"Hannah is dead," he repeated. "That's why I'm back early. She's dead. Had to tell someone. She seemed fine this morning. Fixed breakfast for all the children. Waved goodbye to Elmer and Nat. Said she would bring them lunch in the field, but never came. So they went back to grab a bite and found her slumped over in a chair. The woman who helps with the chores, Annie by name, was doing the washing out back. The children told me their mama was sleeping. I came along just as Elmer was checking her pulse."

"Ohhh," responded Catherine as though in physical pain. "I'm so sorry."

"Elmer is fit to be tied. Can't think. Can't talk straight. Asked me to talk to the elders about the funeral procedure. Wants her to rest in the graveyard beside the Meeting House. Has no idea what's going to happen to him and the children. Hannah was sickly but filled a large place in their lives."

"I know, I know," murmured Catherine, "I'm so sorry."

"Are you on your way home? Is David at home?"

"He and Matthew rode over to Bupee's cabin. They heard that people on the road were staying there and making a mess of the place. They plan to tear it down and use the logs for firewood this winter. That way, they said, they can kill two birds with one stone. They won't be back for a while, but Rachel is here with the children."

Rachel had given the children glasses of milk to drink, had appeared on the porch, and was descending the steps. She informed Jeremy, after a brief discussion, that Hannah Alston would be buried at sunset the next day. Her husband David would arrange for the funeral and Matthew would announce the event. Sarah the cook would go to the Alston place and help with the children. She made these decisions without hesitation and without consulting anyone. In times of crisis Rachel Kingston moved competently and quickly with a sure instinct for what was right and fitting.

2

On the day of the funeral the weather turned cool and cloudy. By afternoon a steady rain was falling and threatened to go on into the night. The women saw that Elmer and his children were cared for and comforted as a coffin was being fitted for Hannah. Speaking quietly with Elmer to learn what he wanted for his wife, Rachel decided Hannah would rest eternally at sunset. Both of them wanted good weather for the ceremony but knew they would have to take what they could get. On this rainy day there would be no sunset that anyone could see. Even so, the days were long in June, and they would have daylight for both the funeral service and the burial. They hoped the rain would stop before the ceremony in the Meeting House was over.

Near seven o'clock people began to gather in the Meeting-House yard. Quarterly meetings allowed for casual dress, but for a wedding or a funeral the people attending dressed in the best clothes they had. Some in their best walked a mile or more in the rain to pay their last respects to Hannah Alston. Others rode on horseback, in wagons, and two-wheeled carts. The sheds that served as stables were full by the time the Meeting-House door was closed. Animals that pulled wagons and carts were hitched to trees nearby. Families went to their accustomed seats on the hard benches and waited for the service to begin. The children dangled their legs, made faces at one another, and squirmed like a hooked salmon. One or two sneezed or coughed but none dared to talk or even whisper. It was a sad and solemn occasion even for the children, and the silence except for the rain on the roof was heavy.

The open coffin rested on wooden frames in front of the gallery at the head of the long middle aisle. It was open according to custom, for Quaker doctrine taught that people needed to see and remember the face of the deceased. Nearby sat Elmer Alston looking downward and lost in grief, crushing the crown of his hat with fingers that refused to rest. Then a kindly male voice, inquisitive and sonorous, broke the silence. The man who was speaking was there to put a period to a life.

"Is it not well to view the face of Hannah Alston whose earthly body lies before us? Shall we do that before words are spoken? Will the family go first and then the elders? Will all the Friends in attendance here file by the coffin to honor this woman in death before we pray?"

The questions were rhetorical and traditional, part of the procedure. In a practical and kindly way they gave instructions to preserve order in a group charged with emotion. They also conveyed an undercurrent of grief and a sense of loss shared by all who had known the Alstons.

Elmer shuffled to the coffin, paused a moment to burn into memory the face of the woman who had shared her life and bed with him, and said a silent prayer. With crushed hat in hand he went back to his seat to let his children view their mother's face for the last time. Each one with dry eyes went to the coffin, peered downward into the waxen face, looked around at everyone present, and went back to their seats. As they sat down, the adults came forward, paused, and passed. Not a word was spoken. Some faces were wet with tears, but no cries of grief disturbed the silence. The only sound to be heard, except for the rain pelting the roof, was the shuffling of feet. As the women came forward, the rustling of skirts softened the sound of the rain. And then it was time to speak.

3

Churches which have a formula for ceremonies such as this often have the advantage when words are to be spoken about the deceased. The Quakers of Blue Anchor had no prepared text, no eulogy carefully rehearsed, not even a rough outline to guide them as they spoke. Each person who stood up was expected to speak from the heart and say whatever the spirit prompted. No person was required to speak, and no person except for the children was forbidden to speak. The very old were given free rein to speak, but when they began to ramble a kindly hand would touch a shoulder as the signal to stop. The ceremony had no protocol dictating who would begin the personal eulogies first and no limit on time. Gender and rank did not matter.

Rachel rose to declare deep and sincere feelings in dramatic testimony, and so did Catherine. Other women and some of the men spoke briefly and simply. When their testimony was over and they had taken their seats, another period of silence ensued. A child coughed into a handkerchief, and muffled weeping came from where the family sat. Outside the rain dashed against the window panes. Then David Kingston announced that interment would be near the Meeting House in a plot standing in readiness according to custom. After a pause that signaled the end of the ceremony, he asked Jacob Darboy to close the meeting when he thought it proper to do so.

Darboy gave the signal for the pallbearers to close the coffin and carry it to the yard. Behind them the men moved in double file and then the women and children. Under black umbrellas, the men gathered in a circle. Women and children gathered in another. Quickly, as the circles merged in symbolic solidarity, the coffin was lowered into the muddy grave. Rich and damp soil, protected by a tarpaulin, was piled upon it to make a mound. A plain gray headstone, dripping with wet, was set in the sod. The rain had diminished to a drizzle when the coffin was lowered into the grave. It soon increased and became a downpour in a wind rising from the east. As Elmer moved out to the road and homeward, shielding his children from inclement weather, the wind was blowing hard and the slanted rain stung his face.

Chapter 24

The second week of June was coming to an end. The countryside flourished under sunny skies, and the farming was good. Elmer Alston had his son and the free black couple to help him with farm chores. David and Jeremy had hired a young woman named Jenny Meyers to keep house for Elmer and look after his children. She was not a Quaker but seemed to have a good heart, and the children liked her. For the first time in months Elmer found his house, on returning from the fields, clean and orderly. She was not the best of cooks, but the food she prepared was edible, even tasty at times. Elmer felt she would improve with practice and gave her all the freedom she desired, even to planning each meal. At first every dinner was much the same as the one before, but gradually she introduced a bit of variety based on what they had in the pantry. Before long even the children were eating with smiles on their faces.

Jenny came to the house every morning and departed when the family was ready for bed. David Kingston was paying her a reasonable wage, and she ate her meals with the family. Eugene and Annie, former slaves and now paid field hands, had signed an agreement to remain on the farm for the duration of the war and beyond if they chose. Free and independent, they were treated as members of the family but lived in a cabin apart and ate their meals there. The Quaker spirit of equality did not extend to their eating at the Alston table, and they preferred it that way. The Society of Friends had pledged their support until Elmer was back on his feet. The contract included Leo Mack who made it known to everybody that he would mend any Alston pot that sprung a leak and do it for nothing.

In the fine weather Mack went from house to house, exchanging gossip and doing business. At noon on a sun-flooded day he parked his rig in the shade of a tree beside Darboy's General Store, left his dog Sparky lying under the wagon, and went inside. The proprietor was talking to a customer about a yoke, but on seeing Leo they both turned to greet him. They expected news of the outside world, something they could pass along to others.

2

"Well, if you ask me, there's a flurry of activity all over," the tinker reported. "Seems to be a fiery, steadfast certainty that secession is the way to go. In the larger towns speeches on every side and people parading up and down in gaudy costume. Young men by the thousands flocking to the colors and swearing to die to preserve the Southern way of life. But signing up mainly for adventure, I hear, and no trouble getting volunteers."

"Flocking to the colors?" asked Alvin Atterbury. A man of middle age, he repaired farm equipment and cultivated a spread of sixty acres.

"You mean the new flag, the one they call the Stars and Bars? I'm having trouble seeing it as a real flag, the colors of a sovereign nation."

"Oh, it's a real flag all right," countered Mack. "You can bet on that. It's flying from courthouses already, and the army's gonna take it into every battle it fights. Everybody is saying it'll be a flag to spark fear in the enemy."

"I've read about flag bearers not being armed," mused Darboy. "If they fall under fire in battle, the soldier next to them must grab the flag before it hits the ground and carry it forward. That's an easy way to die!"

"Well, I guess it is," Mack assented, "but no unit is gonna be without a battle flag, and it's gonna be the Confederate flag in the thick of action."

"I hear there's a shortage of rifles for the infantry," said Atterbury. "And not enough uniforms to go around. And a shortage of shoes. Also chaotic distribution depots and more than enough confusion all over."

"True enough," answered Mack, who now saw himself as something of an authority on the new events. "But these are the early weeks of the war. Officers have to be selected and given their duties. Enlisted soldiers have to be assigned, armed, and trained. Tremendous amount of drilling already going on. The generals and senior officers are trying to find commanders for all the regiments being formed, and that's a real problem right there."

"Well, it's a big and sad undertaking," Darboy sighed, "and perhaps misguided too. Old Thomas Paine could have been talking about us when he wrote about his own day. You remember what he said? Something like this: 'These are the times that try men's souls!' That sure describes us all right. A melodramatic declaration maybe, but it fits."

Mack shrugged his shoulders, sighed deeply, and looked at the ceiling. He disliked fancy quotations from people who read books. Jacob Darboy, the struggling merchant, he favored. Darboy, the pundit and reader of books, sounded too much like Brandimore. And besides Brandimore had already used that little nugget from Thomas Paine way back in March.

"What I know about that," he said, scratching the bald spot on the back of his head, "is about enough to put in a thimble. We can't really say how trying things are gonna get, can we? Just hafta wait, can't see the future."

"I'm saying these are dangerous times," Darboy replied, "exciting right now for the younger folk but deadly later. Mark my word on that, Friend Mack. All these young men with war fever in their blood tramping off to the beat of drums may sorely regret it. Oh, they're eager for adventure all right, but what's gonna happen to the lot of them later?"

"What's gonna happen to any poor lad willing to fight?" asked Mack. "I heard they're marching off to war singing battle hymns written and sung by Northerners. Now that just ain't right."

"Ah, still wet behind the ears. They don't seem to know the price they'll pay for just a little excitement. In another year or two we'll see them paying and paying. Paying the ultimate price!"

Darboy was now talking like a merchant, and Mack remembered he was in the store to pick up an order he had placed weeks before.

"I'm here for the solder you promised to get me," said the tinker impatiently. "Glad to see it came in, can't mend no pots without it, you know. Oh, I almost forgot. You don't happen to have no pots or pans or pails there in your back room that need attention, do you?"

Leo·had been looking for an apprentice to learn his trade and take it over when he grew too old to work. But the word had gotten around that the man was too much a taskmaster to be a good master. A couple years back he had a slow-witted boy who seemed eager to learn but could never remember the details of the trade. One afternoon when his liver was acting up, exasperated and testy but not angry, he lectured his apprentice with so little restraint the boy scampered away and quit. Mack was a good man and a good Quaker, but for reasons unknown to his friends he had never learned patience and calm, commodities prized by the Quakers.

3

At the Kingston farm Rachel and Catherine had resumed preparations for the wedding. The two had turned a piece of cloth into a very attractive gown. It was cut plain and unadorned, but when Catherine slipped into it and stood before the fine old mirror in the living room she scarcely recognized herself. The rich blue of the fine fabric drew attention to her face and made it shine. Her body, lithe and shapely, gave fluid life to the gown. It clung to every curve, accenting and dramatizing her beauty. Examining her reflection in the mirror, she murmured sotto voce and with deep emotion lines she remembered from Keats: *A thing of beauty is a joy forever. Its loveliness increases. It will never pass into nothingness.* In her selfless modesty she was thinking of the dress, but the words applied equally to her.

"It's a work of art," she said aloud, as Rachel stood behind her, admiring their creation, "absolutely a work of art!"

In an old book about her Quaker forebears Catherine had once read a statement that had taken her by surprise: "Their kingdom was not of this world. There was no place for the arts or for the cultivation of beauty in their stern philosophy."

She had shaken her head in disbelief, and now in remembrance she laughed joyously. Who was that pedant, that sour old man, who could write so erroneously about the Quakers? She had taken the trouble to find out, and again she laughed as she remembered. The man himself, at the very time he scribbled that nonsense, was a devout and earnest Quaker.

A day later a deputation of two women, chosen at the Monthly Meeting, came to her with their queries. They talked pleasantly for half an hour and then began to probe. She had never blushed, not even once in her life, but on this day she felt the hot blood rising upward along the neck and into her face. She grew annoyed, for some of the questions embarrassed her, but she tried not to show it. These well-meaning women were prying into her personal life because reasonable Quaker tradition demanded it. They wanted to be certain that while growing up her heart and mind, her blood and brain, her spirit and moral development, had remained unblemished. With incisive questions, they probed to find if she were "clean and clear," and they found a mountain brook flowing into a pristine pool.

At the same time Matthew endured a similar interview. His interrogator asked him questions he felt were entirely too personal. But since he had nothing to hide and respected the tradition, he answered each question with candor. He had not been intimate with Catherine. He had never had fornication with any woman. To his knowledge and understanding, he had no infectious disease he could transmit to his bride. He was fully capable of sexual union with the proper woman, and to the best of his knowledge his seed was sound. In the proper setting he expected to father a large family. And yes, he wanted children. After the interview, a formal announcement of their impending marriage was published.

The Meeting House, which often stood vacant and quiet, was now being used almost daily. Hannah Alston's funeral was the one memorable event of recent weeks, but groups of one sort or another held their meetings there regularly. Selected groups would come in and clean the house and yard, picking up any litter, sweeping the floor, cleaning the windows, and wiping down the benches. Cleanliness in Quaker doctrine was next to godliness. Order and neatness in Quaker life were mandatory. Furniture in their houses was spare and always in its proper place. Each day was carefully divided into hours for work and rest. Rachel Kingston's Monthly Meeting had finished its business, and now the Meeting House was being cleaned again and spruced up for the wedding.

It would take place on June 21, the summer solstice and longest day of the year, at three o'clock in the afternoon. The ceremony would be over in little more than an hour, but no one would be watching the clock. Everyone knew that some weddings had been longer. Early in the morning, well before the hour of the ceremony, several women supervised by Rachel would prepare food and drink for the reception. She would also select her son's wedding attire, keeping it simple and elegant without show. She wanted him to shine in his own right, but also to complement his bride in all her beauty. The bride would be the main attraction, a magnet to draw all eyes, but the groom would assert his presence in the background. His masculinity as given to him by God would highlight and glorify her femininity. All attending would see them as a couple and then as one. So from early morning until late at night Rachel threw herself into a hundred tasks. When the men offered to help she waved them away, saying everything was under complete control. With Rachel Kingston in charge one could be certain of that.

Chapter 25

On her wedding day Catherine Heartwood rose early. The morning sun poured into her kitchen as she prepared a hearty breakfast for her beaming father. They ate in the little nook off the kitchen with only a few words passing between them. Jeremy knew that in times of great excitement his daughter withdrew into pensive silence. She was bright of face and cheerful but anxious and a bit worried. Nothing on this day of hers must go wrong. But what if she tripped ascending the steps of the Meeting House, or in the aisle? What if she forgot the wording of her vows? What if she spoke out of turn? What if someone objected? Didn't Quaker doctrine allow that?

Then as she collected and dismissed all these "what ifs," a thought came to mind that frightened her. What if the ceremony were to be interrupted by troops on their way to do battle? What if armed soldiers came stomping into the Meeting House to desecrate her ceremony? What if some burly soldier picked a fight with Matthew and punched him in the face? She shuddered even to think of that. It was a horrible thought that made her feel cold. Nothing ugly, certainly nothing so ugly as vulgar soldiers making a mockery of her ceremony, must interfere with the beauty of her special day. Nothing untoward must interrupt the pleasant, easy flow of the day. She hoped her God would see to that. She prayed that troops on their way to fight and die would move east of Blue Anchor and leave the village alone.

Catherine rose to pour her father another mug of coffee. He thanked her but she made no reply. She was thinking of the ceremony itself and the behavior expected of her. She would not forget her vows and she would not speak out of turn, and no one would object. But would she and Matthew dare kiss before all those people when they were man and wife? Would someone object to that? Could some disciplinarian like the old Quaker who spoke so sourly of his own kind object? Could some angry voice call the kiss a display of public affection and term it vulgar and forbidden?

Rachel had said the kiss was optional. "Be guided by thy inner feeling, the warmth of thy heart," the older woman had said to her.

But the older rites did not allow for even a symbolic kiss. Could she trust her heart in so tense a situation? Could she trust even her senses? She thought the symbolism of exchanging rings was a beautiful thing, but in the Meeting House there would be no rings to exchange. She would have no simple gold band to grace her finger for the rest of her life, and she couldn't understand why. Some parts of Quaker tradition did not sit well with her.

She cleared away the breakfast dishes, washed them with borax in hot water, and made her kitchen tidy. It would remain her kitchen, but for how long she didn't know. Matthew would live in her father's house until the time came when they could afford a place of their own. His clothing would occupy part of the ancient wardrobe on the south wall of her bedroom. His place at their table was already marked by a setting of blue-rimmed plates and a cup to match. His duty as man of the house, passed on to him by retiring Jeremy, would be to wind the tall clock in the corner every morning, clean it every spring, and make certain its time was always accurate.

When her father went to the barn to feed the livestock and to the field in back of the barn to inspect his vegetable garden, the young woman was left alone with thoughts that seemed to cascade from a cliff. Methodically and without hurry she disrobed and bathed, scrubbing her luminous skin in warm and soapy water until it tingled. Until the wedding hour she would wear something light and loose to remain fresh. Apart from the cleanliness of her body, there would be no feminine fragrance of any kind. Even the bath soap was unscented. She would have no artificial aromas such as perfumes, and none of the summer flowers she often wore as decoration. She would be wearing no jewelry and no makeup on her face or lips, for Quaker morality frowned on baubles and the painted woman. Rachel would help her arrange the mass of blonde hair to make it pretty on her head.

In a room of the Meeting House, set aside for that purpose, she would change into the blue merino that had become her wedding dress. Rachel had said the color might well have been white to show purity, but Catherine had laughed with good humor and said the blue could stand for heaven. She spread the beautiful garment on the bed with her navy-blue stockings, white chemise and petticoat, and linen underwear neatly folded. Under the bed were black shoes that went well with her stockings. For the first time in her life she would share her cozy feather bed, and her eiderdown when colder weather came, with another human being. A male human being, and she was moved by the wonder and the mystery of it all.

2

Early in the afternoon Catherine and Jeremy rode in the gig to the Meeting House. The most joyous day of her life was unfolding exactly as she had hoped. The sky had cleared to a thin hard blue, and a cooling breeze made the gray moss tremble and sway on the live oaks. A bird in one of the trees trilled its song and was answered by another. The bride-to-be and her father were among the first to arrive at the Meeting House, but the heavy doors and some of the windows were already open. The building was old but severely clean and as fresh as the midsummer air.

Jeremy unbridled the aging mare and put her in the nearest shed where she could rest in comfort. Her arms full of clothing, Catherine made her way into the dressing room of the Meeting House. She was in no mood to chat with anyone, not even Rachel, until the ceremony was over. Matthew and her father, and most of the guests, would not see her until the two came forward as planned. Then she would walk down the aisle, lightly and gracefully she hoped, on the arm of her round and broadly smiling father. Matthew, tall and manly in his wedding attire, would be waiting.

An hour later the Kingstons arrived in their coach with Matthew and the children. Moses sat proudly on the high seat, beaming and tipping his hat to people in the yard. Since the Meeting House had no foyer or anteroom, the guests waited near the entrance until the groomsmen ushered them to their seats. The families of the bride and groom sat on opposite sides of the long aisle near the front. Their friends, and there were many, sat behind them. The benches on the Kingston side were quickly filled. When vacant seats remained on the Heartwood side, mutual friends moved in to occupy them.

On a bench near the back sat Jeremy's old friend, Harvey Heckrodt, with his wife Susan. In recent months their troubled lives had grown better. Harvey's tubercular condition seemed to be in remission, and he was doing light farm work in the community. Also the family had managed to get along without harassment from opportunists on the road. Able to show papers to prove they were free, the slave catchers who occasionally came their way did not bother them. And so in the back of the big room they sat in silent expectation and waited. All the guests were properly seated before the stroke of three. Shortly before that hour, Moses left his prized coach and shared the bench with Harvey, Susan, and Sarah. Even though the latter was needed in the kitchen, she was unwilling to miss any part of the ceremony.

Precisely at three o'clock Jeremy Heartwood drew his round form to its tallest height and strolled down the aisle with Catherine. His daughter, a head taller than her father, was a vision of elegant simplicity. The sight of this beautiful woman on the arm of her indulgent and genial father inspired a collective sigh of admiration on both sides of the aisle. The couple marched slowly in delayed step to the front of the cavernous room. With a twinkle in his eye but no hint of the smile he wore when marching, Jeremy Heartwood gave his daughter to young Matthew Kingston and sat down.

He watched intently as the bride and groom joined hands, looked into each other's face, and parted to join their separate families. He saw a tremor on his daughter's lips and a light of wonder in her eyes. He looked behind him and to either side and saw many old friends participating in the moment of silence. Then he shaped a silent prayer for the couple, closing his eyes and bowing his head, and speaking the words only to himself and his God: *"Oh Lord of life, in thy goodness and mercy, send their roots rain!"*

He finished just as the bride and groom rose serenely and separately to meet at the head of the aisle. There they joined their right hands, faced one another, and paused for a moment. That far-off look came back into Catherine's brown eyes and made them moist. Sensing she was on the brink of too much emotion, Matthew spoke to comfort her. No minister was present to conduct the ceremony and no justice of the peace; only the two of them stood alone. Marriage was an ordinance of God, a sacramental decree, and only God could join this man and this woman in holy matrimony.

Then Jeremy heard as if from heaven itself a rich and resonant male voice intoning familiar words. The groom was declaring his vow.

"In the presence of the Lord and this assembly, I take thee, Catherine Martha Heartwood, to be my loving wife. I promise with divine assistance to be unto thee a loving and faithful husband so long as my life shall endure until death shall rend us apart."

The same vow, clear and simple and clean, was repeated word for word by the bride, and she did not miss a syllable.

"In the presence of the Lord and this assembly, I take thee, Matthew David Kingston, to be my loving husband. I promise with divine assistance to be unto thee a loving and faithful wife so long as my life shall endure until death shall rend us apart."

She had not forgotten the sacred words, and she had delivered them with rhythm and cadence from the deepest recesses of her soul and heart. They were in essence an arrangement of musical notes floating upward to the ceiling never to be heard again. They rang to the high rafters in this place without music, moving her betrothed to deep emotion and settling deep in her father's heart. Quaker doctrine urged the putting down of pride. It was, after all, a deadly sin. But on this day, at this moment, Jeremy Heartwood was the proudest man in all of North Carolina. He did not ask forgiveness of his loving God. He knew that his God in mercy and wisdom had already forgiven.

3

Jeremy's gaze was riveted upon them as the bride and groom sat down on a bench facing the congregation. Together they were a living picture to be remembered by everyone present: a self-assured man with dark hair in dark clothes, a blonde and shapely woman in lighter and softer hues, husband and wife in their prime. In what seemed almost a trance to those looking on they turned, embraced one another, and kissed. Not a single person missed this bold display of symbolic union, though it was over in a second. Even Harvey with vision dimmed by the years was smiling, and Moses chuckled.

To Jeremy, sitting only a few feet away, they seemed to kiss in slow motion. He could not be certain that he approved, and yet it seemed positively the right thing to do. Before he could think any more about its moral implications, an usher brought from a table the marriage certificate to be signed. He handed the pen to Matthew who gave it to his bride. She signed her maiden name in the proper space, using it for the last time in her life. From that moment onward she would be known as Catherine Kingston.

The usher held aloft the completed certificate, pausing to let the ink dry and to allow the guests to glimpse it. It was a handsome, gilt-edged sheet of paper looking almost like genuine parchment. He gave it to Jeremy who stood before the assembly prepared to read it aloud. Though the certificate was couched in the legal and wordy language of years gone by, and written in a cramped, ornate hand, Jeremy read it smoothly without missing a syllable. Moses in the back of the room, advanced in age and hard of hearing, caught every word with the help of beaming Sarah.

> *Matthew David Kingston, eldest son of David and Rachel Kingston of Blue Anchor in the County of Prudock in the State of North Carolina, and Catherine Martha Heartwood, sole daughter of Jeremy Heartwood, having declared their Solemn Intention to join Body and Soul in Holy Matrimony at two Monthly Meetings of Friends, and all Things being Clear, have joined in Marriage at a Public Meeting at Blue Anchor this twenty-first Day of the sixth Month in the Year of our Lord, one thousand eight hundred and sixty one. The said Matthew Kingston has taken the said Catherine Heartwood to be his lawfully wedded Wife, and the said Catherine Heartwood has taken the said Matthew Kingston to be her lawfully wedded Husband, she according to time-honored Tradition assuming the Surname of her Husband. Witnesses of the same, on the Day and the Year as stated above, hereby append their legal Signatures.*

At the reception several guests would sign the certificate with their full names. Within days it would be sent to Raleigh and deposited in the courthouse there to resist the ravages of time. Though made of stone, the courthouse burned in 1874. All legal documents on file were lost.

Chapter 26

The ceremonial gathering at the Meeting House was now framed by periods of silence. While the silence reigned, any person with a message appropriate to the occasion was allowed to speak. No time limit hindered any speaker, but all of them spoke briefly and to the point. Jeremy Heartwood, unable to suppress a smile as he stood to address the congregation, wished his lovely daughter and handsome son-in-law the very best in their present life and a most fruitful future. It would please him no end to see them prosper, have many children, and grow old together. With an audible chuckle, he hoped they would have a passel of children in a house of their own. Then Grandpapa would come from his own little house to spoil them.

In the midst of laughter generated by Jeremy's speech, David Kingston, rose from his seat to wish the couple well. Speaking evenly and quietly, he hoped they would accept his benediction. Rachel Kingston faced the young people and spoke in a voice made brittle by emotion. Her love for the happy newlyweds, she said, made both of them an integral part of her. Should they suffer and feel misery, and life inevitably would deliver that sentence, she too would suffer and feel misery. Should they rejoice on many happy occasions, and life would deliver those too, she would most certainly rejoice. When each person had spoken his piece, and many did, silence flowed in again. At length David rose to say, "This is perhaps a suitable time for the wedding company to withdraw." It was the signal for the bride and groom to walk up the aisle to the wide door and waiting coach. Others would follow in the same order they had entered, and therefore no ushers were necessary.

Jeremy rode to the reception at the Kingston house in the coach driven by Moses. Anna sat between Catherine and Matthew, facing her parents and Jeremy. She was glowing with happiness and thrilled by all she had seen and heard. She fidgeted as she spoke.

"I want all of you to come to my wedding. You must promise!"

The adults responded with laughter. She became serious and was a little hurt because they took her so lightly.

"You must promise," she repeated. "And you must promise never to let any more mean boys come near me ever again."

That sudden revelation worried her mother, and not a single person in the coach was laughing any longer. Jesse, who would have had plenty to say, asking how could she marry if no boy ever came near her, was not present to comment. He had the responsibility of harnessing Jeremy's old horse and driving home in the gig.

The rest of the company lingered in the Meeting-House yard, commenting on the beauty of the ceremony, before departing for the reception. The Kingston house with its legendary warmth and loaded tables would be ready to receive them. The marriage certificate would be on display at the doorway with pen and ink beside it. For several happy hours Matthew and his lovely bride would be the center of attention.

2

Exactly one month later in Manassas, Virginia the first major battle of the Civil War raged on bloody ground. The First Battle of Bull Run (a second would come later) was fought in open terrain. Poorly trained young soldiers, many of them away from home for the first time, clashed in an open field. Exhausted by the heat and strain and deadly confusion of battle, it was the first and last engagement thousands of them would see. The Southern troops commanded by General Beauregard, who had fired the first shots of the war in Charleston, sent the Union troops reeling in retreat and won the battle. The dead and wounded, many younger than Matthew on his wedding day, numbered nearly 3,000 on the Union side and 2,000 among the Confederates. Sightseers on holiday, senators and congressmen among them, came out to see the battle from what they thought was a safe vantage point. The Union army, running helter-skelter in furious retreat, narrowly avoided stampeding and killing them all.

All of that, however—young men losing their lives in July—would come later. At the Kingston homestead peace and happiness reigned as the order of the day. Catherine's marriage had taken place with no embarrassment to her or to anyone else. For a few hours a world of violence receded into silence as if in respect for the most important event in the young woman's life. An hour before midnight, as the wedding party continued, she and her new husband slipped away unnoticed in Jeremy's gig. When the festivities were over, Jeremy walked briskly home with

David and Jesse. The two old friends talked quietly of the future as the boy ran ahead of them.

Returning home to the Kingston house that balmy night in midsummer, walking sometimes on the edge of the narrow moonlit road and sometimes in the middle, the curious boy had many questions to ask.

"Jesse," cautioned his father, "slow down."

"Well, if I don't ask questions, Papa, how is a body to learn?"

It was a good question, a legitimate and thoughtful question.

"You will learn in time," said his father.

"Well guess so, but why do I have to wait?"

David did not reply. He was thinking of Tom Bolton. Though haughty and irascible and often flaunting his wealth and power, the man had confronted him only once, and about Edna. For years before that he had been a good neighbor. David didn't want that to change. He was hoping Bolton would cease the rabble-rousing, the inflamed and irresponsible rhetoric, and come to his senses. The times were already troubled enough. Quaker calm and resilience might keep the man in check, but if things didn't go his way anything could happen. David was shaking his head as he approached the house. Jesse's unrestrained energy had taken him far ahead.

3

Thomas Bolton called himself a Christian. His religion, however, had not given him that conviction which mellows into faith and sustains the believer in the worst of times. He had spent most of his life struggling to gain wealth, hoping it would bring happiness. Now when it seemed that elusive state of mind was in his grasp, he was restive and reaching for more. He lived alone in his richly appointed mansion and was often lonely. When speaking of his house, he often said he had not been in some of its rooms for years and did not even know how many rooms it had. His son was there to keep him company, but he wanted female companionship in the autumn of his life. More than once he had gone to Raleigh, hoping to meet a woman who might become his wife. When on occasion he met a person who seemed likely to qualify for that position and perhaps accept it, nothing came of it. No woman wanted to be a substitute for a wife who died too soon.

Twenty-six years before the summer of 1861 he had married a young woman with whom he hoped to sire a large and loving family. She would give him sons, and he would give her in return a life of wealth and leisure and privilege. In the first years of their domestic life they were guardedly happy. Thomas worked many hours each day and did not see his young wife as often as he wished, but whenever he could he paid full attention to her and made her feel wanted. To show his affection he gave her presents, expensive trinkets and costly jewelry. Then a miracle occurred, though he did not recognize it as such. Gwendolyn Bolton became pregnant, and though her labor taxed her body tremendously she delivered a healthy baby boy. It took her longer than usual to recover, but she and her husband were joyous.

"This is the first!" he crowed triumphantly. "After this, we shall have more! I want many fine sons to keep the Bolton name alive, at least five." Gwendolyn loved children and was not reluctant to try again.

"You shall have them, God willing," she assured him.

In the realization of that dream, through no fault of his own, he was sorely disappointed. His wife had trouble conceiving. Two long years went by before she became pregnant again. Then in the middle of a dark December night she gave birth to a blue baby girl who could not breathe properly. The child died before they could even name her. After that Gwendolyn suffered one miscarriage after another until all the juices of life dried up within her. She wanted desperately to give her husband the children he craved, but what appeared to be a hostile destiny decreed otherwise. On the other hand, money came pouring in as if fortune favored them alone, and the faster it accumulated the fonder Bolton became of it and the things it could buy. Yet always he said it was there for the family he hoped to have.

They named their one child Richard Thomas Bolton. He was bright and eager to learn, even bookish at times, but also strong and healthy and athletic. He learned to swim and ride just after he learned to walk. In his teens he could run a mile on a hot day and not feel tired or winded. When he was twelve his father gave him his first rifle. He used it to bag squirrels and other small game. As expected, he became as sure a marksman as any person in the region. At the local sporting events, invariably held in late summer, he earned a reputation for hitting his mark most of the time.

By then the girls in the area were beginning to notice Richard Bolton. One in particular observed him closely and made diary entries on the way he conducted himself. Many years later a newspaper published parts of the diary. She said in one entry, rising poetically to extend a simile, that when he made up his mind to do something he flew like a snipe. By that she meant he would dart in one direction and then another before settling down to an even, steady flight. She admired him for that, and particularly how he held his course tenaciously once he found it. Everyone said he would be a good catch for any girl, but he seemed always too busy to pay attention to the young women of the community. He was being educated at home, and that required several hours of his time each day. His father had brought in a tutor from Richmond to help him with his studies. His mother, living as a semi-invalid, taught him to love books and music and good art.

4

For balance Richard's father encouraged his interest in the outdoors. Together in a small skiff, with fishing gear and rifles slung over their shoulders, they explored the bogs of the Great Dismal Swamp. Thomas Bolton had been drawn to this sprawling natural wonder as a boy and quickly learned how to navigate its intricate waterways. In time he taught his son the mysteries of the huge swamp. They spent happy days and eerie nights there, but as Richard grew older he was expected to help with the family business. Over the years Thomas had acquired a bountiful plantation with many slaves to be supervised. Richard became the chief overseer, keeping an eye on the workers who toiled from early morning until sunset. Though he rode a tall horse and never stooped to manual labor, he worked as many hours as they did, from dawn to dusk. As evening came and went, he struggled with bookkeeping and paper work and sometimes fell asleep trying to read a book.

His father soon came to believe he could in no way do without the competent help he received from his son. The boy's mother had died when Richard was fifteen. Father and son were shattered by her death but vowed to live their lives as best they could without her. Wearing his grief on his sleeve, Thomas went looking for a bride to take her place only months after her death, but found no woman he deemed truly worthy. In time he was compelled to select capable women from the slave cabins to cook his meals in the big house and keep it clean. He found the job of supervision distasteful and difficult; a good wife could have done it much better. The women came to his well-equipped kitchen, set apart from the rest of the house, and went back to the fields as regular as clockwork. He was fastidious in the management of his estate, and particularly with his diet. He brought several cooks to his kitchen and demanded they cook his food to perfection. For most of them that was impossible.

Then Edna came along and for a time served him well. But without his consent she married Dan Becker, who called himself Hambone, and began to cause trouble. Bolton tried to reason with her, emphasizing how pleasant her life had become, but she begged him to let her be with her man. That would have been easy, had the man been a slave, but he was a free man and wanted Edna to be free as well. She ran off with him in the fall of 1860. That left Bolton alone in the big house, except for servants he didn't really need, and a woman of light skin who fried his food with too much grease. Southern cooks were known to fry everything from chicken to okra to green tomatoes, and the food Bolton ate was making his digestive system tremulous. He was also gaining weight and becoming sluggish, and he worried about that. He had heard that rich men often were afflicted with gout. Was that the price he would pay for working so hard to gain wealth?

But losing Edna was for him a bigger worry. It was not losing her value in money that bothered him so much as losing the young woman herself. She was clean, personable, healthy and seemed to like him. She looked after his diet and got along well with servants working under her. By the time she ran off with Dan she had created a warm domestic atmosphere in the big house. Though he didn't recognize it at the time, she brought comfort, competence, and serenity to his household. He lived in the midst of fine objects bought with the money he earned, wonderful things from as far away as Europe and the Orient, and Edna required the upstairs maids to dust each item every day. Bolton had a thousand books in his library, all of them carefully tended, but he was not able to read them with any real sense of enjoyment. It seemed to him that every time he opened a book he thought of his troubles and the lonely life he was living and wanted to drink or sleep to escape them. With Edna gone, only his son had the power to assuage his loneliness. Within a few months, however, Richard Bolton also departed.

Chapter 27

In the summer of 1861, before the marriage of Matthew and Catherine near the end of June, Richard Bolton and his father sat one evening at dinner. The large mahogany table, reflecting rich hues under the crystal chandelier, was set for a formal dinner but for only two people. They sat facing one another, drinking good burgundy and sharing a variety of broiled and baked meats on glistening china. Bolton had instructed the kitchen staff to go easy on the frying, and the heartburn he often suffered was now becoming a thing of the past. The conversation was genial and the mood relaxed. Then suddenly, without notice, Richard announced that he would join the army of the Confederate States of America in another week. Surprised and angry but struggling to remain calm, his father protested, imploring him to reconsider. He was needed at home. He was needed in the fields. He was needed to help run a large, lucrative, complicated enterprise. A man no longer young could not be expected to do it alone.

It was an appeal to reason as well as emotion, but Richard's resolve stood firm. Reluctantly Thomas used his influence to secure a commission for his son. The young man was inducted into the army as a lieutenant and quickly saw action in several battles. As a cavalry officer he served with distinction. Within two years he rose to the rank of major. As Major Bolton stationed in Virginia, he managed to visit his father once in the early spring of 1863. In full uniform, a dashing figure with a sergeant riding beside him, he appeared one day in front of the mansion on a stalwart black horse. His father was sitting on the broad verandah peering in his direction.

"I'm home!" the soldier called. "It's good to be home, Father, if only for a day or two. The prodigal son returneth!"

"Don't come near me!" cried Bolton. "You are not welcome here. Stay away from me!" The man was wearing white and slumped in a large white chair and barely visible. He made no effort to stand.

Perplexed, Richard ran to get a better look at the figure who had cried, "don't come near me!" He was thinking his father's loneliness and loss had affected his mind. In an instant he saw that Thomas Bolton had been shot. A trickle of blood came from under his left arm.

"What has happened to you? Who did this to you?"

Bolton groaned and asked for water. "Cool water," he said. "My throat is parched. I'm burning up. Water, please. And no more violence, please."

He didn't appear to recognize his son. He was speaking in a voice laden with fear as if to a stranger. His brain was burning with thirst, inflamed and sizzling for want of water, and he was walking, walking, blinded by glare and light and trying to get away from something.

"Will you help me into the house? I must lie down. And please, no violence." The man was rasping weakly from loss of blood.

"Father!" cried the young officer, grasping the man's shoulders. "This is Richard. Not just another soldier, it's Richard! Don't you know me? Who did this to you? Sergeant, bring water please."

Bolton drank voluminously and yet could not quench his thirst. Richard gave him three glasses of cool water but refused to give him another. He lay at full length on the bed in the nearby stranger's room. It was a room with an outside door set aside for travelers and supported by Southern tradition. Until the Civil War began, most of the plantation houses had such rooms. Because strangers on the road frequently used them, entering and leaving at will, they were aptly named.

Richard propped his father on pillows and pressed a damp towel against his wound. He opened the window for fresh air and called a servant for help. No one came. He sent his aide in search of somebody. The wounded man's face was drawn and white and his voice feeble, but now he recognized his only son and wanted to talk.

"It happened this morning," he said. "Some of my blacks ran away and I was down by the swamp trying to head them off. I came home to find the door to the stranger's room wide open. I thought a Rebel runaway was there, or a Union soldier. They pass this way all the time, you know."

"Yes, I know."

"With my gun in hand but lowered, I entered the room. A man was sitting on the bed . . . this bed . . . a white man in the same uniform you're wearing, Son, but dirty-looking and plainer."

"Not an officer? A private soldier?"

"Yes, a very young private soldier. He looked sick and scared. Before I could say a thing he seized his pistol and shot me. Then he put me in that chair on the porch. He stood beside the door and looked at me. He shook his head and mumbled, "I'm sorry I shot you, I'm sorry." He mumbled something else I couldn't make out, and then he left. When you rode into the yard I thought the boy was back to finish the job."

His voice trailed off. Then pausing a moment, struggling for breath, he spoke again. He had made a discovery and was agitated.

"So that's what he meant! That idiot boy! That half-wit changeling who died on my property three years ago! Stranger beside the door, he chanted in that strange, brittle voice of his. Pale stranger waiting beside the door. Yes! Inside the stranger's room! Standing beside the door and watching me die. Yes! I see it now! I see it! I understand exactly what he was saying."

Major Bolton did not understand. He viewed his father, a brusque man who harbored hatred as well as love, as delirious.

"The man who hurt you was a deserter. He will be hunted down and shot. I will find someone to look after you."

2

Within an hour, as thunder rolled in the western sky, Thomas Bolton lay dead. The stream of cause and effect that killed him had run exactly as Ethan Search predicted. It all happened just as he said it would that chilly night in October of 1860. Was it coincidence, or did Ethan have some special power to look into the future? Placing speculation aside, it was perhaps a case of preternatural justice. Bolton's uncaring behavior, when Ethan lay senseless at his feet, had not been overlooked by whatever Power keeps the universe in order, nor was it forgotten. The man's lack of compassion had come back to haunt him. The restless spirit of Ethan Search could now return from limbo and swing again on the vines he loved among the creatures he loved.

In recent months, roaming bands of scavengers had slaughtered or stolen Bolton's livestock. His crops had burned and his fields lay fallow. Many of his slaves, even those he had come to depend upon, had fled. He had told them that if the Yankees came to free them, they would be sent to Cuba and sold. Rather than have that happen, they left to find a secure place to hide. Alone and half defeated by events he could not control, Bolton was killed by a son of the breakaway South, which he so fervently supported. At the time of his death in the spring of 1863, his plantation was already slipping away from him, and his fortune was gone. He died a miserable and lonely man, mumbling the name of Ethan Search. His son was on record to inherit the shattered estate, but Richard was there only long enough to see his father buried beside his mother in the family cemetery surrounded by an iron fence. Quickly he returned to duty never to go home again. He had become a responsible soldier in a ghastly war, and its events would soon engulf him.

Less than a month later in that year of 1863, at the Battle of Chancellorsville in northern Virginia, the outnumbered Confederates scored a fantastic victory. The battle was fought during the first week in May and pitted Joseph Hooker's Army of the Potomac against Robert E. Lee's Confederate Army of Northern Virginia. In a brilliant but risky maneuver, General Lee split his army in half to oppose an enemy twice its size, and the engagement became known as the South's perfect battle. Lee's audacity and Hooker's timidity resulted in a significant Union defeat.

Heavy fighting began on May 1. It did not end until the night of May 6 when the Union forces retreated across the Rappahannock River. Casualties on both sides were horrendous, more than 17,000 Federal soldiers killed, wounded, or missing and more than 13,000 Rebels. Instead of open terrain, the battle was fought in a forest. Infantry, artillery, and cavalry tended to get lost in a maze of trees and undergrowth. Horses stumbled and broke their legs. Fires broke out and many of the wounded were burned to death. General Jackson of the Confederates, widely known as Stonewall Jackson, was hit by friendly fire and later died of his wounds.

In high spirits Major Richard Bolton led a cavalry charge against the enemy when the woods gave way to a clearing. On a splendid horse, himself a dashing figure, he urged his men forward. He raised his saber as the signal to move faster, and the curved blade glinted in the shimmering light of a sunny spring day. He could feel the hot blood rushing through his body, and he was more alive than at any other time in his life. He saw himself as a man among men fighting with valor for a just cause. At last he would prove himself as Jackson, Stuart, and Lee had proven their mettle. Young and strong and brave, he was a promising leader but not immortal.

3

As Major Bolton was riding hard to engage the enemy, a bullet struck his mount in the neck. The horse pitched forward, swinging its head, and threw the hapless soldier to the ground. He was trampled by a dozen horses and died the next morning. Without progeny, without anyone to mourn his death, he died in a field hospital as the sun was breaking through clouds. Richard's body was buried nearby. It was just as well, for there was no one in Blue Anchor to receive it. His commander, General Stuart, gave the order to bury the soldier on the field of battle. Two crows crying a raucous caaw-caaw flew across the deadly ground and sank behind the trees.

A cavalry commander under Robert E. Lee, Jeb Stuart fought well at Chancerllorsville. He led the troops with splendid decision when Stonewall Jackson was shot accidentally by his own men. On a gray-white horse with red and gold trappings, Stuart was in the thick of battle for hours but survived. Richard Bolton rode with Stuart at Chancellorsville that day but did not survive. At Darboy's General Store in Blue Anchor, addressing a group of young Quakers near the stove, he had made a stern prediction: "When war comes it will swallow you and your kind. You smirk as I say this, but you will lose everything if you refuse to participate—your land, your freedom, even your lives." He had chosen to participate, had ridden off to become a cavalry officer, had said he would fight for the only life he knew.

He did not say he would die if necessary, and yet he might have. As the field doctors struggled to save the life of Stonewall Jackson, a renowned hero who died a week later, the blood of Major Richard Bolton stained the forest floor crimson. His handsome face was swollen beyond recognition, his head broken, and his stomach torn open. Two strong men placed him on a dirty cot to wait for medical attention, but too many others needed attention. His vital juices soaked the stinking canvas and attracted a swarm of flies. His bowels released their waste, and the flies pounced upon his tattered trousers like a whirlwind. A young soldier nearby cried out in pain, but no one seemed to notice. A man in a uniform reduced to ribbons stood leaning against a tree. His left arm was torn off at the shoulder, and he was bleeding profusely. He stared blankly at nothing, his blue lips quivering. Suffering unimaginable pain, the only sound he made was barely a whimper.

The War of Northern Aggression, as some of the people in Blue Anchor were calling the American Civil War, was the first war in human history to be systematically photographed. A soldier leaning against a tree and dying by slow degrees appeared in one of the photographs. The grainy pictures of Matthew Brady and his team captured the agony and slaughter as no written record could. At the outbreak of the war Brady organized a "photographic corps" to document the hostilities. Often doing their work under fire, his cameramen made hundreds of negatives with cumbersome equipment depicting the carnage of war. Their cameras were not able to record the fast action of a deadly battle, and yet their pictures of the aftermath, displaying mangled corpses sprawled in great abundance on a bloody battlefield cluttered with rifles and other gear, showed war in a new and brutal light. In some of the photographs, the battlefields appear to be stippled with a thousand corpses. A camera placed on a hill could speak when words could not of the blatant cruelty, inhumanity, and horror of war.

4

Reports of savage warfare shocked the Quakers in both the North and South. In Blue Anchor, in Darboy's store, several men discussed what they considered to be a major cause of the war. It was the only informal meeting place the village could offer. They preferred in the warm weather to sit on benches under the shade of trees, but not until many years later did the village have an open square or park. So they sat inside the store or in the shade of the building outside. Because the weather was cool, they arranged themselves in a semicircle on straight-backed chairs with woven cane bottoms. Darboy himself, as moderator, had taken a seat on the counter.

"The Quakers have always argued that America cannot eliminate one evil by resorting to another evil," said Darboy. "It's unthinkable to try to end slavery by waging a gruesome war. I shudder at the thought."

Peter Starkwether agreed with that sentiment and added, "Slavery can surely be abolished without bloodshed. Oh, it won't be as quick maybe but certainly with less pain and loss."

"That's right," asserted Leo Mack. "Look at the British, they sure did it. Why can't our leaders take a lesson from them?"

"They should," answered Isaac Brandimore. "In 1833 the British Parliament passed legislation that emancipated every slave in the West Indies. Within a decade all slaves in all British possessions had their freedom, and the British did it without the incredible cost of major social upheaval."

The leaders in Washington and Richmond knew the facts presented in Darboy's store, but their belief in the righteousness of their cause dimmed their vision. Somehow they convinced themselves that human suffering inflicted in dubious battle would be an acceptable price to pay for ultimate triumph. Later when they added up the number of combat casualties on both sides, and when they took into account the grievous affliction of innocent civilians, they had guilt-ridden second thoughts. But those thoughts were not brought into the open and discussed until after the war had dragged on from the spring of 1861 to the spring of 1865.

The first battle of the war, Manassas or Bull Run, was fought on July 21, 1861 between roughly equal forces. The Union army, marching on Richmond, was met by the Confederate army marching from Manassas Junction three miles away. A five-hour attack by the Union forces resulted in a Confederate retreat. But later the apparent Union victory was stymied by a stubborn brigade commanded by General Thomas Jackson. Holding off repeated attacks, Jackson earned the nickname "Stonewall" in that endeavor. As Rebel forces went on the offensive, Jackson became a hero in the wake of a Rebel victory. The battle sobered the over-confident Union and changed the status of the conflict from a rebellion to a civil war.

Throughout the rest of 1861 most of the action centered in Virginia. The more wealthy North was building an enormous army to hurl against Richmond, which had become the Confederacy's capital in May. In that same month and year Richard Bolton, with the reluctant backing of Thomas Bolton, became an officer under the command of hard-driving and profane Jubal Early. He was assigned to a cavalry unit and eventually served with flamboyant Jeb Stuart. Jubal Early would in time throw his troops against Washington, causing widespread consternation, and then retreat to safety in Virginia. In the spring of 1864 Jeb Stuart, famous for his raids behind enemy lines, would fall mortally wounded in the Battle of Yellow Tavern six miles north of Richmond. A year earlier, in the spring of 1863, a young officer under his command was buried under a tree near the shallow graves of other soldiers who died the same day. His name was Richard Bolton.

Chapter 28

As summer began, news of the death of Major Richard Bolton reached Blue Anchor. According to the report, he had not fallen from his stricken horse to be trampled by other horses. He had died heroically fighting in valiant combat with the enemy. The report was untrue, of course, but since the world began everyone has known the first casualty of war is truth. The men at Darboy's General Store believed the story of high heroism because they had no other story that differed, and they were convinced that Richard was a man of courage. The proprietor was clearly saddened by the news, and the other men shared his sorrow. They remembered the major as an arrogant young man and yet a person of promise who had much to give to the community. If not for the war, he would have taken over his father's estate and done well with it, eventually freeing all workers and hiring them at a good wage. If not for the war, his father would have lived many years perhaps, but no one cared to speculate on that. If not for the war, the Bolton house and plantation would not have fallen into ruin. Eventually the property came up for sale to pay off the taxes.

In the summer of 1863 it passed into the hands of Owen Cooper, a vigorous and active person but a man no longer young. He was not a Quaker, was indeed an agnostic, but soon became a close friend of the Kingstons. Because he was born on one of the islands off the coast of Georgia, he often joked about his "insular mentality" as something that set him apart from others. Yet in no way did he seem insular. Behind his southern drawl and nasal twang lurked a hint of sophistication, an accent more British than American. He said he admired the British because they were islanders too, and he had lived there for more than two years when young. He spent most of his youth in South Carolina, at Hilton Head and Charleston, and went to private schools. His father was a shrewd and wealthy businessman, an exporter of cotton to the British Isles and a traveler to Europe and the near east. In time he amassed more wealth than he cared to have and gave much of it to charitable organizations. He died in his late sixties while conducting business in Europe and passed on to his son a sizable legacy.

In North Carolina, Cooper was educated in the state university at Chapel Hill. Although he studied Greek and Roman literature and thought of becoming a classical scholar, he later bought a sprawling farm east of Raleigh. He ran it profitably in accordance with innovative economic principles. As early as the 1850's he employed only free men and their families, refusing to have anything to do with slave labor. He built small but comfortable dwellings for workers, nothing like the slave cabins of the time. His farmhands paid a reasonable rent, and consistently he made improvements such as deep wells and adequate sanitation. Those willing to work received good wages and were not required to labor on Sunday.

Cooper was not an abolitionist, nor did he openly support any social or political agenda. He made it clear to his neighbors that he was merely a man of business who believed that slavery in the modern world had become obsolete. When farmers in the area heard that he offered good living quarters and shared the crop at the end of the season, they came from miles around to sign on. If they owned their land, they tried to keep it by allowing their sons to work it or by entrusting it to a relative. Most of them were sharecroppers, however, with nothing to lose. Cooper offered them better jobs and a better life than they had ever known.

2

For a time there was no shortage of labor, but when the war came with its insatiable appetite for soldiers, the younger men on the thriving farm left to go into the army. The older men found the work too hard for their reduced number and migrated to nearby towns to find less demanding jobs. At length Cooper sold the operation on easy terms to the workers who had remained loyal and took a commission in the Confederate army. He served with distinction under General Ambrose Hill in North Carolina, was wounded in a skirmish near the coast in 1862, and spent nine weeks in recovery. It was an agony for a strong man, a warrior with the rank of captain, to lie helpless in a military cot day after day. Flinty soldiers, however, were trained to endure such as that, and worse; he passed the time reading. When he could walk again he was discharged with a citation for bravery beyond the call of duty. Influential politicians, friends of the family, recommended more.

They pointed out that he had run across an open field to fire upon a nest of gunners and rout them. Later he was told that his action had spared the lives of many good men. The price he paid for that audacious one-man attack was the shock of bullets tearing into his flesh. The bullets, he later explained, were like wasps stinging his right side and drawing blood. The man had known pain before and did not coddle himself. He made his way back to his unit, running in a crouched position at first, but later stopping abruptly to lean against a tree. His head was swimming, his vision was a blur, and he thought he would surely vomit. As three comrades scurried from shelter to support him, he suffered a sudden spasm of coughing, sank to the ground, and blacked out. Thereafter, for the rest of his life, he endured intermittent pain in his hip and right leg and walked with the aid of a cane. Along with the citation for valorous action in combat came the honorary rank of colonel.

In 1863 he found himself in Blue Anchor looking at the Bolton property. He was able to buy the huge plantation at a fraction of its worth with money in a foreign bank untouched by inflation. As soon as he moved in, he made plans to scour the countryside in search of workers. His aim was to restore the property as fast as he could and make it productive. The plantation in Cooper's hands was not just grain and cotton fields and a stately mansion. It soon became its own little village, including a machine and blacksmith shop, a smokehouse where meat was preserved, a bunkhouse and dining hall for unmarried workers, a large henhouse where poultry was raised, a washhouse where laundry was done, an infirmary for the sick, and the cabins where laborers with families lived. When Thomas Bolton ran the operation, it had stables where thoroughbreds were pampered, a rambling barn where farm animals were housed, sheds for tools and equipment repair, silos for grain storage, and shelters for farm implements. Cooper had all of those again and gardens near the barn to supply fresh herbs and vegetables. Also he planned to construct workshops for artisans to craft barrels, furniture, leather goods, and cloth for use on the plantation. That meant hiring skilled workers, and the word got around.

Some of Bolton's former slaves returned to the familiar fields and were granted certificates of freedom. Blacks on their way north, seizing the opportunity to run in the midst of turmoil, heard about the opportunity to work as free men for good wages and also signed on with Cooper. As the economy became tighter and tighter and jobs more scarce, several young whites and their families began to live and work on the plantation. They labored side by side with the blacks doing the same kind of work, but in after hours they tended to keep to themselves and lived apart. Integration of the races was little more than a theory at the time, and Cooper was not one to experiment with untried social issues. He was running a profitable plantation in the troubled South, not a Utopian community in a place of perfection. If his workers were willing to work hard and produce, he had no quarrel with the status quo. Even so, he encouraged them to get along among themselves with as little strife as possible. It was good for business.

3

About the time Owen Cooper heard Bolton's land was up for sale, Matthew and Catherine Kingston had lived for nearly two years in Jeremy Heartwood's house. In the meantime, in July of 1862, their first child had come along. They named the little girl Emily and made plans to live in a house of their own. But in wartime, thinking of buying a new house was the equivalent of building castles in air. Matthew had his eye on a larger dwelling nearby but had no money even for a down payment. In ordinary times his father would have put up the money. But with the South in deadly conflict with the North, the currency was in great confusion. David hesitated to do business with Confederate dollars, and the money he had in a Northern bank was beyond his reach. Soon after Emily came, Catherine announced after consulting with Robin Raintree that she was in the family way again. If a child came every year, the dwelling would quickly become too small.

Though the little house was already cramped, Jeremy played the roles of grandfather and godfather to the hilt. He began to feel that at long last he had brought under his roof a complete and loving family who viewed him as their patriarch. Often he spoke of building additional rooms to accommodate the growing family, but Matthew reminded him that a divided nation was at war. Building materials for private use were becoming impossible to obtain. Also, as one battle after another devoured more and more soldiers, commands were issued to recruiters to find and enlist able-bodied men of any age, or go to the front themselves. It was likely that Catherine's husband, unless he paid the exemption tax, would soon be called into the army.

That was the conversation at the supper table one evening in May of 1863. Jeremy with a penchant for humor in hard times always tried to bring laughter to the table, but this discussion soon became serious.

"Outside the Quaker community most of the men my age have already gone," said Matthew. "Richard Bolton is a veteran by now, a high-ranking officer they tell me. He came home a month ago and found his father dying."

"Yes, we heard about that," said Catherine. "Mr. Bolton was buried in back of the big house with no rites and with only his son and another soldier attending. So sad. Whoever buys that property will surely respect his grave, I hope, but who knows? Graves of that sort sometimes fade away."

"Richard erected two huge tombstones just to keep that from happening," said Matthew. "His deceased mother is there too, you know, and the site has a sturdy fence around it. Now the place is boarded up, deserted. All the field hands ran away. An old caretaker looks after things, but soldiers sleep there any time they choose. I hear the mansion is a mess. The kitchen table and some of the fine old furniture was burned as firewood."

"Soldiers on both sides come through here so often now one hardly notices any more," volunteered Jeremy. "Gray uniforms one day, blue the next. Both sides living off the land, exploiting the citizens."

"So far they haven't hit us all that hard," Matthew replied, "but the time will come when all of us will have to suffer loss and hardship."

"Time here already," said Heartwood, "hardship already. Yanks more destructive, I guess. But the Rebs can strip a place. Wouldn't surprise me in the least to hear soldiers burned Bolton's house to the ground. They already tramped the crops into dust and took all the livestock."

Jeremy could sense the conversation was becoming too somber. So turning to little Emily, he chucked her under the chin and rubbed her pink little cheek to make her smile. She was not feeling well and did not smile.

The child sat in a high chair that Matthew had fashioned, and Catherine was attempting to feed her. Each time the spoon of mush went into the rubbery mouth she spit it out with a frown.

"Emily is feeling out of sorts," said Catherine, "and I'm a little worried. It bothers me we have no doctor in these parts. What happens when a child gets really sick? We have only midwives. They know about birthing but not much about children after they're born."

"Robin Raintree is good with children," said Jeremy. "If Emily don't perk up soon I'll go over to her place and bring her back posthaste."

"I don't think it's anything serious, she's sleeping all right. I'm worried not so much about her as about you, Matthew. We've been lucky so far. You and I know that. But I hear they expanded the Conscription Act and tightened the exemptions, and what I hear I fear."

4

Now the prattle at supper had taken a serious turn again. The war was foremost in their minds and threatening to throw them off balance. No one could be certain what would happen next. Catherine worried about the recent conscription changes and tightened exemptions. Jeremy chuckled at the rhyme she had made but waited for her husband to reply.

"Yes, the Act is more inclusive now," he said. "A year ago it required every white male between eighteen and thirty-five to serve three years. Not long ago the authorities raised the age limit to forty-five and required the men to serve longer but they didn't change exemptions. Ministers, printers, educators, and the like were exempted. Now exemptions are tighter and I've read quite a number of men older than forty-five are in the ranks."

"And they exempted anyone who refused to bear arms for religious reasons," added Jeremy. "That, of course, includes us."

"The military commanders on both sides have behaved well on that matter. But Jeff Davis wants more and more men to fill the thinning ranks."

"In another year, as thousands and thousands fall in battle, they will enlist any man who can hold a rifle. If the man refuses to shoulder a rifle, they will order him to hold a flag or drum or walk in front of the troops."

"That sounds a little exaggerated, Papa," Catherine scolded. "Perhaps the Romans used soldiers as human shields, and Genghis Khan did terrible things like that, but I doubt any soldier in this war will become a walking shield. Anyway, Quakers are paying the exemption tax to escape conscription. It's extortion, of course, but the reasonable thing to do."

"It's a real burden on poor farmers," said Matthew, "and each year the people in Richmond make it harder to pay. The money from the tax buys supplies for the soldiers, but I would never pay it."

The blunt remark caught Catherine by surprise. Her face and throat grew tense. She responded calmly but with a note of alarm.

"Please don't say that, Matthew. Think of your family. If you don't pay the tax, they'll come for you. If they take you away, we may never see you again. You would never see the child I carry for you."

She placed her hand on her stomach and went on feeding Emily. After a long pause, she added, "We need you here. All of us need you here."

Matthew pushed his chair from the table and stood up. He took Emily from her chair and cradled the infant in one arm. Gurgling, she reached for his face with a tiny hand and grabbed his nose.

"I think Emily is ready for bed. I'll heat some water, love, if you need to bathe her." Catherine knew she could not press her case further.

Chapter 29

Catherine lay in bed that night staring at the streaks of moonlight on the wall and ceiling, her husband beside her warm and breathing deeply. Her life until now, despite the loss of her mother, had been rich and full. She had married the man she had loved in her dreams and now loved openly for all the world to see. She had given herself to him in mutual passion and joy, even when hesitant and inexperienced and scared. Later she found it hard to believe that two people could give one another so much pleasure. Had God in his wisdom planned it that way? She had laughed when he said he couldn't put down the carnal desire to look at her body. With a hint of wonder, for she knew little of such things, she had asked why he thought he had to conquer natural instinct. Her modesty would not allow her to tell him she liked looking at him too. Quickly they decided to obey the biblical injunction to be fruitful and multiply. Within the first year of their marriage a healthy child brightened their world.

In endless conversation, dreaming of their future, they looked forward to owning a spacious house bulging at the seams with happy children. Already they could hear the sounds that children make, and every sound was musical and magical. Catherine would supervise the household, perhaps with a competent servant to help her, and Matthew would earn a good living in agriculture. Until the proper time he would continue to work his father's farm and the portion of Jeremy's land that was under cultivation. Then he would buy some fertile fields of his own and build a house there. Catherine in their comfortable home would look after the children and see to their education. She would read to them and teach them and make them ready for the world even before they went off to school. Anna would read to them too, sharing the stories she loved as a little girl, and so would Rachel. They would also have books for the children to read on their own as they grew older.

Their dream of life, she affirmed in these thoughts, was already coming true. Had she not given birth to a bright and beautiful child? And didn't she have another on the way? Rachel had said her labor with a first child would be painful, and for a time it was. But when the contractions stopped and the child left the womb it seemed as though she were drifting, drifting, sailing in pleasant breezes. And then she heard an infant's mysterious cry and rejoiced. She was so happy at that moment, joyous beyond measure. Exhausted and feeling niggling aches and pains, she was nonetheless so very happy. Her face aglow in remembrance, she turned her back to her sleeping husband, fluffed her pillow, and drifted into oblivion.

2

It was the first week in May in the year 1863, the week of blood and gore at Chancellorsville in Virginia. In the village of Blue Anchor, Matthew Kingston had business at the mill. The large black stallion he called Caesar, on which Anna loved to ride double and the animal he rode when he courted Catherine, no longer belonged to him. In the Kingston stable for years and loved by the whole family, the horse had been seized for service by the Southern army in March and possibly ridden into battle. After the war was over the family often spoke of Caesar, wondering about his fate. Did the horse survive the war? They liked to think he did but had no way of knowing. The chances, they agreed, were very slim.

The Northern government at great expense was supplying officers and cavalry units with strong and reliable mounts. But in the South by 1863 any soldier other than select cavalry and high-ranking officers was expected to supply his own horse. The policy upset the rural populace and generated protests even when everyone knew it was a dire economic necessity. Farmers in outlying districts in particular found themselves victims of the bureaucratic edict, for roving bands seemed to have carte blanche to take their animals. They valued their horses and mules above all other livestock, but the army needed the animals too and was authorized to take them.

In the March raid on the countryside, soldiers were looking for mules and oxen to be used as beasts of burden. The Kingston and Heartwood barns had only horses and cows. Caesar was immediately taken as a prize. The old mare Jeremy customarily hitched to his cart was seized and slaughtered to yield grease for ammunition. Peg, the aging pony owned by Catherine, was declared useless for their purposes and spared. They were looking for horses measuring at least sixteen hands at the withers, but Peg's height was fewer than fourteen. Safe for the time being, she was put out to pasture to nibble the grass leisurely. Still in good health and frisky for her age, she pulled the gig when trips to the mill were necessary. How long Peg would endure no one knew, but this morning in May she was in her element.

Matthew flicked the reins to guide her to the loading dock on the rear wall of the mill. Finding no one there, he brought his cart to the front of the building and looked for others. "That's strange," he told himself. "There ought to be wagons here and at the dock and business going on inside. The place looks deserted." He jumped from the cart and went inside.

3

In one of the rooms he found the miller, Samuel Bradshaw, crouched in a corner behind empty barrels. The rotund man was in his flannel nightshirt, distraught and shivering. Soldiers had come in the middle of the night looking for his three sons. With papers in hand showing the Bradshaw brothers had been officially conscripted into the army, they ransacked the house and the mill. When they found nothing, they demanded to know where the men were hiding. Details of the disturbance, as Matthew quietly asked questions, came back to the miller vividly.

"The penalty for aiding and abetting enlisted men who will not serve," said the sergeant in charge, "is death. You can be shot, old man, or do you want to be hanged?"

"I know nothing, mister. My sons are farmers, not soldiers."

"You will address me as Sergeant. These papers show they are strapping, grits-eating recruits. Your boys are soldiers now, and the army needs 'em. If they run like cowards and hide, they'll be hunted down and shot."

With typical stubbornness Bradshaw told them nothing. They slapped his face with their open hands, and still he refused to speak. Then someone found a length of rope, fashioned a hangman's noose, and tossed it over a rafter. They put it around the miller's neck and lifted him from his feet. When he began to claw at his throat in terror, they let him down.

"Speak, dammit!" the sergeant shouted.

Bradshaw remained silent. He was lifted again, and again the breath of life seeped from him. They let him down to recover from the strangulation, but hoisted him a third time. His feet pointed downward, and the moment he ceased to kick they lowered him to the floor. His middle-aged wife came running from the house, her nightgown above her knees. She was screaming and pleading. A soldier grabbed her by the shoulders and stood behind her. Another threw her gown over her head, revealing her voluminous bloomers. They laughed at their little joke and demanded to know the whereabouts of her sons. She too refused to tell them anything. They were about to lash her to a post and whip her with a thong when an officer intervened.

He told the woman to go back into the house and ordered the soldiers to release Bradshaw. They threw their victim bodily into a stack of barrels. As he lay there groaning, grasping his burning neck, the officer asked if he were the owner of the mill. Bradshaw replied that a local Quaker named Josiah Bosh was the owner. He himself was merely an employee, the manager.

"That Bosh is the one we should be stringing up," said the mouthy sergeant. "Them Quakers have scores of strong sons that ain't serving. They call themselves Southerners and breathe Southern air and own land all over hell and creation but won't do a damn thing to help."

The lieutenant, though calm and polite, was inclined to agree.

"The Quakers," he said to Bradshaw, speaking with only a tinge of anger, "by keeping good men out of the army are making it very difficult for you and me. They could help us win this war, you know. They could be leaders, those people, but they refuse to lead or even serve."

The miller thought it unfair that his sons would have to fight and perhaps die while the big and strong son of Josiah Bosh, simply because he was a Quaker and able to pay the tax, would be exempted. At that moment he might have indicted his employer but said nothing. He knew that if Bosh got into trouble with the authorities, he too would be in trouble and without a job. As they were leaving, the officer urged Bradshaw to persuade his sons to come forward and face their obligation like men.

He lay there shivering among the barrels, sleeping on and off, until Matthew arrived early that morning. They went into the house to find his wife Maggie cowering under a bed. They had to lift the bed to one side and coax her from her hiding place. She was terrified but had suffered no physical harm except for a skinned knee. Bradshaw fixed a spare breakfast for her as Matthew calmed her with quiet talk. She drank black and bitter chicory coffee, ate some griddle cakes, and slowly regained her composure.

4

An hour later Matthew left the mill with three sacks of cornmeal, Peg pulling the cart for home. The day was cool and quiet under brilliant blue skies. The pale-blue morning glories on the posts beside the road were in full bloom. Their heart-shaped leaves were as green as green could be, and Matthew picked one for his wife. An amber-crowned kinglet, startled by a human hand probing its domain, screeched a high-pitched note of alarm and flung itself skyward. A bumblebee was browsing among the flowers, seeking their nectar, and didn't appear to notice either bird or hand.

With a gallant little bow and a flourish, Matthew gave Catherine the verdant heart-leaf, which he had pasted on a sheet of yellow paper. He knew she would be upset when he revealed what he had seen and heard at the mill, but maybe the little gift would calm her. She received it with a gracious smile and fondly kissed his cheek. As she listened to her husband's story, however, the smile slowly dissolved into a frown. Her face turned sallow and her lips grew pale. Though she was often happy and cheerful, she was easily alarmed and prone to worry. It was in her nature, as the war dragged on, to find no respite from worry nor the sadness she felt on learning that her neighbors and friends were suffering.

"The Bradshaws today," she said with growing alarm, "the Kingstons tomorrow. You and Jesse, God forbid, and even your father."

She paused, trying to read her husband's reaction. Her brown eyes were bright with tears, and her voice revealed a little break as she spoke.

"Some of our friends were badgered by Confederate soldiers. Now the Bradshaws have become the latest victims. What will happen to us?"

"Please don't worry about it," Matthew cautioned. "Anxiety is no good even in the best of times."

"When things spiral out of control, how can I not worry?" she asked. "How can I not be anxious? Jesse has heard that a large detachment is moving through the area, Rebel soldiers. They will seek anything they can use, anything, and grab it. He and Anna have gone scouting in the south pasture, looking for a place to hide the heifers."

"If anyone can find a hiding place for them, Jesse will do it. He'll return with a rousing story of a perfect and fantastic place. And don't you worry about Confederate soldiers moving through. They will not be on a rampage. They are not the enemy and they will not harm us. In fact, maybe the worst for us is over. Let's hope so and take things as they come."

He spoke with confidence but was fully aware she would weigh and consider all he said to measure its validity. He hoped his words would lift her spirits, but her wan smile told him she was not at peace.

In the summer of 1861, when Matthew and Catherine came to live as a married couple with Jeremy Heartwood, his barn had several cows, an aging pony, an old and gentle mare, and a steer. As time passed errant soldiers killed the cows for food (except for two heifers hidden away), slaughtered the mare for grease, and harnessed the steer to an ammunition cart. Their neighbors didn't fare any better. Elmer Alston, who had suffered the loss of his wife and was struggling to make ends meet, was not exempt from harassment. Burly recruiters came to impress him into military service and hinted they might also take his underage son Nathaniel. They backed off only when the exemption tax was paid. Harvey Heckrodt had become a victim too. He and his whole family were chased from their cabin one rainy evening by a dozen marauders who needed shelter for the night.

"We'll be coming back to sell you down river," they hooted. It was clearly a joke for them, and they rode off laughing. For Harvey it was anything but a joke. He viewed it as a threat, even a promise.

These wandering bands of Confederates—friendly soldiers they were called—had taken from the Kingstons their horses and cows and even the old coach. It could be used to haul ammunition boxes, they said. Moses, who had served as coachman for several years, was dead by then. He had died in his sleep one morning in early spring, in March to be exact. When he didn't show up for work, Sarah went to his cabin and found him dead. He was buried quietly with little ceremony in a grave near Bupee Mwewa and her son. His exact age was unknown, even to himself, but looking into the old and peaceful face David figured he had to be at least in his early eighties. The old heart, everyone said, just grew tired and ceased to work longer.

Chapter 30

On the Heartwood farm, as Matthew and Catherine were discussing their predicament brought on by the changing times, merry voices came from near the barn. A girl was giggling and a voice an octave lower was laughing. By now Jesse was thirteen and big for his age. His voice was changing too, but he was playfully crowing like a cock. And while his face was boyish, surrounded by flaxen hair, his body was strong and muscular. In height he was only inches shorter than his brother Matthew and weighed almost as much. His mother, looking at her younger son's appearance, worried that he was too big for his age. If recruiters had threatened to take Nathaniel Alston into their ranks, could it happen also to Jesse?

Anna at nine enjoyed blooming good health and was as mischievous and happy as ever. Since the marriage of her older brother, even though her younger brother teased her from time to time, the two had become close. Together in fantasy and secrecy, they had formed a team to cheer the older folk in hard times. Their aim was to make life easier and perhaps better for the people close to them. That motive brought them to Jeremy's home when Matthew was at the mill. Now they were walking toward the rear of the house, carefree and chatting, carrying pails of foaming milk and laughing. Instinctively they were glad to be alive. Every animal, except man in maturity, knows that living is to be enjoyed. For them, in spite of hard times, God was in his heaven and all was right with the world.

2

"Hey, Catherine!" Jesse called as he neared the porch. "Me and Anna found a perfect place for the heifers. They won't miss the barn at all now."

"And we ate strawberries!" piped Anna. "Big, red strawberries!"

"Ripe and juicy too!" added Jesse. "And I milked the cows."

He set his pail of milk on the stoop, and Anna placed hers beside it. Both were feeling a happy sense of triumph. They had accepted a knotty problem to be solved, had found a solution, and had eaten sweet and succulent strawberries as their reward.

"Them heifers won't miss the barn at all now," Jesse repeated.

"In this warm weather I doubt they'd miss it for any reason," said his brother lightly. "Where did you put them?"

"You know that thick clump of alder bushes in the lower meadow? The ones with clusters of catkins near the big magnolia tree?"

"Yep, I think so."

"Well, there's an open space right in the middle. I found it while roaming the fields with Scout a couple weeks ago. Me and Anna cut away some branches to make an entryway. Then we spread a layer of pine needles on the damp ground, and would you believe it? The heifers walked right in and nibbled on some fiddlehead fern! Made themselves right at home."

"How did you conceal the entrance?"

"Oh that was easy! Nearby is a dead tree with yellow jasmine growing on it and hanging down. We arranged some limbs of the old tree to hide the entry and didn't damage the jasmine. Them soldiers can search till kingdom come, but they ain't gonna find no heifers."

"Good for you!" said Catherine, recognizing Jesse's resourcefulness and smiling with amusement. "If your hideout is as good as you say it is, little Emily will have plenty of milk for a long time. And so will her baby brother or baby sister not too far from now."

She glanced at her swollen belly and placed a hand on it. Jesse shifted his weight awkwardly and looked at the floor. Anna smiled but said nothing. The weather was unseasonably warm in May, the beginning of a long hot summer, and Matthew's young wife would be light in August.

"It's far from the house," said Anna after the pause. "Jesse will have to go there and milk them early in the morning or late at night. If he don't do it then, someone might see him."

"Or someone might see *YOU*," retorted Jesse, shouting the last word. "Hear this, everybody. Anna Hope Kingston as of this moment solemnly declares and volunteers to do the milking!"

"Do not!" Anna protested, a frown creeping across her face. "I don't even know how to milk yet. You're teasing me and Mama told you to stop."

"We can do the milking," said Matthew with a wide grin, amused by the pout on Anna's expressive face. "And it does seem a good plan, at least until the soldiers move on through and leave us alone."

"I'm hoping no worse trouble is in store for us," remarked Catherine, her face revealing lines of worry.

A cloud threatening storm seemed to hover over her. An invisible burden, heavier and more troublesome than the child inside her, seemed to be pressing her down. The easy laughter that endeared her to friends and relatives was no longer spontaneous and frequent. For most of her life she had been carefree, looked after by a loving father and happy. As a little girl everything in her world thrilled her senses and honed her appetite for life. But now she felt that some sinister force over which she had no control was being unleashed to test her. She was not at all certain she could pass the test.

3

Everyone in Blue Anchor knew about Oliver Hatcher and Peter Bookbinder, who had refused to pay the exemption tax and were inducted. They had ridden away several months earlier to become soldiers in the Confederate army but not to bear arms. Their families received letters from them, saying one had become a supply clerk well behind the lines and the other a cook. That was good news, for they would not be required to fight or shoulder a weapon. But after one or two letters the folks at home received nothing more, and so worry and uncertainty set in. As for Catherine, her husband did not believe in paying the tax either. She dreaded the day when he would be forced to compromise his principles or suffer unmentionable indignities.

She had heard the horror stories, and she knew some of them were true. Would they persecute him if he refused to bear arms? Would they force him to stand behind a Quaker gun and pretend to be an artilleryman? She knew a log painted to look like a cannon could briefly deter an enemy, but it was also a target. Would they drag him behind a horse if he refused to obey orders? Would they string him up by his thumbs to twist in the wind? Would they tie him to a post and lash him thirty times with a leather whip? Or would they try in more subtle ways to break his spirit? Her painful thoughts augmented her dread, and the dread settled upon her like a leaden cloak.

This stern refusal to bear arms incited much anger among the troops in whose ranks the pacifists were placed. Southerners persecuted Southerners because a few chose to go against the grain. In some regiments the pacifists, or conscientious objectors, were cursed and spat upon, humiliated in a hundred different ways. A grimy cook would hand them food, as they stood in line in the rain and mud, only to drop it before their fingers could seize it. They were assigned ragged tents with holes that soaked them to the bone with the first downpour. Quartermasters deliberately gave them clothing too small to be comfortable and boots that left blisters on both feet. Only the lucky ones had blankets in winter.

A catalog of abuses too long to mention brought intense suffering. Complaints up the chain of command fell on deaf ears even as the abuses grew fiercer and more violent. In one case a man of sixty, claiming to be an educator but unable to pay the tax, was impressed and forced to dig latrines until he died of exhaustion. In another a pacifist was tied to a tree under a hornets' nest, and soldiers struck the nest with sticks as children in Mexico strike piñatas. But instead of candy falling into happy hands, the angry hornets descended in a swarm and covered the man's face and neck entirely. In another case, when a man insisted he would not bear arms, his wife was raped. When the man scorned his tormentors and spat upon them, he was shot in both legs. It was well known that Quakers on both sides were often abused, and yet no Quaker in the North or South, or so the rumor went, had suffered death. While Catherine took comfort in that, she couldn't resist an inclination to worry. Shades of worry on her handsome face found a home there and made her look older than her years.

"Come along, Anna, we must put the milk away," she said with forced cheerfulness as she moved toward the cellar stairs.

The child lingered near her big brother, who stroked the dark hair that fell abundantly to her shoulders. She had placed a tiny bouquet of delicate wild flowers just above her left ear. Matthew plucked one and placed it in Catherine's blonde hair.

"Ahh, look at you!" he exclaimed with genuine admiration. "Now I won't be able to say one of my girls is prettier than the other."

He hoped she would laugh. He had learned that she often revealed her happiness with a soft, musical laugh that was hers alone. If he could make her laugh with his little joke, she might not worry. All he got was a smile.

Anna was happy to share the flowers and laughed merrily as she offered Catherine another artistic work of nature, a black-eyed Susan.

"I used to wear flowers like this at my waist or near my neck all the time," said Catherine wistfully, but in a monotone that Matthew found troubling. "I would decorate the house with them, and with milk-white chrysanthemums from the garden. In the fall when the leaves and berries were brilliant with color I would bring all the colors into the house."

"I know," chuckled her father, who now joined them after cultivating his garden and grooming the pony. "Every season had its own special decoration—flowers in spring and summer, berries and bright leaves in autumn, sprigs of evergreen in winter. I hope to see it again. Our decorated house made life a little more pleasant."

Jesse, loitering in the doorway, noticed the forlorn expression on his sister-in-law's finely chiseled face and spoke up.

"I'll tote the milk to the cellar, Catherine. And I'll do the milking for you and look after the heifers. And even though it'll kill me to do it, I'll stop teasing Anna. I'm sure that's gonna make Mama happy."

Though often abrasive and wayward, Jesse wanted to be liked. He was impetuous and irrepressible, annoying at times, but had a good heart. Catherine wanted to hug him, but was not surprised when he skipped out of reach. He carried the pails to the cellar, poured the milk into pans of pewter, covered them, and placed them in a little spring-fed brook that ran under the house. Its cool water even in summer could preserve perishable food for days. The family, at least for the time being, would have plenty of milk and butter. What tomorrow would bring no one knew.

4

A few days later, in the early morning, a decorated soldier rode up to the little house nestled under the sprawling live oak and smartly dismounted. His gray uniform was sharp and shining in the morning light. It was embellished with colorful ribbons of valor, and he wore them proudly. As he was tethering his horse, Catherine went outside to greet him. She was surprised to see he resembled her husband in height and weight. His hair and complexion were similar too, and the way he carried himself.

With a courteous bow, he placed in Catherine's hands a folded document sealed with red wax.

"For your husband," he affirmed. "Will you tell me he is home? The official paper is to be opened only by him."

Bewildered, nodding her head, she received the document with a sinking heart. Scarcely aware of what she was doing, she made her way inside and to the breakfast table. Matthew was eating a muffin and drinking a second cup of chicory-root coffee. He broke the seal, opened the sheet of thick paper, and read it slowly. A slight frown creased his brow.

"What does it say?" Catherine asked as calmly as she could, trying not to appear nervous or distressed.

"It's an order to report to Richmond for military duty within three days. Either be there to be inducted, it stipulates in the last paragraph in bold print, or pay the exemption tax immediately."

He read through the printed document, with spaces filled in by hand, a second time. Then he looked upward into the face of his wife. It was frozen and pale. The soft brown eyes were luminous with alarm and pleading. She touched the back of his neck as she stood beside him, and her fingers were cold. Her right hand stroked his hair.

"Matthew," she pleaded, her musical voice breaking, "will thee not pay the tax and stay with us?"

Of late when speaking of serious matters, perhaps to assert their identity as Quakers, they used the distinctive and traditional mode of address.

"I love thee more than life itself and want to stay home with thee. But can I really do that? Can I in good conscience pay the tax and see my hard-earned money go to buy rifles that kill?"

"Many of our friends have done so. Dave and Phoebe Cobble and James Baxendale and Peter Whitehurst, and we know the Friends helped Elmer Alston gather enough money to pay the tax."

"I know, but what is thy feeling about it, thy thoughts?"

"I cannot let thee go," she answered bluntly. "I will not."

He rose and put his arms around her. He drew her close to him and became aware of her protruding belly and full breasts, her amazing fecundity. He squeezed her shoulders, firm and strong, and placed his chin against her face. He could tell she was flustered as she nestled close to him. He was her devoted husband, the father of her child and the one soon to be born. He had sworn to protect her in sickness and in health, in good times and bad. It would be inexpressibly hard to leave his wife and children. Yet what could he do? It was just as hard to bend the principles by which he lived.

"I want us to see eye to eye in this matter," he said at last.

"We always have, my love. We never argue, we both know that. But never before have we faced a crisis such as this."

Then she lost the control she had so carefully held captive. She began to sob and to quake and to cry out in pain as though under a whip.

"Oh, Matthew, Matthew, I hurt!"

He held her closer, tighter. Her breath was coming in gasps.

"Does anyone know when this horrible thing will end? When we can live in peace again? Does anyone know? Does God know?"

"Our God will act in due time. Until then we must be strong."

He held her in his arms, letting her head rest on his chest, until the trembling and the sobbing ceased.

"It's terrible," she mumbled. "It's awful. In three short days you will go where? In another month to do what?"

He was about to say something to console her when they heard a sharp knock on the frame of the opened door.

"Has he returned so soon? Why can't he leave us alone?"

"Oh it's not the soldier," Matthew replied as she moved from him and sat down. "It's Papa. He came over to pay us a visit."

"I can't see him just now," she answered. "Please, not now!"

Sobbing, she ran to the bedroom and closed the door behind her.

Chapter 31

David Kingston had come to report hearing prowlers in the night. He and Jesse had gone outside to look around but saw nothing. He supposed a squad of soldiers had been checking the contents of the barn and was nearby. If so, they moved with uncanny stealth and disappeared like ghosts. In the morning he had found nothing amiss outside or inside the barn.

"We had a visitor early this morning," said Matthew, "and he was most certainly not a ghost. A soldier delivering a piece of paper, a decorated soldier in a new uniform with ribbons and medals. With extreme politeness he gave Catherine a piece of paper, thick and pale-yellow, with a red seal."

The summons was lying on Jeremy's little writing desk. Matthew went to the desk and handed the document to his father, who read it quickly. His serene face clouded with growing concern.

"They order you to be in Richmond in three days. They will come to receive you into their ranks, it says here, at my house. We must do something about that, my son. Your family needs you here, and here you must stay. I will pay the exemption tax today. At the last Monthly Meeting, you remember, we decided to pay the tax for anyone unable to come up with the money. If you don't have the means at present, I will gladly pay it for you."

"Elmer Alston is grateful for the kindness shown him. He and Jenny will thank the assembly formally at the next Quarterly Meeting."

Jenny Meyers had served as Elmer's housekeeper for a year before they married. Unlike Hannah, she was healthy and strong and the family was beginning to know happiness again.

"I will pay the tax today," David repeated. "Before noon."

"I know you mean well," replied Matthew, "but I can't let you do that. Paying for exemption does not sit well with me, Papa. Your money would go to assist a deadly cause that you and I know is wrong."

"The money goes to buy clothing, blankets, medicine, and food. It goes for tents and boots and equipment to relieve human suffering."

"And for guns that kill," asserted Matthew.

David could see it was no use to argue. His son was holding religious principle above family, placing a higher premium on belief than on necessity. A man of faith himself, he couldn't deny the righteousness of his son's position. The decorated recruiter in the dashing uniform would take him. Of that he was certain, and there was little he could do. With the women and children watching his every movement, he would ride off with them.

2

As Matthew's family prepared for his departure, something close to them was happening three hundred miles away in Georgia. The traveling Friends from the North, the two men who visited the Kingstons in the fall of 1860, had moved along slowly from one town to another making their way southward. In some of the towns they lived for several days or weeks, getting to know the locals and hoping to win them to their way of thinking. In North Carolina, South Carolina, and Georgia, they preached their abolitionist message to any person who would listen. At times the Southerners nodded politely, remembering their upbringing. At other times pockets in the crowd jeered and walked away. More than once the audience attempted to argue with the speaker and contradict his views. Mifflin was able to maintain his composure, but Pembroke invariably became flustered. When in time they concluded their mission was not reaping the rewards they expected, they decided to make their way northward again. It did not happen. One sunny day in early summer all they had hoped to accomplish came to a sudden end.

In a little town called Euclid, a pretty and pleasant town festooned with flowers, they ran into trouble. Jacob Pembroke, traveling abolitionist, was trying to convince a small group of locals that slavery had to go. He spoke eloquently even as cries of derision split the air. He finished his speech, refused to argue with his audience, and was about to leave. Of a sudden several men, crying angry accusations, lifted him bodily from the ground and hustled him down the street. In less than an hour he was tarred and feathered, ridden out of town on a rail, and left by the roadside to die. John Mifflin, his associate, was able to get him to a farmhouse where good people used turpentine to remove the tar, but the paunchy, feisty, talkative man with inflammatory convictions was too close to death to be revived.

No Quakers had died in the violence of war, or so the story went, but this one pursuing a cause in Quaker gray perished in a riot. He spoke out boldly in the wrong place at the wrong time, and for all his moral earnestness he was crucified by a mob led by slaveholders. His companion, whose convictions were just as strong though less demonstrative, died soon after. Mifflin had lived for months unable to breathe the air the rest of us take for granted. In the throes of advanced tuberculosis, his lungs were gradually eaten away and ceased to do the work required of them. A doctor performing an autopsy when the silent man was dead found only enough lung tissue to cover the palm of his hand.

Pembroke was buried with little ceremony in a pauper's grave. Not a person who knew the man was present to speak for him. Mifflin was too ill to attend and soon followed his friend in death. He had no money and no property and was buried beside Pembroke only when a woman in the town insisted that be done. At one time two small white crosses adorned their graves, placed there in twilight by unknown sympathizers. In less than a year the crosses were gone. Wild grasses blowing in the wind flourished in their place. The burial mounds sank into the loam. The graves of Pembroke and Mifflin surrendered to mother earth and were lost.

In the summer of 1865, after the war had ended in the spring, David Kingston received word from Philadelphia that the two men were dead. Asked to look into the matter, Owen Cooper unveiled the ugly facts. In Raleigh at the state archives, he found a Georgia newspaper that vividly reported Pembroke's violent death. Later with Robin Raintree's help he acquired Mifflin's autopsy and gave it the Quaker elders.

One of them called the men soldiers in a noble cause who died on a battlefield as surely as any soldier in any war. At the Quarterly Meeting held in the autumn of that year, a simple headstone was placed on the edge of the cemetery near the Meeting House. It marked no grave, but read:

JOHN MIFFLIN - JACOB PEMBROKE
SOLDIERS OF PEACE, REST IN PEACE

3

Matthew Kingston's decision to be inducted into the army rather than pay for exemption ran like a thunder bolt through the community. Some of the Friends calmly accepted his decision, for their views were the same as his. Others reacted with alarm. They knew he would be going to Richmond even as the city prepared to defend itself against a Union assault. They had heard by way of Isaac Brandimore, who tried to keep abreast of developing events, that the North was planning to invade and subdue Richmond to end the war in 1863. In a few weeks, according to reports leaked to the public, a huge army would be thrown against the Confederate capital. The Army of Northern Virginia, commanded by Robert E. Lee and not fully recovered from its losses at Chancerllorsville, would be called upon to defend the city. It was half the size of the Union army.

Brandimore believed General Lee would be able to repel the Northern troops, but at a cost of many casualties. He was not privy to more sensitive information, namely that Lee was planning to go on the offensive rather than wait to defend Richmond. To surprise and punish the enemy, perhaps to win a decisive battle, he decided to move his army into Pennsylvania. There, in the first week of July, he would fight a catastrophic three-day battle at Gettysburg and lose. In early summer the fighting was on the Mississippi, near Vicksburg under siege, but Virginia had already become the focal point for most of the battles. In time Gettysburg and Vicksburg would converge to become the turning point of the war.

"Let's hope your son Matthew won't be walking into the fiery furnace," said Brandimore, chatting with David Kingston.

"Reluctant as I am to say it," replied David, "I'm afraid that's exactly what will happen. I pray that Matthew's name will not appear on a casualty list, but he is standing by what he believes. We Quakers are known to husband the golden grain but sometimes, guided by the inner light, we must go against the grain."

"Well put, my friend, no doubt about it. We know that indeed. And we know when good weather comes, so does the fighting and the frequency of it, and the lists grow longer. I believe we can expect a fire storm of biblical proportion come spring. Sorrow, suffering, and loss, but Matthew will come through all right. I'm sure of that."

"Thank you, old friend. His mother and I firmly believe Providence will look after him, but we never quite know, do we? As to what may happen soon, well your vision is just a bit darker than mine."

"God will look after your son," Isaac declared, "I'm sure of that."

He was now sharing his home with a woman named Olga Hannaford. She began her work as a day visitor but soon took up residence in his house. He paid her a small salary, and she looked after him with dutiful concern. He was an old man grieving the loss of his man Seth, but mentally alert and recognized as the settlement's scholar. He bought new books any time he could, and he read voraciously despite his failing eyesight and shortness of breath. His shoulders were bent and his knees feeble, but his mind was as sharp as ever and seemed to govern his health. Every person who knew him said he would gather years like fruit in a basket and live to one hundred.

Steering the subject away from the plight of his son, David asked about Richmond. "How is Mr. Lincoln's Emancipation Proclamation being taken there? It seems to me that really defines the cause of the war."

"Well, as spring moves into summer people are wondering what it really means. The blacks in several parts are celebrating. At Norfolk they marched through the streets cheering loudly behind a Union flag. In Beaufort down the coast they sang freedom songs and gorged themselves on five roasted oxen. It should be obvious, you know, that a slave can't proclaim himself free until Federal troops subdue his master. The North has a long way to go in that respect, and so any celebration by the blacks at this time would seem just a little premature."

"I heard something about a riot in Richmond last month."

"Oh, that. It had nothing to do with emancipation. Just some hungry women rioting for bread. They crowded around a wagon, demanding bread, and then a mob formed and broke into shops. Jeff Davis stood on a platform and tried to speak to the throng. Threw them the money he had in his pockets and they scrambled for it. Distribution system broke down and so there's genuine want in Richmond."

"As far as I can tell, we have widespread want throughout the South," added David Kingston. "Even here in our little corner people are hurting."

4

At that moment Rachel appeared at the end of the long avenue of oaks, and the two men saw her walking briskly toward the house. She had been to Jeremy's place to comfort Catherine and do whatever she could to help Matthew prepare for his departure. She reached them a little winded and greeted Isaac with a smile, asking if all was right at his house. The old man nodded, asserting that Olga was a fine housekeeper and a good cook and made do with short supply without complaining. As he spoke, his eyes grew fixed and turned inward on a fantasy that lived in his head.

"Women are often long on hair and short on sense," he said, mounting his stiff-legged horse, "but not this one. If I was thirty years younger, I'd marry her. But of course one can't turn back the clock, nor the calendar, to the days of wine and roses. All one can do is ripen to the grave and die." He rode off chortling, asking himself if the phrase came from Tennyson.

That was the last the Kingstons saw of their friend. A few days later he awoke feeling seriously unwell. He asked his housekeeper to send for Robin Raintree, but before the woman could reach his bedside he died of a fever. For some time there had been talk of typhoid in the neighborhood, but in those days few precautions were taken against the spread of infection. When a fever was suspected, nobody did anything but hope for the best and wait. Almost at once several people were afflicted by severe intestinal irritation, and one person, Isaac Brandimore, died.

He suffered for a day or two but in the end went so peacefully it was like the blending of sea and sky in a soft and hazy ocean. Because he had no living relatives, his house and all that was in it, and the land too, went to his housekeeper. She claimed he had written and signed a letter bequeathing the property to her, but in the confusion of the hour the document was lost or misplaced. She reported that during the last night of his life Isaac seemed free of delirium and spoke clearly of the look on Seth's face when he understood he would die a free man. Then he mumbled something about tall ships and milky seas and his long-lost youth beckoning, urging, calling.

5

In the weeks that followed, as people spoke of Brandimore's passing, it was common knowledge that Olga was married and a mother of four. Within a week she moved her entire family into Isaac's house—her husband and thin-legged children, her parents, a brother, and three cats. They planted a large garden and sowed crops to be harvested in the fall, the work eventually killing Isaac's old horse. Her brother and husband went into the army to serve in Virginia. Not being Quakers, and not meeting any other provision of the Exemption Act, they had no recourse but to go. With minimal training they fought as infantrymen with Lee's Army of Northern Virginia at Gettysburg. They were killed in battle on the second or third day but listed as missing.

Olga lived with her children in Isaac's house until they were grown. All three of the cats eventually died, but were quickly replaced. With the help of her family, she gathered a meager living from the land. Letters with official seals reported her husband and brother missing at Gettysburg. She never saw either one again. One day in summer when times were harder than usual, she cut down for firewood in winter some of the chinaberry trees Seth had planted. She thinned the grove considerably but preserved his grave among the delicate trees. It was marked by a square stone slab, already green and mossy, with his name and date of death carved on it. The letters were faint and crude but readable: *SETH 1860.* Viewing the headstone, Catherine asked if Seth had ever revealed to anyone his last name. No one seemed to know. Some speculated he never had a last name. Anyone who had known him during his long and productive life knew him only by the one name.

Emily Kingston visited Olga with her brother Ben when both were curious children. Behind a little door in the loft she found all the books Isaac had owned neatly stacked and labeled. Rats had nibbled the edges of some, but most were in good condition and ranged widely in subject matter. Except for their owner, no one had read the books. Emily was amazed to find extensive marginal notes on many pages, commentaries on the text, the gnarled script faded but legible. Equally amazing was a manuscript of several pages setting forth in full and lucid detail the story of Elijah and the ravens. The directness and simplicity of language suggested Isaac as author had children in mind. He had never spoken of any writing he had done.

In a thin book the size and shape of a ledger, the little girl found a folded sheet of paper filled with handwritten words in black ink. Opening the crisp and fragile document, she saw at a glance that Brandimore had bequeathed the house and land to "*one Olga Hannaford, friend and housekeeper.*" The neat and readable handwriting—Emily by then was an avid reader—was the same as that of the manuscript and the marginal notes in his books. For years the village notary had questioned whether the housekeeper had come by the property legally. By accident, rummaging in the loft to see what she could find, Emily Kingston with her brother's help put the matter to rest. As a gesture of sincere gratitude, Olga gave Ben the Elijah manuscript, which became a family heirloom. The poems of Elizabeth Browning in several volumes went to Emily. Isaac had collected them all.

Chapter 32

At the Heartwood house in the first week of May in 1863, Catherine Kingston went about gathering the clothes and personal effects of her husband for the trip he would have to make in a day or two. On his way to Richmond he would be traveling with few possessions, only a few clothes in a knapsack on horseback. She gathered the items in a kind of daze, her fevered thoughts colliding with one another. It seemed so unjust for him to be taken from her possibly to die in a brutal war the North would surely win. He was newly married, a new father, and the couple had a child on the way. He should have let his father pay the exemption tax, but he was a stubborn man and headstrong. Yet in a way, as she thought about it, she admired him for standing on principle, allowing belief to guide his behavior. People had to believe in something, and they had to stand by their beliefs or surely be lost. It would be the first time since their marriage that he would be away from her, and that meant a big change in her life.

His mother wanted to buy him an extra pair of trousers and a new shirt, but the clothing was not available in Blue Anchor. For two years the general store had been separated from its best sources of supply, the industrial cities of the North. Jacob Darboy had used all the ingenuity he could muster to keep his supply lines open, but eventually the steady flow of goods became a trickle and dried up. For reasons no one was able to explain, the distribution of goods in the South was in chaos. Southern cities and commercial centers such as Richmond were enduring severe shortages. Small, isolated places like Blue Anchor were dependent mainly on local resources. Once a thriving business, well-stocked and with little competition, Darboy's store by 1863 displayed bleak and empty shelves. On the brink of closing, the proprietor hoped for a miracle and kept the store open mainly as a meeting place.

In the third year of the war the farmers of Blue Anchor suffered from lost crops, dwindling food supplies, and stolen livestock. Troops from both the North and South marched across their fields, trampling the young plants and leaving desolation behind. When the conflict moved into its third summer, only the basic staples were left. Items such as warm clothing for winter or an umbrella for summer, once considered basic necessities, were no longer available to people without wealth. Self-reliant, even of temper, and looking out for one another, all members of the Quaker community had wood for heating and simple food to cook. Also their homes, seen as rustic and of little value, were largely undamaged by soldiers passing through.

In other parts of the South blue-coated Union soldiers were billeted in fine old mansions and left them in ruins. To wreak havoc upon the South and terrify the enemy, they ransacked and burned many of the antebellum mansions and raped some of the women. Officially rape was deemed an offense punishable by execution, but in the confusion of the times only a few incidents were identified and reported. Incomplete records show only twenty-three Union soldiers were executed for rape, though hundreds were treated for venereal diseases. Federal troops who committed rape while invading the South mostly took advantage of black rather than white women. A few Confederates were charged with raping black women and even Indian women. In New Orleans an 1862 order by Union General Benjamin Butler decreed that any woman showing contempt for his troops "shall be regarded and held liable to be treated as a woman of the town plying her avocation." In other words, if the city's outspoken Southern belles did not hold their tongues, or if (as in some cases) they dumped chamber pots from balconies on soldiers' heads, they would be treated as common prostitutes. After its occupation by Federal forces in 1862, Nashville in Tennessee legalized prostitution and required all prostitutes—and there were many—to be examined weekly. Occupying soldiers viewed the women as spoils of war.

2

Perhaps the people of Blue Anchor were lucky not to live in mansions. Soldiers on both sides took the best of their food and livestock but left their houses standing and their women unmolested. They were seen by the troops as poor, struggling farmers even though some of the Quakers with accounts in Northern banks were well off. David Kingston had an account in a Pennsylvania bank, but during the war the funds were unavailable to him. Kingston resisted using Confederate currency, and with good reason. Rampaging inflation quickly made the Confederate dollar worthless. In May of 1861, a dollar in gold at Richmond cost $1.10 in Confederate money. By the time Matthew Kingston was inducted in May of 1863 and went to Richmond, the exchange rate was $8.00 for one dollar in gold and steadily increasing. On occasion Darboy received an item in demand, but the price in Confederate money was so exorbitant that few in the community could buy it.

Catherine Kingston had always kept an ample supply of linen on hand. However, in the past year constant appeals from needy neighbors had depleted her supply. The spinning wheel that had belonged to her mother, and was brought in a wagon all the way from New England, was dusted and refurbished and put into use. Fortunately they were able to obtain cotton and wool in small amounts, and the two women worked long hours at the wheel and loom. Neither could see Matthew leaving home without a change of underwear and without an extra shirt.

As the man put his affairs in order, they raced against time to create for him a warm and durable shirt. As for him, he persuaded friends to look after his family while he was away. Jesse would care for the heifers and forage in the swamp to fill the wood-box with fuel for winter. Several Friends would help Jeremy gather whatever crops he might be able to salvage, and the women would assist Catherine. About his impending departure, Matthew said little. With a wan smile his wife stated flatly that the war would soon be over, and he would be home again before anyone missed him. She was trying to make a joke, but then a tear appeared in the corner of one eye and trickled down her cheek, marring utterly her struggle to hide her misery.

3

Near the end of the day Jesse came over to the little house under the live oak to milk the heifers hidden behind bushes in the long sweep of pasture. Just as he was picking up the milking pails in the kitchen, he hesitated a moment and fumbled in his pocket.

"Here," he said abruptly to Matthew, "I want you to have this."

He held in his hand the precious pocket knife his father had given him when he turned twelve. Without hesitating, his brother accepted the knife. He knew the gift was the way Jesse had chosen to express his feelings.

"I'll take good care of it, Jess," he replied with just a hint of levity. "One of these days you'll have it back, I promise. I think I may need the knife for all sorts of things. And I thank you."

It was an awkward moment for both, but the boy slipped away without a word and trotted to the meadow. The two heifers came to meet him as he crept through the broken fence. Jeremy had said that repairing the fence could attract the attention of marauders looking for booty hidden away from the house. They wouldn't be looking for livestock behind a broken fence, and so the fence was left unmended.

The rich, thick grass was becoming wet with dew and released a damp and musty odor when disturbed. The crickets, often not heard until June, began to chirp in the still air, emitting a metallic trill pitched an octave above middle C. Jesse squatted on his haunches and worked at the udders of one cow as the other grazed. Streams of milk squirted from under the boy's capable hands and made a slurping sound as they filled one pail and then the other. The second cow swung her head around as he milked her and snorted. He could feel her breath on his face and its smell in his nostrils. The profound repose of the place alerted his senses.

After the milking he drove the heifers to the sheltering clump of alder bushes and rearranged the jasmine that concealed the entrance. As he did so he thought he might be able to chase away some of Catherine's anxiety with a bouquet of flowers. He reached out to pick a stubby branch of the flowering, fragrant plant. Just as his fingers closed on the flowers, two ragged bats darted from the dead tree. Their tightly strung wings nearly brushed his face as they hurled themselves skyward, and they startled the boy. He uttered a loud cry that was not quite a scream. Instantly a burning chagrin rose in his throat, and he chided himself. He would soon be a man, and a little thing like a bat could never scare a man. He laughed uneasily, picked up the pails of milk, and headed for the fence.

A shadowy figure was standing on the other side. In the lingering twilight Jesse couldn't be certain whether the person was a man or a woman. He approached cautiously, the flowers tucked in his wide belt and a pail of milk in each hand. He was thinking that maybe he had given his knife away too soon. He doubted he would ever use it in a rumpus, but to have it would be a comfort. The man looked like a scarecrow and seemed to be dressed in rags. Jesse had heard that deserters, some driven crazy by the horrors of war, were roaming the countryside. Just such a person had shot and killed their neighbor, Thomas Bolton. Was this another? Was he dangerous? He went onward to the fence and set his pails on the ground. The scarecrow man was laughing, cackling, mocking, and dancing a little jig.

"I heard you cry out, you fraidy cat. Fraid of your own shadow, you are! And flowers too! Oh, how sweet! Gimme that milk, dammit! Harland Ebrow loves milk! Harland Ebrow's the name and fighting's my game! But now I'm on the run, hiding from the sun! I'm a poet, don't you know it? I can make a rhyme any time. Woooeeee that's good!" It was the warm milk he was praising, and he was licking his lips.

With the evening air becoming cooler, the gaunt figure stood shivering. He wore no shirt and his trousers were slit and torn. On his right foot was a military boot, but the left foot except for a ragged sandal was bare. Lean of frame with bony shoulders and long arms, he was so thin that in half darkness Jesse could count his ribs. Since he carried no weapon, he was no threat to the boy nor to anyone but himself. He seemed out of his mind running and hiding from the horror of war, and he was hungry. Jesse gave him the milk without hesitating. The derelict drank the entire pail, the thick white liquid flowing from the corners of his grinning mouth and down his chest. He put the bucket down, wiped his mouth with a skinny arm, and smiled broadly. His teeth gleamed white but two in front were missing.

"Gimme that other bucket," he demanded. "Harland Ebrow loves warm milk better than a warm quilt, and he's been cold and hungry a long time. You can keep the flowers, pretty boy. But don't you never tell nobody you saw me here. You got that? Answer me, boy! You got it?"

"Yes, sir," Jesse meekly replied, "I won't tell nobody."

The boy was shaken but not terribly frightened. He knew the difference between jabber and real threats and was inclined to pity the poor wretch. He obeyed the deserter because he had been taught from the time he was a toddler to obey angry adults.

Harland Ebrow was unhinged but not angry. He thrust his haggard face forward, scowled for a moment, and laughed with a loud, cackling, croaking sound. His face was dirty and his forehead above the right eye lacerated. A trickle of blood came from the wound. Jesse could see he had once been a soldier, but who could tell what had happened to him?

4

The boy passed the second pail of milk over the fence. With grotesque facial distortions, the man drank part of it, wiped his mouth again, cackled, and said he would keep the rest for later.

"You don't mind losing the bucket, do you boy? Well, I don't mind if you do mind. To hell with you, pretty boy. Go home!"

Then hesitating as he turned to leave, the fugitive swung around again and blurted, "Gimme that belt! I can use a good belt!"

Jesse gave him the belt but kept the flowers. The wraith fastened the leather belt around his skinny waist and loped eastward along the fence, swinging the pail in one hand. Harland Ebrow was on his way to find shelter in the swamp and perhaps meet other fugitives hiding there. If he could trust them, he would perhaps trade the wide belt for food or a shirt. There in the swamp dwelt men of all ages, from scraggly teenage boys to gaunt old men who had lost all their worldly possessions late in life. They were called swampers and were rarely seen, except when stealing corn or potatoes near dark. Troubled by calamity and often desperate, they were feared by the farming community. No one knew exactly where in the huge swamp they came from, nor where they were going. They were gloomy, seedy-looking characters whom people avoided, though at times a compassionate farm wife would place food on a stump for them. After the war some of these men attained high position in the costly bureaucratic effort to restore the South, but to the end of their lives they wore their hangdog look even when sporting a top hat and a frock coat.

Jesse, who knew as little about the larger world as about the horrors of war, climbed through the wooden fence and scooted in the opposite direction toward his brother's house. Low clouds hanging in the western sky suddenly opened, and it rained hard. He ran in the rain until his first wind was gone and his second came and he could breathe again. He dog-trotted across the meadow and through a clump of damp woods until the house came into view. Then he broke into a sprint, banging the empty bucket against his knees, his shirt and trousers as wet as new wash on a line. The scarecrow man had taken his milk and belt but in return had given him the speed of a swift-running antelope. Matthew saw him tearing into the yard, the flowers clutched in one hand and the pail swinging. The boy stopped near the kitchen door, breathing hard, and scurried inside.

"The cows had no milk?" his brother asked incredulously.

"They had plenty," said Jesse, gasping. "But a crazy man got it. He was half-naked and tall as a stove pipe!"

Now reviewing what had happened, he felt a cold uncertainty running through him. Was the runaway really all that tall? Was it right to obey him with no resistance whatever? Was it a wise thing to do, or cowardly? He couldn't be sure.

Matthew heard the story, quickly told in few words, and invited the boy to sit for a big slice of pecan pie made with honey. He relaxed at the kitchen table to recover from his ordeal, and Matthew assured him he had done the right thing. Shyly, after he had eaten two pieces of pie washed down by a glass of milk, he gave the sprig of flowers to Catherine. She thanked him graciously but with an air of worry.

"It was scary meeting that fellow in that lonely place," he said, getting up to return home. "But I guess he needed the milk more than we do. Said he loved milk, chanted and sang and called himself a poet and danced a funny jig and spoke rough to me. Then guess what, he stole my belt! But I guess I can find another one somewhere."

"You can have this one," said Matthew, removing his own. "You're big enough for it. But it's a loan, mind you. Keep it and wear it until I get home again. I leave tomorrow. You'll keep an eye on Catherine and Emily, and help Jeremy with little things?"

"You bet I will! I won't let you down, Matt! And thanks for the belt. I have to get home now. Mama always worries when I'm out at night."

In a moment he was running homeward. The shower had passed on to the east, leaving a musty smell in the heavy air.

Chapter 33

Early in the morning, before the dew was off the grass, Jeremy Heartwood and his family walked to the Kingston homestead for breakfast. Matthew carried on his back the small pack he would take with him to Richmond. Jeremy bounced chortling little Emily on his round shoulders. Catherine in loose maternity clothes, held her skirts in one hand to keep them from sweeping the damp and sandy ground. Breakfast was almost ready as they came in through the back door to say hello to Sarah. They sat in the alcove near the kitchen and chatted. Matthew would be leaving home in a few hours, but in the midst of good-natured banter not a person mentioned that.

Rachel and Sarah had prepared potato pancakes to be soaked in syrup made of honey from hives on the Heartwood farm. Beside each plate was a large glass of milk. As a special treat they placed on the table a small jar of peach preserves newly opened. Sarah brought from the kitchen a steaming pot of unadulterated coffee, rare and hard to find, and they sipped the rich coffee from earthen cups. The gathering was as festive as any person could make it, considering the occasion, and the bright sun warmed their faces.

Jesse had already given his going-away present to Matthew, and now Anna was ready to present hers. It was a large red bandanna with a white border and white polka dots against the red.

"It's made of cotton and won't get dirty fast," chirped Anna." You can wear it around your neck! Like the railway men."

The little girl had once seen a photograph of a railway crew. They were standing in front of a belching locomotive and wearing bandannas. She had never been near a train, had seen only pictures of trains and railroads, but wanted to buy the bandanna as soon as she saw it in Darboy's store.

"Well, if they put me in uniform I may have to keep it in my pocket," Matthew grinned, thanking her for the gift. "But I'll find a use for it, you can bet on it. And thanks again, sweetie."

"I never bet," said Anna. "It's against my religion, right Mama?" Her mother, smiling and patient, nodded in agreement.

"You would if you could," bellowed Jesse.

"You promised, Jess, no more teasing," chided Catherine.

"You can wear it as a sweat cloth in summer! You can wear it as a scarf to keep your neck warm in winter!" She liked her gift.

Others at the breakfast table gave Matthew small presents, including a traveler's Bible small enough for a pocket and thick enough to stop a bullet. They chatted amicably until Sarah announced that Confederate soldiers on horseback were riding up the avenue.

2

Clad in shades of gray, their weapons and trappings glinting in the patches of light between the trees, they projected raw power not to be resisted. Their horses looked tired as they entered the sandy yard and approached the porch. A man with a mustache, unmistakably the man in charge, dismounted and went up the steps. A knock of strong knuckles on hard wood, neither gentle nor hesitating, sent David and Jeremy to the door.

"I'm Captain Daniel Dawson of the Fifth North Carolina. Your name, I take it, is David Kingston?"

He bowed slightly and touched his fingers to the brim of his hat. He was not a young man but appeared to be in fit condition. His legs were short, his torso long, and his shoulders broad. A proud and militaristic officer, he wore several ribbons of valor. The dignified, simply dressed owner of the house, a head taller than the captain, inspected the man in gray before speaking.

"Yes, that is my name."

"I'm told, sir, that one Matthew Kingston, your eldest son, is ready to go with us. According to my orders, he must come with us to Richmond at once. Since he cannot provide a horse of his own, we have a temporary mount he may use for the trip."

Jeremy stepped aside as Matthew pushed forward to face the Confederate officer. "I am Matthew Kingston. I'm ready to go with you as instructed. But I must remind you I cannot and will not bear arms. Nor will I participate in any military maneuver that engages an enemy in combat. I will build in your service, but I will not destroy."

"I've heard that line before," said Dawson. "Your papers identify you as a Quaker. Well, my advice to you is put your objections in your pocket for now. Join the army like the man you appear to be and fight like the rest of us. If the South is to win, every man available will have to fight."

"I must repeat, Captain, I will not bear arms."

Dawson pointed to a thin, stiff-legged horse that had once belonged to a farmer. A burly sergeant held its reins.

"There's your mount, Kingston. Do you have traps? A bedroll? Extra clothing? Make haste, man. We must go."

Catherine Kingston brought from the house the small bundle of clothing she had prepared for her husband. The dismay she felt on hearing the knock had now become an enduring calm. Her face was serene and a half smile graced her lips. Her large brown eyes were sorrowful but keen and dry. Determined to control her emotions at this crucial moment in her life, she found her strength in Quaker injunction handed down through the centuries.

Matthew slipped his arms through the straps and shouldered the pack. He kissed his wife and child, embraced Jesse and Anna, and shook hands with Jeremy and David. He patted Sarah on the shoulder just as she withdrew to the kitchen, daubing her eyes. He kissed his mother, who had followed him anxiously into the yard, on the forehead and then on the cheek. She clung to him for a moment, looking into his face.

"Don't worry, Mother, I'll be all right."

"Sergeant, bring up the horse," the captain ordered. "Now, Matthew Kingston, your weapon. It's a handsome implement. Take it, now."

He thrust a long Enfield Rifle-Musket into the hands of the man who had warned him he would not carry a weapon. The rifle, lovingly made in England for Confederate consumption, fell to the ground.

"That's no way to treat an object that could save your life some day," said the captain, carefully controlling his anger. "Pick it up. Remember you are under orders now. You may not ignore a direct order."

Matthew did not want a scene to occur in front of his family, and he did not wish to have his behavior interpreted as insolence or arrogance. So he stooped and picked up the heavy rifle and handed it to the captain. With its butt on the ground the weapon stood at least five feet tall. The officer put his hand around the barrel to keep it from falling to sandy soil again.

"We have no time to waste, Kingston, and I will not argue with you. For the second time I order you to take your weapon, mount your horse, and ride with us. I need not explain to you why you must obey my order."

"I am under orders from a commander higher than you, sir," countered the young Quaker. "He tells me not to shed blood. That command I must obey. I don't wish to appear rude or discourteous, but I cannot obey every one of your orders. I will ride with you but without the weapon."

"You speak nonsense that will get you killed."

"I will ride with you but without the weapon," Matthew repeated, looking not at the captain but down the avenue of oaks to the main road.

3

To relieve exasperation, Captain Dawson surveyed Matthew's family as they stood on the porch. They must have seemed quite similar to his own family wherever they lived in some region of the South. He was a volunteer and went gladly into military service for the adventure, the sea change it would bring, and the chance to be a man among men. He wanted to command men, and he wanted to save what he considered a venerable and a gracious way of life. He came perhaps from a similar Southern family but one with different views and a different way of life.

"You are not obligated to go with us," he said after a long pause, looking once more at the papers he had drawn from his saddle bag. "I'm authorized to exempt you, for the present, if you will pay the exemption tax. Are you not able to pay the fee and stay home?"

"I'm able to pay the tax," Matthew asserted. "I've chosen not to pay it because the money collected by that means supports the war. My religion forbids me to support violence of any kind."

"I see that your wife is heavy with child. The papers say you have another child. No able-bodied man should be exempt from doing his duty, but the law is the law and I shall obey it."

"Thank you, Captain. But I have given thought to the matter and don't feel easy buying my way out when other young men newly married with offspring on the way cannot. Also I will not pay for weapons that kill."

Matthew sprang easily into the saddle and waited for the next command. Again he would not accept or shoulder the rifle.

"Sergeant," ordered the captain, "take the rifle and strap it across the saint's back. Tie it tightly, mind you. Put his pack in front. He will shoulder the weapon gladly when the time comes."

The sergeant obeyed with alacrity. Catherine's eyes flashed as she saw her husband wince involuntarily under the rough handling. He said nothing but sat tall and calm on the weary horse, peering into the eyes of the angry officer. When Dawson saw no further resistance, his anger dissipated and he allowed the man a moment with his wife.

She ran into the yard to say goodbye. Matthew's father went with her. She clung to the horse's stirrup, looking upward in anguish, but remained strong. She mumbled words of hope and encouragement and stepped away. With permission from the captain, David stood beside the docile horse and spoke to his son: "Listen to me now. Whatever a man comes in contact with leaves a mark upon him for better or worse. I pray that all you encounter will leave you better. Take care, observe, absorb, and remember. If you do that, my son, today will serve you well tomorrow."

The Kingston family and Jeremy Heartwood stood on the porch waiting for the inevitable departure. They waved as the horses broke into a canter and moved swiftly down the avenue of live oaks. Grasping the reins with one hand, Matthew raised his left arm in a farewell salute. Steeped in biblical imagery as these people were, it seemed to everyone that the long rifle the man bore on his back had become a heavy wooden cross.

Catherine returned to the steps and slumped downward. Motionless she sat with head in hands, elbows on knees, feet on the ground. Already this event, this unforeseen separation, was gnawing at her soul and spoiling her life. She felt heavy, weary, confused, and desolate. Weeping softly, her face concealed, she asked herself: "How long, O Lord, how long? How long shall I cry?" Ringing like a bell in the obscure chambers of her soul, she heard the masculine voice of her husband counseling courage.

When night came she went to bed early. But she awoke in the middle of the night feeling a sad and lonely hunger of the spirit unaddressed by her religion. For half an hour she sat cross-legged in bed staring at nothing. Hope was battling with fear, and when hope got the better hand she slept again. The war had to end soon. Everyone was saying that.

Chapter 34

The distance from Blue Anchor to Richmond was just a little more than one hundred miles. By train the small detachment could have reached the embattled city, capital of the Confederate States of America, in three hours. On horseback the journey was long and arduous, consuming most of two days. The group went first to Forest Junction, and then they followed the path beside the railroad through Petersburg to Richmond. Union forces were bivouacking to the north and northwest of the city and moving closer, but the southern route was open. Though Matthew reached his destination in sound health, he would not remember it later as an easy journey.

At first the soldiers taunted him, jostled him, or kept their distance, requiring him to eat and sleep alone. One or two hurled insults at him, pejorative and vulgar, to gauge his reaction. In time when they saw his behavior was tempered with kindness and patience, they began to treat him with tolerance. After the first day the rifle on his back was removed and strapped to the side of his horse. On the second day as they rode in the hot sun, Sergeant Amos Appleton, gave him a canteen of water to quench his thirst and advised him to keep it. Appleton was the man who strapped the rifle on his back as they were leaving his family.

To begin the following day, Matthew ate starchy rations in the field with his companions, washing the coarse food down with gulps of water that had a vague metallic taste. Later, after they moved into a military camp on the outskirts of Richmond, he waited in line to hold out his tray in a mess tent. A whey-faced young man with dirty hair, a dirty neck, and dirty hands dumped on the dented tray some lumpy potatoes, half-cooked carrots, a slice of dark bread, and a piece of rubbery meat. The food was coarse and unsavory, but he ate it heartily, washing it down with black coffee in a pannikin.

Laughing with gusto, Appleton swore the rubbery substance was horsemeat. When the war started, he said the soldiers ate beef. After a year or so, tough and stringy meat appeared in mess tents and became more and more common. Men calling themselves knackers came on the battlefields when all was quiet and quickly hauled away the wounded and dead horses. What they did with the horses was anyone's guess, though many soldiers believed they were hired by the Confederacy to process the meat.

"When a horse falls in battle, do you suppose they toss the carcass in a ditch and cover it with dirt? Oh no, not on your life! Not in these times!"

Matthew couldn't be sure he was joking, but he noticed the sturdy soldier with muscular arms ate with a ravenous appetite. And he observed as well that Amos Appleton was treating him as a friend.

In Richmond the flags were flying at half mast. The day before, in an outbuilding on the Chandler plantation near Guiney Station, Stonewall Jackson had died. The epitome of efficiency and courage in battle, Jackson was shot accidentally by his own men at the Battle of Chancellorsville. In that engagement, perhaps his best performance as a commander, he led his troops around the Union right flank and routed the enemy. Reconnoitering after nightfall to prepare for another attack at dawn, he was returning to his own lines when pickets standing guard fired on him. Three .57 caliber bullets plowed into his left arm, leaving a gaping wound. The arm was shattered and had to be amputated in a field hospital. Soon afterwards pneumonia set in, and Jackson died of its complications eight days later.

"He has lost his left arm," General Lee reportedly announced in grievous tones, "but I have lost my right arm." Leaders and generals on both sides were conscious of history when they spoke, but often as with Jackson the final words of a soldier were poignant. Jackson died on May 10, 1863 murmuring these last words: "Let us cross over the river and rest under the shade of the trees." With little concern for historical remembrance, his longing for respite was speaking.

The city was in mourning. Flags all over the South would dip in mourning. The Confederacy had lost one of its best commanders but had gained a legend. The general's widow, Mary Anna Morrison Jackson, never remarried. Until she died in 1915 she campaigned to keep his legend alive.

2

The morning after their arrival Matthew went with Captain Dawson to report to another officer. Though unofficially inducted when he refused to pay the exemption fee, he was now offered a last chance to take advantage of the Exemption Act. When he formally refused the offer, he became officially a private soldier in the Army of Northern Virginia under the command of Robert E. Lee. Without delay he was assigned duty in a regiment stationed on the outskirts of the city, one prepared to defend vital industrial targets against any attack. The quartermaster gave him boots and a belt and a wrinkled uniform that appeared too small. Politely he pushed the neatly stacked clothing back across the counter but kept the boots and belt.

His refusal to wear the uniform of the regiment caused little stir. Confederate uniforms were in short supply, and his durable costume of Quaker gray blended well with the soiled and tattered clothing of soldiers in the field. Some of them scoffed when he identified himself as a Quaker man of peace, but he quickly became an object of curiosity rather than animosity. Many of the men were from the same area back home, had even known each other as friends in civilian life. So as Southerners in a common cause the regiment became their second home. They could see at a glance that Matthew Kingston was a Southerner of similar ethnicity and background, and they could hear the familiar twang when he spoke. Maybe it didn't matter that his thoughts were different.

He made friends with several of the soldiers, for they liked his open and honest manner and the strength he seemed to take from his simple faith. In camp he did what he was told and worked as hard as anybody, but when other soldiers were cleaning their weapons, he was reading or writing a letter. On occasion in the quiet of evening he read aloud from his Bible as half a dozen men listened with rapt attention. Knowing they could die the next day, the profane young soldiers wanted to make peace with their Maker. At the very least they wanted to hear comforting words of hope.

At the beginning of June, Matthew's unit became engaged in a bloody skirmish that left too many young soldiers dead. Union forces had the area under surveillance and attacked in fierce ambush when least expected. In minutes the Rebels saw themselves cornered and victims of raw power. In the grip of destruction, they fought as best they could but to no avail.

A barrage of small-arms fire killed several men before they could hunker down. Amos Appleton ordered his squad to take cover as he himself fought with skill and courage. He was dragging a wounded man to safety when a rifle ball smashed into his skull. The moment he fell, another soldier grabbed his loaded weapon and fired. As the soldier reloaded, his bravery noticed by the others, several bullets struck him in the face. He spun around with a loud shriek and was dead before he hit the ground.

Unarmed and repulsed by the thought of killing another human being, but not willing to die if he could help it, Matthew crouched behind a boulder. Yet when Sergeant Appleton fell, the young Quaker darted across open ground and dragged him and his comrade to safety. The wounded man survived to fight another day, but Appleton died instantly. Another soldier who survived said Matthew might have saved the sergeant's life had he grabbed a rifle to fire it when Appleton went to the wounded soldier. In the smoke and confusion, he had not seen Matthew risking his life to save the fallen sergeant. No one else lucky enough to be alive when the skirmish was over had seen it either. Charges were quickly brought against the Quaker pacifist, and he did not deny them. The next day Matthew Kingston was arrested and placed in the stockade. Three days later he was brought before a court-martial and sentenced to hard labor in a military prison for the duration of the war, plus ten years of confinement after the war.

3

When they led him from the dingy room to a patrol wagon outside, he was not able to walk like a man. His hands were bound behind him and a short restraining chain was locked to each ankle. All he could do was shuffle in small steps, bouncing to keep his balance along the uneven floor. Sitting in the gloom of the wagon with two other prisoners, he was taken to a dark and severe prison on the east side of the city of Richmond. During the half hour of travel to get there, the three of them chatted to pass the time. Orville Henderson and Robert Lipton were separated from their comrades when the ambush ended, and as they tried to hide they were captured.

As they talked, Matthew suddenly realized that through some twist of an unkind fate their guns had killed Amos Appleton. They were reloading, according to their story, to kill a tall soldier in plain clothes who carried no weapon. Their rifles were leveled and ready to fire when they were ordered to fall back. They lowered their weapons and waited for their unit to move, but waited too long and were captured. In their dirty blue uniforms, these men chatting amicably with Matthew were Union soldiers and the enemy. If he could believe their story, they had killed a good soldier who had treated him kindly. And they had come within the blink of an eye to taking his life too. Matthew had every right to hate these two haggard men who spoke of warfare as a grand adventure to ward off boredom. But unlike little Timothy Swope who badgered frightened Anna in Blue Anchor, he had never been taught to hate. They in turn felt no animosity toward him.

"It's just a deadly game," said Henderson, "exciting as all git out but deadly. There's no real emotion involved except maybe excitement."

"And like any game," added Lipton, "there's an element of luck. Some see the game right through to the end, some don't."

For them the game was over. Many of their comrades would die, but they would live. If they survived the prison camp, if their luck held as it had in the impromptu engagement that killed Amos Appleton, they would go home after the war with colorful stories to tell. In prison, working at a menial job with plenty of time to chew the cud and remember, Matthew often thought of these two easy-going men and wondered what had happened to them. Even though all three were housed in the same prison, after they left the processing room he never saw his would-be killers again.

From their iron cage on wheels they shuffled to a holding room inside the prison. The dark and smelly room had one window partly open. It had only two benches and both were occupied. A dozen men on the brink of exhaustion stood waiting. Two or three were talking in a thick southern drawl about nothing. Another man from the Dutch country of rural Pennsylvania was speaking with an accent. A dilatory clerk with a pale face and gibbous eyes was attempting to process the new prisoners. He was a choleric, anemic, self-important little man who moved at a snail's pace. A fat deerfly bit into his moist neck, and with fisheyes glaring he tried to swat it. After an hour a guard with short legs and a big belly led Henderson and Lipton away, but Matthew waited in the stifling room more than two hours.

The officious clerk explained he was not able to move faster, adding that the place was miserably understaffed. When the sun was low in the sky, the same guard hustled Matthew through a dark and rank corridor to a tiny and damp chamber. Night came on fast, and in the darkness he lay down on the hard cot. Feverish and not able to sleep, he could hear a distant church bell tolling the hours one by one. Near midnight when the bell clanged 144 times instead of twelve—or so it seemed—he sat bolt upright and broke into a cold sweat. He was reliving the anxiety he had felt when Catherine dropped the heavy quilt on his head in the autumn of 1860. His prison cell had the same oppressive effect, plus a pungent odor, and the stale air was hard to breathe.

4

Belle Isle Prison took its ironical name from a small island of fifty-four acres in the James River, which ran through the heart of Richmond. The camp was located on the flat and damp east end of the island near the buildings of the Tredegar Iron Works. The cemetery where twenty-five Confederate generals were eventually buried, Hollywood by name, was nearby. The island was an ideal breeding ground for biting insects. At one time it had trees to mitigate the heat and humidity, but to make the camp larger for more prisoners most of the trees were cut down. In the prison yard in summer the blazing sun was almost tropical. Sweating, unwashed men in ragged clothes, most of them captive Union soldiers, endured primitive conditions in hot weather and severe, inhumane conditions in the cold of winter.

In the warmer seasons the prison was tolerable in spite of the huge mosquitoes called gallinippers by the inmates. In all seasons it was sadly overcrowded, unsanitary, and reeking of putrid odors. Prison food was coarse and poorly prepared and lacking in nutrition. It cut the lining of the stomach, producing bloody stools and diarrhea. The latrine system, crude even for that time, adequately served only a fraction of the men in the camp. A pervasive stench, worse than rotting flesh, struck the nostrils like a slap in the face. The harsh and bitter prison could be suffered patiently by strong men, but among the sick and weak disease was rampant. Every hour around the clock skeletal men were dying. Even healthy men died from exposure to the elements, particularly the weather in winter. Regulations required small tents for prisoners to sleep in, but only 3,000 were available in 1863 for more than 10,000 soldiers. The place had a few run-down buildings with spartan cells, but no sheltering barracks were ever built. New prisoners came every day or so, making the camp even more crowded. In their battered uniforms they looked all the same, like drops of water or breakers on a beach.

When winter came Belle Isle Prison quickly became unendurable. It was notorious for the number of inmates who died there in the wintertime. Without proper food and shelter, and weakened by disease, as many as thirty captive soldiers died every day. Belle Isle was a place of confinement for ordinary soldiers and more brutal than Libby Prison. The latter, only a few miles away, was smaller, more comfortable, and reserved mainly for Union officers. Unlike most of the other prisoners in the teeming prison camp, Matthew was given a cell in a ramshackle building. The size was about the same as the impromptu sleeping chamber Jeremy Heartwood had made for him in happier days. As he lay on the smelly cot, he remembered the quilt hanging from the ceiling beam and the smooth, hard leather of the deerskin couch.

After a day or two of idleness, waiting to be assigned a job, he asked if he might send a letter to his family. His keepers replied if he could find a way to have it delivered, there would be no objection. But how could he do that from a prison cell? For more than a week he languished in a tiny room with a hole for a window. He had to stand on the bed to look out and found it difficult to see the ground. It was just as well, for men were dying on that ground. Most of the time, glancing at the hole that served as a window without panes, he saw only a little patch of blue sky, but quickly he learned to read the weather. Once in a heavy rain a bluebird fluttered to the opening. It cocked its head as it perched there, and looked inside. Then it uttered a shrill tweet and flew away. Preparing for flight the bird seemed to shudder.

Chapter 35

Days of gloomy idleness went by, and then a kindly guard gave Matthew a scrap of paper on which to scratch a message to his family. Standing by, he hinted he might be able to find someone to deliver the message. In the confusion of the times, particularly in the South, one could not expect a dependable mail service. However, a traveler passing through a town would sometimes leave a packet. Matthew passed the smudgy letter through the grating the next day. To encourage the guard to place it in the right hands, he offered the man his red bandanna, the treasured neck scarf Anna had given him.

"Not enough," said the turnkey, pursing his lips tightly to show he was irritated but open to another offer. "That little rag is no good for an old fart like me! Don't you have anything of value? I'd do it for nothing, of course, but times are hard."

Matthew rummaged through his pockets and found the small traveler's Bible. He remembered his promise to carry it with him at all times.

"I would like to give you this. It could do you a world of good. But I need it myself. I promised I would carry it with me wherever I went."

The guard laughed and shook his head. He would never be able to read the fine print, he said, and he had no time for reading anyway. He believed in the Bible and truly loved all that was in it but had no time to read it. He was too proud to admit he was not able to read.

Then Matthew's probing fingers touched the hard steel of the knife, the sacrificial gift from Jesse. Involuntarily he drew it from a pocket and looked at it. The guard was looking at it too, his beady black eyes squinting in the rugged, bearded face and missing nothing.

"Hand it over," he said, grinning. "That and the bandanna will do. But if you get some kind of package from home, and I sure hope you do, I'll be asking for that too. Postage don't come cheap in this place y'know."

With a pang of guilt Matthew gave the man the gift from Jesse, but not the bandanna from Anna; he was not able to part with both gifts. It seemed a long time ago when he assured Jesse the knife would be a loan. He would keep it and use it but return it later, he had said. It troubled him to break his promise, but getting the message delivered was vital. His relatives in Blue Anchor had to know that so far, though languishing in prison, he was not in great danger. He would have to relinquish the knife, but the bandanna and Bible he would keep on his person as mementoes of home.

A few days later the turnkey, who called himself Otis Hinkle, reported that a group of blacks on their way south would deliver Matthew's letter. He had come with a tin tray on which was a bowl of watery soup with flecks of onion skin floating in it and a piece of dark bread. The gray soup had no layer of grease on it, a sure sign the cook had boiled only raw vegetables in a large pot with no meat. Curiously, the soup had a fishy taste but no smell. The turnkey complained of severe shortages and high prices and said the prisoners were eating "just about as good as us guards." If that can possibly be true, Matthew was thinking, the war would have to end soon.

"They took the letter when they heard you was a Quaker," Hinkle remarked. "Said the Quakers went and helped them once in hard times. Now it's their turn to help. Least they could do was take the letter, they said. Seemed glad to do it and didn't ask for any kind of pay."

"But why were they traveling south?" the prisoner asked, a bit puzzled. "Shouldn't they be trying to get across the lines of combat into the North? Seems to me they're traveling in the wrong direction."

"Oh, they're going to a place near Blue Anchor to find jobs on a new plantation. It's a big spread with level fields of cotton soon to be turned into corn and wheat and stuff. Former owner got killed in the war, and now a man named Owen Cooper needs field hands and pays good, they say. Only free workers and no slaves need apply."

"That sounds like the Bolton farm. It's a plantation I know," said Matthew, "but the last I heard the whole place was in ruins."

"I wouldn't know," replied the jailer wistfully. "All I heard is what a good place it is for a good life. Kinda wish I could go there myself."

2

At about the time Matthew went off to prison Owen Cooper bought at auction the property of Thomas Bolton and became acquainted with the Kingstons. A man who seemed to have unusual power when it came to dealing with bureaucrats, he quickly became a valued friend. His goal was to bring the huge plantation from the brink of ruin back into active production. He would plant cotton first and then rotate the yield to keep the soil fertile and eventually bring most of the acres into food crops. Those the government needed most and would be a willing buyer at just about any price. He would own no slaves but made it known he was ready to hire at good wages any displaced person, black or white, who was willing to work hard.

It was rumored in the community that he was a very rich man with a fortune untouched by inflation and with powerful friends in high places. The story went that he had visited Jefferson Davis in Richmond and had met also with Robert E. Lee. He was always doing business in Raleigh, and in a short time acquired enough livestock to plow and till and seed large tracts of land. In his stables were excellent horses and sturdy mules, not one of which was ever stolen by prowlers from either side of the conflict. It appeared that military units, moving through the region and living off the land, had been ordered at their peril to leave undisturbed any property owned by Owen Cooper. Civilians on the prowl were also alerted to stay away.

One morning in June he paid a visit to the Kingstons. In a crisp, white suit and black boots, he rode into the yard with a saddled horse tied by extended reins to his cart. David and Jesse were already at work in the fields, but Rachel with a dish towel in her hands came out to meet him. The sun filtering through the trees cast irregular patterns on the sandy ground and gave to the man's white suit a dappled effect. It picked up the gray in Rachel's hair and made it shine like silver, but at the same time it softened the tone and hue of her skin and the lines of gentle aging on her face. Cooper in the new-looking trap pulled by a fine horse was looking at her.

"Good morning, Mrs. Kingston," he said politely, tipping a jaunty, well-made hat. "They tell me that a roving band took your horses sometime back. I'm sure you know you need a horse to get around these parts, even to visit your neighbors. And you could use an animal for plowing. In a few days I'll send over a mule with some hay."

Astonished, Rachel twisted the towel in her hands and gazed at the man. For a moment she was unable to speak. Then, hesitantly, she replied, "We are certainly in need of livestock, Mr. Cooper, but I doubt that my husband would accept such a gift. He's a staunch and stubborn man and believes that ultimately our God will provide."

"Call it a loan," said Cooper, smiling "As your neighbor and friend I want to help whenever I can in these difficult times. May I stable the horse? A good barn needs livestock in it, and I think I can help you with that."

"My husband and son will be home at noon," said Rachel.

Alone with Cooper, though outside and several feet from the man, she felt a sense of unease. He looked every inch the gentleman, but something about him did not sit well with her. She could not put her finger exactly on what she was feeling but knew he made her slightly uncomfortable.

"I want to see them and will come again soon. I'm told your son was inducted and taken to Richmond but refuses to bear arms. The Confederate army doesn't like objectors of any stripe. Already he may know that better than I, but I may be able help him."

He led the horse to the barn, his lame right leg requiring the use of a cane. In minutes he was back and springing lightly onto the seat of his trap. Touching the brim of his hat with two fingers, he flicked his horse for a sharp turn and rode swiftly down the avenue of oaks to the main road. Rachel stood in the yard and watched him leave. Little clouds of dust rose from the metal rim of each wheel.

3

Catherine had taken the shortcut to the Kingston home and entered the yard as Cooper left. On her head was a white linen bonnet to shield her face from the sun, and because she was pregnant and the day hot, she wore a loose-fitting dress with short sleeves. Her infant was asleep at home in the care of her father. She had assured him she would not be away very long, only long enough to speak briefly with Rachel Kingston. She carried in her hand a tattered envelope delivered an hour before by one of Owen Cooper's men. Inside was the hastily penciled letter from Matthew. The men looking for work had kept their promise and given the letter to Jade Scurlock, Cooper's aide. Rachel invited Catherine to take the load off her feet and relax in one of the white rocking chairs on the wide verandah. Gladly she eased into the chair. A gentle and cooling breeze came from the southeast.

The climbing rose bush on the lattice was brilliant at this time of year and fragrant with budding yellow roses in the midst of deep green. Rachel remembered the time her son had plucked a faded rose from the bush and presented it to her with the air of a cavalier. She smiled as she recalled the image of her handsome son on that day in autumn, so manly and so gallant and so thoughtful. She remembered pressing the rose in an old book to hold it once again in her fingers some day. And then looking downward to her lap, she felt a crumpled piece of paper in her hands. She had a premonition it was important and nervously opened it. Her lips moved as she deciphered a message in smudgy, barely legible handwriting.

> *My dearest wife and friend, I write this in haste from my prison cell in Richmond. I love thee more than ever I can tell and hope all is well there. Please convey my love to all our relatives and friends and particularly to Emily. I have decided that our second child will be named Benjamin if a boy. If a girl and it becomes thy wish, I leave it to thee to name her. I will not be there to share thy pain and joy, but will think of thee every minute.*
>
> *Believe me, I will come home to my family when all this is over. Everyone I meet is tired of this war and everyone hopes it will end soon. We came into Richmond and saw the flags at half mast and were told Stonewall Jackson was dead. He was shot in one arm at Chancellorsville and died a week or so later. They say the battle was a great triumph for the South, but how can anyone say that when so many lives were lost?*
>
> *The food is not good, but I manage to eat whatever they give me to keep up my strength. I'm here because I would not do violence against my fellow man when a skirmish erupted. My friend Sergeant Amos Appleton, the man who strapped the tall rifle to my back in Blue Anchor, was killed in that savage little battle. How long they will keep me here I don't know, but I will not lose faith and will not have you do so either.*

The letter was on a scrap of gray-white paper, wrinkled and soiled by sweaty hands and signed in bold black. Matthew had scribbled the words on front and back with a stubby, blunt pencil. Neither Catherine nor Rachel had trouble reading his paragraphs or recognizing his handwriting. He closed the message with a terse avowal of undying love and a benediction. Then as an afterthought he added a word of advice to his young wife, hoping to soften her misery: *You must insist on the value of life, my love, even when plowing through that dull gray mist that often comes down on life.*

Rachel nodded her head with a quickening heart, tears blurring her vision. Adversity had made a man of her little boy.

She sat in silence, rocking back and forth, staring at a hitching post in the yard. Then suddenly immobile but trembling slightly, she became the image of Adam staring at the apple or Kant with unblinking eye looking intently at the church steeple. The note fell from her numb fingers into her lap. Her back and shoulders trembled as she read the message a second time. Then she composed herself, smiled brightly, and put the letter in Catherine's hands. It would become a precious possession the woman would keep for the rest of her life.

"Matthew will be all right," Rachel asserted. "He's a man now, strong and capable. He can take care of himself. God looks after those who look after themselves, that we know. He will come back to us."

4

Catherine was about to make reply when Anna from within the house called out to Rachel, "Mama, the cornmeal is nearly gone."

Then aware of who was on the porch, she ran from the large storage closet off the kitchen to greet her next-favorite person and hug her. The child couldn't know how deep were the chords of feeling she touched in that instant. Catherine said not a word but hugged her tightly.

"Jesse will be taking the corn to the mill tomorrow," said her mother, speaking to Catherine. "He had planned to borrow Peg, but I suppose he can use the horse Mr. Cooper left with us. He won't be going again soon."

"That was kind of the man, and so generous."

"Yes, but it makes us feel beholden."

"These days we can't stand on pride. We have to be thankful."

"Well, I'm wondering how long we can hold out. The last company of soldiers that went through here rode down the new corn. But we have plenty of potatoes and will soon have peas if soldiers don't trample them."

"Papa has a corn field and a small garden. If the soldiers stay away and don't tramp through our place, we can certainly share."

Suffering from a deep longing for her husband, the young woman fell silent again. She missed him terribly, feared he would be mistreated in that noisome prison camp, and desperately wanted him home. He had said keep the faith, value life, and be strong. She made up her mind to enfold herself in calm as though it were a woolen blanket. No one would see her misery.

As the days passed she found herself working about the house, trying to imagine what he was doing at that moment. He was in a prison. No Quaker she had ever heard of, except the founder of the Society of Friends, had ever been in prison. So how was she to take that? How would the village take it? How would God himself in all his mercy take it? Was it not a shame? Would it become a blot on the family name and on the Quaker faith itself? Did Matthew do something terribly wrong? Or was he thrown in prison for doing the right thing? She wanted answers. His letter lacked details.

Catherine had her father and daughter to keep her company. Routinely she presented her most pleasant self to them even when she felt an emptiness only Matthew could fill. A tinge of bitterness, foreign to her temperament, was seeping into her soul and sinew. When the politicians decided to go to war, did they know she would suffer? It just wasn't fair, but whoever said life is fair? With studied calm and with patient acceptance of her lot, she did her housework as usual. She had been taught by experts, the Quaker elders, never to buckle under adversity. Yet some nights when the owl hooted into the wee hours and sleep would not come, she wept.

Chapter 36

In late afternoon near suppertime, Jesse came in from the fields hungry as a bear and washed his face and hands at the pump in the yard.

"I'm in the mood for fried chicken," he said, walking into the kitchen and licking his lips. "But I guess we don't have no chickens young enough for the frying pan."

"You could get us one of them old hens," Sarah said, pointing to one clucking and pecking in the yard. "That old hen would make a good stew. Don't do nothing but cluck. Don't lay no eggs no more."

"The clucking could bring the soldiers down on us," said Jesse, advancing Sarah's argument and going to the yard. "Then no more hens at all."

"And no more eggs," said Anna, who was shadowing her brother. "We could shut up the hen house at night and let them roost in the bushes. A prowler would have a hard time grabbing a chicken in the bushes out there in back of the barn."

"But not them foxes and wildcats," muttered Jesse. "There's a moldy cellar under the barn. Maybe we could put them there."

"Yeah!" said Anna with animation.

"We could put up perches and drive them in every night maybe. But they're ornery critters and hard to control."

As he spoke Jesse was edging closer to the targeted hen. Then suddenly with a powerful lunge he threw himself in her direction, reaching out with both hands to grab her. He missed and sprawled face down in the dirt. She squawked loudly and flew over their heads to the roof of a nearby shed, scattering feathers and droppings in her flight.

"Well, there goes our stew," sighed Anna. "Clumsy Jesse scared her so bad she flew away like a bird."

"Yeah, and dropping poop all over just like a bird!"

"Would of been too tough to chew anyway," said Sarah.

"Never mind. I'll shoot her when she settles down a bit. Too much work trying to run her down, and too hot."

"Don't even think about shooting that hen," said his mother in a tone he had learned to respect. She had come outside when she heard the cackling. "I detest guns, Jesse, and I will not have you shooting any of our domestic animals, not even a scraggly old hen."

"But we have to eat, Mama," said Jesse defensively. "I s'pose I could wring her neck if I could catch her. Would that be all right?"

"No, it would not be all right!" Rachel exclaimed. "You know better!"

"I saw some quail down in the south pasture. Too fast to shoot. Do you think I could catch a quail sprinkling salt on his tail?"

"Hey, that rhymes!" Anna hooted. "Sprinkle salt on the tail of a quail!"

"No one ever caught a bird with salt, Jesse. It's just an old wives' tale. Now go inside and clean up."

"What's an old wives' tale, Mama?" Anna asked, her curiosity getting the best of her. Sitting by the window, her mother patiently explained. Even as she spoke she worried about Jesse's love of guns and wanting to shoot them. And yet she knew the time might come when he would have to be skilled with a gun to keep food on the table.

Rachel deplored the taking of any kind of life even when it was sometimes necessary, and the thought that young men were killing each other in senseless battle made her miserable. In debate with herself, she had asked more than once whether war was ever the answer to any problem. To correct a problem as far-reaching and as evil as the institution of slavery, perhaps the war had to be fought. As fire can be used to fight fire, perhaps evil is necessary to fight evil. No, that line of thinking she would never endorse. Wisdom on the side of good could have been used to spare human lives. Then her thoughts came back to the matter at hand. Jesse was hungry and wanted fried chicken, but that was not available. So what to do? Well, there were other ways to solve the problem. On this day the hen would live. Some other day, depending on necessity, maybe not. For supper they would have fresh garden vegetables, potatoes, corn pone, and a rabbit caught in a trap. Sarah had already prepared the rabbit for cooking and had placed several pieces, dipped in a batter she had made, in a skillet. Rachel would give her share to Jesse. He liked the taste of rabbit deep fried to a golden brown and crispy. He liked the taste of anything fried.

2

In Jeremy Heartwood's household the family ate hot buttered cornbread with rice and beans, fresh new tomatoes, okra, and steamed squash. Beside each plate was a big glass of milk. They still had the two heifers producing milk which could be churned into butter, but their supply of meat was gone. The garden by now was producing vegetables of several kinds, and the cornfield would soon be giving them corn. Until summer ended, no one would have to worry about going hungry.

After supper, and after her kitchen was clean, Catherine wrote a letter to her husband. She answered his letter word for word and added concerns of her own but concealed as best she could her unrest and worry. He knew already that everyday life at home was becoming harder, and so she told him many of their friends had fallen on hard times but would survive. Then with tears blurring her sight, she conveyed to him a love that had begun in the depths of her hidden heart to grow like a weed and flood her life with sunshine. The love he gave in return had made the sun even brighter and her life complete. It had come deep and strong when she needed it most, and its warmth, she confessed, made a woman of her and taught her desire. Then quickly she changed the subject.

She wrote that a man named Owen Cooper, called Colonel Cooper by his workers who praised him highly, had bought the Bolton property after the death of Bolton's son. She was not certain that Matthew knew Richard had died in a battle fought somewhere in Virginia. Cooper had confirmed the news, she explained, corroborating the rumor spread earlier by Leo Mack. The community was told that Major Richard Bolton had died a hero, bravely charging into battle and urging his men onward. No one seemed to know the exact details, but Cooper had heard that Bolton was shot in the neck as he broke through enemy lines.

Leading his men into battle and riding ahead of them in a daring display of courage, he quickly became an easy target. Mortally wounded, so went the report, he continued to charge headlong into the fray until he died. Catherine, who had no reason to disbelieve the report, admired the man's valor but begged her husband to do nothing heroic. Save the heroics for someone else, she cautioned. A dead hero, though honored to high heaven, would be of little use to his wife and children. She closed with a benediction and a promise of eternal love.

Then she folded the letter, placed it on the mantelpiece, prepared for bed, and checked on Emily. Though the child was sleeping with not a care in the world, her mother was agitated. She had written the letter as carefully as she could, but who would deliver it? The newspapers often published stories of letters never received by soldiers. The wife of an infantryman wrote to him every day, but not one letter ever reached him. A few came to her from him and one from the War Department. A few words on stiff paper edged in black informed her that her husband had died a hero in the performance of his duties. Later she learned he was run over in broad daylight by an ammunition cart. Well, even if a trusted person tried to deliver her letter, Catherine was thinking, would it reach her husband? Would he read her words and feel close to her? Would he value his safety and come home soon? Again her thoughts were so weighted with worry they numbed her brain.

Changing into her night clothes, she crept into bed hoping to find solace in sleep. In the cozy little house only one stubby candle dispelled the darkness. The ponderous wheel of slumber turned slowly. For an hour she struggled to work its machinery, and then fitful sleep came and went. Half awake, she thought she heard the muted sound of unshod horses ridden hard. Then suddenly, as sharp as a bell ringing, came the snuffle and stamp of a horse nearby. To affirm her suspicion, her heart racing, she sat up in bed to listen. A night bird in the still air was breaking into song. A leathery bat fluttered past her window, uttering a barely audible "chip chip." Somewhere in the distance a cow was lowing and a dog barked plaintively. From near the barn came the sound of a hoot-owl hunting mice. She listened, sorting the sounds, and they seemed to fill the night like down in a featherbed. In the next room her father, sleeping soundly on his back, was snoring and wheezing softly.

3

In Blue Anchor in 1863 the June weather was hot and dry. The rich soil in the level fields was good for planting, and the farmers were making a courageous attempt to cultivate a crop. Jeremy Heartwood, without the means to employ Harvey Heckrodt as in past years, resigned himself to tending his garden. Except for a small potato patch and a plot of corn, his fields lay fallow. In late afternoon, with David and Jesse home from the fields, he often visited the Kingston farm to hear the latest gossip and war news. Sometimes early in the morning he would appear on the kitchen steps of his neighbor's house with a gallon of milk.

Standing at the back door, even when the door was open, he would hesitate before crying out, "Anybody home?" If he got no answer, he entered the kitchen gingerly and yelled his question again. By then the Kingston cook would be on hand to supply an answer. On this morning he handed the pail of milk to Sarah and asked his usual question. The servant put the milk on her sideboard, wiped her hands on her apron, and looked into the back yard.

"The men folks am in the fields, Mistah Jeerme, and Lawd knows where the chillen are. Guess both gotta be somewheres round here."

Then she remembered that Rachel was in the front yard talking with Colonel Cooper. Jeremy wished her good day and walked around the house to see Cooper in his signature white clothing astride a splendid horse. One of his men, holding the reins of a strong mule, stood nearby. Rachel Kingston was talking faster than usual and seemed unsettled.

"Really, Mr. Cooper," she was saying, "under no circumstances can we accept such a gift. You must understand that we cannot and will not receive charity. Our general condition, at least for now, is not all that bad."

"But there's plowing to be done, and I promised to lend you that mule. It is not a gift, Mrs. Kingston, only a loan. As neighbors in times like these I firmly believe we must help one another. I was brought up as an islander, you know, and on a tiny island we always assisted each other. It made life more pleasant for all of us. Would you deny that Blue Anchor in a time of war and rumors of war is something of an island?"

He caught a glimpse of Jeremy approaching and touched the brim of his hat. It was a gesture smartly executed that resembled a military salute. The round little man smiled, his face beaming, and nodded.

"I wish you could speak to my husband directly," said Rachel before acknowledging Jeremy. "I will have my son give him a message when he goes out to help with the hay."

"Very well, Mrs. Kingston, if that's your wish."

"Right now the boy is on his way to the mill, riding that horse you loaned us, with corn to be ground. He should have done it yesterday but put it off until this morning. Now I'm sure he'll have to wait."

A shade of concern darkened Cooper's face. He shifted his body in the saddle, looked directly at Rachel, and spoke with just a tinge of excitement.

"I don't wish to alarm you, Mrs. Kingston, but a contingent of recruiters stopped at my place last night. They rode off at dawn, saying they planned to scour the countryside for able-bodied men of any age. Your Jesse is a well-grown lad for his age. I wouldn't want to see him run into trouble."

"But Jesse is only a child!" Rachel urged, her mother's voice rising in pitch. "Just barely thirteen. He's just an innocent boy, a child!"

"Child or no," said Cooper cautiously. "If he's big enough to carry a weapon and big enough to shoot it, he could attract their attention."

"Ah, no, Mr. Cooper. No recruiter would even look at Jesse!"

"One thing you must understand, Mrs. Kingston. These recruiters must fill their quota, and it's getting harder every day. If they don't do it, they can be sent into battle themselves. They were eager to take a few of my workers, even the older ones, but I persuaded them to look elsewhere."

Rachel was silent now and clearly worried. Jeremy, standing nearby and hearing all that was said, could see that she was becoming nervous.

"They left feeling mighty disappointed," Cooper went on, "and a bit desperate I might add. I think it wouldn't hurt if I rode over that way to see how things are going. Will you stable the mule, Mr. Heartwood?"

"Of course I will do that," replied Jeremy in his friendly way, "but how will your man get home?"

"Jade? He can trot along beside me, or cross through the woods. He's the fittest person I know and good on his feet."

"I'll trot," said Jade Scurlock. "You might need me at the mill."

As they disappeared down the lane Rachel walked with Jeremy to the barn. She wore a frown but was glad to be in the company of an old friend.

"Now that's a handsome mule," said Jeremy, "good teeth, good coat."
"Do you really think there's any danger?" she asked.

"I don't believe so. But I hear the recruiters are becoming as bad as the scavengers. If anyone can help us in these unsettled times it's Cooper. The man is a lot more powerful than he lets on to be."

"Do you really believe that?" she asked. "Do you think he could do something if Jesse happens to be in danger? I worry about Jesse and about Nathaniel Alston. I've heard Nat actually wants to go into the army. Said if they take him, he would fight like the two Quakers from Iowa who fought with John Brown at Harpers Ferry. Foolish, foolish boy!"

"Cooper will look after your son," Jeremy assured her. "The man said he 'persuaded' the rascals to look elsewhere. Hah! That's an understatement if I ever heard one! He has connections in high places, mind you, and the rabble are not about to cross his path without permission. But I think he likes you and David and maybe me."

"I know. He and David are already close friends, but I feel uncomfortable around that man. Don't ask me why, Jeremy, but I do. White suit and black horse and honorary title? He's proud, mind you, and putting on a show. More than that, he's making my family feel beholden."

"You don't like him because he's wealthy. And because he was a soldier, bore arms, led men into battle, caught a bullet in the right leg. Do you know he walks with a limp? They say he came down with pneumonia and nearly died. Then one morning, like a miracle, he's up and about hale and hearty and ready to fight again, but they gave him a discharge."

"I don't dislike the man, I really don't. It's just that he makes me feel, well, uncomfortable somehow. I feel tense when he comes into the yard, when he sits on that fancy horse and looks at me."

"He's a man of mystery," said Jeremy. "You can't figure him out. Can't read him like a book. Maybe that's it."

Rachel returned to her kitchen shaking her head with aggravation. Jeremy was a sweet man with a delightful sense of humor, and she loved him dearly, but he ruffled her feathers at times. "Why didn't he try to understand?" she was thinking. "Oh, the man didn't even try. He just wanted to see my reaction, wanted to see if he could get my dander up. Oh well, he is what he is—exasperating—and one must be charitable." She glanced over her shoulder to see him entering the barn. He put the mule in a stall, gave the animal some hay, and sauntered whistling back to his house.

Chapter 37

Jeremy Heartwood found his daughter in an oversized calico dress, cradling her bulging stomach and wiping the sweat from her brow as she worked at the spinning wheel. She wore a worried look and her face was pale.

"Papa," she asked, "do you know we have but a hundred dollars left? I went through your desk and Matthew's papers, and that's all I could find. We're running out of money!"

She knew the power and value of money very well, and she knew that many worthy people were suffering as their money lost its value day by day. Her father could read the distress on her face, hear the anxiety in her voice, and he tried to respond as cheerfully as he could.

"Well, Katie," he said with quiet assurance, "it's good money, not that Confederate stuff. That hundred dollars will keep us through the winter and well into spring and summer. With goods so scarce, there's not a lot we can spend it on. So don't fret, my dear. We have a roof over our heads. We have food and clothes and fuel from the swamp. If the candles give out, as the oil has already, we can burn some sweet-smelling pine knots for light."

"Oh, no you don't, no!" she replied with mock sternness. "I'll sit in the dark, and you will too, before I smoke up the house with pine torches."

"Well, the tallow dips we have are bad enough. Poor in quality, you know, and burn too fast and don't really give much light. They stink when they burn, too, and smoke. Not much better than the soap we have. If we could find some grease, we could make our own soap. But to get grease you need animals, and they're in short supply too."

"After the war do you think we can raise pigs again?"

"Of course, Katie, lots of pigs. I been thinking about that too."

"Then we can have sausage for breakfast," she said, smacking her lips. "And we can have ham for lunch and pork chops with yams for dinner!"

"It's good to see you dreaming again, Katie. Warms my heart!"

"Cheap candles and rancid soap and skimpy bits of meat we can put up with, Papa, but what if basic foods—you know, really basic foods—become so scarce we can't feed ourselves?"

"Ah, daughter, you worry too much. We'll have food to eat." He was beginning to think that worry was a part of her character as a woman and would stay with her even in good times. As a child she never worried.

"We seem to be coming to the end of our tether, Papa. I can't help but worry. There's no breaking loose."

"We'll have food to eat," Jeremy said again. "Your papa will see to that. The Friends will see to that. Even Jesse will see to that."

"Jesse, Papa? His mother will not have that boy shooting guns. There's probably nothing to shoot anyway, and no ammunition left."

"The swamp has game aplenty. Oh, not as much as before the war but enough. And even though his mama don't like it, Jesse is uncommonly good when it comes to shooting a fat duck."

"I know, he's already a good marksman. He wanted to shoot an old hen for a stew, but Rachel wouldn't let him."

"Well, maybe when we need it she'll let him aim at a fat duck. I can scald it and pluck it, and you can roast it to a golden brown. And you think we won't have enough to eat? Why that's the best eating anyone can have. As for coming to the end of our tether and not breaking loose, where in the world did you get that idea? Trust me, Katie, no tether, no rope, not even chains will ever tie us down. I came to these parts to live free, and I will insist on living free—and so will you."

2

Jesse in his usual good humor was whistling a tune as he rode up to the mill. Daydreaming as he whistled, in spite of his mother's dread of warfare he saw himself as a famous general. In a spiffy uniform with brass buttons and golden epaulets, he marched with high-lifted feet that pounded the dust of a barren plain. Behind him was an army of gray with flags and swords and long rifles, a phantom army silent and menacing. When he stopped, the gray army halted but quickly grew pallid and bewildered. For a moment the army held its ranks, and then sighing a soft farewell dissolved into a gray mist. Jesse was in front of the store. In his haste to get his job at the mill done, he didn't bother to notice four men in rough clothing lounging against the wall. He hitched the horse to the rail in front and threw a sack of corn over his shoulder, intending to return shortly for the other sack. Before he could reach the doorway a lanky young man with big hands and a sunburned face stepped in front of him and blocked his way.

"Why ain't you in the army, fellow?" he blurted, spitting a dollop of tobacco juice in the dirt, and moving closer to the boy. "And where did you get that fine-looking horse? You didn't steal it, did ya?"

"I'm a Quaker," said Jesse with fine simplicity, "and Quakers don't believe in fighting or stealing."

He forgot to say he was only thirteen years old but remembered to answer the questions about the animal.

"That horse? Well, that horse belongs to my papa's friend, and I didn't steal him. It's against my religion."

"Is that so?" said another youth, taking hold of the horse's reins. "This prime animal now belongs to us. And you will come along to help us defend the capital of the Confederacy, whether you like it nor not."

They encircled the boy and pressed against him. The sack of corn fell to the ground and lay in the dirt. He could smell the chewing tobacco and the dank, unpleasant odor of their unwashed bodies. He tried to retrieve the corn and move into the mill, but they pinned his arms behind him and were ready to shackle his wrists. At that moment Owen Cooper on a black stallion with a huge black man trotting beside him rode into the yard.

"You will leave the boy alone," he said, "and you will move out of these parts right now or take the consequences. Do I make myself clear?"

His voice was calm and even and just loud enough to be heard. Unmistakably he had given the Rebel soldiers a command. And soldiers they were, though in rough civilian clothes and looking only slightly older than schoolboys. Would they obey the order or merely laugh in his face?

For a moment Jesse thought they would seize the man in the fancy white suit and take his fancy horse and shoot him if he stood in their way. Then he saw Jade Scurlock approaching them and showing something in a box to the soldier in charge. It appeared to be a badge or medallion of some sort reposing on cotton in the small box. They released the boy, placed his sack of corn back on his shoulder, and quickly apologized. In the shade of the building the four of them huddled in conference.

"Get your corn to the miller," said Cooper, pointing toward the loading dock. "Do it now, make haste."

When Jesse went inside the building the recruiters were tensely conversing with Cooper, even trying to argue with him. Jade stood near the horse, his arms folded across his massive chest, ready for action. In the yard again for the second bag of corn, Jesse found only Jade sitting at leisure under a tree. The big black man did not get up but threw him a salute. Half an hour later when Jesse emerged with his sack of cornmeal, without speaking Jade helped him secure it to the horse.

"Where did Mr. Cooper go?" the boy asked, hoping to see him nearby. "I wanted to thank him for getting me out of trouble."

"It's *Colonel* Cooper," came the gruff, laconic reply with emphasis on the military rank. "He went home and that's where you wanna be."

3

A bit shaken by his close encounter, Jesse returned home as fast as he could. The spirited horse wanted to break into a gallop, and so did Jesse, but the meal had to be delivered safely. He tried walking the horse, sped up to a trot jostling the sack behind him, and eventually settled on a faster but smoother canter. He dismounted in one great leap, grabbed the heavy sack of meal, and ran into the house to report what had happened at the mill. He spoke simply without embellishment, trying not to be excited.

"I said I was a Quaker and wouldn't fight. They got surly after that and closed in on me. At first I thought they were gonna beat me up. Then I realized they were gonna tie me up and take me with them! That's when Colonel Cooper showed up with his man Jade. It was pretty amazing. All he said, sitting there on that big black horse of his in that white suit and floppy hat, all he said was let the boy go. Real slow and not very loud he said it—'let the boy go.' They backed off and started talking amongst themselves and then to Cooper, and when I came back out for the second sack they were gone and so was Cooper. But he left Jade to keep an eye on me."

"Oh, Jesse!" exclaimed his mother. "Can't you be more careful? Were you showing off to attract attention? Why didn't you keep quiet? At the very least you could have told them your age."

"They didn't ask, and besides it didn't matter to them. They said I was big enough and strong enough and ugly enough to be a rifleman, and they needed fresh horses and new men for the army. I'm pretty sure they wanted Cooper's horse more than me, and they already had it. But he put the fear of God in 'em, Mama. You could just see it, the fear of God. And I didn't show off none, just went about my business."

"*Mister* Cooper," corrected Rachel. "Call him *Mister* Cooper."

"No, Mama. Jade told me to call him Colonel Cooper. And that Jade is one big man I don't wanna cross. I never saw muscles bigger than his."

"I'm told that some call him Captain," David remarked. "That was his rank as an officer with General Hill. But I've heard him referred to as Colonel too. Must be that honorary title Confederate officers with influence are sometimes given. When all's said and done I think he prefers Mister."

"Well, the captain of that bunch of recruiters, or sergeant, or whatever they call him, seemed to know Mr. Cooper real well after Jade showed him something in a little box. They listened when he told them I was under age. He said he would make trouble for them if they took me. They were pretty sulky about it, but they let me go and got out of there real fast."

"You won't have to go to the mill again for some time, Jesse," said Rachel protectively. "That's the last of the corn to be ground. Well, at least for a while. Put the meal in the pantry, please."

Jesse braced the bag on his hip and set it down on the pantry floor. He looked at the shelves and found them nearly empty. As long as he could remember the pantry with its shelves had been a special place of plenty, holding all the good and tasty things he liked to eat, but no longer.

"That pantry scares me," he said on emerging. "It's as bare as Mother Hubbard's cupboard. If we don't start laying in supplies soon, we'll never make it through the winter."

"The Lord will provide," said Rachel with Quaker conviction. "Now as soon as you eat something I want you back in the fields with your father, and take that mule with you."

"We can use that mule all right," chortled Jesse. "That Cooper is a straight shooter. I'm glad he's on our side!"

"*Mister* Cooper," said his mother patiently, "*Mister* Cooper."

"Fine, Mama, *Mister* Cooper. But why do the soldiers hate us? They looked at me real ugly like when I said I'm a Quaker and don't believe in fighting or stealing. We're Southerners too, just like them. So why?"

4

Until now Anna had said nothing. Then she recalled the incident with Timothy Swope when she was seven and the war not yet begun. The boy had persecuted her and frightened her, and he didn't even know her. He knew only that she was a Quaker, and someone had told him that Quakers were no good. He was acting out a hatred others had imposed upon him and losing his innocence in the process. If he came into the world trailing clouds of glory, at the moment he threw his first rock he lost it all. It was a concept Anna did not understand at that time and could not understand even now when older. But she remembered the searing pain and the lesson she learned that day. It was a lesson she would never forget.

"Quakers are different," she said, "and people hate us 'cause we're different. I don't wanna be different, do you Jesse? I wanna be just like everyone else and be happy."

But Anna was destined to be different. Somewhere deep within the little girl a secret ambition was stirring and striving to grow. In fewer than twenty years she would become one of the first female physicians in the nation. In the next ten years she would become well known in medical circles as one of the foremost authorities in her field. She would move with her husband, also a doctor, to the mountains of North Carolina, open an innovative sanitarium for tubercular patients, and gain a sterling reputation on the national scene. She would become a scientist but remain a Quaker.

Before returning to the fields, David and Jesse ate a simple lunch served by Rachel with the help of Sarah. The talk was about Owen Cooper.

"We must thank the man somehow," said David. "We must thank him with more than mere words, but I don't know with what. We are truly indebted to him. Because of him we have livestock to work the soil, and because of him happy-go-lucky Jesse is safe. I wish Cooper could do something to help Matthew in prison, but that's really too much to ask."

"When it comes to helping my son," rejoined Rachel, "nothing is too much to ask. Already he has said he will look into the matter."

"I'm told he goes to Richmond regularly," said David. "He may be able to find out something about Matthew, even see him, and he could take along a letter or two from us. I know Catherine is desperate to correspond. But if he doesn't volunteer to help us that way, we have no right to ask for help."

"We mustn't worry about rights, dear. We don't have the luxury even to think about rights in our situation. I do believe Mr. Cooper will try to help us. And I believe Matthew as a man will find a way to help himself."

She was finally convinced that her blithe little boy—married and a father and now an unwilling soldier standing on principle and facing grave danger—had put his childhood behind him to become a man. It would soon be Jesse's turn to go through the same transformation. How would she handle it? How would he? Why did life have to be so difficult?

Chapter 38

On the verandah of Bolton's restored mansion, in the heat of a sultry afternoon in summer, Owen Cooper relaxed in the shade with a glass of clear, stinging, honey-yellow bourbon. The silence was broken only by the buzzing of bees in nearby flowers. Two gigantic butterflies, symmetrical and ablaze with color, were inspecting the flowers. Then suddenly the pounding of horses' hoofs on hard sand stamped out the buzzing and scattered the insects. An officer in a gray uniform, accompanied by half a dozen soldiers of lesser rank, rode into the yard and asked to see the master.

"I own this place," replied Cooper, "but I don't call myself the master. Times are changing, man, and we have to change with them. I employ no slaves here, and I don't expect a servile obedience from any worker. I'm not his master, only his employer. What can I do for you?"

"May I speak with you in confidence?" asked the officer. "My name is Colin Stroud. I have a bulletin for you."

"That sidearm you're wearing, Captain. Please leave it with one of your men. A revolver similar to that killed the former owner of this place. A terrible waste of life, let's not repeat it."

The soldier complied without comment, and the two men withdrew from the porch to the stranger's room. For an hour they spoke to one another in private. Cooper read the wire from Richmond and asked a few questions. Captain Stroud explained the circumstances to the limits of his knowledge and offered instructions. Cooper could ride with a group of soldiers on their way to the city, or he could take a train loaded with ore for the Iron Works near Belle Island. It would be uncomfortable and noisy but faster.

"I prefer my own horse to any smoke-belching iron horse," Cooper retorted. "I will ride with you in two days' time. In the meantime my home is your home. Jade will show your men to their quarters."

At the Heartwood home, Catherine was thinking Cooper might be able to deliver the letter she had written to her husband. She placed it on the mantel above the fireplace, expecting to see it there a long time. But

Owen Cooper had the reputation of being something of a miracle man; if anyone could get it to the right person, he could. Those thoughts were alive and active as she drifted into sleep. She was up with the sunrise the next morning and was bathing Emily when the tall clock in the corner struck seven. At that moment Cooper was instructing Jade Scurlock to pay a visit to the Heartwood house. He would be there to pick up the letter Catherine had written, and he would pay a similar visit to the Kingston homestead.

Any envelopes gathered at the two farms would be placed in a special pouch, and either Cooper or his man Scurlock would make an effort to deliver them to Matthew in prison. Cooper had the authority to call in couriers for special delivery of important documents, but this time he chose to do it himself. He and his aide would be in Richmond soon, and so he felt no need to entrust the letters to a courier. Sometimes, despite their best efforts, the couriers were not able to complete assignments. Also these were personal letters, not official documents. With the letters in the leather pouch he carried with him on special assignments, he would meet with Confederate leaders to do business cloaked with secrecy.

2

In the bleak confines of Belle Isle Prison, Matthew Kingston was thinking of his wife and family and home. He wanted to be present when Catherine gave birth to their second child, but even if he survived the war he could remain in prison for years. That was his sentence: the duration of the war plus ten years. Each time he reviewed his situation he came to the same inescapable conclusion—he was not guilty as charged. He had done nothing to cause the death of Amos Appleton despite the claim against him. He had no animosity toward the person who filed the claim. He simply believed the man had not seen the full picture. His conversation with the blue coats Henderson and Lipton, as the patrol wagon was hauling the three of them to Belle Isle, convinced him that Appleton was meant to die on that day. Nothing anyone could have done would have saved him. The Union soldiers admitted the sergeant was targeted as the leader of the squad and shot as soon as possible. He himself was to be next. Had he fired a weapon at the hidden enemy when Appleton ceased to fire, it would have been a waste of ammunition. The Union riflemen were well protected by an outcropping of rock as they fired in ambush. Not one of them was wounded or killed that day.

As for refusing to pay the tax and allowing himself to be thrown into combat, his thoughts were the same as when he left home. He was not able to compromise his beliefs, not even for his family. To pay the exemption tax meant contributing money to a war machine that obliterated young men in their prime. It meant paying money to a government bent on perpetuating slavery throughout the South and hanging Lincoln when the war was won. From the beginning few Quakers believed the South could win, and so the prospect of punishing Lincoln was academic at best. The slavery issue, however, was not. Though a Southerner, Matthew was not able in good conscience to support and defend an economic system nurtured by slavery and oppression. And so he languished in prison, trying to adapt to harsh conditions and counting the dreary days as one dissolved into the next.

Each day was much like the one before it. Each morning, just as the sun was coming up, he was rousted from a fitful sleep on a hard cot and marched outside to stand in a line of unwashed men at the mess tent. Sitting on a crude bench or squat-legged on the ground, he ate a watery breakfast that sometimes smelled of spoiled food. Then he was hustled into the work yard where he labored in the heat of the day, assembling carts and weapons carriers and rebuilding damaged equipment. At noon he rested in the shade after a meal of black bread and watery soup. Half an hour later he went back to work and toiled until supper. Given half hour for supper, he ate stale bread and beans and sticky, poorly cooked rice. After that interval, with blisters on his fingers, he struggled with the hard labor that was part of his sentence until nature offered release in darkness. The guards were often rough in their handling of prisoners, but he did what he was told and was not mistreated.

He was allowed to bathe in the river once a week, but was not able to eat as much as his body demanded. The food was spare, greasy, starchy, and tasteless, but he ate it nonetheless. His work made him hungry, and he knew if he didn't eat he would sicken and die. Day by day he could feel himself losing weight and becoming weaker. He could see that others around him, lacking proper nutrition, were in the same condition. Some would vomit soon after eating, unable to keep the rough food in damaged stomachs long enough to benefit from it. Others suffered from galloping diarrhea. Yet they arose at daylight to work in sun and rain and frost, or to sprawl idly on the ground when men outnumbered jobs. Many with bulging, bloodshot eyes and swollen stomachs were not able to work. They were skin and bones, pale and worn, cadaverous and waiting to die.

At night Matthew slept on a narrow cot made of wood. Its only accessory was a thin blanket used mainly as a pillow. He wondered whether the flimsy blanket was intended to provide warmth in winter. He had heard that the prison camp was cold and damp and unheated during the winter months. Exposed to the weather, both summer and winter, many soldiers found conditions unendurable and died. Inside the shelter in the cold of winter a frigid wind seemed to blow always down the corridor. Prisoners came to Belle Isle in fairly good health but rapidly grew weak of hunger or disease and died. Matthew was sheltered in a tiny cell, but even in the brightness of a summer day it was damp and dark.

He learned that by lying on the hard cot in a particular position he could rest better and fall asleep faster. And because he was dead tired when evening came, he had no trouble sleeping. But the mornings rumbled in too fast and too abruptly with the noise of a freight train. The authorities had opted to waken the prison population with a loud siren-like horn that penetrated every crevice of the camp. The raw noise of the klaxon jangled the nerves of every prisoner and made a gentle awakening impossible. On one occasion a small group protested the noise but were quickly silenced. Ten minutes after the raucous horn sounded inmates had to be on the move.

3

For several weeks Matthew occupied the diminutive and barren cell alone. Because he was away from it many hours each day, he found it tolerable. The solitude didn't bother him because fatigue after work took care of that. Then returning one evening, he found a pale young man with freckles and sandy hair sitting on his cot. He was not more than seventeen.

"The name is Raymond," he said curtly, extending his hand. "Raymond Tucker. I'm to be your new cellmate. I'm supposed to get a cot in a little bit, and I guess it'll have to be side by side with this one."

"I'm not sure the cell is big enough for two cots," said Matthew.

"Oh, they'll find a way even if they have to stack 'em. This cot is hard as the floor but maybe not as slimy. Are you pestered by bugs? I mean I been sittin' here and lookin' and all sorts of insects are crawlin' around."

"Well, this is the South," said Matthew with a half smile, "and one can expect insects in this climate in summer. They'll leave you alone if you leave them alone." He could see that Raymond was talkative, gregarious, a bit awkward, and nervous in the new place.

"Well, I'm not sure I can! Some insects came into the world to be swatted. I'm convinced of that! I hate mosquitoes and big ol' bugs like the one that just skittered across the floor."

He was trying to make a joke, but Matthew did not respond. He was looking the boy over and wondering how he had managed to get himself in such a predicament.

"Where you from?" Tucker asked abruptly, standing up.

He was tall and thin and wore a ragged shirt half tucked into blue trousers too big for him. His leather boots were in good condition, but he wore no socks. Another soldier had stolen his socks, he revealed later.

"Not far from here," answered Matthew. "I live in North Carolina, a village called Blue Anchor near the Great Dismal Swamp."

"North Carolina?" Tucker whistled incredulously. "That's Southern territory, man! What you doin' in this godforsaken place? Did you kill some poor bastard on the wrong side?"

"I refused to bear arms and refused to buy exemption."

"Refused to bare arms? Refused to buy redemption? Wooeeew!"

The long whistle seemed to relax him, but he went on talking. He ceased to make jokes and became curious with many questions to ask.

"What do you mean by exemption? You could buy it, you say? And they said you had to bear arms, but you wouldn't do it? I didn't have none of them choices. I had to do what they told me or be shot."

"That is exactly what they said to me," Andrew, interrupting.

"They made me a sapper. You gotta have guts to be a sapper! One of us got blown to hell first day on the job! And nobody said nothing to me about buying my way out, 'cept this crook trying to fleece me. Said Lincoln was a friend of his, and he'd write and get him to let me go home if I paid a hundred dollars. 'Course I didn't have that kind of money and wouldn't of paid it anyway. My family is dirt poor and as far as I know my two brothers are dead already in this crazy war."

"Where are you from?" asked Matthew, repeating the boy's question, curious to know which state.

"I'm from Williamsport. It's a town in the mountains, not really a port, nowhere near the sea, but on a river."

"Williamsport? Is that in Pennsylvania? My family has friends in Pennsylvania, in Philadelphia mainly. Most of the prisoners here seem to be from that state but from other Northern states too."

"That's because we got the tar kicked out of us at first, but we're winning now. Did you hear about that? The North is gonna win, you can bet on it. And I know about Philadelphia but never went there."

He spoke hesitantly, but with a show of pride and with just a hint of a swagger. Sitting down, he slipped into a monotone without emotion.

"We lost bad at Chancellorsville, and they rounded up a bunch of us and shipped us off like cattle to Richmond. And then a week ago my platoon ran into a bunch o' Rebs and retreated, but I didn't move fast enough. They say I'm to be here for the duration, whatever that means. I don't expect to get home again. I hear they shoot prisoners when the place gets too crowded. Hear even strong men die like flies in winter."

"No, that's not really true," said Matthew. "At least not the first part. Just don't get any of the guards upset, and try to eat the food, and try to rest any time you can when they put you to work in the hot sun."

"Oh, I'm good at resting," he said with a wry smile. "At home I could sleep on the wood pile all night and not even turn over. And I don't mind the sun all that much. Kinda like it in fact. I'm used to working outside."

With a bang the grated door opened and a second wooden bunk was shoved into the cramped little room. On it was a thin and soiled pad that served as a mattress. It didn't have a blanket. Tucker placed the bed opposite Matthew's, and curled up in a fetal position facing the dirty wall.

"He's no bigger than Jesse," Matthew thought, lying on his bunk and looking at the damp ceiling. "The boy should be in school. Certainly not in this awful place. Hard to believe, but they tell me he's the enemy. Soldiers exactly like him, maybe even the same last name, were trying to kill him. And he was ready to kill them. Hard to believe."

Within minutes the young soldier was sleeping on the dirty cot like a baby on a pristine cloud, and snoring.

"O Lord, deliver us," murmured Matthew in a little prayer, amazed at man's inhumanity to man. "And please, dear Lord, keep Tucker safe and send him home again."

Then rising to look at the still form curled on the cot and facing the wall, he decided to give the boy his blanket. He had heard he would be leaving the prison shortly and would not be there to suffer the cold.

"Tucker could die in this place come winter," he told himself, "but at least he's alive for now and facing a moldy wall instead of guns."

4

Raymond Tucker survived the winters of 1863 and 1864. During the first, he came down with a severe case of bronchitis but somehow managed to get over it. During the second, he wore a heavy wool coat night and day that had belonged to a prisoner who died. When the war ended, he languished for months in the prison before he was finally released in late summer. Then with a few dollars in his pocket he made his way back to Williamsport. There he married, got a steady job with the railroad as a signal man, raised a family, and lived in Lock Haven for half a century. He often spoke of a tall Southern soldier, in prison for disobeying orders, who had given him a blanket before going into battle. To the end of his life he breathed the sweet air of the mountains like a prisoner newly set free. He died at seventy-two in 1918, just as another war was beginning.

Chapter 39

As Matthew struggled to remain sane and strong in the prisoner-of-war camp, Colonel Cooper arrived in Richmond to meet with important people. The next day he sat face to face with none other than Jefferson Davis, President of the Confederacy, and several members of his cabinet. He informed them that certain agents under his command had intercepted critical information that required their immediate attention. Instead of remaining near Richmond to defend the city against a rumored Union assault, General Lee had decided to move through the Shenandoah Valley into Pennsylvania. Lee was hoping for a surprise offensive, but Union intelligence was clocking his every move, and the Army of the Potomac was poised and ready. Both armies were gravitating toward a little town called Gettysburg. Should Lee decide to do battle at Gettysburg, Cooper asserted, there would be no element of surprise and no advantage on good ground. Union forces would quickly seize the high ground and gain the power to repulse and defeat.

"I cannot recommend a Pennsylvania campaign at this time," said Cooper with quiet assurance. His face calm and his steel-gray eyes steady, he looked into the face of each man at the table and made eye contact.

"We all know General Lee is a genius when it comes to military strategy, but all the information we've gathered strongly suggests that offensive action in Pennsylvania at this time is ill-advised."

The dignitaries listened politely to what he had to say but with an air of surprise. They knew the man in the white suit was a military strategist with a network of agents gathering useful information. They had been told he was a gifted theoretician who weighed the variables of military maneuvers meticulously to predict their outcome. He played, as it were, a game of chess and he was very good at it. He moved his pieces only after considerable study in the light of all he knew. More than once his advice to generals in the field had proven invaluable. Now he was saying that General Lee, the greatest military leader the South had ever produced, was playing with fire as he flirted with a major engagement in southern Pennsylvania.

"If the North secures a position on high ground and waits for Lee to attack, in a pitched battle the South will lose. And Pickett? You have to watch him. The man can be reckless at times."

"What about Jeb Stuart?" one man asked. "He's a juggernaut of undisputed power, and he's under Lee's command."

"Stuart is good, no doubt about it. But a cavalry assault alone cannot be expected to turn the tide in a battle so complicated as this could be. If Lee's infantry forces attempt to charge uphill, the North entrenched on the hills will mow them down like corn stalks in a cornfield. You can't imagine the number of casualties. Lee's army would be decimated."

Davis and his cabinet were amazed at what Cooper was saying. How could he know so much about Lee's plans? And to announce dogmatically that Lee in all his genius would fail seemed the essence of effrontery. This man sitting before them, a man with impeccable credentials but unknown to any of them except through hearsay, seemed clearly out of line. He was telling them, with only charts and maps to prove his point, to rein in Robert E. Lee, the best of the best. Did he really think he was better qualified to plan a military campaign than Lee? Ludicrous, but they would listen.

Cooper insisted that Lee should remain in Virginia and let the enemy come to him. His remarks sounded reasonable, of course, but in the final analysis they were based on theory. One could view them as argument based on opinion discounting the value of Lee's own thinking and planning. To wait for the enemy to come to him, Lee had already said to Davis, meant giving the Union forces valuable time to regroup, gather strength in numbers, gain momentum, and build morale.

"Keep Lee in Virginia," Cooper was asserting, pointing to his map. "Keep the main forces of Hill and Longstreet nearby and ready to strike in a flanking attack." They listened, and yet in a way they did not listen.

It was too large a proposal for Lee's civilian superiors to act upon. On the heels of a risky maneuver that brought victory at Chancellorsville, Lee had seized the initiative by reorganizing his army and invading enemy territory. Virginia was already picked clean, and he thought he would find ample provisions for his army by moving northward. His maneuvers, he declared, would confuse Northern forces and throw them off balance. In his own good time he would pounce upon them and achieve one defeat after another. The fighting in Pennsylvania could be the turning point of the war.

Lee had convinced Davis, in secret messages, that meeting the enemy on his own ground was better than waiting for him to move. In the June weather he could march his troops into Pennsylvania with little resistance. A showdown between him and General Meade, now commander of the Army of the Potomac, seemed inevitable. And what better place than Pennsylvania? At the eleventh hour Jefferson Davis was unwilling to change the pattern of events that was shaping the future. It was too risky even to try. Besides, Lee was brilliant in battle and would surely chastise the Union army as he had promised. Had he not done that a few weeks ago at Chancellorsville?

Most of the men sitting around the mahogany table paid lip service to the man in white, often nodding their heads in agreement, but did nothing more than talk. Even as he spoke Cooper knew his proposal was being rejected. He left the meeting shaking his head, convinced he would not be able to do anything to change the course of future events. The lumbering war machine had become a living entity, an organism moving on its own, and too powerful to be halted by the men who made it.

The leaders of the Confederacy would follow the general's movements closely but would not interfere. They would wait until three days of slaughter decisively determined the outcome of the crucial battle of the Civil War. Afterwards they would become alarmed, even despondent. But not one of them would admit, either then or in later years, that all of them had been duly warned. Owen Cooper, for his part, would remain silent about the matter for the rest of his life. He had come to Richmond to execute a formidable task, but the opposition was stronger than he had calculated. Despite his power and influence, he had failed. Now he would look into lesser matters before returning home.

2

"We must go to Belle Isle Prison," he said to Jade, "and see if we can obtain the release of Matthew Kingston. If we don't get him out of there now, he could die in the tumult and confusion. I hear that men there are deprived of necessities and dying of disease, malnutrition, and exposure to the elements. Even now Kingston could be sick with diarrhea and slowly starving. They have a way of making a prisoner's life even more miserable when he falls sick. The Quaker could be shunted outside with no shelter."

"More than a hundred Union captives were sent there only last week," Jade replied. "The prison camp was already full, more than full. So where did they put them? When a box is full you can't put no more in it."

"That's what worries me. The place is ripe for violence. Men quarrel and fight when deprived of space. A man can be as easily killed there as dying there. But Kingston could be gone by now. The new policy is to put the objectors on the battlefield to shift for themselves. If they refuse to fight, they can't expect to be fed and housed at public expense. It seems a reasonable policy, I suppose, but it could reap barbaric results."

They rode on through the streets. The day was bright and clear, but the city was congested, noisy, and dirty. From Byrd Street they went southward on Seventh to the James River, turned right on Tredegar Street, passed the Iron Works, and crossed the bridge to the island. They came to the odious camp, flashed their identification at the gatehouse, and entered. It was a gloomy, forbidding place even in the stark sunshine of late June. In addition to the main house they saw a few shacks within the confines of the prison and many tents. Half-naked emaciated men lay listless in the shade of a few trees. The yard was muddy from a heavy shower, but the prisoners didn't seem to notice. In the air was the stench of an overflowing latrine. Some men were digging another.

Cooper and his aide wiped their boots on a mat at the door and went inside the main building. An orderly led them to the office of the chief administrator, the commandant of the prison. He was a pale, paunchy, balding man in glasses too small for his face and hidden behind a large desk piled high with paper work. As he rose from his chair he looked like a mole emerging from its burrow. He introduced himself and extended his hand.

"I am the commander here," he said with not an inkling of pride. "What can I do for you? Your man will have to wait outside."

He took off his glasses and polished the lenses with a handkerchief that needed washing. Beads of sweat stood on his forehead. His face was somber, almost thoughtful, and his right eye twitched.

Jade Scurlock glanced at Colonel Cooper, the man he had sworn to protect, and stepped back into the hallway. He stood outside the door, looking down the dark corridor, his sharp eyes alert for any movement from any direction. In the office the two men huddled over the desk, poring over papers the commandant had retrieved from a file.

With a look of hard intensity on his chiseled features, Cooper appeared to be questioning the captain closely and receiving answers he didn't wish to hear. Matthew Kingston had been released from the prison and assigned to an infantry unit moving northward. By now he would be in a regiment under the general command of Robert E. Lee. Confederate battalions were perhaps near Harrisburg, the riverside capital of Pennsylvania. If they could subdue the defenders and capture the city, it would mean not only another victory but a decisive psychological blow. One soldier in the midst of thousands, Matthew would be hard to find even by a courier.

"I have letters," said Cooper quietly but firmly, "important letters from Kingston's family and pregnant wife. Letters that must reach him as soon as possible. Tell me how they can be delivered."

"Oh, don't worry about that," the commandant replied officiously. "I will have my adjutant forward the letters. I can assure you that in time they will get to the man, if by then he's not already dead."

He was looking at Matthew's prison file, flicking through the documents in the folder. With mild surprise he mumbled, "Some letters in the man's folder, six of them. Seem to be in sealed envelopes."

He drew the envelopes from the file and spread them like an oriental fan on his desktop. They were letters to Catherine, Jeremy, David, Rachel, Jesse, and Anna. An attached note recorded the date and made a plea for fast delivery by persons unknown. Matthew had learned that Southerners regularly came to Richmond looking for Northern relatives taken captive as prisoners of war. He had the presence of mind to write the letters when told he would be leaving for military duty, and he hoped they would fall into the hands of someone able to take them to his family.

3

Owen Cooper was not surprised to find all six of the letters filed away in a folder. Indolence and incompetence ran unchecked in just about every department of the war machine. Added to that was a stultifying indifference, a lack of concern, that pervaded any prison camp. It began with the commandant, who soon lost confidence in running the place properly, and trickled down to the lowest guard and eventually to the prisoners. Every day was taken as it came, every man cautiously looking over his shoulder, looking out for himself and only himself, and the devil take the hindmost.

"I will not leave the messages I have in my possession with you," Cooper asserted. "They could be lost in your files and be found a hundred years from now as historical documents. I'll find a courier for them, and I myself will take those lost six letters to his family and wife in North Carolina."

"Suit yourself," sniffed the commandant, returning the folder without the envelopes to his files. "In these crazy times you could be right about documents getting lost. Happens all the time."

Cooper wished the man good day, turned on his heel and joined Scurlock in the hallway. He left the unproud military officer polishing his spectacles again. They rode across town to a red-brick building, its three stories colorful in the sunlight but somehow shabby. His aide sat in the shade of the cool steps, surveying the activity in the street. Two Confederate soldiers wearing sidearms stopped and looked him over.

"Where's your master, boy?" asked one.

"Boss inside," said Scurlock, refusing to stand.

They hesitated but went on down the dusty street, muttering. The big black man remained seated in the shade, calm as a buddha on a mountain top. He could have swatted them like flies on a tablecloth, but swatting a fly leaves a stain. He didn't want to tangle with them, nor they with him.

Cooper made his way to a drab office with a squeaky floor and unwashed windows. He spent an hour there in tense conference with bureaucrats. He emerged with an air of guarded satisfaction.

"I'm fairly certain," he said as they rode away, "that Kingston will receive his letters from home in three or four days. I persuaded the bigwigs to assign a special courier. Also they will process a hardship discharge for the man. That could take some time even though they stamped *URGENT* on it."

"Do they know even where the man is?" asked Scurlock.

"They assured me they know the general location of his unit, and the courier will be riding that way tonight. I'm hoping the bureaucrats will send him back to Blue Anchor before summer is over, but who knows?"

"Well, that's the big question, Boss. Who knows what them bureaucrats gonna do? They don't know their left hand from their right. Nobody knows from day to day what they gonna do."

Cooper acknowledged Scurlock's cynicism with a chuckle and nod of the head. Then smiling, he replied that one must not lose hope even when dealing with self-important bureaucrats in wartime.

"Can you can really get the army to release him?" Scurlock asked.

"As I said, I hope I can. The record will show that Kingston received no favored treatment. Cause of discharge will be hardship at home. Wife alone in a remote place, you know, about to give birth, and a crop to be harvested."

Chapter 40

Early the next morning the two men left Richmond on their way southward. Their horses were rested and well-fed and sustained a canter mile after mile. The pebbled path beside the railroad, pitted but dry, seemed to glide by under well-shod feet. Moving like that, the trip would require only one night of rest before reaching home. The men would go into Starkville, have a meal and a good night's sleep at the inn there, and get back to Blue Anchor by late afternoon the next day. That would give Cooper plenty of time to visit the Kingstons before the long summer day faded to darkness.

It was drizzling when they rode into the village. A raindrop fell on Cooper's face and cascaded down his cheek. He flicked it away and felt a prickly stubble of beard. He would have to shave before arriving home. As the rain began to fall fast and hard, they reached the "Purple Onion" standing low and broad on the main road. The inn's swinging sign, flecked with water and dirt, offered immediate hospitality. Inside a billboard called their attention to *The Finest Southern Cuisine East of Raleigh—Meats and Seafood, Soups and Stews, Vegetables and Salads—authentic Italian Bread, delicious Desserts, and More (including Barbeque) to Delight the most Discriminating Palate.* In time the men discovered the inn could boast no such abundance; only the most basic of Southern foods were available.

In turbulent times the establishment was losing its suppliers and losing its guests, mainly commercial travelers, and becoming shabby. A room with a large bed and faded wallpaper could be had for a modest fee, and yet the inn had no accommodations for Jade Scurlock. He was a black man and the proprietor catered only to whites. Pressed to explain, the corpulent innkeeper cited laws he had to obey. Scurlock could not be a guest at the "Purple Onion," could not eat in the dining room, could not share a bedroom with a white person, could not sleep in any of the beds reserved for white guests, and could not use the toilets reserved for guests. He would have no problem stabling his horse. The rules did not apply to horses.

When paid extra, however, Tobias Smit was not adverse to giving Jade a clean and comfortable cot in a small storage room. Cooper's husky aide also had a hearty meal of fried catfish, hush-puppies, slaw, potatoes, and iced tea. Even though he ate at the common table in the kitchen, he found the food tasty and satisfying. It was the same as served to Cooper in the dining room. Topping off the fried fish was a platter of pulled pork from the barbecue pit in back. An hour later a scruffy boy with watery eyes and a pimply face, wondering why a big black man was being treated so well, placed the cot in the storage room and two fat bottles of beer on a shelf. With a nervous laugh he said the man could use the outhouse in back if needed. Scurlock drank the beer with gusto, savoring the robust bitter-sweet taste, and used the outhouse. Though the sturdy little cot was too narrow for his bulk, he slept well. When morning came he ate well, but in the kitchen.

2

Their ride home taxed their endurance but was uneventful. The weather was hot and humid, and the horses sweated but were not abused. They were delayed for more than an hour when Scurlock's horse threw a shoe. Fortunately they found a blacksmith nearby who did a skillful job replacing the shoe. Cooper paid him well for his work, and they rode on. Along the way they passed many displaced persons stumbling along the railroad track as the best open and level road they could find. Some appeared to have bedrolls or camping equipment. Others carried bundles on their backs and even pieces of furniture. Little children plodded along with filled gunny sacks. A skinny boy with a club foot and nothing to carry was plucking on a banjo. A pregnant woman, sweating in the heat, sat on shaded ground, leaned against a tree, and rubbed her belly. Farther on Jade's hawk eyes spotted here and there little things people had dropped—a clock too heavy to carry, a teacup with a golden rim, a silver spoon.

As in any war, most segments of the civilian population in the third summer of the Civil War were paying a heavy price. Signs of struggle, deprivation, and sheer confusion were everywhere. Extended families were becoming separated, and children were losing their parents. Charitable organizations, even those lacking adequate resources, directed their efforts to orphans increasing in number. Scalawag preachers, pretending to preach the gospel, attempted to profit from the plight of others by holding open-air meetings and persuading anyone present to give whatever they could. "In these bad times, dig deep in your pockets," the opportunists cried, "and give! Give, dear friends, to those poor wretched souls less fortunate than you. Give what you can and pray for us all! Armageddon is upon us!"

The times were bad, and yet evangelists like Stephen Hawke made them easier for some. He went through the countryside preaching sermons of doom and gloom but also of hope. He spoke with a profound air of conviction, and his listeners hung on every syllable he uttered. When his deep and resonant voice clapped like thunder, some of the ladies fainted. Others, rolling their eyes to heaven, began to speak in unknown tongues. Some of the younger people caught the rhythm of Hawke's exhortations and began to dance in a sort of trance with a jerking motion. All for a time were delivered of any burden that weighed them down, set free of stress and worry.

The two horsemen reviewed all this as they discussed the temper of the times. Then as they came to the plantation once owned by Thomas Bolton and now the property of Owen Cooper, the countryside seemed more prosperous and the people not quite so deprived. A profitable business was in operation, and workers had jobs and were free of want. Food crops, already bought by the government, would soon be harvested. A generous portion would go to every worker to inspire him to work harder for the next harvest. The men rode into the spacious yard fringed with green lawn near suppertime and quickly dismounted.

A servant led the horses to shade and cool water and fodder. The chief cook in Cooper's kitchen, Eileen Norwaite, brought out a bottle of brandy with barrel-shaped glasses. The riders sat in silence on the wide verandah, sipped their brandy, and smoked brightleaf cigars. The man of mystery and his trusted aide had talked quietly along the way and now had little to say. Both were tired. In the still air the blue cigar smoke curled upward to tease the nostrils. Cooper was thinking that after supper he would select another horse and ride over to the Kingstons. They would be happy to hear fresh news about their son. He would not be able to tell them precisely what they wanted to hear, but he could offer them hope. Perhaps he would be able to convince them that in time Matthew would be coming home.

3

Colonel Cooper took a bath after eating and slipped into a fresh suit of clothes. A stable hand brought out a black stallion with a brown mane, and the colonel sprang into the saddle. He was a striking figure as he rode through the village and up the long avenue of live oaks to the Kingston homestead. A harlequin boy in the main road, a merry-andrew, gawked at him as he passed, did a little jig of mockery and amazement, and waved vigorously. Instinctively he knew that a man on a splendid horse was equally splendid. Cooper had not been given an abundance of humor when born on an island, but the boy made him laugh. The Kingstons heard the clatter of hoofs on the hard ground and came into the yard to greet him.

Quickly and without effort he dismounted and walked toward them with a slight limp, a sturdy walking cane in his right hand. Because his day had been a long one with strenuous exertion at times, he was feeling some pain in his right leg. Prefacing his greeting with a ceremonious bow, he opened a saddlebag and produced the precious envelopes. As his neighbors received the letters, he said it was his belief they would see their son again in a few weeks. Certainly in a week or two they would have new correspondence from him. Arrangements had been made with the courier service to pick up his letters and take them to Richmond for delivery in Blue Anchor. The old war wound was throbbing, aching.

When the Kingstons began to tear open their envelopes, calling for the children to come and receive theirs, Cooper told them of their son's release from prison. He wanted the news to sound like good news, but his easy laughter seemed a little forced. When pressed for details, he explained that Matthew was again a reluctant soldier somewhere in northern Virginia with a regiment under the general command of Robert E. Lee. He had been released from prison only to be placed in the front ranks. The new policy decreed that any person refusing to carry a weapon could find himself in the thick of battle without one. Cooper knew that General Lee and his forces were on the move and preparing for battle, but that was classified information not to be divulged to civilians.

"Don't worry," he said, smiling, attempting to make light of the matter. "Matthew will be returning before you finish stacking the hay."

He could sense the uncertainty of the news he was giving them, even its gravity, and so he was trying to reassure his Quaker neighbors. They responded with sighs of relief but with some anxiety.

"Maybe we can't celebrate our son's return just yet," said David Kingston. "My old friend Brandimore, in that blunt way of speaking I always admired, would have said, sizing up the situation, that Matthew has jumped out of the frying pan into the fire."

"Yes, you could say that," Cooper affirmed. "But I'm working to get him home before hostilities begin."

"At least our son is alive," said Rachel, speaking mainly to David. And where there's life there's hope. We do thank thee, Mr. Cooper, and our daily prayers go with thee."

"Yes, we are grateful for all you've done," David added.

"It's only a matter of time now. Bureaucratic wheels are creaky and slow at best. Your son will be coming home, believe me."

"I do believe thee," Rachel asserted. "I must believe thee."

The man in white, who had the ability to read the pulse of perilous times and seemed to have powers beyond ordinary mortals, was really neither omnipotent nor omniscient. He didn't know that Matthew's regiment was already in Pennsylvania. Lee's Army of Northern Virginia had met little resistance and was moving northward faster than anyone expected. His forces would soon engage the Army of the Potomac, led by General George Meade, near a pleasant and pretty little town named Gettysburg.

4

Encamped in the rolling fruit-orchard country of southern Pennsylvania, Matthew read the letter from Catherine over and over. He had not heard of Major Bolton's death. As a teenager he had never liked Richard. The youth had been too proud, too haughty for his own good, but his untimely death as a man in his prime was tragic. Catherine gave the usual account of Major Bolton dying in battle as a hero, for that was the only account she knew. No one in Blue Anchor, with the one exception of Owen Cooper, knew the cavalry officer was mortally injured before the Battle of Chancellorsville began. No one anywhere, except for a handful of military inspectors, knew the young officer had been thrown to the ground and trampled by his own horses. The official report said he suffered a bullet to the neck, but the bullet actually pierced the neck of his mount. Only a few cavalrymen, in full gallop in dust and smoke, had seen the incident. They did not live to talk about it. Matthew was privy only to the heroic account given by Catherine. Had he known the exaggerated glory embellishing the man's death was false, it would have saddened his senses as much as the gore.

He wanted to reply immediately to her letter and those of his parents. He was of a mind to send all of them a long and personal response to let them know he was alive and well and no longer in prison. Perhaps he could tell them, without fear of censorship, that he was bivouacking with Confederate troops poised to do combat. He was thinking that maybe he could do that if he didn't mention a particular location. However, when he asked the captain about sending letters home, he was told it would not be possible. No letter from any soldier, even those of high rank, would be leaving the encampment any time soon. Only the most trusted couriers would ride out on fast horses with dispatches in a special pouch. Rumor had it that a Union army was in the area and ready to fight. It seemed inevitable the two armies would clash. Security was therefore tight.

Early in the morning at the end of June in 1863, the day Matthew was able to read his mail from home, a contingent of Confederate troops approached Gettysburg on the old Chambersburg Road. They had left camp at Cashtown and were marching toward the town in search of badly needed shoes. All the men knew they were in enemy territory but marched along in lively rhythm, breathing deeply the fresh and fragrant air in balmy weather. Their plan was to enter Gettysburg, loot every store they could find, and return peacefully to Cashtown. Their leader, Brigadier General James Pettigrew, was admiring the high morale of his troops when he began to sense danger. Prudently he halted his men and rode on to Seminary Ridge to get a clear view of the town and the land around it.

In the distance he could see the blue-gray softness of hills and ridges running north and south to form a basin. Between the ridges stretched fertile fields and lush pastures of vivid green. In the center, like a skillfully precise sketch on a drawing pad, lay the streets of Gettysburg. A mile and a half west of the town, meandering through a grassy swale, was a sluggish little stream the locals called Willoughby Run. Riding near the stream, the general's scouts reported a column of Union cavalry closing in fast. Under strict orders not to initiate a battle, Pettigrew managed to get his troops back to Cashtown without incident. There he gave a detailed description of the encounter to his commander, Lt. General A. P. Hill.

The next day, to investigate the arrival of the Union cavalrymen and gather important information, two divisions left Cashtown for Gettysburg. At five o'clock in the morning on July 1, 1863, in the dawn haze of a summer day, they tramped eastward. When the two divisions met only minimal resistance, two brigades were ordered to occupy Gettysburg. Unknown to the Confederates, the town was already occupied by two brigades of Union soldiers commanded by General John Buford. They were deployed northwest of town just east of Willoughby Run and ready for battle. The first ranks of Confederate skirmishers trod through fields of wheat and across pastures with guns blazing. The Union troopers, near the creek and protected by rocks and trees, trained their seven-shot Spencer rifles on the enemy and waited. As the Rebels splashed through Willoughby Run, the water glinting in the sun, they were hit by a terrific burst of small-arms fire and artillery salvos. The ferocity of Buford's attack sent the Rebel soldiers reeling back across the creek to reorganize and regroup for another assault. A minor skirmish was quickly turning into a major battle. The battle spawned fighting that raged for three days.

Chapter 41

Ugly times have plagued America in more than two hundred years, but the Civil War brought the worst of times. It was human slaughter on a grand scale, dwarfing in its savagery all that went before or after. It was a time Americans would like to forget but cannot forget. It shook the nation and shakes it still. During those three horrific days at Gettysburg, young men who might have become great leaders died in agony before their time.

The fighting began on the morning of July 1 west of the town. By late afternoon Union forces were in pell-mell retreat. Too many of their officers had caught Rebel bullets in the head and chest and died. The first high-ranking officer to fall was Major General John F. Reynolds, commander of the Union First Corps. One of the ablest of Federal generals, he was killed at the edge of McPherson's Woods as he led his troops into the jaws of Rebel fire. The battle on that first day raged for hours.

As night fell the sounds of conflict slowed to a murmur. Only sporadic musketry, like firecrackers going off, could be heard. Exhausted soldiers of both armies collapsed beside stone walls and fences, rifles in their laps, and slept. In the fields and woods they sprawled. In the streets and alleys of the town they lay. Slouching against any wall they could find, they sought rest and sleep as they waited for the fighting to resume on the morrow.

2

In camp a few miles from the action, Matthew had been assigned a tent so small that when he lay down to sleep that first stuffy evening in July, his feet protruded. He found it necessary to curl up on his side, using a thin blanket as a pillow. The night was warm and still and the ground was hard. He could hear as he dropped off to sleep the mournful strains of a tortured harmonica in counterpoint to a banjo. Blending with the music and becoming part of it, were muffled sounds that seemed to come from a distance. Troops and their equipment were on the road, moving with precision into position. Two armies not fully aware of each other were preparing to clash by first light.

Matthew slept fitfully for an hour and then like a stone all through the night. He awoke to a misty morning in summer to stand in line for a field breakfast of grits, bacon, hoecake, and coffee. Commonly the soldiers had eggs with their bacon and grits, but in Pennsylvania and on the move eggs were scarce. As they were sitting down to eat, a messenger galloped through the camp with news of a skirmish that had quickly become a battle. The crucial combat of the Civil War, the Battle of Gettysburg, was already in its second day. With sustained ferocity unusual even for that war, it would drag on for three days. Coupled with Vicksburg's collapse in the west, the battle would become the turning point of the war favoring the North. Casualties for General Lee would number between 25,000 and 28,000. Some of his men would live to do battle another day, but never again would the Army of Northern Virginia launch a major offensive.

On that first day Confederate soldiers drove the Union army back to a strong defensive position on Culp's Hill and Cemetery Ridge south of the town. They also occupied Gettysburg and Seminary Ridge to the west. The front was as wide as three miles along Cemetery Ridge and heavily fortified. On the second day Lee attacked the Union flanks, aiming his main assault at the left flank. The fighting was fierce with many casualties on both sides, but Meade held on to Cemetery Ridge. The assault on his right flank at Culp's Hill also failed to dislodge him. His forces were dug in on high ground and determined to remain there. On the third fateful day, Lee ordered General George Pickett to charge the Union lines in the center with as many men as he could muster. Pickett sent 15,000 infantry soldiers across open terrain into ferocious enemy fire from a fixed position. They fell like blades of grass under an iron heel. Fewer than 6,000 survived the repulse.

Lee's attempt to weaken the enemy with Stuart's cavalry, which had arrived the night before, also failed. As Owen Cooper had predicted at Richmond, Gettysburg was a terrible defeat for the South. It was a logistical disaster of biblical proportion, and it came in the same week that Vicksburg fell to General Grant. Unprecedented losses brought suffering and humiliation not just to Lee and his loyal army, but to all citizens in the South. The summer of 1863 had become a time of crisis. If it can ever be said that anyone wins a war, the North at great cost was now poised to win this one. The pundits were already saying the North would soon end the war.

3

On July 1, the regiment Matthew Kingston had been assigned to did not enter the fray. The opposing armies maneuvered for position on that day, the Southern forces taking the town and the Northerners securing a position on high ground south of town. On July 2 the fighting grew more intense, with Lee confidently attacking the enemy's right flank, while Longstreet went for the left near the wheat field and peach orchard. The South fought hard on that second day but failed to break the North's defensive line. It remained intact and without a single breach when the day was over.

Many of the soldiers in Matthew's infantry unit were killed that day even though they fought with courage, verve, and tenacity. As their ranks thinned, the Quaker pacifist was ordered to grab a rifle and fight. When he refused, the captain quickly issued another order.

"Shoot him!"

Then as three rifles were leveled at the young man, the riflemen waiting for the order to fire, the officer had second thoughts and issued a third command. If the able-bodied Quaker would not bear arms, he would care for the wounded on the battlefield or die.

"They also serve who bear stretchers!" the captain shouted. "It's more deadly than running with a weapon, but you will do it now!"

Matthew reasoned that by obeying the order he would be helping his fellow man rather than doing violence against him. He knew the wounded and dying needed all the help anybody could give them. Then suddenly he found himself in the midst of battle, removing broken bodies as fast as he could to a field station behind the lines. It was hard and hazardous work, but altogether necessary, and he could do it without compromising his beliefs. He was exhausted when that second day at Gettysburg was over but had survived unhurt. Though every muscle ached with fatigue and his body cried out for rest, he was not able to sleep.

On that last day, July 3, his regiment became part of Pickett's charge. Stalwart but hapless soldiers marched across an open field and up the slopes of Cemetery Ridge. Knowing they were easy targets, but knowing also they could do nothing about it, they ignored the enemy fire. With no weapon to encumber movement, Matthew went with them. In minutes soldiers around him were hit by enemy fire and falling, shattered like clay ducks in a shooting gallery. Through the acrid smoke he could see blurred figures in gray and blue firing point blank into sweating, distorted faces. Men in the prime of life, boys not fully grown, old men pushing sixty spun like whirling dervishes when shot. Ripped apart and spinning, they were flung to the ground, their guts staining the grass and dirt red. Most of them, thrashing in agony, held on to life as long as they could.

The air was full of sound, a farrago of discordant sound, but Matthew could hear bullets whizzing close to his head. He could hear them splat with a dull thud into human flesh, and then the screech of artillery shells drowned all else. He was forced to decide in a moment whether a man was dead or alive before lifting him to a stretcher. If a fallen soldier cried out, he and his assistant (a young man he knew only as Tom) tried to render aid. If he did not cry out and lay still, they judged him dead and went looking for the living. The corpses cluttering the battlefield became a hindrance. So many young Americans died that day, falling on top of the stricken when they themselves were struck, it took many hours to clear the battlefield. Hundreds who might have been saved by rescue teams such as Matthew's were hidden beneath dead bodies. They either suffocated or bled to death.

Facing impossible odds, only a few of the Southern troops reached the top of the ridge. Before they could feel triumphant, before they could tussle with the enemy or even level a rifle at him, they were killed or captured. Fewer than half the original force managed to survive. Lee with his usual show of magnanimity took full responsibility for the slaughter.

"All this has been my fault," he mumbled over and over. "All this was my fault. I must surely take all the blame." Racked by utter dismay at so colossal a failure, the general was sincerely distraught.

Owen Cooper had said Lee would lose and had spoken of Pickett with words of warning. General Longstreet, who initially opposed the charge as the height of folly, eventually acquiesced. If Longstreet had firmly stood his ground to explain his position, Pickett's charge might not have happened. If the Confederate leaders in Richmond had listened to Cooper, the battle itself might not have happened. General Lee had listened only to primitive instinct and his own voice. The force of the man's personality trampled reason and left it bleeding. The men of state in Richmond were obliged to share some of the blame, but none did.

4

By late afternoon on that third day both sides, bloodied and weary, began sorting out the wounded and getting them to shelter. Earlier that same day the white flags of truce appeared over Vicksburg on the Mississippi, signaling the North had won. Even though much work was needed to bring order out of chaos, the long siege was over. Meanwhile at Gettysburg, cleanup squads picked up the muskets left on the field to be used again. They fitted each weapon with its bayonet and stuck the rifle into the ground. More than 26,000 tall rifles, standing in gaunt relief against a menacing sky, made the battlefield look like a ravaged forest. Casualties on both sides were staggering, at least 46,000 and perhaps as many as 51,000. The full number of Confederate casualties numbered at least one third of Lee's army.

On that third horrendous day Matthew came through without a scratch. Bullets whizzed within inches of his ears but never struck him. One came so close to the back of his neck it tore his collar. Another creased the heel of his boot. Tom was not so lucky. He caught a bullet in the face and spun to the ground, his young blood spurting skyward.

"If I don't make it," he whispered, "tell my papa I died in the midst of battle doing my job. And tell him this, please . . . dying ain't so hard." He was wrong. Dying is hard, especially for the young. Any leaf turning yellow in autumn cries out in silent pleading for sap.

Matthew carried his assistant on his left shoulder to the medical tent, stepping over contorted bodies on the scarlet ground but not attempting to duck the bullets. The gray shirt his mother and wife had made for him turned wet and smelly and red. A sharp tang of something monstrous and ugly was in the air. Caustic battlefield smoke, hanging thick and blue-gray like swamp gas in the early morning, burned his nostrils. A cloud of vivid green vapor, its origin unknown, whirled, broke, and vanished. The reek was so strong he found it hard to breathe. Gasping for breath, he found a cot and placed the limp body on it. The boy's blonde hair, matted with blood, glistened like ripe strawberries in sunlight. A large, black horsefly settled on his forehead and moved down his nose to his lips. Matthew flicked it away. In the heat and rampant confusion, he was not able to learn Tom's last name.

5

On July 4, 1863 General Pemberton and 29,000 defeated Confederates surrendered to General Grant at Vicksburg. On that same day, realizing his battered army could no longer remain in Pennsylvania and rightly believing that Meade would not pursue, Lee began wearily to withdraw to Virginia. From Seminary Ridge a long wagon train of wounded men and supplies moved slowly in the late afternoon southwest and southward. Lee's infantry and artillery fell in behind, increasing the column to great length. Military crews loaded into wagons as much equipment as possible, and yet a huge amount remained on the battlefield for the victor. As the defeated army trudged in bitter withdrawal under a serene sky, storm clouds began to appear in the western quadrant and claps of thunder rolled across the hills.

A heavy rain began to fall, nature weeping as in pastoral elegies for the loss of so many gallant souls. Even though the downpour soaked the retreating soldiers, tired to the bone and now wet to the skin, it did little to cleanse the good land of carnage. The rain turned the ground muddy and the heavy wagons sank into the mud and made for slow and arduous movement. Infantry with shoddy boots too large or too small sloshed in the mud and suffered blisters on wet and tired feet. In later years the rolling wheat fields near Gettysburg became a national monument where tourists for more than a century found the bones of fingers, arms, legs, and sometimes a skull. A little girl, visiting the dedicated ground in 1968, heard the tortured cries of the dying.

In the small town after the third day, thousands of wounded men filled churches, barns, and private homes. Union medical teams, exhausted by three days of bloody battle, were left with an overwhelming number of Union and Confederate soldiers needing care. These were the men too severely wounded to move southward in retreat. Even with the help of citizens and Confederate surgeons, who had remained behind to care for their wounded, the situation seemed hopeless. However, medical personnel soon arrived with equipment and supplies and established a hospital with clean beds east of Gettysburg. When a soldier was no longer in critical condition, he was sent by rail to a permanent hospital in Philadelphia or Baltimore. General Lee made it back to Virginia to fight another day. The double file of walking wounded, trudging in sullen silence across alien ground, extended several miles. Matthew Kingston, tired and hungry and shaken by the slaughter, by the promiscuous heap of carnage he had seen and smelled and touched, walked with them and shared the long agony of the march. The aching men had heard that on the battlefield this young Quaker, a Southerner like themselves, had behaved with honor, dignity, and bravery. All of them to a person accepted him as one of their own, and yet never in his life had Matthew felt so much alone.

The effects of the battle tormented the citizens of Gettysburg and all of Pennsylvania. For a long time after the two armies left to wreak havoc in other places, the routines of daily life were not in tandem. A poignant account of the aftermath was recorded by Sallie Myers. She had grown up in Gettysburg and had lived there all her life. During the summer of 1863, at the age of twenty-one, she was a teacher in the public schools. Rather than hide in her cellar when the Confederates occupied her town, she went out to comfort the wounded soldiers in the Catholic and Presbyterian churches.

"On the pews and floors lay men in agony," she wrote. "The groans of the suffering and dying were heart-rending. I knelt beside the first man near the door and asked what I could do. 'Nothing,' he replied, 'I am going to die.' I went outside the church and leaned against it and cried. The wounded man died on Monday, July 6."

Less than a year after the battle that placed her hometown in the history books, her brother David Myers, a private in the 87th Pennsylvania Infantry, was captured as the Wilderness Campaign began. The date was May 6, 1864 and the wild flowers were already in bloom. Strong and brave and lucky to be alive, David Myers was sent to Andersonville Prison in Georgia, notorious for its harshness. He died there a few months later on Tuesday, September 27, 1864. The official record does not show the cause of death. Unofficially he died of disease and malnutrition. The day was warm and sunny in Georgia, and some of the trees were just beginning to show the colors of fall. In Pennsylvania near Gettysburg a soft morning haze cloaked the hills.

Chapter 42

"It's only a matter of time," Owen Cooper had said, speaking to the Kingstons after returning from Richmond. "Matthew will be coming home before you finish stacking the hay." He gave them hope they would see their son again, even assurance, but with a show of confidence he didn't feel. Cooper was an honorable man and a man of influence, but he was helpless before untoward events that had taken on a life of their own. Though insensate and mindless, they seemed to move with purpose and direction on a scale beyond human understanding. Only time and circumstance would stop their movement through levels of horror to reach calm and peace.

In a scheme involving thousands, those awful events could not be expected to notice the welfare of one young man. So Matthew Kingston, slated to return home on a hardship discharge, endured the most deadly battle ever fought on this continent and survived without bearing arms and without injury. Coming through the deadly conflict alive, he told himself, was clearly a miracle and proof that his God had protected him. Trudging southward with Lee's battered troops to safety in Virginia and not pursued by a large enemy force was also a miracle.

Thousands of ragged, wounded, exhausted, and hurting soldiers walked away from Gettysburg without fear of being chased by Northern troops. After the war, politicians and pundits chastised General Meade for not pursuing Lee's army and finishing it off. Had he done so, they claimed, he could have helped to end the war much sooner. They didn't know that sheer exhaustion, an inability to move, hampered Meade's troops by the thousands. Plainly speaking, the men were too tired to move and too shocked by the horror of it all. Only desperation and a fear of more slaughter drove General Lee's men to move. Matthew came through the agony unhurt physically but with emotional scars that made him somber before his time.

At camp in northern Virginia, he scribbled in black ink with a scratchy pen a letter to Catherine. For days he had carried the crumpled paper in his rucksack, and now he struggled to make his words legible. In a calm and sad voice he spoke of his burning experience on the battlefield, of the thousands who had died at Gettysburg, and particularly of Tom. He wanted to speak truthfully of what he had gone through but was careful not to alarm her with vivid details. She would be pleased to know he survived the nightmare in one piece, but with a sorrowful heart. The bloody, visceral, violent death of Tom, and the mindless slaughter of so many brave soldiers, rent him, he said to her, as lightning splits a tree. The whole experience came back to him as he thought of what to say in the letter. Prudently he spoke vaguely of the stinking battlefield, the blood and gore and violence.

Though he wanted to speak of the full experience, he would not give his loving wife more cause to worry. By God's will and some good luck, he asserted, trying to sound cheerful and positive, he remained whole in body and mind. He had run the gamut of the brutal ordeal without visible wounds. The hurt inside, the sadness mingling with fury, he mentioned only in passing. He confided that even though he had raged against mankind that terrible day, his God had forgiven him and protected him. In future, he said to her in closing, he would put down the rage and replace it with gentle compassion. But the healing, he told himself as he sealed the letter, could take a long time.

In North Carolina and particularly in Blue Anchor, the third summer of the Civil War was hot and humid though with little rain. Except for a few days when the skies opened in late afternoon, and the cooling downpour made gullies in the sandy soil, the roads with ruts from heavy wheels were dusty. Even so, summer for many of the people in the village was easier than other seasons and a time to enjoy life if one could. It was also a time to look after those who couldn't. So when Matthew Kingston refused to pay the tax and rode away in May of 1863, leaving behind his wife and daughter, the Quakers in the community went out of their way to enact little kindnesses to make life easier for Catherine. Everyone knew she was "in the family way" and would soon reach the end of her term, but the head of the family when the big event came would be faraway and facing the ugly reality of war. When he would return was anyone's guess.

2

Near the end of June, six weeks after Matthew's departure, a figure as thin as a shadow appeared in the yard and called Catherine's name. Her father had gone to the open market with Emily. He had repaired an old baby buggy the Kingstons had given him and had attached large wheels for the uneven ground. When Jeremy placed her in the contraption and pushed her briskly along, the child screamed with delight. So when the dark apparition appeared in the yard calling her name, Catherine was alone in the house with no companion nearby. Taught by the times to be cautious, she stood behind the partly opened door and peered outside. The figure did not move.

Apprehensive but curious, she stepped onto the porch and looked into the yard. The man called her name again, walking in a half circle as he did so. Though she was now only a few feet from him, he didn't appear to see her. At a glance she had recognized her visitor as Harvey Heckrodt, their friend of many years. He was a free man but had once been owned by her father and before that by a German immigrant whose name he had taken. Prematurely old and half blind, he ceased the half-circle walking and stood very still. In his hand he held a small basket of ripe tomatoes.

"We want you to have these," he replied. "The missus done said, 'Git over there with them tomatoes 'fore they rot, and don't lose yer way comin' home again.' So I hope you'll take 'em, Miz Catherine, and like 'em. They good tomatoes, ripe and juicy. I know yer papa is gonna like 'em."

Catherine placed a hand on his thin shoulder to reassure him, and took the basket. She thanked him sincerely and asked about his family. Looking downward, he scraped his foot in the sand and replied "jus' fine, Miz Catherine, jus' fine." Then after a pause he shook his head and spoke softly of plans to move northward and freedom.

"But Harvey," said Catherine, her oval face wearing a frown of concern. "Surely you must know you're already free and have been for a long time. My father just won't hear of this. You and Susan and the children don't belong to us, nor to anybody. You were given your freedom a long time ago. You don't have to go looking for freedom in some other place. Please reconsider, old friend, I beg you."

"Well, thank you much for yore interest, Miz Catherine, but we done decided. We 'spect to go north along the shore wit' a large group. No one is likely to stop us coz no one seems to care no more."

"People do care, Harvey. We care."

"I know, and I thank you again. But for a long time I feared bein' sold again, and not long ago them rascals come to my place and threw me and my family out and threatened to sell us all, they did. I wan' some peace of mind, y'know, 'fore I go to that golden shore."

He tipped the brim of his ragged hat, turned on his heel, and began to walk away. Catherine knew there was little she could say to help him change his mind. In unsettled times, he and his family would join the displaced and trek along dusty roads in the hot sun to another place hoping for a better life. For many desperate people the North had become the promised land, a place of milk and honey where halos rested on rainbows. To get to that favored place with his wife and family and a few treasured possessions was Harvey's dream. He would find a way to support his family when he got there. It was a dream shared by many others, and for many it quickly lost its luster.

Day after day they moved through the countryside, these refugees of a an insufferable war. Dazed and confused and hungry, they made their way northward living off the land. They were farmers who had lost their land and their livelihood, slaves without a master seeking security and freedom, former slaves like Harvey, half-mad deserters who had walked away from their military units, young and old, black and white, civilians in tattered clothes, and soldiers in motley. All were on the move, blinking in the hard sunlight, trekking northward with wavering hope, looking for a rainbow and gold.

Heavy with child and now heavy of heart, Catherine returned to the porch and sat down on the steps. In the distance she could see her father returning with little Emily. A gunnysack bulging with potatoes was slung over his shoulder. In the child's buggy was a bag of lima beans.

"We didn't find very much at the market," he said with an air of disappointment, "but Emily had a good time."

The child was gurgling and sputtering "Ma Ma!" and raising her arms to be lifted from the buggy. She was wholesome and happy, clean and chubby in spite of the short rations dictated by the times. She was unaware of evil in the land, and she didn't know that every day, regardless how gray, she gave her mother internal joy. That sustaining joy made the woman's longing and worry easier to bear.

"Old Harvey was here," said Catherine sadly. "He plans to move north along the coast and won't hear of anything else."

"I know," replied Jeremy with a sigh. "I met him on the road. Urged him to reconsider but couldn't talk him out of it."

"I tried the same but he wouldn't budge. His mind is made up."

"He's been thinking about it for a long time, ever since the war started."

"He grew old too fast and he worries too much, even more than I do."

"Maybe it's with good reason, Katie. A band of no-good varmints came one night and ran him out of his house and threatened to sell his whole family farther south in spite of his papers. He's been a wreck ever since."

"Come inside," urged Catherine, changing the subject and snuggling the baby to make her laugh. "I'll put these potatoes and that bag of beans away for now. Then later we'll have some good eating."

3

A few days after the Battle of Gettysburg, the community of Blue Anchor heard all about it. Colonel Cooper rode over to Darboy's store with a full account. Earlier Leo Mack, making his daily rounds, had broadcast snippets of newspaper articles he had seen. The news that Vicksburg on the Mississippi had fallen to General Grant after a long siege came later. Both were regrettable disasters for the South. In several meetings the Quaker elders agreed the war could not last much longer. Two crucial military campaigns, collapsing in defeat at the same time, had brought the Confederacy to its knees. Yet the war went on, the Rebels ignoring hardship and fighting fiercely.

Into late summer of 1863 it seemed to all concerned that the South was losing the war and teetering on the brink of economic collapse. Federal armies had destroyed factories and foundries and railroads. The infrastructure of a sound economy was in chaos. The transport system and the distribution of goods had ceased to work, and commercial activity was grinding to a halt. Everyone knew that inflation was out of control and running rampant. The Confederate dollar had depreciated in a drastic and alarming spiral downward. Before the war began Richard Bolton paid a few pennies for the candy his stooge Swope ate by the handful in Jacob Darboy's general store. The same candy, if available at all, would have cost in 1863 several Confederate dollars. A year earlier most of the people in Blue Anchor had resorted to bartering. Only Colonel Cooper had money to pay his workers, but that too was hurt by inflation and rapid devaluation.

As August came with muggy weather and warm winds from the sea, the village people went about their daily lives as usual. Any conversation, however, always came around to the war and the fallen. Many young men had gone off to war, including the three sons of Samuel Bradshaw. A shocking number would not return. Two of the Bradshaw brothers fought and died at Gettysburg. The third was killed in a skirmish near the coast when Confederate defenders were overwhelmed by Union gunboats and driven inland. The husband and brother of Olga Hannaford had fallen also at Gettysburg. Samuel was told his sons died as gallant heroes, and every soul in the village mourned their passing. Olga heard only that her loved ones were missing. Peter Bookbinder was also missing in action and so was Oliver Hatcher. Did that mean they too were dead? The summer weather was fair in Blue Anchor, but in every household clouds of gloom shut out the sun.

Leo Mack, tinker and talker, went from house to house in his old wagon reporting news that was mostly horrific. His faithful dog Sparky, a constant companion for more than a decade, was now dead and the man was alone. He had found that Cooper was privy to special news from time to time, and so he frequently went to the old Bolton spread to pick up what he could. The innovative planter believed the more people knew about current events, the better for the welfare of all concerned, and so he was happy to have Mack publish unclassified news that came to him. Classified information, anything deemed undesirable for civilians to know, Cooper kept to himself. Working together, the two of them reported the outcome of recent battles and kept the casualty lists current.

Between their monthly and quarterly meetings, Quaker men often discussed events at the general store. Like the barbershops in larger towns, the store had become a gathering place for men. The women were expected to concern themselves with matters of the house, but of course they also talked about the war any time they met. The belief that sensitive women prone to hysteria had to be shielded from things so ugly as war had yielded to the moment and the times, and was going out of fashion. Rumor held that some women were disguising themselves as men and going off to fight. A Raleigh newspaper reported that doctors were amazed to find that a wounded soldier, shot in the stomach and dying, was a woman. Other women risked their lives and distinguished themselves as nurses. A few served as spies. The women knew as much about the war and the setbacks suffered by the South as the men. Certainly they suffered as much, or more, when a loved one was killed. And they worried more than the men about what their children would eat for the next meal. The adversity spawned by the war, especially in the South, brought suffering to women as well as men and even the children.

A newspaper reported that many children in the South were not getting enough to eat and were dying of malnutrition even as they labored on hardscrabble farms to bring in a crop. Other children as young as nine or ten worked in the mills and factories to sustain the war effort. A ten-year-old was asked why he was not in school. Did he prefer to work rather than go to school to learn reading and writing and arithmetic?

"I would like to learn to read," he replied, "but how can I when I'm working all the time? I even have to work at night sometimes."

Other children went to war and fought as soldiers or served as drummer boys in the thick of battle. Most of them did not survive. Many died on the battlefield and many more died of disease. The drummer boys were the first to go. Any boy with a fife and drum was a good target for the enemy.

Chapter 43

In the Heartwood house rations were not as plentiful as in the Kingston house. Cooper had fallen into the habit of supplying his friends with necessities even when they protested. When invited, he came sometimes for dinner and often brought rich foods impossible for them to acquire. He wanted to bring a good bottle of wine to enhance the taste of the food but prudently declined to do so, knowing that Quakers drank no alcohol of any kind.

"I'm an islander," he said with a wry grin as they chatted over dinner, "and islanders, as you must know, have a need to converse with intelligent people. It's the only way for us to know the larger world. Not only that, but I enjoy your company. I hope you will practice, as I know you will, a bit of kindness and tolerance toward a lonely man. Until I find a wife and start a family, you will have to put up with me."

"Oh, I can help you with that," said David with a chuckle, reading Cooper's remarks as a joke. I know three or four comely widows who might show a bit of interest."

"Then of course you must introduce me!" Cooper replied, laughing.

The planter, businessman, government agent, and military strategist was speaking with tongue in cheek but not joking. Rachel had heard that he was seeking a wife in Raleigh, the state's capital. She thought he was too old even to think about marriage but would not judge him.

The stories Cooper told delighted the men, Jeremy and David. But the women, Rachel and Catherine, were never quite at ease in his presence and wondered why. The man was not a Quaker, not even a Christian so far as they knew, and yet in classic Christian tradition he seemed eager to help those less fortunate than himself. Except when relaxing at home, he wore white clothing, a dark hat, a slender black tie, and black alligator boots as a badge of identity. At all times he rode a splendid black stallion with a brown mane. He was dashing on horseback, chivalrous, and masculine but didn't seem unduly proud. Perhaps the islander made the women uncomfortable without even knowing it. As they thought about it, they decided he was a lonely man and no threat to anyone.

The sprawling mansion had no family to make it a home, no children to run and play in its hallways, no female voice to chide the children. And so Cooper, the women reasoned, developing their theory, went from his comfortable but cold house to the warmth of a home. When he was not busy with arcane projects as some kind of agent, he visited the Kingstons regularly, and they welcomed him warmly. Because their home was missing a family member, he became something of a substitute though vastly more experienced than Matthew. He was a reservoir of good stories and told them well. Jeremy encouraged him to talk about his war experience, but when that happened the ladies excused themselves and left the room.

At the Heartwood dwelling where the tall clock in the corner ticked and ticked, tolling each hour of every day with chimes that counted the hours, the family prepared for another arrival. Though the infant would come wailing into a very imperfect world, the little boy or girl would not go lacking and Catherine was confident he or she would flourish. As her pregnancy came closer and closer to term, she felt more and more complete. She was happy in her condition and yet sad at the same time. She needed her husband safe at home, not somewhere in a camp or on a battlefield. Her soul as she waited for him to return seemed to be sleeping, but at times it would awaken to open the gates of memory and let her relive the joys of childhood, courtship, and the day she married. Also indefatigable Jesse and sprightly Anna managed on most days to keep her spirits from sagging. On this day they came asking about firewood.

"You wanna get in a good supply for winter," said Jesse, "and do it 'fore cold weather comes. August ain't too early and this is a fine day to do it."

"They know all about that," Anna scolded. "You don't have to tell them stuff they already know. They know to gather wood before winter comes, and plenty of it. They don't have logs from Bupee's cabin like we do."

"Oh, yes, we know," laughed Jeremy, "and I've been planning to do it for sometime now. We need to hitch Peg to that cart in your barn and stack as much wood on it as we can."

"I can take Peg and hitch her to the gig," Jesse volunteered, "or I can make that old long-headed mule do some work now that plowing's done. Just me and Anna can do it. We ain't afraid to go to the swamp in summer."

"I don't know," said Catherine, "I don't think it's a good idea, you and Anna alone on the road and in the swamp. Runaways are known to be there, all kinds of people, crazy people. I worry even when Papa goes there. I still remember how scared I was one night in the swamp in pitch-black darkness. A violent storm too, but I won't elaborate."

"I wouldn't let them go alone either," said Jeremy with dry amusement. "A ghost might grab the littlest and most talkative even in the day time, even in the middle of a sunny day like this!"

He made a face like a monster, howled like a banshee, and lunged at Anna. The little girl screamed above high C and skipped away.

"Papa, you're awful!" chided Catherine in mock alarm.

"Oh, she knows I'm only joshing. Don't you Anna?"

"No, I do not know!" the child replied emphatically, pouting just a little and keeping her distance.

"We can take the trap and have plenty of room," laughed Jesse. "And the mule can pull it coz that old mule is stronger than Peg."

So in the middle of an August afternoon two children and a round little man went searching for firewood to be cut to size, dried, and burned for winter heat. Catherine Kingston, heavy with child and feeling lazy, remained at home with Emily. As the baby slept, her mother read Byron's "She Walks in Beauty" to bolster her emotional strength. The poem reminded her of that magical evening when Matthew draped a fleecy white shawl over her shoulders, asking her to look into the fine old mirror in the Kingston parlor. "Look at thyself!" he had murmured. "Thine eyes have seen the glory!" She longed for the glory again. Why did it have to pass so fast?

2

A breeze rose from behind them as the mule pulled the cart along the road that went into and through the swamp. They came to the entrance marked by the bay tree, entered the tangled and wondrous swamp, and went onward for about a mile. Jeremy made a mental note to gather on leaving the swamp some of the aromatic bay leaves for cooking. On either side of the road, as they got deeper in the morass, they saw desolation left by armies passing through. Fires had been kindled along the gray road. Dead trees had been chopped down to feed the fires. Blackened tree trunks stood gaunt and menacing in the cinder-covered ground. Anna shuddered perceptibly, frightened by the thought of Jeremy's gloomy ghost suddenly reaching out to grab her. Jesse laughed and called her fraidy cat. Refusing to break down and cry, she scolded him. When Jeremy took her side, Jesse was silent.

An eerie pale-green light inside the swamp, caused by a thick canopy of trees shutting out the sky, put both of the children on edge. Insects, dark purple and yellow, skimmed across the black water beside the road. The cool breeze, not able to penetrate the thick growth, remained outside. The air was pungent with damp and decay. A rich, elemental odor came in whiffs, and they could almost taste it. The heavy silence of the place was oppressive. Nothing stirred in the swamp except for a bird or two. A snowy egret, white as an angel, winged its way along the canal. Nearby high on a limb of a crooked tree a red-tailed hawk looked down with raised crest and keen eyes. The hawk screamed, suddenly splitting the eerie silence and startling the intruders. Glaring in their direction and screeching hreeeeee! . . . hreeeeee! the flustered bird seemed to be judging them.

"That sounds like a wagon wheel scraping rocks," said Jeremy.

"Or like fingernails on a blackboard!" offered Jesse.

"I'm not afraid," whimpered Anna. "There's not one single ghost in this place, not one single ghost! That's only an old bird of prey."

"Well, pray he don't get you!" her brother taunted. "You shiver like a little girl before a big lizard!"

"Don't say that!" Anna shrieked.

Sensing she was genuinely afraid, Jesse relented. "Well, I think this is one dreary old place. Let's get to work and fill the wagon. I don't like this swamp, it's lonely."

"It's not remarkably cheerful," affirmed Jeremy with a chuckle. "That's why they call it the Great *Dismal* Swamp."

The three of them went quickly to work and soon filled their vehicle to overflowing. Jeremy was pleased to have so much wood so soon. He would store it on the south side of the barn and do all he could to keep it dry. And if this one load turned out to be not enough, he would make another trip into the swamp. It seemed to have an endless supply of wood, peat, small game, even medicinal herbs. The peat was sometimes harvested by farmers for use in their gardens. Equal parts of peat and sand made a good mixture for cuttings. Swamp peat would not become a commercial product until later when it was cut and dried for use as fuel. Most of the wood the trio gathered would have to be split and chopped before stacking. That would be hard work for an aging man, but Jeremy would offer Jesse a pocket knife as payment for the job. It would replace the heirloom knife the boy had given his brother.

3

On their way out of the swamp, its dank smell in their nostrils, they encountered a gathering of blacks heading eastward. Near fifteen in number, the group was bent on crossing the boggy marshland to reach the coast and move northward. Less than a mile inside they had stopped on the road and were gathered around an object that lay on the ground. Moving closer, Jeremy and the children could see a little boy about ten years old curled in the fetal position on a little patch of grass beside the road. The boy had become too weak to walk, and they were told his companions had no way to carry him. Several perplexed men and women stood nearby quietly talking.

"Is he sick?" asked Jeremy, addressing a tall and powerfully built man with shaggy gray brows above dark, intense eyes.

"Yessah," answered the man, "he bery sick an' what to do we don' know. Spec' somebody oughta tote 'im but it ain't easy. He jus' a little fella, but nobody here strong enough to tote 'im. We be in a cleft stick, can't go back no mo' and can't go fo'ward."

"What does that mean?" asked Anna, her curiosity getting the best of her. But before anyone could answer she was asking more questions. "Who does he belong to? Does he have a mama? Does he have a papa?"

"Don't 'long to nobody," replied one of the women. "His mama and his papa left 'im sometime ago and run away wit' the railroad people, an' I took 'im. He walked 'long right bravely to where you see 'im, but I guess he done fo' now. The fever done took 'im and I reckon he's a dyin'."

The boy lay still with one small hand under a pinched cheek. His large and liquid eyes were dull, his thin face in a grimace. He showed no willingness to move. A turkey vulture with a red head and wide wings perched heavily in a tree nearby, flapped its wings as if to move in flight, and then settled down. As the boy caught sight of the bird a look of apprehension sprang into his face, and he tried to speak.

"What is it?" asked Jeremy, stooping to catch the faint words. "What are you trying to say, boy?"

"Don' let 'im git me befo' I die. Jus' don' let 'im git me."

"No buzzard will get you, son, either alive or dead."

"Don' let 'im git me," he said again, weakly lifting a hand.

"Let's take him home with us," said Anna. "Will you let us take him home, please? We can make him well again!"

She was looking at the woman who thought the boy was dying. A crystal tear left one eye and crept down her cheek. She turned and looked at Jeremy with pleading eyes, asking him as well.

"We can't do that," said Jesse. "He's not a rag doll, you know, and he's not a pet like old Scout."

"That's a good insight," said Jeremy, patting Jesse's shoulder. "The boy is not a pet and not a thing either. He's a sensitive human being with dignity and has to be treated as such."

He paused, removed his hat, and wiped his brow, all the time looking at the small, inert bundle on the ground.

"Please?" whined Anna. "Can't we do something? I wanna cure him!"

"We sure can't take him home," said Jesse.

"Well, maybe we can," said Jeremy, "but only if he's willing and only if his guardian is willing."

"It's a mighty kind thing to do," said the woman. "Bless you."

Then kneeling beside the boy she asked gently, "Maris, will you go wit' these good people? Will you go wit' them and git well again?"

The boy seemed not to hear the woman's inquiry. For several minutes he lay there, his eyes wide open but without expression. The woman put the question to him again, and he nodded. Quickly Jesse removed some wood from the cart, and Jeremy placed the boy in a corner.

"Did you call him Morris?" asked Jesse.

"He done call his self that. His name be Maris Whitelaw."

"Morris Whitelaw?" Jesse asked again.

She nodded. To Jesse, and even to Jeremy, it seemed an unusual name for a black child. Its origin just had to be shrouded in mystery, and Jesse was already imagining how he got it. The boy himself probably knew nothing of his name, and they would not ask about it.

As they rode homeward, Jeremy flicked the mule's flank to make the animal move faster, but the mule in typical stubbornness resisted. Morris lay curled in the corner and seemed barely conscious. Looking over his shoulder, Jeremy could see the refugees trudging blindly eastward. They moved like sheep without a shepherd beside the sluggish canal on the damp, gray road. When Jeremy looked again, they were out of sight. The buzzard on the dead tree craned its neck, flapped its wings twice, rose in flight, and glided away into the gathering shadows. The round-shouldered driver in a wagon pulled by a stubborn mule passed the sentinel bay tree, looked it over, and inhaled its aroma. He did not stop to pick the leaves.

4

Anna was thankful when they reached the house. Twilight had closed around them, and that was the time of day people spoke of seeing spectral shapes floating among the trees in the swamp. Twilight and early in the mornin, they said, ghosts would rise from the bogs and settle in the trees. The spooky apparitions were nothing more than methane gas, but Anna didn't know that. She was delighted to be out of the scary swamp and home again. She jumped from the cart and ran inside, yelling for Catherine.

"Not so loud, honey bun, not so loud. I just put the baby down to sleep. Why all the excitement?"

"Come outside! We have a boy in the cart!"

"A what?"

Catherine eased herself down the steps and into the yard just as her father and Jesse were lifting Morris from the cart to carry him inside. The boy lay in their arms like a sack of meal.

"I'll explain later," said Jeremy. "Right now we need to make the little fellow comfortable. We must lay him down gently and give him something to eat. If he'll take it, give him some cool milk to drink."

"And let me take care of him," pleaded Anna. "I wanna care for him and make him well again!" Something lying dormant within her, an inherent will to help others, was sputtering into flame. She was too young to know that already a pattern of set behavior was making her life important.

They put him down on the rug in their living room and put a cushion under the limp head. He was sweating profusely but shivering at the same time. Catherine spread a light blanket over the boy and fluffed the cushion to make it more comfortable. He lay there a few minutes, then stretched his arms and legs, rolled his eyes, and motioned he wanted to sit up.

"Well, that's a good sign!" cried Jesse with a hoot. "There's life in the skinny little rascal after all."

"Don't talk like that!" Anna scolded, her instinct for caring and curing asserting itself. "We brought Morris home to make him well again. Can't you see we have to be kind to do that?"

She gave the boy the mug of milk Catherine was holding. A thin hand took it feebly, and the boy drank from it hungrily. The milk relaxed him and brought a half smile but no attempt to talk. He glanced around the room, looked askance at the faces in front of him, and drifted into sleep. Morning found him much better. A breakfast of milk and hoecake, fed to him as he sat in the kitchen, made him noticeably stronger. He was soon smiling and hoarsely speaking a few words.

Jesse and Anna had gone home for the night, but early in the morning both children came asking excitedly about Morris. They found him propped up comfortably on the deerskin couch, a blanket over his legs.

"We think he's better," said Jeremy, "but we really need someone to make sure. Maybe Jesse can ride over to Robin Raintree's place."

Chapter 44

Robin Raintree was the local midwife in Blue Anchor. When medical or pharmaceutical help was needed, she was the one person everyone depended on. The village was too remote to boast a physician, and so this woman in her late forties made her rounds like a country doctor checking on the condition of her patients. Before she met her husband she had lived in a larger town farther south, and somehow had gained a knowledge of midwifery and medicine. For twenty years she had practiced her craft in the white community of Blue Anchor. Every person in the county seemed to know her.

In the afternoon she returned with Jesse and quickly entered the small house. She carried a leather satchel containing instruments and medications. She placed it on the floor and knelt to check the boy's pulse. Anna looked at her curiously with rapt attention. She could learn from Robin.

"He's weak," the woman said, "but not dying. Can't tell right now if he caught something. Could be just plain exhaustion and not enough to eat. With rest and plenty of food I think he'll come around."

"What are we do with him?" asked Catherine. "We don't have room for him in this little house."

"And he can't live with us in our bigger house," added Jesse. "He's black and we're white, and the law says he has to live with black folks."

"That shouldn't matter at all," said feisty Anna, speaking her piece. "If he's sick we have to care for him, and that's all there is to it."

"Molly Danmar will probably take him," said Robin, nipping in the bud a developing quarrel. "She's got a comfortable cabin and lives alone."

Molly was a free black woman who lived near Cooper's estate. She was a midwife herself and valued by the black community. Whenever she was needed, when bringing a child into the world or helping someone leave it, she did her job as well as Robin did hers. Often they worked together.

"I'll take the boy home with me and keep an eye on him. I don't think my husband Jonas will mind. Then I'll talk to Molly."

"I think we'll need you here again soon," said Catherine, looking down to her full and round belly.

"I can see that!" Robin retorted. You look big as a barn door! You and me and Molly, and maybe your papa to help on the side, will have to get together in a week or two to make you light again."

It was her way of saying that Catherine was ready to give birth. In the meantime she would help Morris regain his strength and find someone willing to take him in and look after him. For more than a week he slept in the back room of Robin Raintree's house, and her husband cared for him when she had to be away. When his strength returned and he was well enough to walk about, he went to live with Molly Danmar who was happy to have him. Quickly she began to view him as her one and only son.

Morris Whitelaw grew strong and tall living with her. He ate bannock for breakfast, unleavened bread flavored with sorghum. Molly baked it on a griddle made slick with bacon grease from Colonel Cooper's kitchen. In the middle of the day he guzzled wild strawberries and honey found in a hollow tree. Rambling through the countryside in summer, he ate blackberries and wild grapes called muscadines. Sometimes for supper he devoured with an amazing appetite Molly's golden-brown cornbread with pinto beans, turnip greens, and half a rabbit deep fried. He washed the good food down with milk when they had it and with spring water when milk was scarce.

Molly found her life's purpose in raising the boy, and he added years to her life. In the little cabin they shared she discovered he was eager to learn, and she taught him how to read. She asked if he wanted to be called Danmar, but he liked the unusual name someone had given him and didn't want to part with it. A few years after coming to live with Molly in her two-room cabin, they added another room. Owen Cooper had given Morris Whitelaw a well-paying job repairing farm equipment. With three rooms the tight little cabin became a house and quickly a home.

2

In late August the weather in Blue Anchor continued hot and muggy. A cooling breeze came sometimes from the southeast, and anyone with a few minutes of leisure found a place in the shade to catch the breeze. On Monday, the 17th of August in 1863, at three o'clock in the morning, Catherine Heartwood's water broke. Robin Raintree was on hand to deliver the baby with the able assistance of Molly Danmar. Jeremy was there too, but all he could do was care for Emily and heat water while the women performed the important job. They called for hot water and towels, and he hovered over a pot simmering on the stove. When they came for the water, he quickly refilled the pot as soon as they returned it. Later he found out the water and towels were for cleanup, but one larger towel was wrapped around the pot to make it warm and ready to receive the infant.

Rachel Kingston was present but did not participate in the delivery. She was there to support Jeremy and do whatever she could should anything go wrong. Anna with insatiable curiosity concerning all things medical wanted to be present. Rachel thought it over and decided she was too young.

"You will grow up to become a woman yourself," her mother explained, "and then you'll learn what it's like to have a child."

Though Anna was disappointed in not being allowed even in the same house during the birthing, nothing of any magnitude went wrong. Rachel and Jeremy waited in the kitchen, and then without notice they heard a slap on tender flesh and the faint cry of a newborn child. A moment later the cry became louder and more sustained, and Robin Raintree called out, "It's a boy! A smooth and velvety baby boy!" Just as young men in their prime were dying or about to die, Catherine was giving birth to a healthy son. His coming into the world was a link in that great chain of being. As some links turn weak and begin to break, others quickly come forward to take their place, keeping the chain intact. As people die people are born and life goes on.

The infant's father at that moment was lying on a bed of pine needles somewhere in Virginia in a tent too small for his frame. His feet protruded and his boots were shabby, but the season was late summer and the night was warm. By some miracle he may have known with certainty that his son had come wailing into the world. He would say in later years that he woke in the middle of the night, perhaps near three in the morning, with a sense of something happening, something important affecting his life. Resting on his elbow in the darkness, he thought of home. In the past he had never been able to gauge how much he loved his wife. Now, caught up in events that could take him away from her forever, he was able to fathom the full measure, and he was astonished that he could love a woman so deeply. More than once, as he reviewed their life together, they had disagreed on little things but never anything big, and not once had he spoken to her in genuine anger—exasperation perhaps but never anger. And she had reached out to him to offer her love and tenderness and understanding even when he refused to buy exemption from the horror. He honored her for that, and in his thoughts he wrapped himself in her fair and fecund radiance as in a garment to keep him warm through the coldest of winter nights.

Catherine remembered her husband's request and named the child Benjamin. Her love for her father made it easy to choose the boy's middle name. Benjamin, she had learned, was the youngest son of Jacob and Rachel and the brother of Joseph. Beloved by his parents and brother, his name meant "son of my right hand" or "son of the south." He founded the Israelite tribe that came to be known as the Benjamites. They were famous warriors known for their courage and daring in battle. Now thinking about her son and his namesake, she wanted him to grow up strong and brave but never to become a warrior. Her dream was to see him grow tough as a pine knot and become the cheerful right hand of his father. And of course he would be a loyal son of the South, working with his father to wrest a good living from the good earth and helping to restore the South to prosperity.

In the family Bible she recorded his full name, the date and place of his birth, and a little prayer: *Benjamin Jeremy Kingston. Born wholesome and healthy and sound of limb near dawn on August 17, 1863 in Blue Anchor, North Carolina. Watch over him, dear Lord.*

Benjamin Kingston inherited his mother's love of nature and spent his childhood in happy enjoyment of natural things. He learned to read the secret signs in the western sky and spoke of the wind as a living thing. He could tell you the name of any tree or shrub or flower, and he delighted in the special fragrance of the swamp. His mother wanted him to be a botanist, but he went off to college and came home again to practice law in Blue Anchor for half a century. By the time he retired and gave the practice to his eldest son, the struggling bucolic village had become a pleasant little town. He passed on the Kingston name to numerous favored descendants who became solid citizens of the South.

Benjamin's sister Emily went to a Quaker college in Greensboro, graduated near the top of her class, and later served for many years in the state capital as a schoolteacher and prominent agitator for women's rights. She gave her time and energy, after teaching school all day, to seeking freedom and equality for women in the workplace. Advanced in her thinking and the author of a groundbreaking book titled *Women at Work*, she cried out against policies that discriminated against female teachers. Particularly she sought to repeal the rule requiring women in the classroom to remain single. Declaring in fiery speeches and pamphlets that women deserved the same rights, the same pay, and the same quality of life as men, she managed to bring about important changes in school policy but did not marry.

3

Four people now lived in the little house where only two with the big clock in the corner had lived earlier. Jeremy was older and less agile but somehow managed to be cheerful most of the time. The children were infants together, though Emily was fast becoming a toddler. Their mother was again prétty, shapely, and healthy but went to bed each night worried about her husband. In her bedroom where she had experienced the joy of being one with the man she loved as much as life itself, she slept not with that man but with two little children dependent on her. It was not the best of times for Catherine Kingston, nor was it the worst of times. Though longing for her husband and sometimes hurting, her children brought her joy.

On the day Benjamin was born, Rear Admiral John Dahlgren, whose son would die in a Union raid on Richmond, renewed the attack on Charleston's defenses. On that day his gunners fired more than 935 shells into Fort Sumter, but again the fort held. At the end of August the Federal batteries once more inflicted heavy damage on the fort, but the Confederates dug out their guns and kept on fighting. The valor of Sumter's defenders would be glorified and taught for generations in Southern schools. Except for sporadic action now and then, Virginia remained quiet. When Catherine heard from Leo Mack that almost no fighting was going on in Virginia, her mood began to improve. Perhaps the troops had become too exhausted to fight, and the war would quietly end. She spent her days nursing her baby, caring for the older child, keeping the house neat and clean, cooking for her father, and helping him in the garden. Sometimes for an hour or two she walked down country lanes to collect her thoughts and be close to nature.

Jeremy helped with the household work and like the squirrel that scampered in the sprawling branches of the live oak, he went about stocking their larder with food for winter. As autumn came he stored in the cellar three bushels of apples picked from a tree near the creek. He placed clusters of peanuts, damp from the tangy soil, on the tin roof to dry in the sun. Later he stored them in a canister near the milk in the cellar. Wearing a hat, a veil, an over-sized coat and gloves for protection, he removed the honey from his hives. Honey was a good substitute for sugar and also a delicacy, a delicious treat for breakfast or any meal. On the south side of the barn Jeremy stacked up a good supply of firewood for cooking and heating. An overhang and the sun would keep it dry. If no band of hungry marauders came with demands, the family would get through the winter comfortably.

At the Kingston farm, with Cooper's help, they began to bring in a good harvest. The colonel had assisted them all through the summer, sending over men to drop off some hay and sharpen the plow. David and Jesse worked hard during long and languid days and were now ready to enjoy the fruits of their labor. Most of the people in the community seemed to be better off as autumn settled in than when the summer began. As fall came and went the year 1863, horrendous in the annals of American history, would soon be over. Everyone hoped the war would end soon.

Catherine and Jeremy thought of Harvey Heckrodt who had left with his family in the summer to trek northward, looking for a better life. Did they find their land of milk and honey? In a dream one night Jeremy saw Harvey, half blind and stumbling along railway tracks, with his family behind him. A train billowing fire and smoke bore down upon them, and he couldn't be sure they stepped out of the way. Then he saw them standing safely beside the tracks and watching the cars flash by, and he could hear their clatter-clatter-clap-rap as though he were there. As the dream ended, Harvey and his children—he couldn't be sure about his wife—were limping along the tracks in a heavy rain that washed their faces and soaked their clothing. That image, somber for a man who cultivated cheer, disturbed Jeremy Heartwood and jarred him awake. He comforted himself with the thought that while old Harvey seemed to be suffering, at least he wasn't bleeding. It was almost dawn before he slept again.

Chapter 45

At the autumn Quarterly Meeting, the Quakers of Blue Anchor spoke of the deprivation so many had suffered since the war began. During 1861 most of the farmers were not bothered by troop movements, only by scavengers displaced by events and roaming through the countryside. Near the end of 1862 soldiers on both sides came on the scene and made their presence felt but fought no destructive battles in or near the village. Closer to the coast they fought, and the town of New Bern on the Neuse was occupied by Union soldiers from 1862 until the end of the war. On more than one occasion Confederates tried to retake the town but failed. In the fighting some old buildings dating from the beginning of the eighteenth century were damaged or destroyed, and civilians were killed. Blue Anchor was spared, but as events escalated in 1863 the rural folk suffered indignities and loss.

Soldiers tramping through the region ransacked their homesteads, seized their food, confiscated their livestock, and ruined their fields. A squad of blue coats came to Deeter Haartsook's house in early autumn, demanding food and drink for themselves and fodder for their horses. They stacked their rifles one against the other to construct a cone and placed their kits in a ragged circle around it. The brawny sergeant entered the farmhouse without invitation, made a point of not removing his cap, and quickly made himself at home. In the tight little room he smelled of sweat and leather and raw strength. His dark blue, floppy-crowned forage cap was made of broadcloth with a leather visor. Above the visor and visible to the Haartsooks were brass letters identifying the sergeant's regiment and company. Placing a big revolver on the kitchen table, he warned them not to make any sudden moves, and asked them many questions.

After Deeter's wife Abigail fed the soldiers, using most of the oatmeal and cornmeal they had put aside for winter, they sprawled in the yard under the shade of the live oaks and smoked their pipes. Some went to the barn and returned with bundles of hay for the weary horses tethered with drooping heads to the fence. The lonely little house and its surrounding yard seemed turned into a military camp. Deeter was certain that his house and yard would become a battleground should Johnny Reb happen to come that way. The laughing blue coats assured him there was nothing to worry about. "If any pathetic butternut steps foot on yer property," they said as one, "we'll blast him to smithereens! So don't you worry your little head about it."

That night the farmer's barn went up in flames. Even from a distance, as he gawked in helpless amazement, a searing sword of heat singed his eyebrows. Deeter Haartsook wanted to believe it was all an accident. Maybe a careless soldier, gathering hay, had dropped burning tobacco from his pipe.

Others, including Jacob Darboy, complained that while cornmeal was still available, many commodities often taken for granted in peace time had dried up and disappeared. In fact, supplies of all kinds were growing more and more scarce. Roasted peas had taken the place of coffee, though chicory roots were a better substitute. Sassafras leaves were being used for tea, or one could boil the dried root bark for a richer flavor. Sugar was available to the rich, but who in a time of violence and war was rich? Only Owen Cooper and maybe the governor of the state could afford sugar. Ordinary citizens, unless they had hoarded a few bags, had to rely on sorghum or honey. When pressed, the sorghum yielded a sweet juice that could be turned into a passable substitute for molasses or syrup. The sticky sauce mixed with meaty pecan or walnut pieces made hoecake palatable.

Potatoes were to be had on most of the farms surrounding Blue Anchor, and in the swamp one could find gamey animals for meat. Before the war came along it was easy to find deer and even bears in the swamp, but now the larger animals were gone. Soldiers moving through the region had hunted them almost to extinction, or had driven them deeper into the swamp. The same was true of the geese migrating from Canada for the winter. So many were killed by soldiers and locals they soon became scarce. A scholar in Raleigh contended that the geese were flying all the way to the Caribbean rather than land anywhere in the South and risk being killed for food. He couldn't explain why the ducks didn't follow the same procedure.

Like the Kingstons, some farmers in the community had managed to bring in a harvest. And while the small harvest in war time was nothing at all like the cornucopia of good years in peace time, those who had the means to share would certainly do so with those less fortunate.

"We have always taken care of our own," said David Kingston at the autumn Quarterly Meeting to a nodding of heads. "In times such as these we must and will look after each other. Therein lies our strength."

After a short interval of silence, Zachary Bookbinder stood up to speak. His son Peter had been inducted by the military at about the same time as Matthew and had not been heard from for several months. He reminded his brethren of the burden persons in war time must shoulder.

"Any war brings deprivation," he said, "but we shall endure."

He was about to sit down again, but prompted by a new thought he rose to his full height and paused. The aging farmer and cabinetmaker remembered an old German fable he could use to drive his point home. His listeners shuffled their feet and waited.

He spoke of the time when God created the birds, giving them soft and beautiful plumage but no wings. Then as the creatures hopped about on the grass their Creator laid before them feathered wings of all sizes, telling each to take a pair as a special burden. Without hesitation each bird lifted the heavy wings, content to carry the load as instructed. And then a wonderful thing happened. The wings they had lifted quickly became attached to their shoulders, and that which had seemed a burden to fasten them forever to the ground allowed them to soar to great heights in a blue heaven.

"And so it is with us," asserted the pious man."We lift and carry our burden today to become stronger tomorrow."

2

It was early in the morning in late October, and Rachel Kingston was setting the table for breakfast. "I do hope the quiet in Virginia means the war is winding down," she observed as her husband entered the room. "Maybe it's a good sign Matthew is coming home soon. I certainly hope so."

"Well, many Southerners," said David, "are glad to know Confederate troops are fighting on despite being defeated at Gettysburg and Vicksburg. They don't want to believe the South is running out of men and supplies and teetering on the brink of defeat."

"It's an attitude of quiet desperation," Rachel said, "or maybe not so quiet. Seems to me the South will fight to the last man before it surrenders. And the soldier-scavengers will grab every pig, calf, sheep, and chicken they can lay their hands on. Oh, I worry about Jesse. The recruiters tried to get him once and will try again. And I worry about you, David. Even a man your age is not exempt."

"Unless, of course, I pay the exemption tax," he remarked with a half smile, "and that I won't do. Our son did the right thing standing up for his beliefs. If push comes to shove, as they say, I'll do the same."

This was the first time Rachel had heard that from him. Alarmed, she was about to tell him that under no circumstances would she see her husband leaving home on grounds of principle, religious scruple, or whatever. In her pragmatic way she wanted to assert that God and religion come first in their lives in normal times. But in times of danger and need, when people of free will must act on their own merely to survive, the family must come first. Before she was able to speak, however, Sarah called out from the parlor. Soldiers had appeared in the yard and were striding toward the porch.

"Two sojers here wanting somethin' to eat," she called. "Jes' two sojers. Should I send them away?"

"We certainly can't do that," said Rachel, walking from the alcove off the kitchen into the living room. "Hungry soldiers can't be dismissed with a wave of the hand Sarah. We have to give them something, or they could tear the place apart. The corn bread you were ready to put on the table will go to them. No, we can't send them away, I will have to invite them inside."

"Are they blue coats or gray?" asked David, rising from his seat in the alcove and walking toward the living room.

"Blue coats," Rachel answered from the porch. "They tell me they were separated from their unit and are trying to get back to it but have no rations."

"I don't remember seeing blue coats in the area," said David *sotto voce*, "but let's invite them in and get rid of them soon as we can."

The soldiers were already walking through the door and removing their caps. Rachel had heard that many Union soldiers never bothered to do that. Later she learned the two removed their caps to hide insignia that someone might identify. From New Hampshire, they were looking out for themselves rather than paying respects to Southern courtesy.

Sarah brought in a plate of golden corn bread and Rachel followed with a pitcher of milk. The men were young, rangy, and thin. Lines of exhaustion and stress creased their faces. They were polite but cautious. In the same situation Southerners had killed blue coats. They thanked their host for the food and eagerly drank the milk as they wolfed down the tasty bread.

"Do you have any eggs?" asked the younger man. With dirty blonde hair and pale blue eyes, he looked like any one of their friends but spoke with a different accent. "I really need some ham 'n eggs. I need a lot of ham and a dozen eggs! And I could use a bath and a good bed."

"We have no pigs," David bluntly replied. "Those were taken from us a long time ago. We have some hens that lay eggs, but the few we had on hand went into the bread."

"Hens," said the other man, chewing his corn bread and looking at the last piece on the plate, "chickens. They say southern fried chicken is the best in the world. Could you whip up some fried chicken?"

The question went to Sarah, who smiled broadly. Curiosity had gotten the best of her, and she had not as yet retreated to the kitchen.

"Hens are no good for fried chicken," David replied, "too tough, you know. They have to be boiled. I do wish we could offer you ham and eggs, or fried chicken, but in our present situation we can't."

"You do have milk," declared the older soldier who seemed to be in charge, a cunning half smile on his tanned face. "That means you have a cow, a fine healthy cow."

"Sure does," assented his companion, grinning widely.

As they spoke, Sarah eased away from the wall to return silently to the kitchen. The children were playing outside and she wanted to be there when they bounced into the room unaware of the visitors.

"Oh, no you don't!" the older man cautioned. "Go back to the kitchen, but don't try to sneak no cow away from us. Our unit will take us back gladly if we show up with a cow that gives milk. No one else leaves the room till Luke here searches the premises."

He drew his pistol and placed it on the table. He was more experienced than Luke and clearly the one in command. Without waiting to receive the order, Luke bounded toward the barn to look for the cow.

All this time Jesse and Anna were somewhere outside the house, and now they came into the kitchen with cheerful chatter and the usual clamor of young feet on the oaken floor.

"Shusssssh, chillen," warned Sarah, her finger on her lips, "we have blue-coat sojers in the house!"

Anna remained in the kitchen, wide-eyed and curious. Instantly Jesse was back in the yard and running toward the barn. He didn't have to worry about the cows, for they were already in the pasture, but the horse and mule were in the barn and he thought he might be able to hide them.

Suddenly Luke appeared in the boy's path, laughing at his efforts to reach the horse and mule and make them secure.

"That ain't gonna do at all," he said. "The mule you can keep but we need that horse. I'm surprised to see such a fine animal after three years of war. Can't believe you still have him. Anyway the horse belongs to us now."

"That horse belongs to Colonel Cooper," replied Jesse. "He won't be pleased to learn you took it."

"Cooper?" queried Luke, his eyes blinking. "Colonel Owen Cooper? We heard of him. Heard he lives in these parts and not to mess with him. Heard he has connections in Richmond and Washington. Some say he knows Jeff Davis and Abe Lincoln both. What proof you got the horse belongs to him?"

"Here," said Jesse, pointing to a small yellow tag attached to the horse's right ear. "He don't brand his animals like some do, says it's cruel to do that. He tags 'em and this is the proof."

The rogue soldier scrutinized the tag, nodded in agreement, and quickly returned to the house. Jesse could see that he seemed nervous.

"No heifers in the barn," he said in an undertone to his companion, "and no horses we can ride. We need to get outta here fast."

After a brief discussion in private, the two Union soldiers thanked the Kingstons for their hospitality and departed. Jesse walked part of the way down the avenue with them.

"It's sure a poor country to forage in," said the older man. "I reckon your mama wouldn't care to see *us* again."

"I reckon not," said Jesse, speaking the same idiom but with a down-country drawl that amused them. "Good luck finding your way back, fellas. I hope you get back with no more problems."

He couldn't be sure the men were lost as they claimed. More than likely they were deserters, and could be executed if caught, but he would take them at their word. They were the enemy, and yet he rather liked them.

3

During September and October of 1863, Virginia saw limited cavalry activity and only occasional infantry skirmishing. In Charleston mortar fire and the guns of ironclads hammered Fort Sumter again and again. The buildings of the fort crumbled in smoke and dust, but the garrison shored up the shattered remnants and remained defiant. In Mobile, Alabama a group of women driven by hunger marched on food stores with placards reading BREAD OR BLOOD and ransacked them. In New Orleans, General Grant, tipsy from too much boozing, was injured when his horse shied and fell on him. He would have to swing on crutches for several weeks.

In North Carolina pernicious rumors of war and peace spread like wildfire. Confederate soldiers by the score, or so the story went, were defecting to the Union. Even worse, according to unconfirmed reports, a band of insurgents led by a man named Gideon Smoot had raised the Union flag above the courthouse in Wilkes County. Then drinking heavily and shouting obscenities, they cheered their achievement before dispersing. In the state capital, at about the same time, Rebel soldiers raided a pro-Union newspaper and reduced its offices to smoldering shambles.

Near the end of September, in the Georgia woods southeast of Chattanooga, heavy skirmishing morphed into a full battle that went on for two days. The Federal Army of the Cumberland under General Rosecrans, positioned along a ragged three-mile line, clashed with the Army of Tennessee under General Bragg. The Southern fighters were furious and unrelenting as they charged the Union line. The fighting went on for many hours, ceasing at dark on the second day. When the Battle of Chickamauga ended, the Confederates had won a tactical victory but with heavy losses. The casualty rate was estimated at 28% for both sides.

As the third autumn of the war came around, the South was fraught with problems and under constant attack. But Southerners seemed to be in better spirits than in midsummer when Confederate forces suffered humiliation and defeat at Gettysburg and Vicksburg. That was because the Confederates had managed to bring the Federal assaults on Charleston and towns in Texas to a stalemate, and had won at Chickamauga. In Virginia, believing the conflict had shifted to a new locale, both Lee and Meade sent troops to the west. In Blue Anchor the people wondered what would happen next. Catherine worried that her husband would be deployed in the west and would never make his way home again. Her father-in-law tried to console her with comforting words, asserting that Owen Cooper was acting on her behalf to get her husband home before Christmas. In the meantime, unknown to David Kingston and his family, a detachment of soldiers was on its way to his house.

Chapter 46

They came in the afternoon of a windy day in November, six of them with an officer in charge. They rode smartly up the avenue of oaks into the yard, and one man dismounted. A lieutenant in his mid forties, his temples already gray, knocked with some force on the door. When David opened the door, he asked the master of the house to identify himself and gave him a sealed document. It was a summons for him to report to military duty no later than one week from the present day. David's son had been given only three days to pay the exemption tax or go to war, but the older man, as a special courtesy, was granted more time to get his affairs in order. The Confederate officer, lean and fit in a clean uniform, bade him good day. Turning on his heel to leave, and flicking two fingers to the brim of his hat, he said his detachment would return in one week.

This second summons to military duty triggered consternation in the Kingston family, particularly in Rachel. It was bad enough that her son was called upon to leave his native place and perhaps die in a terrible war. Now her husband would go also? Her son riding off with a rifle strapped to his back, as though crucified on a cross, was more than she could bear. Now in slow recovery, she would have to ratchet her suffering to another degree because her stubborn husband wouldn't pay the exemption tax. How could she respond to that, with anger or with sadness? He wouldn't listen to her even when she argued he was too old to become a soldier, even a noncombatant. He was fifty-five and close to Lincoln's age. Would Lincoln exchange his desk in the White House for a Spencer rifle and a military camp in winter? She knew Lincoln was a brave and formidable man, but in similar circumstances would he do as her husband was doing? Of course not! So where does bravery leave off and foolhardiness begin?

David replied quietly that changes in the Exemption Act had brought about this state of affairs, and there was nothing he could do about it.

"Before long, mind you, any man of any age will be required to serve in the ranks if he can walk and fire a rifle or ride a horse."

"The Friends will pay the exemption tax, and gladly," Rachel urged.

"I can't allow them to do that, I really cannot."

"Your friend Cooper has already said that father and son in a small family should not be risking their lives at the same time."

"Father and son have the same beliefs, dear Rachel. And what about the three sons of Samuel Bradshaw? All three were under fire at the same time. Old Sam believes they died as heroes in gallant battle at Gettysburg. But of course any person slaughtered in the most minor of skirmishes dies a hero."

It was useless to argue with him. His mind was made up. So Rachel Kingston went about the dreary task of preparing for her husband's departure as she and Catherine had done for her son. She knew he would not be wearing a uniform, and so to pack warm clothing for him was important. Matthew had ridden off to Richmond in early May of 1863 to endure a long, hot summer. Now his father would go near the end of the same year to suffer uncertain weather in winter. Rachel knew full well that warm clothing was essential for the man's survival, but new clothing of any kind was not to be found in Blue Anchor.

David owned a good coat and warm trousers, but she would have to make him a shirt. She hoped father and son would find themselves in the same regiment and support each other. Then as she thought about it she decided their not being together would be safer. Though Cooper had assured the Quaker elders that Matthew would be coming home soon, no one dared speculate. Whether the two would ever meet again was anyone's guess. And what about Jesse? Would the boy be the next to go? And Nathaniel Alston, so desperately needed on the farm. Since he was older than Jesse, in time he would surely go. But maybe he would find a way to stay out of the sight of recruiters. As night came, the wind blew hard and the rain turned to sleet. The bad weather made Rachel's thoughts even more dreary. Could her obstinate husband endure such weather in a military camp? Could a ragged tent provide shelter for survival? Could someone convince that stubborn old man that he is no longer young? Rachel's heart was heavy.

2

General Lee's army in Virginia had settled into winter camp along the Rappahannock and Rapidan rivers. Some of the soldiers had pets, and Lee was said to have a pet hen that laid an egg for him every morning. Most of the high-ranking officers were quartered in comfortable houses, but the enlisted men had only flimsy tents to shelter them from the cold. Junior officers and some of lesser rank occupied captured Union tents of better quality. Other lucky soldiers made do with Union blankets, canteens, and haversacks collected after a battle. Some of the men owned coveted rubber blankets manufactured only in the North. They used them as ground cloths. Any time they fought, Confederate soldiers combed the field for Union equipment to use later. It was invariably better made and more durable. Some Union weapons jammed in use, and a scandal erupted over a shipment of shoddy blankets that caused rashes and provided no warmth, but on the whole one could find less graft and corruption in Union factories than in the South.

In the winter camps the erratic weather soon became as much an enemy as Federal troops. Cold weather often moved in early, and countless soldiers fell ill from exposure. The cold was a living thing, a demon-presence with an icy hand touching everybody in one way or another. Harried physicians in the field hospitals were compelled to turn soldiers away, even those who had to be carried there. Epidemics of influenza, in addition to a litany of other ailments, ran through the camps. The medical staff had no effective medicine for the flu and no vaccine. Diarrhea and dysentery, caused by an inadequate diet and not enough rest, claimed young lives on a daily basis. Hungry soldiers suffered from night blindness, depression, and lethargy and were constantly foraging for food. Physicians spent most of their time treating frostbite and a host of diseases common to exposure in winter. Pneumonia and tuberculosis ran unchecked through the winter camps. A malady widely known as "camp fever"—a combination of several fevers—struck hard with pronounced chills followed by flushing heat and general debility.

The remedy for the ills that plagued them, the soldiers were told, was activity. No soldier had the leisure to recuperate more than a few days from an illness, and no soldier could sit and wait for the next battle to begin. He and his comrades were ordered to keep moving just to stay warm. Winter was a time for equipment repair, restoration of personal strength, and intensive training. It was the time for incessant military drill—often for hours in cold, windy, and rainy weather—but important for discipline in the ranks when heavy fighting began. Cavalrymen drilled with their sabers, on foot and on horseback, while artillerymen drilled with their cannons limbered and unlimbered and ready to fire. Sporadic skirmishing took place in winter, but spring and summer saw most of the action.

Leisure activities in all seasons included reading, writing, chess, checkers, card games, and skylarking. In favorable weather many soldiers pitched horseshoes and engaged in team sports. They played a version of football so rough it was later monitored because too many were injured. Much of a soldier's free time when not on campaign was spent writing letters home. Soldiers of the Civil War were prolific letter writers and wrote to loved ones whenever they could. It was the only way for them to inform the folks at home of their condition. For reasons of security, they were not allowed to reveal exactly their position or what went on from day to day. Most of them obeyed that order, but censorship was lax and sensitive information often went home to relatives. While a major campaign demanded time to develop, hostilities could erupt at any moment. Military maneuvers were sometimes reported to the press and sometimes not.

An explosive situation was averted when Meade threw his troops across the Rappahannock at Kelly's Ford, but for reasons known only to himself went no farther. In the dead of winter and for the moment, Virginia was quiet because the focus was on Chattanooga and Charleston. Thousands of rounds of artillery were thrown against Fort Sumter during the winter of 1863, but the garrison stood firm in the midst of ruins and the Confederate flag, faded and frazzled, continued to fly month after month. The stalwart resistance in that one place heartened the entire South and kindled hope.

In Richmond, only days before David Kingston's arrival, officials were alarmed by a report that 13,000 Union prisoners on Belle Isle were planning to escape the island by night. The authorities wanted to know who leaked the report and why, but had too little time to find answers. Artillery was quickly set in place to surround the prison, and riflemen were placed on rooftops. Any prisoners attempting to escape would be shot. The revolt never materialized and the guns were never used. If thousands of prisoners were indeed planning to escape the hellish place by wading the shallow rapids of the river, they had second thoughts on seeing the gun emplacements. A slow death in the prison was preferable to being cut in half by a cannon ball, or shot to ribbons by a score of rifles firing at once.

3

David went to Libby Prison nearby and sat outside a dingy office similar to the one his son had visited when the weather was warmer. He waited more than two hours for the ponderous bureaucratic machinery to move. Then before witnesses he formally refused to pay the exemption tax. Minutes later he became a soldier in the Confederate army. A guard was hustling the tall Quaker to a holding tank for more waiting when an officer called them back. "We can send this man to Petersburg with a unit going there today," he said. "Have the clerk process his papers immediately."

"I'll tell him, sir," answered the guard with a slow and lazy salute.

The order persuaded the machinery to move faster. In less than an hour David was on his way to board a train. Near the middle of November he went by rail with a contingent of soldiers to a fortification that soon earned the name Fort Hell. The railway cars were cold and drafty, bulging with soldiers, cramped, and confining. The cars had seats, rough benches without backs, but David had to stand. His appearance, for all to see, indicated that he was a conscientious objector who would not fight for the cause.

He could tell that some of the soldiers were casting sour glances, but all but a few lacked the energy to show open hostility. A pale and pimply young man in a soiled and rumpled uniform made an effort to confront him but was seized by a fit of coughing and sat down again. He could only frown and stare at David and hack into a dirty handkerchief. A sergeant, struggling through the crowd, stepped on his foot. It hurt but he told himself it was an accident. He went on standing, bracing himself against the clatter and the movement, until the journey was over. Cursory glances in all directions told him that Petersburg was well fortified and ready to mount a ferocious defense against any force that dared to attack. Engagement with the enemy was inevitable—that he could see—but no one knew when. Several battalions of the Union army, encamped within easy marching distance, were expected to bide their time until winter was over, but that was not a certainty.

David's son Matthew was in the battalion of Lee's army known as the Brick Lane Dragons. It was a nickname, of course, but a mystery. Not even the commander knew how the battalion got its name. Their camp was beside the Rappahannock River, and they were prepared to rebuff any assault by Meade's forces encamped on the other side. Artillery was placed in a semi-circle and aimed at the middle of the river. The gunners were convinced that any force attempting to cross would be utterly destroyed by cannon fire. Meade had pushed across the river in a couple of places, but the action had not become a major offensive. Matthew's unit was poised to do battle with the first bugle call but was spared when Meade withdrew.

The weather was cold, and many infantrymen lacked appropriate clothing. Officers were required to buy their uniforms and dressed warmer. During the first week of November the river close to shore became encrusted with ice. On the grass near the shore lay a thin white rime of snow and frost. President Davis returned to Richmond on November 9 in the midst of an early winter storm. President Lincoln in snow-flecked Washington went to the theatre that day to see John Wilkes Booth in *Marble Heart*. Later, as fate would have it, their paths would cross again. In Blue Anchor a group of women who met to talk about the war decided to observe Christmas quietly.

Ten days later on a festooned platform at Gettysburg, Edward Everett in the major speech of the day spoke on the history of men at war. He was a well-known orator with far-ranging knowledge and a distinguished reputation as a compelling speechwriter. His riveting oration, nearly 14,000 words in length, began with poetic praise of divine silence and natural beauty:

> *Standing beneath this serene sky, overlooking these broad fields now reposing from the labors of the waning year, the mighty Alleghenies dimly towering before us, the graves of our brethren beneath our feet, it is with hesitation that I raise my poor voice to break the eloquent silence of God and Nature. But the duty to which you have called me must be performed. Grant me, I pray you, your indulgence and your sympathy.*

More than two hours later his speech ended with the following:

> *But they, I am sure, will join us in saying, as we bid farewell to the dust of these martyr-heroes, that wheresoever throughout the civilized world the accounts of this great warfare are read, and down to the latest period of recorded time, in the glorious annals*

> *of our common country, there will be no brighter page than that which relates the battles of Gettysburg.*

The speech of the day was erudite, moving, well-delivered, and well-received. It was skillfully structured and spoken with perfect timing to place all emphasis where it belonged. Everett's audience appeared to be hanging on every word, on every syllable, but a week later only a few people could remember what the gentleman had said. That was because the next speaker on the platform was President Abraham Lincoln.

In what later came to be called the *Gettysburg Address,* he dedicated in his high-pitched, twangy Kentucky accent a part of the battlefield as a cemetery for those who had lost their lives in the battle. His speech was fewer than 270 words and was over in two or three minutes. Immediately after the address, shaking his head and shrugging his shoulders, Lincoln called it a "flat failure." It was later judged one of the most eloquent and moving and memorable speeches ever written. Simple, inspired words defined the Northern States as one people dedicated to one principle—equality. To uphold that principle, brave men had fought and died on hallowed ground.

In Blue Anchor, Isaac Brandimore, had he lived to see that day, would have repeated, with some reservation, these ringing words from the speech: *The world will little note nor long remember what we say here, but it can never forget what they did here.* Indeed. And what did they do? Pausing to pull on his beard, Isaac would have answered: "During those three terrible days at Gettysburg, in the heat of high adventure, young Americans slaughtered one another by the thousands. Let the world remember and let it never happen again."

Chapter 47

When 1863 came to an end and 1864 began with plangent wintry winds, the human condition in the South was fast becoming intolerable. In Richmond an inadequate food supply was tormenting residents. In just a few months the sleepy town of 40,000 catapulted to more than 140,000, and hungry people in crowded conditions were becoming desperate. Runaway inflation increased the price of flour from $20 a barrel in January to $250 a barrel fourteen months later. Some parts of the South had enough food, but Northern forces were wreaking havoc on the infrastructure required to move goods. Transporting and distributing food supplies had become a major problem.

On Owen Cooper's plantation in Blue Anchor a tall warehouse was full of sweet corn, but not even Cooper could find a way to get it to the people who needed it most. He sent wagonloads to the station in a nearby town for shipment by rail to Richmond, but the railroads were unsafe, subject to sabotage, and monopolized by the war effort. Also desperate scavengers haunted the railway yards to steal whatever they could. Cooper's heavy and slow wagons were easy targets for predators unfazed by his reputation. They were stolen, plundered, and the drivers were beaten. Though swift vengeance was meted out to any thief unlucky enough to be caught, many got away.

Depreciation of the currency went on without hindrance. Those on fixed incomes or no income at all were hit the hardest, but even the government was finding it difficult to buy necessities. To some extent the shortage of commodities was solved by using impressment agents. These men had the authority to seize a prized commodity and pay the lower government price instead of the market price. Producers objected to the practice but were powerless to change the policy. Making matters worse were many dishonest agents who fleeced the government whenever they could to fill their own pockets. Corruption as the war became more savage was patent and rampant. The fighting was extending too long and taking a fearsome toll on civilians as well as soldiers. When the armies in conflict settled into winter quarters to remain there till spring, the Confederacy breathed a sigh of relief. It had managed to keep the enemy at bay another year.

Matthew Kingston, refusing to bear arms and refusing to fight, had survived in dangerous situations eight perilous months. In camp he drew upon his prison experience to repair moveable equipment. He soon learned that a soldier's job amounts to more than fighting. All the men worked at a wide variety of jobs when not fighting. When skirmishes broke out—there had been no major battles since Gettysburg—Matthew once again became a medic. His performance in that capacity won the admiration of his comrades, and no man persecuted him because of his beliefs. In fact, he became a favored comrade among them even though he kept mainly to himself.

As the months slowly came and went, his sturdy Quaker attire began to wear thin. The tall clock in the corner at home went on ticking and ticking, and the calendar marked each day that passed. But Matthew was losing track of time. The months were becoming years, and each day was a week. The minutes were becoming hours, and there were no moments in his life. He knew the reality of time only when his body began to stink. For weeks he went without a bath but somehow managed to shave. In time he was obliged to wear whatever clothing he could obtain. A comrade gave him a warm shirt once owned by a Union officer—no bullet holes, though it's collar had spots of blood—and a pair of trousers from a Confederate officer.

He began to look like a soldier but never wore a complete Confederate uniform. Shoes and boots were in very short supply, and so he wore his own boots as long as he could. Some of the higher ranking officers were able to buy alligator boots, considered a luxury, made in Louisiana. Coats and trousers for cold weather, products of Southern factories, were poorly made and wore out fast. Matthew's original clothes had lasted twice as long. As the months passed, he lost weight and suffered from headaches and blurred vision but remained in relatively good health. Then one day without notice he received news that eventually he might be going home. He did not rejoice. A comrade had received similar news only to die the next day in a skirmish.

2

As Matthew thought of home with renewed hope, Jeremy Heartwood ventured once again into the swamp to gather firewood. It was near the end of November and the day was cold. Because the Kingston children were in school and the Christmas break had not yet come, he went alone. He was thinking as he went how angry Rachel Kingston had been when she learned her children had been given new textbooks explaining and justifying the Confederate cause. A bankrupt government had somehow found the funds to print and distribute new books that bulged from cover to cover with egregious propaganda. The children of the South were expected to see Abraham Lincoln as a wicked and withered old man bent on destroying their way of life. Jeremy sadly shook his head as the aging pony slowly pulled the cart, snorting puffs of steam in the wintry air. Desperate scavengers, risking the wrath of Owen Cooper, had taken the mule in the Kingston barn. They wanted the cart also, but earlier Jeremy had removed a wheel and replaced it with a broken one. The cart looked disabled and the ruse worked.

In the swamp the little black pools where insects skated in summer were covered with ice, but his work and a thick woolen sweater kept Jeremy warm. Though the gaunt trees stood dripping from an icy rain, in the tangle of ferns and brush he found wood that he could burn without drying. Now he was on his way home with an ample supply to last through the winter. He would have gathered firewood for the Kingston family, but they had the logs from Bupee's cabin. The logs had been sawed to fit the huge fireplace in the living room, split to burn hotter, and stacked beside the barn.

Jeremy pulled into the yard of his home and dumped the wood near the barn before returning the cart. At the Kingston house he called out to Sarah who stood on the back steps and waved to him. He parked the cart in its usual corner of the barn, removed the wheel, and put the broken wheel in its place. He was taking no chances, for at any time of the day or night foragers might hitch the precious vehicle to an old horse and make it their own. At the back door with Peg in hand he stopped to chat with Sarah.

"Come in, Mistuh Jeremy!" she scolded. "You gonna catch yo' death o' cold in this kinda weather."

He thanked her for her concern but replied he had to be home for supper. It was late afternoon and the days were short, and he had work to do.

"Give my regards to Mrs. Kingston," he said.

"She done walked to the school to meet Jesse and Anna. She don' like the road people, say road people talk crazy to the chillen. Anyway maybe it ain't my place to say it, but Mistuh Matthew comin' home!"

"What?" asked Jeremy, astounded. "What did you say?"

"He comin' home!" Sarah repeated loudly, as if Jeremy were hard of hearing. "Mistuh Cooper's Jerome done brought over a letter. He gonna be released and will be here in time fo' Christmas! It was mighty official looking and so you can believe it. Jerome done took it to Miz Catherine at yo' house. I bet she smilin' and happy by now."

For once in his life Jeremy was speechless. He climbed on the pony and rode the short distance home as fast as he could. The little horse was too infirm to trot, and so the man in his excitement had to be content with a fast walk. In the yard he jumped off and bounded into the house. The pony, left untethered, sauntered away and nibbled on wild oats at the edge of the yard. Inside the house Catherine sat motionless in disbelief but wearing a radiant smile. Quickly her father found his spectacles, gently pulled the document from her trembling grasp, and began to read its formal language:

> *To all to whom these presents shall come, Greetings. Be it known that Private Matthew David Kingston, having served honorably near One Year under the general command of Robert Edward Lee, and having been commended for Valor on the field of Battle, is hereby relieved of Duty without impending Restriction to attend Hardship at home.*

The certificate rambled on with more words, but these were the ones to remember. It was an honorable hardship discharge secured by Colonel Cooper. The same printed letter, with blank spaces to accommodate Matthew's name and rank, the signatures of appropriate officials, and the date, had gone to his parents. The War Department had learned early in the conflict that one document of such importance, sent to one person at one address, sometimes did not reach its destination. And so they fell into the habit of sending more than one. In near collapse the government continued the practice.

3

There was joy in the Heartwood farmhouse that evening. Little Emily had not heard her mother laugh for a long time and thrilled to the sound. Though an infant, her son Ben caught the excitement with a burble that mimicked laughter and spit up his supper. Jeremy danced an Irish jig and urged his Katie to join him. Politely she declined, but laughed without restraint to see him joyously dancing. To celebrate the good news they brought up from the cellar a few lumps of brown sugar she had hidden away months before. She baked a batch of cookies from flour also saved for just such an occasion. They ate the cookies with sassafras tea and merry, animated talk.

Catherine was prone to worry even when good news made her burden lighter. She wondered whether some unforeseen event might interfere to negate the good news and prevent her husband from coming home. If all went well, just when would he be coming? Would it take him long to travel from where he was stationed? Would he be home to celebrate Christmas? The document did not make that clear. So many things could go wrong. If all went right, he would soon be able to pick up his life again with his wife and daughter and the son he had never seen. To comfort herself and ward off the chill of the November evening, Catherine put another log on the well-stoked fire. In the iron grate it blazed greedily, sending fire stars up the chimney and mollifying doubt. She would look on the bright side and plan a cheerful Christmas for her children and father even if the good news proved false.

If it did not prove false and was indeed good news, she would live again and love again. She would build for herself and family a shining future in the midst of troubles that would certainly fade away in time. She had learned even as a schoolgirl that calm presages storm and comes again when stormy weather has passed. At the end of the storm she was certain she would find a bright and sunny sky and the soft, silver sound of a lark.

Chapter 48

The middle of December brought frigid weather. People in the North, during this third winter of the Civil War, found it hard to believe their troops were suffering exposure and frostbite from the weather. They had been told the South was a sunny and temperate place with a gentle climate the year round. The misinformation was a reference to the deep South. It did not apply to Virginia, where the Kingston men were stationed, nor to Tennessee, and not even to Charleston. In Virginia's climate, life in a military camp in winter was hard even for the strong and sturdy. For the hapless soldier on short rations, and weakened by the ravages of war, it was often unendurable. Even though in winter there was little fighting, the soldier had to wait and speculate when the fighting would commence, and that in itself was torture.

In the encampment established to defend Petersburg, David Kingston occupied a tent that offered little protection from the weather. A cook in the mess hall gave him some tallow, and he rubbed it into the grain of the canvas to make the cloth more rain resistant, but in a downpour or steady rain the tent leaked. He considered himself fortunate to have warm clothes and a good blanket. His wife had seen to that. But without notice his situation could change. His consistent and steady refusal to join the daily military drill was infuriating his officers and particularly the drill sergeant. That loud and tough old soldier had convinced him that blankets, shoes, and coats had a way of disappearing in cold weather.

A short, burly man with a short fuse, the sergeant had to look upward into David's face for their eyes to meet, and that alone made him angry. He disliked the Quaker because the man was tall and fit and rugged with broad shoulders, but spoke softly of nonviolence. He looked every inch the soldier but was not a soldier and clearly despised soldiering. He was willful and disobedient, sloughing off orders even from the brass. The sergeant, married to the army and viewing it as a good home, made it clear that such behavior would not be tolerated for even a day.

"You are in the army now whether you like it or not!" he bellowed, sidling up to David who was standing in the review line but not at attention.

"If you know what's good for you, fella, you will put that religion of yours in your pocket for the duration and obey orders."

He went on down the line and David could hear him berating a man of low intelligence who had tried his patience more than once.

"You are not in order, soldier!" he exclaimed sharply. "Your uniform is not in order and your pack is not in order. How many times must I say this to you? Everything here must be in order!"

As this was going on an officer approached David and urged him for his own good to obey every command issued to him.

"You can be shot if you don't."

"I can't expect thee to understand," David replied calmly. "I must obey a commander of higher rank than thee. I cannot disobey the rules and substance of my religion. I can't in good faith participate in military activity, not even the daily drill. It prepares one for hostility and violence and death."

"Hostility and violence and death," the captain repeated without mocking. "That's as good a definition of war as I've heard anywhere."

David was looking directly into the man's face. Perhaps the officer expected him to say "thank you," but he did not reply.

"You appear to be a sensible man," the captain continued. "But your insubordination must be corrected. In wartime we do whatever we have to do. Obeying orders is the first rule. I shall issue a command to place you in the front ranks when we fight again. Make no mistake. Your mortal body, despite your God Almighty, will quickly become a feast for crows."

It was not an idle threat. The officer, though speaking calmly, meant exactly what he said. It would be David's punishment for disobeying orders, a serious offense. Because the troops were in winter camp, in hibernation as it were, no battle was likely to occur any time soon. Also Colonel John Gibson, the ranking officer and commander of the regiment, had heard of David and wanted to talk to him.

2

One evening the colonel sauntered down to a copse where soldiers lounged around sheltered campfires. Though December, the temperature on this particular day was pleasantly mild. David was sitting apart, leaning against a tree and reading in the half-light what appeared to be a small book. As the evening glow faded, a blue haze crept up from the valley and the hills grew dimmer. The campfires cast shadows on the trees nearby, and their languid smoke curled upward in the still air in columns of gray ribbons. He put down his book as the colonel approached.

"Good evening, Private Kingston," called the colonel in a friendly voice. "No, don't get up on my account. I wanted to ask a few questions, wanted to chat with you informally in a neutral setting. It's awkward talking to another soldier from behind a desk."

David wanted to say he was not a soldier, and should not be addressed as one, but refrained. He was not inclined to argue the point, for refusing to pay the exemption tax he had been officially inducted into the Confederate army to perform as a soldier. He spread his blanket closer to the fire and invited the colonel to sit on it.

John Gibson was a decade younger than David. He had once been a schoolteacher in a small town in Georgia where he grew up. With the outbreak of war in the spring of 1861 he went into a Georgia regiment when the school year ended in June. He left behind a wife and two young daughters and expected to return within the year. He had no way of knowing the war would drag on and on, but he did the job he was called upon to do and rapidly rose in rank. His promotion to colonel had occurred two months after the fall of Vicksburg as he traveled eastward from Tennessee. He had seen fighting there but was not a career soldier. He dreamed of home and family and looked forward to being home again soon. He wanted to be with his friends and colleagues doing a job he liked better than soldiering. His blue eyes were intelligent but tired.

Though he spoke courteously, all who listened could detect an air of command. Quickly he made it known to David why he wanted to talk.

"Do you really believe, Private Kingston, that your God will protect you when you go into battle?"

"I do," came the ready response.

"Oh come now! Surely you know by now that you'll be put in the front line to take first fire. I'm told if you had shown a little more cooperation you could have avoided that."

"Somebody will have to go in front. If others go, why not me? I've heard it's no picnic under fire wherever you happen to be."

David hoped his remark had not come across as flippant. He was relieved when the colonel replied, "I'm beginning to see a blend of compassion and logic in you. And I agree, no battle is a picnic."

"Rather than trusting a piece of hardware, I prefer to place my trust in God. If I'm to walk through the Valley of Death and survive, one crude musket will offer no protection at all. God Almighty, as unseen as the spoke of a spinning wheel or a bullet cleaving air, may or may not protect me."

"I'm not one to know much about your religion," said the colonel, "but I do know one thing for a certainty. If you go into battle unarmed, you will die. Nothing short of a miracle will save you."

"Yes, nothing short of a miracle. I believe that."

"And you truly believe in miracles?"

"Yes, I do. I know a lot has been written on the subject recently, and I admit I haven't read it all. I know science and religion in our time appear to be in conflict, but I do believe in miracles."

"Will you tell me why? Will you show me the evidence? A rational man like yourself must surely have evidence."

"My evidence is my faith," David replied. "He who made the sun and moon and stars came down to earth in the form of an ordinary man. While on earth he worked many miracles. My belief is not based on reasonable evidence, Colonel, but on faith."

Gibson glanced at his comrades sitting cross-legged in a half circle. It seemed to him they were becoming restive but ready to listen to his reply out of respect. He chose to speak quietly but rapidly.

"Whatever you believe, Private Kingston, the story that Christ was executed, came to life again, and was carried through clouds into the heavens is very hard for me to believe. And that makes it difficult for me to believe the other miracles of the New Testament."

David was primed to make a fast reply, but the darkness of night had come and a few stars were already visible. Though the day had been warm for December, the night was becoming chilly and the campfires were sputtering into embers. Soldiers were drifting away, headed for their tents and what they hoped would be uninterrupted rest. A few junior officers remained near their commanding officer to saunter back to their quarters with him. Colonel Gibson could sense they were growing impatient.

"Let's continue this at another time," he said to David. "It's getting late and all of us could use some shut-eye. The morning will be here faster than quicksilver, faster than a bullet."

Kingston nodded, stood, and saluted, wishing his commander good evening. Then he picked up his blanket, rolled it under his arm, and helped the other soldiers bank the campfires for the night. A gentle breeze was beginning to stir as he walked alone back to his tent. In the distance was the rumble of heavy wagons on the road, a rustle of endless activity like the murmuring of bees in a hive. "Supplies moving in," he muttered to himself, "or maybe more troops."

As in former times, Petersburg was facing a very uncertain future. During the War of 1812, the town had become known as "Cockade City" because its soldiers wore jaunty feathered hats and because it was a lively, carefree, proud little town. Now by contrast the city was becoming "the last ditch of the Confederacy," the defensive moat and back door to the capital. Every soldier assigned to defend the place knew well that if Petersburg were to fall, so would the city of Richmond. With its capital lost, the South would collapse and the war would be lost. The hard work to fortify Petersburg against any assault seemed to be going on industriously around the clock.

3

On the banks of the Rappahannock, not far from Petersburg, morning broke with a steady rain. Matthew Kingston walked in the rain to the old farmhouse that had become the headquarters of his battalion. He had been summoned by his company commander, Captain Bradley Hawkins, and the messenger could tell him nothing more than to be in the man's office at the appointed hour. That meant he had to finish his breakfast, such as it was, and be on his way. He drank the thick, bitter coffee with its dash of sugar for warmth and energy. He ate the lumpy grits, limp bacon, and fried potatoes on his tin tray but left half a piece of Johnny Cake. Cornbread fried on a griddle in bacon grease, he tossed it to a comrade.

In the mess tent food was never plentiful. It was the practice for a soldier to eat everything on his tray or have someone else eat it. The rough, starchy food lacked nutrition and was poorly cooked. It lay in the belly like lead, but no one had to beg any soldier to eat. As the war dragged on, many acres reserved for cotton went to food crops, but Southern larders were never quite full. In camp, especially in wintertime, the men needed many calories each day to sustain health but some went hungry. Most of the soldiers lost weight, and the average weight during most of the war was not more than 145 pounds. The average height was well under

Matthew's six feet, and so the young Quaker was taller than most of the men around him.

At the doorway Matthew identified himself, stated his business, and was led to a small office in the back of the house. Captain Hawkins, behind an improvised desk and wearing spectacles with wire frames, pointed to a chair and asked him to sit. Any number of questions were running through Matthew's mind. Was he there to be transferred to another unit? Would he be given another assignment? Would he have to answer to some kind of complaint? He could remember no personal conflict nor confrontation and was fairly certain no reprimanded was looming. He had done his job on the battlefield as a medic, bearing a stretcher instead of a rifle, and had done it well. Now when no battle seemed to be brewing he worked daily as a carter moving supplies and equipment to specified sites and repairing equipment.

The captain shuffled some papers on his desk, looked them over through spectacles perched on his nose, and spoke with a slow southern drawl. He was still in his forties, but his thinning hair, developing paunch, and pale complexion made him look older. His home was in Alabama.

"I see you were commended after Gettysburg. Served with valor it says here. You were offered a medal in ceremony, the papers show, but refused the medal and did not attend the ceremony."

The captain was smiling, amazed by the audacity of the young Quaker. "And when the time came for a reckoning, the men you served with affirmed your bravery, petitioned for clemency on your behalf, and no punishment was meted out. Is that right?"

Matthew nodded, and his commanding officer went on speaking.

"Well, at least you accepted the commendation, would've been foolish to refuse that too. Patience with Quakers wearing thin, you know."

"Yes, I know, sir. I have not deliberately tried to cause trouble."

As Matthew spoke, he continued to wonder what the meeting was all about. The commendation had come in the heat and haze of an August day a month after Gettysburg. It was now December, misty and cold, and August seemed faraway. He remembered the fancy envelope and the red wax seal but scarcely more. He waited to hear why he had been summoned.

Once more the captain looked over papers spread on his desk. With a linen handkerchief, he polished the lenses of his glasses vigorously. Then he picked up a document scrawled by hand in black ink.

"This," he said, "is a letter releasing you from duty. Delayed by several months. Got lost, it seems, in the Richmond maze. Dated a few weeks before Gettysburg, official signatures, you know, all very official. This document grants you an honorable hardship discharge. Reason, wife pregnant in a remote place, farm I suppose, and in need of help."

"She's no longer in that condition, sir," answered Matthew bluntly. "The baby was due sometime in August. If all went well, the child is more than four months old now. I haven't been able to receive a message from her."

"All the more reason for you to be going home," said the captain. You need to be there with your child before you become a stranger to him or her. Notice of your discharge, according to these papers, went out to your family about a month ago. They'll be expecting you. Farewell and God speed."

Matthew stood, saluted, turned on this heal, and left. The captain sat musing. Would the man go home now? Or would another bureaucratic blunder send him into battle again?

Chapter 49

Walking back to his unit, Matthew remembered the captain had said his discharge had been approved in Richmond several weeks before the Battle of Gettysburg occurred. Officially free of any discipline the military machine could impose upon him, he had gone off with Lee's army to Pennsylvania, marching mile after mile in the heat of summer, to be placed in harm's way at Gettysburg and possibly to die. Because some inept clerk in Richmond had misplaced a piece of paper, he stood as an unarmed civilian in the midst of the most ferocious battle of the war. He could see the irony of it but was in no mood to appreciate it. He thought he had every right to be angry, and yet he felt only a deep sense of sadness and resignation.

Within a week of his meeting with Captain Hawkins, Matthew Kingston was on his way to Richmond. From there he would go by train to Raleigh. In Blue Anchor, Owen Cooper had been informed of the arrangement and intended to meet the young man in the state's capital with a fresh horse for the ride home. It was not the shortest route, and Matthew questioned this roundabout way to reach his destination. He was told that Federal troops were bivouacking in a wide area south of the Rappahannock and to the north of Prudock County. To ride in that direction could mean capture and imprisonment for the duration of the war, his discharge papers notwithstanding. So gladly he accepted the long way home. To languish in prison for a second time was not a pleasant thought.

In a boxcar half full of cornmeal and guarded by two men who worked for the railroad, he went to Richmond. A fat rat nibbled on the corner of a sack and paid no attention to the men in the car. The next day in a passenger car Matthew went by rail to Raleigh. He passed the time, in the unheated and clattering car, reviewing his military experience and looking forward to picking up his life again at home. A gentleman of middle age, well-dressed and smoking a big cigar, sat opposite the young man. He wore muttonchops on either side of a florid face, and his abundant belly displayed a golden watch chain. He might have been a politician, a planter, or a merchant traveling to the capital to do business. Pretending to read a newspaper, he looked over the edge to observe his companion.

"Why aren't you in the army, young fellow?" he asked abruptly. "You could be hard at work killing the enemy."

Sadly Matthew leveled his gaze at the man but did not reply.

2

The weather in Blue Anchor, as Christmas approached, was not good. By late afternoon a drizzling rain was turning to sleet and the day was dark and cold. At the Cooper estate, relaxing near the hearth, two men sat talking. In the spring Owen Cooper had planted food crops on the acres once reserved by Thomas Bolton for cotton. That fall with the help of well-paid workers he brought in a good harvest. He gave some of it to his workers, took some for himself, and sold the rest to the Confederate government. At the end of 1863 the army needed food as much as ammunition. Impressment agents came to the plantation to take the crop at deflated prices, but sullenly withdrew when Cooper insisted on being paid in English pounds. Richmond wrangled with him but eventually relented and paid for his harvest in good money. At a time when other planters were pawns of the government, Colonel Cooper had the power to bargain. He planned to do better the following year.

The conversation turned to matters more immediate. Word had come that Matthew Kingston was being discharged from the Army of Northern Virginia and would need assistance getting home. There was nothing more in the message, but Cooper could read between the lines. He had been instrumental in obtaining the release of Kingston, and now the authorities supposed he would be on hand to bring the man safely home. Privy to classified documents, the Confederate strategist knew exactly where enemy troops were deployed and suggested the roundabout trip to Raleigh. He had planned a trip to the city anyway, and so the mission to pick up Matthew would not be a time-consuming bother. Jade Scurlock, his loyal henchman, would ride with an extra horse and go home again with their friend while Cooper remained to transact business. He would in fact mix business with pleasure, for a comely young woman was waiting for him to visit her house and have a drink with her father.

"Do you think the weather could be a problem?" asked Scurlock. "It's a long ride. Won't bother me none but might be a problem for him."

"You can spend one night on the road."

"Gonna be cold camping in this weather."

"No, not in a camp but in a snug and warm house owned by a friend of mine. You will take a letter of introduction."

"I'm black," Scurlock replied tersely.

"You think I don't know that?"

"What I mean is I can't stay in no roadside inn and no private house with a white man. You know that. Don't you remember how it was at the 'Purple Onion'? They call me a free man but I'm not free. I don't think I'll ever be free, even when the war is over."

"Not in your life time, my friend, but in a hundred years the race problem will no longer be a problem. Lincoln is forward looking, progressive."

"In the meantime a black man must say look at me, I'm black! And he can't live like a man oughta live."

"The color of your skin, Jade, will not matter in this instance. Let me put your mind at rest on that. You will sleep in a good bed in the same room as the Quaker, and no one will complain."

"Do you think we should notify Kingston's relatives?"

"I'm not sure. Perhaps his mother but not his wife. I would like to engineer a big surprise for his wife, something exciting."

The next morning in a milky mist that stung his face Scurlock rode over to Rachel Kingston's house and told her the good news. He asked her not to share the news with anyone else, not even the children. His boss wanted to make the homecoming a big surprise. But Rachel could not contain herself. She had to tell someone that her son at long last was coming home safe and sound. She told the children, and they told their teacher, and their teacher told others. Beginning at the school, the news of Matthew's impending return swept through the community like an afternoon storm in July.

In the little country school many children of varying ages were taught by one teacher. Her name was Prudence Goodwin. Her students called her Miss Goodwin or Miss Prudence, but a few young women she named as friends called her Prue. She was unmarried, thin as a rail, gossipy and lonely, but eager to learn and glad to teach. One day a pupil known to have very little at home put a gnarled and twisted apple on her desk. It looked hard and sour and she thought of tossing it away even as she thanked him for it. But at lunch time she bit into it and found the ugly little apple crisp and sweet. She took another bite and found it juicy. Instantly she became one of the few to know the value of twisted apples. Jeremy Heartwood had made that discovery in his youth and had passed it on to his daughter.

In the little house under the sprawling oak, Catherine and her father heard the news and rejoiced. Then as they thought about it, Catherine had doubts about its reliability. Jeremy tried in his fatherly way to reassure his worrisome daughter, but she speculated that many things might go wrong.

"Maybe he won't be coming home at all," she said, "or maybe something could happen to hurt him. On frozen ground his horse could stumble. At the very least Matthew could suffer from the cold."

"It's possible but not likely."

"It's winter, Papa, and frigid. Also desperate people are on the road."

"Don't worry, Katie. Everything will be all right. Scurlock will be with him, and that man is strong enough to take on an army."

"It's well known the road people can be dangerous, even violent."

"There you go building imaginary events to worry about. Don't think about it. Just be happy your man will soon be home."

"Even with Jade Scurlock riding with him, something could happen on the way home. His horse could throw a shoe. They could be robbed at gunpoint, even shot if they resisted. Jade is not invincible, you know."

Jeremy's consoling words fell on deft ears.

3

Matthew arrived in Raleigh nine days before Christmas of 1863. Cooper and Scurlock sat in the waiting room to meet him. They stabled their horses at a reputable hotel selected by Cooper and checked into comfortable rooms. The black aide was not allowed a standard room at any cost. He spent the night in quarters reserved for black cooks, bellboys, and stable hands. Not even Cooper had the power nor the influence to buck the custom that separated the races. It would endure for a hundred years and more until Congress in its bumbling, roundabout way would finally pass a series of Civil Rights Bills. On the day of Matthew's arrival the Confederate army, revealing dissension within, announced command changes in the military echelon. Skirmishing broke out along a creek near a village called Free Bridge in North Carolina. A destructive fire—deliberate sabotage many thought—laid waste to a regimental hospital, an arsenal, and a bakery at Yorktown, Virginia. It was another loss the South could ill afford.

The next day Matthew and Jade Scurlock rode eastward from the hilly piedmont region to the flat coastal plain. They got off to an early start in good weather to reach the halfway point Cooper had designated. Just before dark as the weather was turning colder, the two found themselves approaching a town called Willow Creek. On a quiet, tree-lined street they knocked at the door of a modest house. A black woman opened the door, glanced at the letter of introduction, and invited them in. The Quakers had helped her in the past, she said, and now she was ready to help them. They slept through the night in warm and comfortable beds and awoke to a good breakfast. Scurlock gave the woman a sum of money that she at first refused to take.

At the end of their second day on the road they cantered into the yard of Cooper's mansion. The owner of the estate had remained in Raleigh and would not be home for several days. A kitchen girl served them a sumptuous supper, by Confederate army standards, prepared by Eileen Norwaite. It was the best meal Matthew had eaten in many months. Scurlock joked that if he could eat a few more like that he would have meat back on his bones in no time. Another servant gave the horses fodder and water and stabled them, and still another led Matthew to his guest room. Tired but happy to be in his native place, he lost no time jumping into a warm bed to slumber. A stiff breeze came up during the night and whistled around the eaves, making a shutter clatter. Oblivious to all around him and floating on a cloud that sailed briskly in a blue sky, Matthew heard nothing.

4

In Raleigh, sitting comfortably at a huge oval table in the center of an ornate room of the state capitol, Colonel Cooper was talking with quiet intensity to the Governor, a general, and other dignitaries.

"The man is fifty-five years old," he was saying, "and a farmer. He's far more valuable to you producing food on fertile acres than standing somewhere in the front ranks to be shot."

"He's a Quaker," said the Governor, examining some papers in front of him, "and he refuses to pay the exemption tax."

"He's a good man and cannot be punished for his religious beliefs. He will not pay the tax because it supports the war effort."

"We don't see it that way. The law was willing to exempt him if he paid the tax. When he chose not to pay, he knew he would have to take the consequences. The man is against the war and deserves what he gets."

"Anti-war demonstrators in Alabama were jailed," said another man at the table. "Anti-war newspaper offices right here in Raleigh were raided and destroyed. I'm not sure we can release a protester without cause."

"Any protest this man feels is hidden by a cloak of calmness. He is not a troublemaker. And certainly he can help us more at home than doing some menial job in a military camp. I know the army needs men, but men are needed in the civilian sector too. Given a chance to farm, he can bring in a crop of food to feed the hungry. Will you deny that?"

"Where is this man stationed?" asked the general.

"He was sent to Richmond and later to Petersburg."

"Oh, that's a powder keg!"

"He is there to help with fortification. We know sooner or later the Union will hit Petersburg with all the force it can muster."

"It will and soon."

"And you know thousands will die. It will be the final assault to end the war and a blood bath. After that Richmond will yield without a fight."

"By his own account," said the general's adjutant, "the man will not carry a rifle, will not even wear the uniform. In this situation, military justice demands that he fight or die. Prison for such a person is folly."

"He will not fight and he will die. We must not let that happen."

"But why?" demanded the general. "Why is this Quaker's blood more precious than mine or that of any of other Confederate soldier?"

He directed the question with a sardonic smile to everyone in the room, wanting them to think about it, but pointedly expecting Cooper to reply.

As the gentlemen at the table waited for him to answer, the man in white hesitated for a full minute and drew a deep breath. Then with calm dignity, not in the least ruffled by his opponent's abrasive self-importance, he looked the general squarely in the eye and spoke quietly.

"Every soldier has a job to do, General. As you know, it's a job every volunteer chose, though perhaps not the conscripts. Like the volunteers, you have a job to do, one that you chose. If your blood is spilled—and I doubt sincerely that will happen—it factors into your choice. My Quaker friend, on the other hand, has a productive job at home, his choice. Standing up to military force, friendly or otherwise, is not his choice."

The discussion went on for another hour, and most agreed Cooper had skillfully made his point. Although the general and his aide were reluctant to show special treatment of any kind, the civilian authorities understood that David Kingston would be of more value bringing in a food crop than being shot for insubordination. They promised to look into the matter and get back to Cooper as soon as possible. They never did.

Chapter 50

For Matthew in a clean and comfortable bed for the first time in months, morning came faster than a bird in flight. The icy morning was bright and fresh and the eastern sky tinted with gold. Sunlight flooded his room and finally awakened him. Two young women came with hot water and a tub for his bath. One offered to scrub his back and shoulders with a soft brush, but he refused the offer and bathed alone. Clean after many weeks and dressed in fresh clothing laid out for him earlier, he went down for a breakfast that stuck to his ribs for the rest of the day. Scurlock rode with him to the Kingston homestead and turned back as they reached the avenue of oaks. On a fine horse owned by Owen Cooper, Matthew made his way up the lane and into the yard. Rachel must have seen his arrival from inside the house. In great haste she scurried out to meet him, stumbling in her long skirts, overwhelmed by excitement. He jumped from the saddle and ran to embrace her. She was crying but radiant and speaking with unrestrained excitement.

"I know you want to see Catherine and the children," she said in muffled tones, her face against his chest. "This old woman will not stop thee, not for a minute. Go to thy wife and children, my son."

He was torn between staying a few minutes to comfort her and riding on. She urged him to ride away quickly before the children came.

"If Jesse and Anna get to you, they'll keep you here for the rest of the day. Go to your home, Matthew. Your life and your wife await you there. Go home to Catherine. She's been miserable without you."

It was a Saturday morning and the children were in the barn doing their chores. Jesse never forgot his main chore, filing the wood-box. But at times he tried to shirk the others with the same skill as St. Michael trying to dodge his combat with the dragon. On such occasions Anna would chide him and threaten to tell on him, but if it were summer he would mosey off to the fishing hole to catch a trout. That was a lot more fun than cleaning stalls of manure even if he got into trouble later. He hated making the barn tidy with a besom—sweeping was woman's work—but on this day the weather was cold and the barn doors were closed, and both of them worked steadily to stay warm. In the yard Matthew flicked the flank of his horse and rode away without their knowing he had been there. A few minutes later he was in the sandy yard of the Heartwood house.

2

Before dismounting he glanced at the front of the house to refresh his memory and was pleased to see the white lace curtains in the windows. He was about to knock on the heavy oaken door when Catherine flung it open and threw herself into his arms, shrieking. He caught her around her slender waist and lifted her from the floor and kissed her. With his wife in his arms he crossed the threshold and walked inside.

"My love, my love. My love is home again!" she repeated over and over, her heart racing. "My darling husband is home again, here to stay!"

He kissed her again and they drew apart to look at each other.

"My goodness, how pretty you are!" he exclaimed. "Not just pretty, mind you, beautiful! I never forgot how beautiful! Ah, my lovely wife!"

She was smiling and laughing and crying all at once. It was the fullest moment of her life. She couldn't remember another occasion, neither her marriage vows nor childbirth, that had brought to her such joy. Deep within she felt a surging influx of new life. It gladdened her heart and made it sing. Now she drew back and frowned as she looked him over from head to toe.

"Oh, how thin you are! How thin! Didn't they feed my honey husband even once during all that time?"

"I've put on five pounds overnight," he laughed, "eating rich food at the Cooper place. And these new clothes are not an exact fit."

"You are thinner than I remember but clean and rested looking."

"Clean because I had a steaming hot bath this morning! First in a long, long time! Also I slept in a clean and comfortable bed last night."

Then becoming serious he assured her he was in good health and strong despite losing weight. By then Jeremy was on the porch and opening the door. A little girl stood close to him, grasping his leg and peering around it. Matthew hugged his father-in-law probably for the second time in his life. Then he stooped to reach out to the little girl, her pretty eyes wide with wondrous unknowing.

"Emily, Sweetheart, Emily. Your papa's home!" She moved gingerly into his arms and he lifted her high above his head.

Squirming and squealing, she called out "Papa!"

It was the first time Matthew had heard his little daughter speak. Then he remembered the other child, and they went to his crib. Little Ben was lying against a tiny pillow sound asleep, his head and tiny hands peeking from under a pale blue blanket. He wore a frown and then his rosy lips puckered into a fleeting smile. His father was smiling too and laughing inside. Was anything more beautiful than the soft, crooked smile of this sleeping child? Beauty had come again into his world, and for a moment all the ugliness of war faded into the dim mist of a December morning.

Catherine bent down to lift the infant so that his father could hold him and be close to him, but Matthew gently demurred. Once when he was a child himself his mother had said to him, "There is no pet quite so fascinating as a baby." Now after many years of wondering what she meant by that remark, he thought he understood. He wanted to feel the tiny hands of the infant grasping his fingers. He wanted to lift the child high above his head and talk to him and play with him and put him on display and spoil him, but fought against the impulse.

"No, no," he said, "not on my account. Let my son sleep, let Benjamin sleep and grow strong and tall."

"Don't you want to hold him?" Catherine whispered.

"When he wakes up all of you will introduce me to him. Then before you can blink an eyelash, he and I will be plowing the south forty."

From the crib they went into the next room. The tall clock, decorated with evergreen, stood like a patient sentinel, its tick-tock clearly audible but muted by Catherine's thoughts. *Our dream is still alive! Everything we have dreamt of, in spite of the horror, will come to us now. Our dream of life will never be crushed by the reality of life. Dreams have a way of becoming real when people work on them. Are we not proof of that?* Her thoughts swirled upon themselves like confetti in a brisk wind, but one by one they were collected and repeated as songs of thanksgiving. She could not remember a time when she felt so at peace with herself.

Then touching her arm, her husband drew her back to the moment. Together, hand in hand, they walked over to the familiar fireplace. Matthew could see that in the little house very little had changed. The same ornaments sat on the mantelpiece, and the same fire tongs leaned against the wall. In the corner of the room the clock—ticking-tocking, its pendulum swinging back and forth—remained the same, and the furniture was just as he remembered it. On the dining table the blue-rimmed plates lay face down as though locked in time and undisturbed all the weeks and months he was gone. The yellow-pine walls, bare except for a calendar and a fringe of evergreen, had a richer tint. Catherine's seasonal decoration seemed spare this year.

Turning to her husband, as they stood in front of the fire, she looked upward into his face, drew him close to her, kissed him full on the mouth, and spoke in a serious but joyous tone.

"All my worry is now a thing of the past. In my grief and loneliness I never thought it would happen, but you want to know something? My reality at this moment goes beyond my dreams!"

3

In a small community good news travels fast. Before noon on Sunday every person in Blue Anchor knew that Matthew was home. They asked about his health and whether he had been mistreated. The word ran like wildfire that he had survived a major battle without a scratch. They didn't learn of the bravery he had shown on that day and the commendation he had received until Owen Cooper spoke casually of it with Jacob Darboy in the presence of Leo Mack. They were glad to have him home safe and sound. Peter Bookbinder, another Quaker who had refused to pay the exemption tax, had not been so lucky. He was listed as missing in action. No one knew whether he was dead or alive. And Oliver Hatcher? His family had received notice that he was killed in action. When they asked the War Department for more details, they were told he fell off a wagon loaded with soil for an earthwork and was crushed under its wheels. He was performing his duties at the time, and so was listed as killed in action.

As Leo Mack spread the news of Matthew's commendation, he speculated that Bookbinder was also dead and explained why.

"He's just gotta be dead. They didn't hear nothin' from him for a long, long time. I hate to say it, but he just gotta be dead. Soldiers always find a way to write home. Peter Bookbinder didn't, he's dead."

His listeners tended to agree with him. And yet if any of them had thought as Isaac Brandimore often did, they might have said, "You speak in theory, man. Do you have facts supporting your theory?"

Shortly after Matthew came home, just a few days before Christmas, the Quakers decided to hold a special meeting of welcome. The ceremony was cheerful, pleasant, and profoundly sincere. Several young men and women and some of the elders rose one by one, after the customary interval of silence, to express their goodwill and friendship. Invariably the speeches they delivered were spare of language but moving. Matthew sat stone-faced, trying to contain his feelings, and listened to every syllable. He couldn't trust himself to speak but managed to thank them all.

After the meeting some of them went to Rachel Kingston's house for the usual holiday dinner and celebration. The times were hard now, harder than ever, but thanks to Colonel Cooper the table groaned with good things to eat. Matthew made a little speech, something he was unable to do in the heavy emotion of the Meeting House. He thanked all his friends and all his relatives for all the kindness they had shown him during all his life. He thanked his loving God for protecting him in perilous times, and he thanked the man in whose mansion he had spent the night for all the help he had given.

Someone asked him what he planned for the future now that he had walked through the Valley of Death to stand hale and hearty in the sun. He answered calmly but with few words.

"Work and serve."

After a pause he said by way of clarification, "Work to come closer to God. Work for you and my family. Farm and hope the weather cooperates."

Smiling listeners, knowing the caprices of nature, nodded. The merrymaking continued well into the evening. Candles lit up the living room and threw dancing shadows on the ceiling. Oil for the lamps had gone the way of many common necessities and couldn't be bought. Jesse and Anna, on instructions from their mother, had kept a low profile. But now they came to their brother for his attention, and they had much to talk about. Then Matthew remembered the red bandanna Anna had given him so long ago. He pulled it slowly from his pocket, as a magician pulls a rabbit from a hat, and knotted it around her slender neck. She giggled with delight.

"It's yours now, sweetie, and thank you so much."

The beaming little girl skipped away to show off the bandanna and to tell an imaginative story, made up for the moment, of all that her gift had gone through when her brother was a soldier.

From another pocket Matthew brought out a wide, black, leather belt with an oval brass buckle so shiny you could see your face in it. Jesse recognized it immediately as standard-issue military and beamed.

It was the belt issued by the quartermaster in Richmond with boots and socks but no uniform. On the buckle were two bold letters, **CS** in bas-relief. It now belonged to Jesse. He removed the belt he was wearing, the one Matthew had loaned him when he lost his own to a crazy man, and returned it. Wasting no time, he pushed the imposing military belt through his trouser loops and strutted. Though it worried his mother, for to her it was a symbol of violence, it was the best present anyone could have given him.

The celebration was marred somewhat by the absence of one man, a leader in the community who had gone off to war rather than compromise his religious beliefs. Rachel tried not to think of David as she and all her friends honored Matthew, but with persistence the image of the person she loved most in all the world pushed its way into her mind and heart. She had not heard a word from him since he went away more than a month ago. She was certain he had written letters to her, but she had not received them. Owen Cooper had offered to help her learn his whereabouts, but as yet had told her nothing. Even so, as she worried about her husband, the man in the jaunty hat and the white suit was attempting to secure his release from the army and bring him home.

The day after Christmas, as Matthew relaxed at home, Jerome rode over to tell him the horse that came from the Cooper barns now belonged to him. "It's a special Christmas present," the man said. "In the spring, maybe for Easter, the boss gonna send over a mule."

"I really can't accept such a gift," Matthew responded, astonished.

"Well, the boss ain't gonna take no to that," Jerome chuckled. "He's a very stubborn man 'bout things like that. He say keep the horse till you bring in a good crop and can buy one fo' yourself."

During the Christmas season and into the new year the deadly drumbeat of war was almost silent. Though skirmishing was reported in a number of places, no major battles were fought as 1863 came to an end. In Petersburg, in the harrowing discomfort of winter, a tall and quiet man read his Bible and thought of home. His commanding officer, in the relative comfort of an old house that had once been a farmhouse filled with laughing children, was thinking also of home. He had noticed the wooden floor in his office creaked as he moved about in the room. He told himself he would have to screw down the floorboards to make them tighter, but only the ones at home.

Shortly before he left to go into the army, his wife had asked him to do something about a pesky creaking of the floor as one entered their sitting room.

"I'm embarrassed when people come here and step on that spot and jump back in surprise when the floor creaks so loud they think they stepped on the cat's tail. I want you to find some screws, John, and roll up the carpet and tighten the floorboards. Don't do it just for me, dear, but for the house and all of us."

It was a task he could do in half an hour, and he said he would do it just as soon as he could find some screws. In an old toolbox he found a handful and made ready to use them, but it never happened; he went off to war. It would be one of the first things he would do on returning home. His wife would not have to ask him again.

Chapter 51

The third January of the war came in 1864 with icy winds and cold. In the frigid weather, soldiers on both sides huddled around makeshift stoves in canvas "cabins" and suffered from the cold. Despite the weather, some light skirmishing and guerrilla activity went on daily. No important military action had occurred since early November, and none appeared imminent. Armies on both sides, waiting anxiously, knew it was only a matter of time. In Blue Anchor, at the house that seemed empty without him, Rachel Kingston received a letter from her husband. It had been severely subjected to censorship and revealed no information about his present location. Cooper had told her the city of Petersburg had become a last-ditch fortification awaiting attack. David was in the thick of it, as far as could be determined, but with changes taking place one could not be certain.

On the adjoining farm Matthew and his family got through the winter without difficulty. During those months marauding gangs of looters came and went but found little to steal. The family had plenty of wood to keep the little house warm, and they had enough food so as not to go hungry. The tall clock in the corner was now being wound daily by Matthew, who had taken over the task after his marriage but had to give it back to Jeremy when he went off to war. The old clock was noisy at night, in a musical sort of way, when it counted the hours as it tolled the time. At midnight, twelve mellow bongs woke every occupant in the house, even the baby. It was a nuisance but also a comfort.

Catherine brought out the spinning wheel once owned by her mother and was able to spin wool she found in the loft into threads for the loom to make warm clothing. Matthew and Jeremy helped around the house as much as they could, but it seemed Catherine was always busy with more duties than they. She did the cooking and the cleaning and the sewing, and she cared for her two small children with meticulous concern. The men planned to put the acres Jeremy had allowed to go fallow into production as soon as the first days of spring. It was a happy and hopeful time for the family, especially for Catherine. The lines of worry that had settled upon her face to wrinkle her brow and sadden her mouth and lips were now lifted. She was able to laugh and joke, and her skin was becoming radiant once more. Her mirthful wit, inherited from her father, was at play again.

At the Kingston farm there was hope as well, and yet the elegant old house where once the inhabitants and their guests had shook the rafters with gusty laughter was losing its grace. Rachel's son had returned from the war, and for that she was glad, but he now had a home of his own and was seldom in hers. Her stubborn husband, whom she loved beyond measure, was somewhere in a military camp in harm's way. He was too old to be in the army, she kept telling herself, not as strong as in youth. He was fragile and liable to injury and would not heal as in youth. Though he called himself a Southerner, he was foremost a Quaker. That would soon get him into trouble, for neither side in the conflict seemed to have much use for Southern Quakers. Her bittersweet thoughts were quite accurate except for David's being too old. By the time he went off to war in late 1863 hosts of men his age were fighting and dying in combat.

Even though her emotional state was gloomy, her engaging children and grandchildren were sunshine to warm the heart. She saw them as unreservedly delightful even in the bleakest of times. Jesse was irrepressible, incorrigible, irresistible, and funny. Anna had all the qualities of her older brother but in a package made brighter by her gender. Jesse was the warm autumn moon hovering above treetops; Anna was a shining star, hard like a diamond in its brightness and growing brighter every day. The children knew their mother was often sad, and they went out of their way to comfort her. Political events had no power to stir them, even to touch them. The conflict pitting brother against brother and generating unspeakable misery in so many families seemed faraway to them.

Yet on occasion both could be scared by incidents generated by troubled times—Anna by young Timothy Swope and Jesse by the recruiters and the runaway. Rachel believed that Jesse was just too big for his age. His father had told him more than once to spend his time growing bone and muscle. "These will be more useful to you than Latin or Greek or even your sums," he had said, and the boy took him at his word. At the time Rachel was in full agreement with her husband, but now she worried. Jesse was young and innocent, impressionable and too big for his age. She warned him to keep a low profile. The thugs that badgered him once before could return.

2

As for lighthearted Anna, she must never be friendly with strangers. In love with life and as pure as the driven snow, she thought every person was as good as she. Well, not every person, not Timothy Swope and not her brother who often teased her and called her "Miss Know It All."

Well, if she knew it all, she told him once, he knew next to nothing. "You know yesterday and tomorrow and Tuesday but not a day more. You don't even know Sunday!"

Jesse didn't catch the full drift of what she was saying but secretly thought it clever, laughed, and retorted as only he knew how: "Now poke your tongue out when you say that, Miss Know It All!"

Anna had found her vocation looking after Emily and now caring for Ben. When Emily tripped and skinned her knee, Anna was first on the scene to cleanse the wound and put healing herbs on it. Even at ten she must have been dreaming of becoming a doctor, of leaping over any obstacle that stood in her way. It didn't occur to her that because she was female, it would be a gargantuan hurdle to make newspaper headlines. Given the circumstances, Rachel did all she could to encourage her children as they dreamed of the future. She had serious conversations with them. She read to them and listened with a show of interest when they read to her. She tried hard to make her house a haven for her children, pleasant, playful, and happy.

A few miles away the rooms reserved for entertainment in the Cooper mansion were happy and cheerful, for a celebration was taking place. At the beginning of the year the planter had returned from Raleigh with a lovely bride. Now several dignitaries and their wives had come by coach to celebrate his good fortune. They ate together a sumptuous meal made better with vintage wine and punctuated with a vast amount of talk. After dinner the men withdrew to smoke fat cigars and drink amber bourbon in squat little glasses. As the men grew tipsy, the women drank the wine and chatted until servants came in to clear the table. By then all the sherry was gone and several bottles of bourbon stood empty. That was the signal to join company in the drawing room where the guests would continue to chat among themselves while a string quartet from Raleigh teased from cello and violin a soft and willowy chamber music. It was the sweet undulating music, the servants recalled later, that made the place a wonderland.

The colonel had married Lucy Wingate, a dozen years younger and the daughter of Judge Jonathan Wingate, sooner than her friends expected. They had planned a wedding for June but decided not to wait. Their courtship was simmering even before Cooper bought the Bolton spread in Blue Anchor. A lively young woman who taught Latin in the new high school in Raleigh, she visited the plantation once or twice during the summer, and he went to Raleigh many times. Now the community would know why he went so often to the state capital after settling in Blue Anchor. Few would know, however, that each time he made the trip he was also there on business in one identity or another. He was mixing business with pleasure and loving both. For him the Civil War was stupid, brutal, senseless, and unnecessary; but it was also a way to make money and therefore tolerable.

3

While Cooper had found a way to amass wealth in hard times, others operating small businesses were not so fortunate. The general store, owned and run by Jacob Darboy for so many years, was by 1864 almost out of business. He kept the store open only because people liked to gather there to exchange gossip and chat. They wanted to hear about all that was happening in the deadly conflict between North and South, and they wanted news of the latest battle or event. The store had become an informal meeting house for Quakers and non-Quakers alike, and it promoted a sense of brotherhood among the residents of the rural community. A huge potbellied stove sat like a self-important pooh-bah holding court in the middle of the room. Its beckoning warmth drew talkative men from all over the county. At its base was a pile of cobblestones held in place by thick boards nailed to the floor. The small, round stones absorbed heat and helped warm the room. Leo Mack was there almost daily. He was a walking encyclopedia of small information and always drew a crowd when he came in to talk. That was because the outside world had penetrated the customary complacency of Blue Anchor and made it vulnerable. Thereafter the settlement would never be the same.

Josiah Bosh, pompous owner of the village mill, was a regular at the store. He would arrive in a comfortable old phaeton and promptly monopolize the conversation. James Baxendale and Mordecai Wagner wanted to know why the phaeton was never taken by scavengers. Did

Bosh have some kind of special influence to ward them off? The two of them managed on a regular basis to create an uproar with speculative and personal opinions. Dave Cobble came to the store, and so did Peter Starkwether with his guitar. He always sat away from the other men and strummed his instrument softly as they talked. Deeter Haartsook and Elmer Alston liked the give and take they found at the general store and often chuckled when arguments grew heated. Neither had much to say as participants but appeared to listen carefully. Calvin Swope was absent of late. He had gone into the army, had caught a bullet in the spine, and was in a hospital in Richmond. Samuel Bradshaw and Zachary Bookbinder were of a mind to stay away. In mourning for their sons who had fallen in battle—the Bradshaw brothers were dead and Peter Bookbinder was missing—they lacked the stomach for small talk and didn't want to hear another word about the war.

The winter of 1864 saw occasional fighting in several parts of the South but nothing major. People were saying the cold weather had brought the war to a stalemate, but that was wishful thinking. In Charleston Harbor, off Sullivan's Island on February 17, a new-fangled Confederate submarine sank a Union ship. But in the aftermath, before anyone could cheer, the submarine itself sank with its crew of eight on board. To this day why the vessel went to the bottom of the harbor remains a mystery. It was another loss the South could ill afford. On land, as warmer weather crept into view, guerrilla activity increased and was often fierce. Even as the fighting resumed, however, a nation engaged in civil war was tired to the bone and yearning for rest. In the churches of North and South people prayed for the war to end soon.

To the west, in the state of Mississippi, General Sherman was leaving camp to destroy Confederate railroads and wreak havoc upon the enemy in and near Meridian. His troops captured the town on Valentine's Day, rested for a while, and marched eastward. With orders to annihilate everything in their path, they decimated 115 miles of railroad, 61 bridges, and 20 locomotives. Except for sporadic cavalry harassment, they encountered minimal resistance. The movement of the army toward the east was the beginning of the infamous long march to the sea that would take Sherman's men into Georgia to sack and burn all in their path, including Atlanta.

4

Shortly after Valentine's Day in 1864, captive Federal troops began arriving at an unfinished prison camp in Georgia. For several months as many as four hundred men a day were sent there. Officially called Camp Sumter, the prisoners called the place Andersonville and the name stuck. The camp quickly became the harshest prison of the war. Belle Isle where Matthew Kingston had languished was hash and even deadly in winter, but Andersonville was worse. The prison was spread over twenty-seven acres of barren ground with a slow-moving stream running through it. The creek was meant to supply water to most of the camp, but it soon became so contaminated it was little more than an open sewer. A prison wall made of pine logs firmly placed in the ground and standing fifteen to twenty feet high enclosed the camp. Built largely by slave labor as "a stockade for Union enlisted men," it had sentry boxes on the wall—called "pigeon roosts" by the prisoners—at strategic places. Guards were ordered to shoot anyone who crossed the deadline, a wooden railing placed nineteen feet from the outer wall.

Allotted just enough coarse food to remain alive, prisoners were condemned to suffer inclement weather, a foul and pervasive stench, dirt and disease, hunger and slow starvation. No clothing was provided and many prisoners were reduced to rags or nothing at all. The monotony of one miserable day after another took its toll, and many soon fell sick. Some of the men, after only a few days at Andersonville, withdrew into themselves, began to hear celestial voices, and slowly slipped into insanity. Prisoners were housed in makeshift huts, a few shabby tents, trenches made by teams of diggers, and holes in the ground dug by individual occupants. They drank fetid water contaminated by sewage and brown in color. The stench in summer was so unbearable it burned the nostrils and sickened new arrivals.

Designed for 10,000 inmates, by August of 1864 the sultry prison held 32,000 wretched men, making it the fifth largest city in the Confederacy. At its peak the monthly mortality rate from disease, malnutrition, and exposure to the weather reached 3,000. During one day near the end of August a prisoner was said to have died every twelve minutes from dysentery, gangrene, diarrhea, scurvy, or starvation. A soldier from Ohio wrote in his diary: "If I had the tongue of an eloquent statesman, I would describe this hell on earth where it takes seven occupants to make a shadow." Another described the prison as a brutal place that no human being, nor animal, should have to endure. From the beginning the hastily built camp lacked adequate food and shelter as well as effective medical care. Desperate prisoners attempted to dig an escape tunnel under the stockade posts, but their effort ended in failure when several posts collapsed into the tunnel.

The records show 49,485 prisoners endured cruel conditions there during the camp's fourteen-month existence. Of that number, more than 13,500 (28%) perished. Their bodies were buried by other prisoners in shallow mass graves near the camp. A grave patrol went out daily to check on the damage done by nocturnal animals clawing at the dirt. Captain Henry Wirz, a Swiss immigrant who had attended medical schools in Paris and Berlin and was practicing medicine in Louisiana when the war began, was put in command of the prison in March of 1864. He remained there as commandant for more than a year, working against impossible odds to maintain order. Contemporary accounts describe him as domineering and abusive, so hated by the prisoners he was afraid to go among them even with bodyguards.

After the war Henry Wirz was tried, convicted, and executed for crimes against humanity. Innocent of some of the charges, he gained the dubious distinction of becoming the only Confederate soldier to be executed for war crimes. Confederate authorities, who failed to provide the prison with adequate food and other essentials, were as much to blame as Wirz. However, as Owen Cooper often remarked, no official would blame himself if he could find a scapegoat. Captain Wirz was just the right person for that role. A lengthy and highly publicized trial appeased public anger caused by photographs taken of starving prisoners when the camp was liberated in May of 1865. Andersonville was abominable, to be sure, and yet Northern camps such as Johnson's Island in Sandusky Bay were close contenders. In winter fierce winds howled across the waters of Lake Erie, turning the camp into a place of cruelty and misery. Prison camps on both sides were intolerable dumping grounds, grim and cruel, where healthy men were sent to die. Thousands waited for the end in prison and yet the war went on.

With the coming of spring, Lee and Meade were in the throes of planning campaigns and marking time. Richmond in warmer weather was thrown into consternation by an audacious Union cavalry raid. Anyone who could fire a rifle rallied to defend the city—office workers, factory workers, shopkeepers, wounded veterans, boys and old men, and women.

Faced with heavy resistance, the cavalry withdrew in the dark of a rainy night. The raid on Richmond sputtered and died but left horses and men squirming in agony. Later in early spring, General Grant was given the authority to take command of the Armies of the United States. When word of his promotion came, he was in Virginia assessing the Army of the Potomac commanded by General Meade, who seemed to be showing a lack of drive. At the end of February in 1864, skirmishing broke out in Louisiana near a quaint little town called Nackatish by the locals but spelled Natchitoches in the records. The fighting presaged the precipitous and uncertain Red River Campaign. It began on March 10 with ambitious objectives but ended in failure.

At Charleston the Northern batteries fired again on Fort Sumter, inflicting heavy damage. Even though the fort was reduced to little more than a pile of rubble, the garrison stood firm and refused to surrender. In places spread far and wide guerilla activities were picking up. Observers were turning toward Virginia and speculating whether that state would again become the focal point of the struggle. Grant was now the driving force behind Meade's army, but opposing him was the formidable Army of Northern Virginia commanded by Robert E. Lee. Just a few miles to the southeast was Petersburg, preparing to defend itself against a blistering assault that would surely come when the weather grew warmer. That was the bloody thorn that pricked the regiment in which David Kingston found himself.

Chapter 52

The soldiers of the Ninth North Carolina, most of them volunteers, saw themselves as special and were known for their bravery in battle. They were clannish but eventually began to accept David, who was older but came from the same state and seemed like one of them. Moreover, he practiced consistent kindness among the men, talked with them, and made them think. Even the bluntest among them, facing danger and knowing they could die the next day, argued questions involving life, death, and immortality. When on occasion Colonel Gibson verbally sparred with David, they listened with rapt attention. Their initial contempt of the simple but dignified man who called himself a Quaker, the outsider who refused to wear a uniform or carry a gun because of his religion, eventually turned to respect. He was strong and well-built with broad shoulders, and that impressed them. His mental faculties, as displayed in argument, were as sharp as those of their commanding officer. Grounded in the principles of equality, his bearing among officers was that of an officer. When he walked among enlisted soldiers, he was a common soldier equal to them but never above them.

They knew that David Kingston would be placed in the front lines when the first conflict began. The fatal order had not been rescinded and the man would surely die. They knew from experience that his bloated body, turning stiff and purple in the sun, would be pecked by crows. Yet the man whose destiny they often talked about seemed undisturbed by his predicament and was always even of temper. So they listened to David when he spoke, even the drill sergeant and the officer who in anger gave the command. They were hoping to learn the source of his strength and perhaps his reason for being unafraid. Was he really as calm as he seemed?

Again the soldiers found themselves lounging around campfires in the copse after their day was spent. The weather was much improved, almost balmy compared to December. It had rained for several days and the ground where soldiers tramped was muddy. In the grove of trees a thick layer of pine needles carpeted the ground, making it a favorite place to sit down and rest when the day's work was over. As the weather grew warmer, more and more soldiers gravitated to the hospitable atmosphere of the place. The thicket of trees and shrubs shut out the wind, and the sheltered campfires in the quiet April evening gave enough heat and light for comfort.

Colonel Gibson in the midst of other soldiers was sitting on a cushion of pine needles and leaning against a stump. He invited David Kingston to join the group. The tall Quaker sauntered over and sat down facing the colonel. He knew the man wanted to discuss issues on which they would disagree. He expected a vigorous but civil contention, and so he greeted his opponent with a friendly smile. They chatted amicably a few minutes, and then Gibson mentioned the Bible.

"Do you believe in the Bible?" David asked, dropping the Quaker plain language for the benefit of those who were listening.

"In a way I do, some parts of it. I'm not able to call it the inspired word of God by any means, but its moral teaching seems strong enough."

"You believe in the parts that teach morality but not others? Is it not the inspired word of God to be taken literally?"

"No, I can't agree with that. I know the King James version is a work of genius and a work of art, but it's man-made and perhaps not entirely accurate. A Unitarian clergyman in Boston recently called the Bible 'a book of many mistakes.' And why? Because obscure and difficult languages had to be translated and the translators sought to make the work poetic."

"A book of many mistakes," murmured David. "And you are willing to take a book of many mistakes and have it guide you in this life and the next? I'm not sure I would use such a book as a guide even from here to home, and certainly not for my life. As for the authenticity of text, well that becomes a scholarly problem. The rest of us must take the holy word on faith."

"Thoughtful persons find it difficult indeed to take anything on faith. In our time, thinkers readily admit they have lost their faith, particularly scientific thinkers such as Huxley and Darwin."

"Many people in all walks of life claim a loss of faith. It may be a sign of the times. But let me ask you another question. If you believe in parts of the Bible, as you say, do you also believe in a divine Creator?"

"I suppose I can say I believe in God," said Gibson, "though at times I wonder how a loving God can possibly permit the horror of war."

"I have those same thoughts," David replied, "but then I tell myself that mortals must not question the ways of God to man."

"I could never understand that pronouncement. Why not question the ways of God? Would he strike us down with a thunderbolt if we did?"

"I doubt that would happen. Nature and natural law are part of God's domain, of course, but God lives beyond nature. Unlike the pagan god Thor, my God does not use the forces of nature to punish."

"Then why does your God permit hurricanes, floods, and fire—natural disasters that certainly do punish as they bring people loss and pain."

"As I have said, I believe God lives beyond nature and does not interfere with the workings of nature or try to control it."

"Well, maybe not," said the colonel, "but people do wonder about that. It seems to me that religion is part of the personal baggage we carry with us, and my God is manifestly not the same as yours. If I see God as the soul of nature, rather than living above it as you say, I have no trouble believing. I can apprehend God and nature through all my senses. I can smell the flowers and taste the salt of the sea and hear the wind blow. I can feel the cold in winter and these damp pine needles under my rump."

"And so can I," laughed David. "Perhaps we need a bit of levitation."

"Ah, now you're talking about miracles. I don' believe in miracles. If God doesn't interfere with nature, it's logical to suppose he doesn't interfere with our lives to make miracles happen. Are we not a part of nature?"

2

Instantly David knew that Gibson wanted to resume their earlier discussion of miracles, the one interrupted by the coming of night. He was not certain he wanted to move in that direction. In books and magazines and newspapers too much had already been said about miracles. So how to respond? He knew the colonel was waiting. He marshaled his thoughts and spoke.

"Miracles don't just happen, you know. That implies circumstance or happenstance, not cause and effect and not Divine Mind working with direction. Miracles, I believe, are created by a supernatural power with mind and will and purpose. Why do you not believe in miracles?"

"Because they're contrary to nature," came the ready reply. "They defy natural law. What power in all of creation can waken the dead, give sight to the blind, or levitate you and me while the others sit?"

"What power you ask? What do you suppose is the definition of 'miracle' as given in a good dictionary? Anyone have a dictionary? Anyone have a dictionary in his pocket instead of a Bible?"

That lightened the mood, and a wave of laughter rippled through the group. The chaplain, at rest on the ground nearby, pulled a small dictionary from his coat pocket. His doing so caused another flush of laughter.

"Chaplain Orville Westbrook carries a dictionary with him instead of a Bible," a young officer joked. "I'm not sure I want to listen to his sermons any more. And yet I must admit they're couched in the best of words!"

And still more laughter.

Chuckling and with a flourish, the chaplain displayed a Bible to balance the dictionary. In fading light he read the definition slowly.

Miracle (noun). An event that appears to be contrary to known laws of nature. An event or an action termed amazing, extraordinary, unexpected, and marvelous. An event not explicable by scientific law and therefore considered the work of a divine agency.

The soldiers were no longer laughing. Every person heard every word. The chaplain smiled, nodded, and returned the book to his pocket.

"Is that not exactly what I've just said?" asked Colonel Gibson.

Kingston spoke again, quietly, presenting his point in a question.

"You cannot believe in miracles because they are amazing, extraordinary, unexpected, and marvelous?"

Laugher somewhat out of place rose from the group, and Colonel Gibson showing a hint of impatience waited for silence.

"Oh I can believe miracles are extraordinary, but I can't believe they are the work of divine intervention. Must I point out to you that you ignore the first part of the definition, the main part?"

David thought it best to parry the colonel's intuitive question and thrust with solid questions of his own.

"Does any marvelous event require explanation? Do we have to submit an extraordinary event, a double rainbow for instance, to endless scientific analysis because it appears to be more than a dull, gray, ordinary event? Why can't we take the double rainbow as it is and rejoice?"

"You ask a lot of questions, my friend, but you do not answer mine."

"I understand your point of view, Colonel. But do you understand mine? It may be that you and I will never see eye to eye on this. The Jews could see no miracle in the raising of Lazarus and the feeding of the five thousand. Only the faithful could perceive it, only those who believed."

"Oh, I think we may come around," the colonel replied, "but only if the war doesn't end tomorrow! But back to definitions. I may define evil as the absence of good. The dictionary will perhaps define it as whatever is sinful or wicked or wrong in opposition to good and right. Does that mean, because my definition differs, that I believe evil does not exist?"

"Can you say, perhaps, that evil is in the world to help us come closer to God? There's an old canard saying if you add a letter to God you get Good. If you add a letter to Evil you get Devil. So if the devil is in the world, could you not say that God is in the world to oppose his presence?"

"That I wouldn't deny. I suppose it's 'the stern dichotomy of right and wrong' as some evangelist once called it. But let's get back to miracles. Do you have proof that a miracle ever existed? Some churchmen get nervous when the talk comes round to miracles."

The chaplain shifted his weight as he sat on the ground and cast a quizzical glance at his commander. A soldier nearby chuckled.

"Let me ask you this," said David. "Can we define a thing that does not exist, has never existed? The chaplain's dictionary concisely defines miracles as extraordinary events that do exist."

"Ah, but all kinds of things can exist in the imagination."

"Can you imagine something you've never seen, heard, smelled, tasted, or touched? Something never apprehended through the senses?"

"Composers must surely imagine melodies before hearing them. Beethoven composed music after he lost his hearing."

"But they've heard melodies, musical compositions similar to what they imagine, and that inspires them to seek differences. Beethoven is a good example. No art, whatever the form, can be totally original."

"I can imagine a centaur though I've never seen one."

"Again you've seen sketches of that mythical creature, or you've heard it described. And of course it came into being when imagination welded half a human body to a horse, two known things."

The colonel, while not winning the argument, was becoming interested in its substance. He was an educated man, a former schoolteacher. He liked to engage in mental gymnastics with a worthy opponent, but he liked exchanging ideas even better. This Quaker who had come unwilling into his regiment—this calm, quiet, strong-looking man who in a few days could be dead—he now recognized as clever and quick.

"I find that you're given to funambulism," he said with a chuckle, "but you must not invite me there. I'm too old for tightrope walking. Now if you don't mind, let's get back to miracles. If indeed God devised the laws of nature, why would he capriciously suspend them?"

"Do we have proof that any law of nature has ever been suspended?"

"Well, that's my argument. If natural law is suspended we get a miracle, but you contend the laws of nature are seldom if ever suspended."

"Does a bird suspend the law of gravitation when it hovers in mid air or flies upward? I think the bird is working with the law, not against it, and with other natural laws too."

"Ah, but the bird's flight is not a miracle, simple mechanics, physics. Some among us say man was not meant to fly. One day he will."

"And will it not be a miracle?"

"No, of course not. Man will discover the mechanics of flight and fly. Oh, not physically, mind you, but in a contraption of some sort."

"Now that's my point. A tribesman in the wilds of Africa would see a miracle in what we call a mere contraption. What you and I see as ordinary another person will see as extraordinary. For centuries, of course, men have envied the flight of birds as something beyond the ordinary. Modern science limits God's power to the laws displayed in nature and then asserts he violates those laws when he performs a miracle. I believe the execution of a miracle does not violate any law."

"I would like to see a miracle," said a young officer wistfully. "Then one might believe."

"That, of course, is the reasonable or rational response," David asserted as a final thought. "If every generation had to see a miracle to believe in it, then raising the dead and letting the blind see would become so common they would no longer be miracles, now would they?"

Again quiet laughter swept through the group. It stirred a few soldiers to stand and stretch themselves. The hour was getting late. Tomorrow would be a long day, and the colonel rose to return to his quarters. Neither David nor Colonel Gibson had won the debate. All agreed it was a tie.

3

A sergeant gave orders to bank the fires. The chaplain, standing on a stump to be seen, raised his hands and pronounced a benediction over uncovered heads. The soldiers filed out of the copse to return to their tents for the night. Both the colonel and the chaplain shook hands with David Kingston and bade him goodnight. Quietly conversing, the two men climbed the hill and took a path to the officers' quarters.

David lingered a few minutes before returning to his tent. He touched the textured bark of an oak tree not unlike the trees on his land at home. On its north side a gray-green lichen clung to the trunk. He pressed his fingers into the plant and it yielded like rubber to his touch, releasing a mossy scent. He looked upward to view the tree's branches. They were beginning to sprout new leaves and twigs. The earth at the base of the tree was already green. New living blades of grass were pushing up, prodded by an insistent but invisible hand. Spring with its rustling diurnal rhythms was poised once more for a new beginning. It had come again with the miracle and the mystery of new life and new growth. Surging and burgeoning in a world of green, new and vital forms would flourish, run through their cycle from birth to death, and be replaced by new life—another miracle.

Alone he walked slowly up the hill, listening to the night. Somewhere in the distance a nightjar chirred shrill and undulating, its distinctive call rising above the groaning vehicles on the road. That identical song was heard by Caesar when he entered Gaul, was heard by Nero as Rome burned, and now again in turbulent times it cleaved the night air. Yet miracles in nature do not occur? A miracle to be a miracle must contradict nature? The colonel was quick and bright. Why had he not opened those tired, intelligent eyes to see? From a far corner of the camp, dismissing the song of the bird and interrupting David's thoughts, came the strains of an old hymn. Black workmen, slave laborers erecting earthen ramparts and shaping redoubts, were singing in harmony as they worked. Resonant and sweetened by distance, their lyrical music floated like ribbons of sound on the balmy air: *My Lord, what a morning! My Lord, what a morning! My Lord, what a morning! When the stars begin to fall.* With each repetition of *what a morning*, voices blended, rose in harmony and volume, and fell with the last wondrous line like a clatter of dishes on a stone floor. The plaintive, insistent, melancholy rhythm of the old slave song haunted a lonely man of peace who wanted no part of war. David was sick for home.

Chapter 53

The year was 1864 and the war had dragged on since the spring of 1861. When the month of May came to Blue Anchor, just as Matthew Kingston and Jeremy Heartwood began to prepare their fields for planting, a rumor went round that the war was nearing an end. There had been no major fighting in Virginia for a long time, and the Confederacy was running out of resources and the will to fight. It was losing men and supplies at a prodigious rate and suffering a loss of territory daily. Many Southerners appeared to be losing faith in their president, Jefferson Davis. Some were already calling for his resignation. People in Blue Anchor were saying this most uncivil of civil wars just had to end soon. Yet with the coming of spring weather the war effort gained new momentum and went on with vigor. The North was winning but dead tired and disillusioned. The South in its stubbornness had become sacrificial. Surrender was not an option; the troops were determined to fight on to the last man and to the last drop of blood. The conflict in 1864 became ruthless, relentless, and more barbaric than in previous years.

At a formal session of the Confederate Congress in Richmond, President Davis condemned the barbarism of the Union armies. They were plundering the property of private citizens, taking their lives, and destroying their dwellings. The North, he proclaimed, had deliberately planned and implemented a policy of scorched and salted earth as cruel as that of Genghis Khan. Northern troops were sacking and burning places of worship, places of commerce, even entire cities. They were shooting unarmed citizens on sight and inflicting horrible outrages on women and children. Reports were coming to the Congress of gently bred Southern women being humiliated and brutalized, even raped, tortured, and killed. One story depicted Union soldiers stripping babies naked and playing a game of football with them. Another claimed depraved soldiers were tossing infants into the air, as their hysterical mothers watched, and catching them on bayonets.

It was crafted propaganda, of course, with barely a modicum of truth but effective among those who believed it. And yet, as in any war, ugly atrocities did occur to shock the public conscience. The fiery speech by Davis, an official condemnation of the enemy's war-like behavior, was widely publicized in the North as well as the South. Davis thought his speech would give the enemy pause, for the Union had broken all the rules, but it brought no changes. The North was determined to end the savage conflict as soon as possible even when it meant more savagery. The cost in human life and dignity would escalate. The war by 1864 had become a game without rules.

Early in May of that year orders went out from General Grant through General Meade to move the massive Army of the Potomac across the Rapidan River, march around the right flank of Lee's Army of Northern Virginia, and head once more toward Richmond. On May 5 of the fourth year, a gorgeous spring day with wild flowers in bloom and robins wheeling in the pale blue sky, the gruesome work of the Wilderness Campaign got underway. In a wooded area called the Wilderness, about fifty miles north of Richmond, General Lee with fewer than 70,000 soldiers met the first Union attack.

At the end of fighting on May 6, as many as 18,000 Union soldiers lay dead. Before the campaign was over, nearly 60,000 were killed, but despite the heavy losses Grant moved closer to Richmond. At about the same time, in the mud and rain of hostile weather, Sherman began his infamous march to the sea. On that campaign he was always fighting in the rain, sloshing through mud, and building pontoon bridges across rivers. Anything built by his troops was later destroyed. His army laid waste to everything in its path. As Sherman scorched the earth and made headlines in Georgia, the fighting in Virginia became more and more intense. The rumors in Blue Anchor that the war was nearly over were clearly false.

2

Sitting beside one another on the wide verandah, Owen Cooper and Lucy were enjoying the fine June weather at home. They were now in the sixth month of their marriage. The day was gorgeous, and they were looking intently at a ruby-throated hummingbird dipping its beak into flowers nearby. The tiny bird hovered in mid-air, its iridescent wings a transparent blur. As it wheeled backward and flew away, the couple began to banter with witticism and laughter. Cooper was animated as he talked about his plantation and how well the operation was going. Food crops instead of cotton and tobacco had already been planted, and he was expecting a rich harvest in a few months better than the year before. Also he had spoken to a prominent cattleman about turning some of his acreage into grassland for several hundred Herefords. Confederate soldiers and the populace in general were in dire need of red meat. A strapped War Department would find a way to buy good beef. But raising cattle would take time and the war could end soon.

Lucy agreed it could be a profitable business venture, but he would have to keep a close eye on events before investing their money. He laughed and changed the subject, asserting the day was too fine to talk about business or money. Attired in casual summer wear, shirt sleeves and sandals, he relaxed in the wooden swing attached to the ceiling of the porch and spoke of their future. His young wife in a colorful, loose-fitting gingham dress snuggled close beside him and placed his arm around her shoulders. She was pregnant now and was expecting their first child before the end of the year.

Her father and husband were in agreement that when the time came for her to deliver the baby, she would receive the best care available anywhere. The state capital had the most advance medical procedure, and from Blue Anchor she would go to Raleigh for prenatal care and the delivery. Before her labor pains began, she would return to her girlhood bedroom in her father's house on Walnut Street not far from the capitol. The birth would occur in another bedroom specially prepared for the event. A well-known physician, with nurses to help him, would be on hand. Years later Lucy's children would deliver their babies in a well-equipped hospital.

In Blue Anchor, as her pregnancy advanced, her house would be open to Rachel and Catherine and others in the community. She was not a Quaker but hoped to be friends with all the good people of Blue Anchor, especially women of taste who shared her interests. Modest and unassuming but quick of mind, she was already the friend of many people in the community. In fewer than three months she had come to be known as "the colonel's lady." At times the sobriquet pleased her. At other times, asserting her identity as a woman, she thought it patronizing. She regretted giving up her job as a teacher in Raleigh, but was pleased to learn that she could tutor students in the local school as a volunteer.

"Maybelle," her husband called, "would you mind filling our glasses? Lucy would like a little more lemonade, and I could nurse another brandy."

"Of course, Colonel," said the smiling kitchen girl as she came with a pitcher in one hand and a magnum in the other, "too bad we don't have no ice for the lemonade."

"Oh, we'll have ice again," Cooper assured her. "They'll be cutting the blocks on northern lakes in no time and shipping them south in straw-packed cars. Until then cool water from a deep well will do."

Ice was expensive in any season other than winter, and only the affluent could afford it. During the war, especially in the South, it was a luxury not to be had even by the lucky few whose money was secure in foreign banks.

Maybelle, a sprightly black girl of seventeen with clear skin and bright eyes, had been hired by Lucy herself. The girl worked with the chief cook, an older woman named Eileen Norwaite, to prepare wholesome meals for her employer when he was home. She lived with her parents and two brothers in a new cabin on the plantation. All of them worked for Cooper and all were free. Jade Scurlock, Cooper's trusted aide, was her kinsman.

As the couple talked, enjoying the cool summer breeze that swept across the porch, the conversation shifted to other matters and became serious.

"I must go to Raleigh again, perhaps even Richmond, and look into getting David Kingston released from military duty. A dangerous situation is developing at Petersburg. I can't give you details, but something fierce will erupt there any day now. The man should be home."

"Can you really get him home again?" asked Lucy.

She had heard from several reliable sources that her husband wielded unusual influence, but remained incredulous. To her mind he was a manly farmer and businessman with a pleasant Southern drawl and the manners of a gentleman. He was by no means an enigmatic man of mystery with arcane powers, as some were saying. He was schooled in the classics, as was she, and that alone boosted the compatibility they enjoyed. She knew even before marriage that he was complex and difficult at times, but was he really anything more than a prosperous planter? She had posed that same question to her father. He was in his study at the time, relaxing and reading a newspaper by gaslight. He lowered the newspaper to his lap, paused for a moment as he looked at her, and nodded with an unspoken yes. Before she could make reply, he raised the newspaper to obscure his face and went back to his reading. Its black headlines spoke of war.

3

Early on a Monday morning near the middle of June, Cooper and Scurlock rode out from Blue Anchor to conduct business in Raleigh. The weather was pleasant and the road peaceful, but heavy skirmishing was going on in Virginia. The fierce and final campaign to seize and occupy Richmond had begun. With secrecy and efficiency the Army of the Potomac, numbering more than 100,000 men and led by Grant and Meade, was pulling out of positions near Cold Harbor and crossing the James River. As Cooper was trying hard to secure the release of David Kingston and bring him home from Petersburg, the first assault to bring the city to its knees was already underway.

But for a series of mistakes and missed opportunities, the attack might well have succeeded. With better planning and precision the "back door to Richmond," as Petersburg was now being called, could have swung wide open, but that didn't happen. Indecision and bungling on the part of Union forces, and a staunch Southern defense, saved the city and prolonged the war by many months. The Union assaults continued for several days, and then the siege began. Grant had decided that Petersburg could not be taken by force. It would have to be surrounded, "invested" in military jargon. All roads into the city, including the railroads, would have to be blocked.

Colonel Gibson's regiment of 262 men lay in wait for the battle they knew would come soon. The time was only a few days after the conversation that kindled a friendship between the colonel and David Kingston. Gibson was moving among his men, making sure that all troops were in order and ready. His presence alone was enough to boost their morale. A quiet nod of approval as he encountered individual soldiers improved morale even more. He paused to speak to David, already in a protective position but in appearance nonchalant and uncaring.

"Private Kingston," he called, dismounting and coming closer. "As a personal favor to me, will you carry a rifle today? You may not have to use it. Our position is defensive. I can't put a man into battle unarmed."

David stood up, placed a hand on the reins of the colonel's horse, and quietly responded. "Thank you, Colonel Gibson, for the concern you show. But as I've said before, I listen to a different drummer. Nor can I ignore the injunctions of my supreme commander, my shield and buckler."

His face was earnest, his tone sincere.

"May I remind you once again, my stubborn friend," said the colonel with a trace of aggravation, "your faith is not bulletproof!"

"It is all I have, sir. If Divine Providence chooses to protect me today, so be it. If not, so be it. The ways of God to man cannot be questioned."

Astride his stallion again and reining in the horse to ride off, the colonel had the last word. "Did you not speak those same words to me once before? Well, if you and I come through this day's work alive, Private Kingston, I will have another talk with you."

Moments later two rangy soldiers approached David Kingston, each taking one of his arms. "You are to come with us," one of them said, "the captain's orders." They frog-marched the man of peace over rough ground to a company positioned in the vanguard. Three platoons were there as a defensive buffer, but if a charge became necessary his platoon would be the first to plunge into battle. Of the four squads in the platoon, his would be in front and followed by the others. A dozen men would march in close order into a wild volley of bullets, and many more would follow. Other troops, perhaps the entire company, would quickly enter the fray. David, as ordered, would be in front of them all. His sergeant had offered him a wooden facsimile of a long rifle, but not a weapon and nothing resembling a weapon would he carry into battle. He made up his mind to march unarmed should the battle become an assault. His faith in himself and his God would not let him cower in a ditch or run like a rabbit. Moreover, refusing to march, he would be trampled to death or shot as a coward.

Chapter 54

In Raleigh in the well-appointed study of a comfortable home in a favored neighborhood, Owen Cooper was in conversation with his father-in-law. In their hands were finely crafted glasses of vintage wine from the judge's cellar. On the mahogany desk with its surface of hard leather was a tobacco canister, a platter of finger food, and a bowl of fruit. On the shelves of the study were leather-bound law books, and the comfortable stuffed chairs were covered with soft and durable leather. Firelight from the wide fireplace softened the gaslight that lit up the room.

"Is there nothing you can do for Kingston?" Cooper asked. "He's a friend and I want him home again. The man is somewhere near Petersburg in Virginia and the Union forces are assaulting the town even as we speak. Already they hold two of the five railways into the city and several roads. The Confederates have turned back the Union attacks, but I doubt they can hold out for long. I'm told they have as many Quaker guns in the fortification as real cannon. Also I've heard David Kingston was placed in a forward position as punishment for not bearing arms. He could be dead already."

Judge Jonathan Wingate, wearing a silken, ornately embroidered smoking jacket, was puffing thoughtfully on his meerschaum pipe. He knocked the ashes out, put it down gently in it special saucer, and replied.

"About the only thing we can do is have a talk with his commander and maybe get your Quaker friend to a place of safety behind the lines."

"I thought of that, but how do we get through enemy lines? Chances are good the commander would listen, but the logistics at the moment don't seem to be in our favor."

"The campaign against Richmond has already begun and Petersburg must fall before Grant can go to Richmond. If I read my reports rightly, the Union sees this as the final onslaught to end the war. I'm sure confusion is the reigning monarch there, but Grant will stop at nothing."

"My sources tell me the North is strong but suffering a vast number of casualties. Grant and Meade are throwing more than 100,000 men against 60,000 Southerners, but the Confederate line is well established and holding. Advancing Union soldiers are falling like Rebel soldiers fell at Gettysburg. The latest report from our man there singles out one heavy artillery unit from New England. It suffered horrendous losses in one of the assaults, more than 200 fatalities in a unit numbering fewer than 300."

"If the count is accurate," observed the judge. "We can never be certain that such information, gathered in the heat of the moment, is correct. Truth, as the ancient saying goes, is the first fatality of war."

"When I look at these dispatches and read between the lines," Cooper affirmed, "I can see the attempt to take Petersburg by main force will not work. It's a situation similar to the conflict at Gettysburg. The South fought valiantly there and so did the North, but the North on high ground simply waited. The guns chattered, advancing soldiers fell. If my friend seeks protection in a defensive position he may survive."

"We do know that brave men on both sides are fighting at Petersburg. And brave men are dying there too," mused the judge. "Your friend could possibly survive if he hunkers down. If they expose him as punishment, probably not. His name could be on a casualty list by now."

2

Every person in Blue Anchor knew that David Kingston, by refusing to pay the tax, had placed himself in a perilous situation. The Quaker elders worried about his welfare but found themselves powerless to help him. All of them, their wives included, signed a notarized petition with a very official-looking red seal and sent it to Richmond. They waited for a simple acknowledgement that the petition had been received, but heard nothing. It was either lost in the confusion suffocating bureaucratic Richmond, or more likely the petition numbered among hundreds and was ignored. The elders agreed it was futile to send another petition, for it too would be ignored, lost, or tossed in the trash. Hostilities were heating up, Richmond was under threat of imminent invasion, and the day-by-day clerical work was becoming haphazard at best. At the same time, something was happening in Blue Anchor to lift the gloomy mood of the village.

Private Peter Bookbinder, missing in action for many months and thought to be dead, had returned home. As with David and Matthew

Kingston, he had refused to pay the exemption tax and went into the army as a conscientious objector refusing to fight. He was told to obey orders and do the right thing or be shot. The right thing for him was to stand by his beliefs, and so he would not obey the order to shoulder a weapon. It was no surprise when his refusal to do so brought anger and punishment. He suffered severe treatment daily, but somehow managed to survive. At home again, when asked to speak of his experience, he described a meeting with an impatient officer who demanded he wear a Confederate uniform and carry a rifle. The officer sat behind a small desk in a barren room and required Bookbinder to stand as he delivered an ultimatum.

"You will remain silent as I speak, and I will say this only once. If you expect to return home alive, you will obey orders. If you do not, you will be strung up by your thumbs to twist in the wind. If you continue after that to go against the grain, you will be shot into strings. Do I make myself clear? You may speak, Private Bookbinder."

"I will do whatever I'm told to do short of wearing a uniform and firing a weapon. I don't wish to cause trouble for anyone, sir, but I must stand by what I believe, by what my religion teaches."

From that moment he was viewed with high suspicion by officers and men alike. Southern soldiers treated another Southerner as though he were the enemy or worse. Day after day he ate food so coarse it cut the lining of his stomach and injured his health. He was never given enough food, and what he got was seldom nutritious. He lost weight, suffered from lethargy and poor vision, and a loss of strength. His bones ached and even walking was difficult. Yet any time his unit found itself in a skirmish, he was placed forward of all the others. Catherine had asserted her father exaggerated when he said conscientious objectors would be ordered to walk in front of the troops as a shield. Now Peter Bookbinder was saying on more than one occasion he had suffered that indignity and had lived to tell his story.

He went on to inform the Quakers in his village that he began to hope a bullet might end his misery. He was going to die anyway and so why not sooner than later? It did not happen. In a skirmish near the coast he was taken captive by Union soldiers. His body was skeletal by then, but as a prisoner in the ranks of the enemy he ate food that slowly restored his health. While enemy rations were not abundant, they were better than any food the Rebels ate. Contrary to what he had heard, the Federal soldiers did not require him on pain of death to exchange allegiance and fight on their side. He was sent to a Union prison camp for the duration of the war. It was harsh, but he slowly adapted and endured. At length he was told that a group of Quakers visiting the prison were negotiating for the release of all brethren being held there. Because the prison was grossly overcrowded their voice was heard, and they helped him make his way homeward. In the early morning of a balmy June day, he came trudging along the road with only a small rucksack on his back. He was walking toward his father's farm but losing strength and becoming disoriented. Then he saw on the road an old horse pulling an old wagon with an old man sitting stiffly on the spring seat.

Leo Mack, tinker and traveler and purveyor of news, caught up with him and slowly began to pass him. At a glance he could see a thin man in tattered clothing and took him to be a deserter. He had heard deserters were often wild and unpredictable in behavior. So hoping to avoid trouble, the tinker gave the lone pedestrian plenty of room on the road and did not speak as the wagon moved past him. Suddenly to his surprise he heard the tramp call out, "Leo! Leo Mack! Don't you recognize me?"

With some misgiving the tinker stopped his rickety wagon, and the young man climbed onto the seat beside him. Only by looking carefully into the man's face could he recognize a native of his village, but to his chagrin he could not remember his name. It was a sad, lost feeling because he prided himself on recollecting names. Always he called his customers by name. Then slowly like a wave flowing in from the horizon it came to him. Always curious and eager to gather information of any kind, Leo asked Peter Bookbinder many questions but found the man was too tired to talk. In silence he drove his old horse as fast as he dared to Jacob Darboy's store. There as the curious gathered around him, Peter waited for someone to notify his pious father. And there he told his story of courage and endurance.

Before the day was over all the people in the village knew of the family's good fortune. Matthew Kingston rode over to visit Peter and to welcome him home. They had gone through a similar ordeal and had much to talk about, but that would come later. When the weekend came, a younger group of Quakers celebrated Peter's return with a picnic in the yard of the Meeting House. A formal welcome home, with even the children attending, was scheduled for the next Monthly Meeting. Peter had suffered, but now he was home again and ready to live again. The community bravely looked forward to the return of David Kingston, but no one could read the future to be certain whether that would happen.

3

At Petersburg in the front ranks of a defensive formation, David shared the peril with other men placed there as a form of punishment. To his left was Henry Hunt, a flaxen-haired boy not older than fourteen. To his right was Paul Fletcher, a man in his fifties with bulging, bloodshot eyes and a wild, fierce aspect. Both had known trouble adapting to the discipline of army life, but now both were ready to fight with all they could muster. The day was warm and sunny and the pale blue sky flecked with wispy clouds. Blue battalions were on the run, coming wave on wave across the valley. Shimmering waves of blue, their steel glinting, rumbled in the midst of green and gold. Hundreds and hundreds of look-alike men moved with precision and vigor in close-order formation. With colorful flags and banners flying, they were yelling, chanting, and singing as they marched.

A jumble of fiery thoughts crowded Kingston's mind as he viewed the scene. He couldn't believe what his eyes were seeing. It was like some calamitous act of nature: a forest of tall trees lashed and leveled by a tempest, a meadow ablaze with wild flowers plundered by hailstones. One disturbing question after another raced through his head. How could a powerful country abiding by the rule of law come to this? How could a great civilization equip men of the same blood to destroy each other? What could these men possibly be thinking? And what do they feel? Have they been told they will reach the enemy, defeat Johnny Reb in minutes, and sing hymns of triumph? Or were they told honestly that Confederate guns will mow them down like a rusty scythe ripping through ripened grain? Surely they must know they are running at full pace to meet a ghastly death. Do they see themselves as indestructible simply because of their number?

Unbeckoned and racing beyond the questions, the words of the prophet Jeremiah flashed through David's mind. *A wonderful and a horrible thing is committed in the land. The prophets prophesy falsely.* When he applied those words to the deep distress of the entire nation, they seemed indeed prophetic. Surely horrible things were being committed all over the land, particularly in the South, and more so in 1864 than ever before. And did not the prophets fail in their endeavor? He was certain the terrible suffering and waste of human life in a monstrous war could have been prevented. Wise and methodical legislation carried into effect years before Lincoln's inauguration could have made all the difference.

Absorbed in the spectacle of a pastoral setting in the act of becoming a battlefield, and moved by wondrous thoughts that ran unmarshaled through his mind, he was suddenly jerked back into horrendous reality when bullets began to splatter around him. For a moment he hated the earthy, cynical, brutal reality into which he had come willy-nilly without consent. That sentiment quickly yielded to thoughts involving the event. He gazed across the valley and could see nothing but a blue haze of smoke. Then through the smoke he saw with a sense of something catching in his throat a thousand blue coats rampaging up the hill. The stench of gunpowder invaded his nostrils. A roar and rumble assaulted his ears. On either side and all around him his comrades in gray were blasting away, firing their weapons as fast as they could reload and fire again. The ferocious volley, deafening and making his ears ring, failed to check the onward rush of Union soldiers.

The man to the right of him leveled his long rifle, aimed carefully, and fired. Reloading with a broad and toothy grin that relaxed his sweating face, Paul Fletcher cried out triumphantly, "I got one of them dirty bastards! I got him good! Down he went! He's kissing the ground right now!" He went on swearing, as voluble as Matthew was silent, rocking slowly from side to side and grinning seraphically. His vital organs began to throb, his broad body to shake. His toothy smile grew wider and wider and his fierce eyes gleamed. He was clearly feeling the exultation which often accompanies hard fighting.

With thick, spatulate fingers he worked rapidly to reload, sweat streaming down his face and neck. Vigorously chewing his cud of tobacco, he spat a dollop of amber juice on the ground and fired again.

"Let the bastards come!" he cried. "It's hard to kill an old thing like me! If I go down, a hundred of them will go with me!"

Fletcher was in the fight for the fun of it. He was taking pleasure in the contest. The boy on Kingston's left, Henry Hunt, was already down and groaning. Shattered by a volley but refusing to die, he was writhing in pain with a puzzled expression on his smooth young face. Old shadowy fears rose within him, mingling with blank and bleak confusion—fears of the dark, of the unknown, of his father's anger when he had done something wrong, of being eaten by wild beasts. An icy loneliness seized the boy, and he found himself standing apart, watching all he had ever known fade away from him.

"I'm hit?" he asked, his eyes beginning to water. "I'm hit?"

David stooped to comfort the stricken boy, raising his voice to be heard above the din and holding him by the shoulders.

"You'll be all right, son. Hold on! You'll be going home now."

"I'm hit?" the boy asked again, hoping to get an answer. "I'm hit?"

His face was already drained of blood and very white. He had ceased to thrash and writhe on the ground and now lay still. So this was how young warriors died? In whispers shaping questions?

"I don't feel anything at all," he mumbled. "What happened?"

"You're going home," David repeated.

But Henry Hunt did not go home, not to an earthly home. He lay there looking upward, his young blood spurting from his neck and chest, a bird with both wings broken. David looked into the boy's eyes. They were hideous now and rolled back. Only the whites were showing, and the face red with blood. Crimson spittle dribbled from his mouth and nose. He was lying now in a pool of shimmering blood, his unseeing blue eyes blinking. He moaned again and was quiet. Before a medic could reach him, he was dead.

Chapter 55

As the afternoon wore on, Colonel John Gibson rode up to David's defensive position in the vanguard. Alarmed by all the excitement, his mount was wheezing and snorting but under careful control. For an hour the leader of the regiment had been riding among his men to bolster their morale. Now he saw from the corner of his eye a tall figure standing in the midst of the fray with hands clasped behind him. As calm and pensive as a minister in a pulpit, he seemed lost in thought or prayer. Soldiers in gray on either side of him crouched and fired. Others in blue not far from him were falling like blades of grass under an iron wheel. Bewildered by the savagery of men at war, and peering into a cauldron of human slaughter, David Kingston shuddered imperceptibly. Gibson could see him shaking his uncovered head as if to make sense of it all, and he could feel the man was sick with pain.

In an instant the tough colonel became the caring schoolteacher of happier times. Moving in close to be heard above the pounding uproar, and rising a little on his stirrups, he shouted at the top of his lungs a direct order.

"Kingston, go to the rear! You will not stand there to be shot!"

"Oh, but I'm shot!" cried a man nearby. Struck in the face and neck and pitching forward as under a terrible blow, he cried out, "I'm hit! I hurt!" Again David stooped to help a young soldier, but his heart burned hollow at what he saw. Half of the man's face was missing.

"He's gone! You can't help him!" yelled the colonel over the rampant noise. "Go to the rear! It's an order!"

David turned to obey, but suddenly with great force a fierce volley of new fire knocked him off his feet.

The colonel yelled again, "Are you hit? Do you hear me?"

David staggered to his feet and was about to reply. A hail of bullets tore up the turf under his feet. Blinded by the smoke, he could hear the frantic cry of an animal in pain. Colonel Gibson lay motionless on the ground.

"Colonel, are you hit? Do you hear me?"

The horse was galloping away, bolting and foaming at the bit, bridle flying and blood streaming along its side. Again David Kingston stooped to assist a fallen soldier, his commander. The gray uniform, saturated with blood and soiled by dirt, was now the color of rust.

He hoisted the man's body to his broad shoulders and walked slowly along the line through the smoke and noise to the rear. Bullets were splatting all around him. A pang like a bee sting ran up his left leg.

In seconds his leg was numb and he fell almost to the ground. On his feet again, he tasted something bitter dribbling from his mouth. He stumbled onward, stopped at a tent, and released his burden. Slipping to the ground as he did so, he drifted into an Alpine meadow of wild flowers and soothing breezes and children in lederhosen laughing and dancing on the green.

2

Back on the forward line two men loaded their rifles to fire again.

"Hey, Chiggers! I thought you said that man was a coward," observed one of them. His sweating face was covered with dust, and smoke lingered on his neck and shoulders. He was speaking to the rifleman beside him.

"Don't look like it to me!" yelled his comrade.

"Looks to be pretty damn brave to me!" said the other.

"Coward or hero, sinner or saint, what does it matter? He's dead now. But I wish I felt as calm as he looked, stepping over them dead bodies with that bleeding man on his shoulder."

"You said it, Chiggers. Just strolling along like he's taking the air on a summer day, except for the sweat and blood and that burden on his back."

"Looked like the colonel. Was it?"

"I dunno, couldn't tell. Watch it! Here they come! Looky yonder!"

"Wahoo! It's gonna be close! If I don't make it, Wilber, you can have my pipe and tin of tobacco and anything else of my stuff!"

"You'll make it, Chiggers, and so will I. We'll drive them crazy Yanks back to the hell they came from and then some!"

He aimed his rifle, squeezed the trigger, and began to reload. "Death!" he shouted. "Death is coming! Let's give back what we take! If you and me are gonna die in the dirt, so will they!"

"Maybe you got it wrong!" yelled Chiggers. "Maybe it's life that's coming! Twenty minutes of fighting is more life than you can scrape together in fifty years of farming! So live it, man, shoot!"

Wilber never got that pipe and tobacco. They held the line until the few surviving Union soldiers faltered, flinched, and retreated. The attack had failed. Petersburg would not fall into the hands of the Northern army that day, nor the next. Grant's strategy to run roughshod through the rail center and subdue it by force had failed. His plan to move quickly from Petersburg to conquer Richmond and end the war had failed. He would now lay siege to Richmond's back door until Fort Hell, as its denizens were now calling the place, finally surrendered.

As soon as the battle ended the cleanup squads began to sort the dead from the wounded. After the rumble and roar a sudden and sweet stillness drifted across the battlefield. A crow called from a distance, but not a single moan came from any of the bodies on the field. Death with an iron hammer had hit this place hard, and all was silent. The Northern forces in their camp were tending their wounded and counting their losses. When they retreated the sun was hanging in the sky like a huge red ball streaked with blood. It was barely visible through the smoke that lingered over the battlefield, and it soon plunged behind the quiet hills. As the sun sank the damp mists rose and mingled with the rancid smoke. The hush of evening crept over the battlefield, and the still air with no breeze to stir it was thick and heavy. Slowly rising in the remote and empty sky, a blue moon hung faint and pale above the smoke. In the southwest the evening star trembled into view. In both camps exhausted soldiers slumbered.

3

For David Kingston there was no sleep. He lay on a cot in the hospital tent with a lead rifle ball in his left leg. He was dead tired and aching all over. His leg was numb and throbbing but no longer on fire. He might have slept but for the moaning and the screaming of the wounded and dying. In the middle of the night a young soldier stood on his bed, screamed profanely with his last breath, and collapsed. Another seemed lost in a dark pit and was calling for loved ones to come help him, pleading in stifling pain all through the night. Close to him three wounded men sat on a cot and played a game of cards. In that house of death they had lit a lamp and were playing euchre with obvious delight. Their easy chatter blended with cries of agony. David lay there waiting for help, counting the hours. When morning came, doctors removed the bullet from his leg. It was lodged against the bone.

In the half-light of dawn the chaplain walked through the hospital tent to comfort the suffering. He was a capable man but corpulent and looked out of place in this setting. He carried a Bible in one hand and a damp towel in the other, using both to assuage pain. The cool towel went to sweating faces and brows burning with fever. The Bible was for the hand of any soldier who wanted to touch it. He paused at Kingston's cot and looked down at the ashen face frozen in a grimace. The doctors had given David no anesthetic when they operated. All they could do was pour whiskey on the wound, put a piece of hard leather between his teeth, dig out the bullet, and swab away the blood. The searing pain had taken his breath away and lingered on and on. Still in pain, David managed a smile of acknowledgment as Chaplain Westbrook approached and spoke to him.

"Is thy God whom thou servest continually able to deliver thee from the lions?" he asked, adopting the language of Daniel.

In like manner David responded, "My God hath sent his angel providing succor in my time of need. I scorn the teeth of the lions."

After a momentary pause to cope with pain, he added with a wry smile, "But one of those wretched lions pawed me just a little."

"I heard," said the chaplain, showing concern. "You seem to be in great pain right now, and for that I'm sorry. So many died yesterday, so many young men died! No more pain for them."

"Have you seen the colonel since they brought him here?"

"I'm told it was you alone who brought him here. An eyewitness account it was. You will be commended."

"Is he all right? Will he recover?"

"The doctors were with him when I left to look at the dead. I fear he's seriously wounded. That other tent, unlike this one, was solemn and quiet. The bodies lay there on bare boards in peace and comfort. But not one face wore a smile. Not one face. A few attendants were in the tent trying to identify the fallen, gathering personal effects to send home."

Again David asked, "Is the colonel going to recover?"

The chaplain paused, then shook his head. "Not from what the doctors tell me. They give him twenty-four hours. Internal injuries, paralysis."

"I'm sorry to hear that. The pain in my heart dwarfs the pain in my leg. Perhaps the old saying is a just one, *the good die first*."

"Too many of the good died yesterday," Westbrook mumbled. "I grieve for them. I . . ." His voice trailed off into a whisper.

The chaplain moved on in the performance of his duty. He looked exhausted and stricken but went from bed to bed in a twilight of physical fatigue, consoling each soldier as best he could. David saw him bending down to swab the forehead of a man in high fever, offering his Bible to a faltering hand, heard him reciting formulaic kindness in monotones.

4

The next day Kingston's wound seemed to be on the mend. The bullet had been removed before infection could set in, and he believed he had every chance for a full recovery. He wasn't able to walk, not even on crutches, but hoped that within a few days he would be ambulatory. He couldn't wait that long, however, before speaking with the man he tried to save. An attendant went looking for a wheelchair, but since nothing of the kind was available in a primitive field hospital, he brought in a litter. On that, after his pain subsided, David went to the colonel's cot in a separate part of the tent. Because of rank and office, the commander's accommodations were more private and comfortable than in the open tent. His cot appeared wider and was certainly cleaner. The wounded man was lying quietly on his back with eyes wide open but fixed on nothing. The strong attendants lifted David from the stretcher and placed him in a folding chair beside the cot. Unlike his own, it had sheets and a light blanket. At first Gibson seemed not to notice, but then a look of recognition crossed the commander's haggard face.

"Stand up and salute, soldier!" he demanded in a raspy voice, trying to sound fierce. Though paralyzed on one side and not able to smile or even to swallow, the man was trying to make a joke. An intolerable pulse pounded in his head, but he put it down to speak to a friend.

"Oh, come now!" he said with authority when David looked puzzled. "At ease, soldier, don't even try to get up. No ceremony is needed here."

Smiling, Kingston spoke words of encouragement. "The colonel will be up and about in no time at all. A little lead won't keep thee down, my friend, too much work to be done."

"I don't believe I thanked you for toting me off the field yesterday. I think I have a bullet in the spine, can't seem to move."

He really meant the day before yesterday, but it didn't matter. David had carried the limp and bloody body to a tent behind the lines before he himself collapsed and was placed on a cot.

"No thanks are necessary," he answered simply. "It was the least I could do. Is there anything I can do for thee now, my friend? I'm strong and vigorous and full of pepper."

"Well, for one thing, you can drop what you call the plain language. It was never plain to me. I find it just a bit confusing."

"You seem irritable at the moment, Colonel, but it's your right. I guess we both have earned the right to be as irritable as we please."

The laughter was anemic but shared. For half an hour they talked of faith and the role it plays in a man's life. David could sense that Gibson was in critical condition but eager to talk.

"Ah, my friend, have they not told you that I am dying?"

"You will live to be one hundred, Colonel. Pray with me and have faith in all that's good and godly."

"I have faith, my friend, though not in the supernatural element of the Christian religion."

"We will not argue. Pray to become hale and hearty again. Set your mind to it and believe a miracle could happen."

"I know I shall never be hale and hearty again. I'm paralyzed. But to ease your mind I will certainly pray."

"One moment for a silent prayer," said David. "God hears all."

And then the talk turned to home and family. Colonel Gibson was a man who took religion lightly but loved his family. Above all he wanted to go home again to the warmth and peace of home and hearth. He had a lovely wife and two young daughters, and he desperately wanted to see them again. They were in need of their father, he said of his daughters, and in need of guidance. They were delicate and pretty, so young and alive, but not happy with their father away from home. The life coursing through them had always spilled onto him and made him stronger. He wanted to be with them now to see what miracle they could perform.

David chatted with him for an hour until the colonel became very tired. With the help of an aide he withdrew to let the man rest and be alone with his thoughts. He lay there reviewing his life, his face grim and pale and one arm limp at his side. He wanted to live and love and work to a mellow old age but knew he was dying. He had always thought he would die quietly, surrounded by family, and melt into the immense design of things. Now another plan seemed to be unfolding, and he would have to go along with it. The war, the war—he would not die thinking about war. He would think of home. His thoughts of home stirred chords of feeling deep within him, and the pain all but disappeared. Then suddenly a visionary light settled upon the unblinking eyes trained on the canvas ceiling. Quickly the spark of life became a flame and burned brightly for a moment. Closing his eyes but not his mind he slept. He died the next day at forty-seven.

Chapter 56

The death of Colonel John Gibson was a grievous loss to his regiment. Without him his men felt they were wandering through an unknown forest in an alien country. Soldiers under his command knew him to be highly competent and concerned with the peril they faced daily. In a crisis he was cool of head and able to make quick decisions that saved lives. He was a man who did his job in the face of danger, not ignoring the danger but not running from it either. He did not go eagerly into battle, nor did any of them except the foolish, but in the heat of conflict he was fearless. That quality he passed on to his men. In a brief ceremony at the end of June in 1864, they honored their fallen commander and mourned his passing. David Kingston, who had sternly resisted becoming a soldier, had formed through an unusual circumstance a friendship with the colonel. He too was in mourning that day.

Grant's siege of Petersburg had already begun, and the Southern defenders never quite knew what tomorrow would bring. They did know that another assault would come any day, and yet launching those assaults in May had cost the Union dearly. Four days of fighting had brought disastrous results. More than 8,000 Northern soldiers were killed or wounded. In its defensive position, the South suffered casualties too but remained on alert as the siege was put into place. No further attempt was made to take the city by force. The siege went on for nine horrific months, slowly wearing down the defenders but prolonging the war. In the meantime David recovered from his wound and began to walk again but with a limp that was eased by a cane.

One rainy afternoon, leaning on a crutch, he went to see Colonel Gibson's replacement in the rickety farmhouse that served as battalion headquarters. Lieutenant Colonel Robert Winters was older than Gibson had been, but was at present of lesser rank. He had been a minor politician in South Carolina before he joined the Confederate army in 1863. Though in his early 50's and no longer a young man, he told his friends he wanted to serve the South as best he could. They joked that he was trading ballots for bullets. He replied that ballots are sometimes more dangerous than bullets, and so it would not be a fair trade. He hoped to fight with the brave men defending Fort Sumter, but eventually he found himself in Lee's legendary Army of Northern Virginia. After the war he expected to return to his home state and run for a position in the state legislature. He accepted military service as an honor and worked hard at being a good soldier.

In one year, through rapid though necessary promotion, he rose in rank from lieutenant to lieutenant colonel. The loss of so many good officers at Gettysburg and Vicksburg meant swift promotion for an educated man with the skill to lead other men. This man had run for political office and knew how to get things done without offending. Politics had made him a vain man highly conscious of image but with little to be vain about. In his new position he was cultivating a rough and tough exterior, which he believed to be an asset for a military leader. He wanted his men to like him, but earning their respect was of greater importance, and he was working on that. When the man began to talk, David could see that he lacked the nimble intelligence of Colonel Gibson as well as the polish. To fill the shoes of his predecessor he would have to learn as rapidly as he could.

2

He was blunt as he began to speak but seemed honest and open with only an echo of self-importance. As he spoke he rubbed his forefinger across the polished surface of a malachite paper weight and seemed more absorbed in the trinket's color than in what he was saying.

"I'm your new commanding officer," he announced abruptly as David entered. "I've heard of you."

"I hope it's not all bad, sir," David replied smartly, emphasizing the "sir." He leaned heavily on his crutch until instructed to sit down.

For a few minutes Winters studied some papers in front of him. Despite his rank and uniform, David thought he resembled a side-whiskered clerk in an accountant's office. Though his manner was mild, he spoke in a firm tone of voice like a politician on a podium.

"I see that you're a Quaker, a conscientious objector, a pacifist. I see by your record you refused to pay the exemption tax, refused to bear arms when conscripted, and refused to wear a uniform."

"Yes, sir. My religion does not permit me to do violence against my fellow man. I am all that you see there."

"Here's a notation about something recent. You tried to save the life of my predecessor when his horse was shot."

"And when he himself was shot in the shoulder and back and left side and lay motionless on the ground, sir."

David was not a soldier and would never be one, but he had learned quite early that the way to get along with officers was to use the respectful 'sir' whenever possible. However, the interruption appeared to irritate his new commander. It interfered with his stream of thought.

"Yes," he said after a long pause, looking up and over his eyeglasses. "Those were fatal wounds, fatal. Good man, Gibson, good man."

"I agree, sir. Colonel Gibson was a very good man."

He waited for Winters to make his point. He couldn't understand why his new commander had singled him out for this meeting. Surely the man didn't have the time in his present situation to talk with all the private soldiers under his command.

"Oh, yes. I'll explain why I sent for you," Winters said, as if reading David's thoughts. "You are to receive in ceremony a commendation."

He paused to see what effect this announcement would have on the tall Quaker whose wound was only partly healed.

"I don't understand, sir. I'm to be commended for what?"

"Although you were not shouldering a weapon, you behaved with uncommon valor on the battlefield. You showed calm presence of mind in combat. You risked your own life as you tried to save the life of Colonel Gibson. Rank and file soldiers were impressed by your behavior."

"Thank you, sir. I did what any other man would have done."

"Perhaps, I will not disagree. You set a good example for other men to follow. You will be commended in ceremony for gallantry in action. It was service above and beyond the call of duty, and you will be promoted."

All of this was delivered as if rehearsed, as if memorized for a political rally. The colonel stood up to receive David's salute. It signaled the interview was over. David struggled to stand stiffly and saluted. Earlier Gibson had taught him not to offend an officer by not saluting.

Returning to his tent after a summer shower, he found it difficult with a lame leg to avoid the puddles. The water seeped into his shabby boots, but the wet feet didn't matter. He was thinking over what the colonel had said, and then he remembered what the chaplain had said: "I'm told you alone brought him here. You will be commended."

So that's what he meant—a formal, ceremonial commendation. Well, he would not be the only one to receive a medal. Many brave men had struggled through that day and managed to survive. How could he not stand with them to honor them? Though Quaker teachings cautioned against the sin of pride and told him to put it behind him, he was proud to be in the company of such men. He would not disgrace them, nor himself. He would attend the ceremony, accept the commendation, and wear the medal on his Quaker shirt for all to see. It was the least he could do.

3

In July of 1864 General Sherman was moving closer and closer to Atlanta and already planning his march to the sea. Many square miles in Georgia had already been put to the torch, ravaged and plundered by a juggernaut Union army. In Virginia, General Grant's army was pounding Petersburg from trenches surrounding the city. It was tightly under siege. General Lee's weary troops were also in trenches and repelling every assault thrown at them. The regiment in which David Kingston found himself was on daily alert. Because the wounded leg made him semi-ambulatory, he had been assigned a desk job helping with paper work.

Historians had advised the Confederate army, as well as its nemesis, to keep meticulous records. That did not always happen, and yet the Civil War was the first in American history to be so well documented. If an army marches on its stomach, as Napoleon once said, the Confederate and Union armies marched on reams of paper. David wondered, as he shuffled dispatches and read daily records heavy with stiff and murky English, how any correspondence could be important in a war that seemed to have a momentum of its own. Owen Cooper with unrestricted access to sealed documents marked SECRET could have told him.

At the commendation ceremony, which he attended with some embarrassment, David had received a promotion in addition to a medal. It came as a surprise. Vaguely he remembered Colonel Winters had concluded his remarks, that rainy day when they talked in his office, with "you will be promoted." Those last words had not registered at the time. Perhaps because of his age, his mind was becoming less agile. Certainly because of his age, his wound was healing slowly and becoming a nuisance.

He had been told it was only a matter of time before he would be released and sent home, for it was the practice on both sides to discharge men seriously wounded in battle. Then one day he opened an official brown envelope and found a medical discharge inside. Its contents surprised him. Although he had never been a combatant, the document identified him as a wounded soldier with the rank of corporal. It went on to say he had served with distinction, had performed his duties with exemplary competence and dispatch, and was now receiving an honorable discharge. Those appending their signatures to the document thanked him for his service. A smile crept across his face as he read the florid prose of the paper, and then he realized he was no longer in the Southern army. He was free to go home.

A few days later he was told to pack his belongings and be ready to move out when the time seemed right. Everything he owned, including his medal, he packed into a knapsack. That with the clothing on his back and the walking cane that had replaced the crutch were the only material items he would be taking home. His memories of the military experience were in a different category, but they too would go with him. Like the deep and jagged scar on his left leg, they would be a source of pain well into old age. He couldn't deny, however, that the sentence written by that experience was neither dull nor pompous. It ended with an exclamation mark.

The problem confronting him now was how to get home. Though a Southerner, he had never viewed Union soldiers as the enemy likely to kill him on sight. Many Quakers lived in the North, more by number than in the South, and they were obligatory friends. Some of his kinsmen lived there as well. Pembroke and Mifflin, who had visited his house in 1860, had lived in Philadelphia. Nonetheless, an army identified as the enemy stood between him and home. He had to reckon with General Grant's forces on alert in trenches surrounding Petersburg and other forces to the southeast. If he attempted to exit and cross the lines without expert help, most likely he would be shot to ribbons. The Union had put a virtual fence around Petersburg, but the fence had a few holes that men of courage might squeeze through.

David went on working daily, filing papers and filling a ledger with figures that came to him. Then one day in late afternoon he was told he had a visitor in the yard. During all the months he had been on duty with the Confederate army, he had never received a visitor. In fact it was unheard of for a soldier, except for officers of high rank, to receive visitors. With the curiosity of a young man, and with mounting excitement, he went into the yard to see a black man in peak physical condition sauntering toward him. Immediately he recognized Jade Scurlock, who led him away from the building. Mincing no words and spare with comment, Scurlock informed David that his boss, Colonel Owen Cooper, had sent him to show the way.

"You going home now. I will help you get there."

When asked how he had managed to come through enemy lines to reach the fortified camp, Jade mumbled a few words that revealed nothing. When asked what procedure would get them out of the compound and beyond the enemy to safety, again he didn't explain but gave instructions.

"Be ready, Corporal Kingston, to leave this place tomorrow night at ten. Meet me under yonder tree. Wear dark clothes like mine if you got any. Travel light, some walking to do before we ride."

Chapter 57

The date was July 14, 1864. David Kingston, on a lively stallion, was riding up the avenue of live oaks to the sandy yard of his house in Blue Anchor. In France it was Bastille Day. In Mississippi in sweltering weather the Battle of Tupelo was raging with heavy Confederate casualties. In Virginia warfare more severe than a skirmish was occurring at Malvern Hill. In Leesburg thirty-three miles away, Jubal Early and his infantry corps relaxed in safety after their daring raid on Washington. During the fright and confusion of the raid, fearing the enemy might penetrate the environs of the summer White House, Lincoln moved with his staff and family to the traditional White House for greater security. Now on this day he went back to the summer place north of the city. Midsummer was thought to be cooler there.

The weather in Blue Anchor was oppressively hot and humid. The outlying roads in sultry weather were dusty and deserted. In the spacious yard surrounding his house David sprang from his tired horse, forgetting the muscle damage and stiffness of his left leg. It gave way and he fell heavily to the ground, but quickly sprang to his feet and ran with a pronounced limp toward the porch. Jade Scurlock had said the sleek brown stallion, courtesy of Colonel Cooper, now belonged to him. With courage and drive, Scurlock had led the way as they skirted the enemy lines on foot at Petersburg. Then before dawn, with the help of secret agents, they found fresh horses waiting for them and began to ride. When night came, they camped in a thicket of trees and made their way to the railroad the next morning. The path beside the railway was in good order, but the rails at intervals lay in ruins.

Now David was home again and eager to see his family. The broad horse stood silent and still without a tether, nibbling on a tuft of grass. A blue jay squawked in a nearby oak, and a susurrous bumblebee flitted from flower to flower. In the distance a dog was barking. From his position in the yard the house looked weather-worn. The grain on the heavy front door had turned gray and the bronze knocker green with patina. He searched his pockets for the key he had sewn into them so as not to lose it.

For months he had carried that key, and now its smooth fit unlocked the door. Until the war began, the door was left open even when no one was in the house. Later when soldiers and scavengers began to roam across the landscape, that practice was abandoned. He was not surprised to find the door securely locked.

Inside the house he found no wife, no children nor guests, and not even the cook. It was an ordinary day, a Thursday, and he expected the usual activity in and around the house that he had known for years. Jesse and Anna were not in school during summer recess, and so where were they? And Rachel? And Sarah? The servant was now getting on in years and was seldom away from her kitchen, but she too was gone. That puzzled him, for any time the family went away, Sarah stayed behind to look after the place. When they returned their home would be clean and orderly, and they would find inviting food waiting for them. Today, to his surprise, the house he had lived in for many years was locked, empty, and silent.

Well, maybe someone belonging to the house was in the barn. Using his cane with a skill that came of practice, he walked down the path of strewn wood chips, passed the logs from Bupee's cabin (still in use and not yet exhausted), and approached the barn. The sturdy doors with new leather hinges were closed and locked. A healthy mule stamped inside and a few chickens loitered in the barnyard. He stopped at the well for a drink of water. Then he brought his mount to the well and gave the thirsty horse a pail of cool water. He looked around the area as the horse was drinking and was consoled to see that little had changed. Both house and barn needed a coat of paint, a job he should have done before leaving home. But paint was another commodity in short supply and would be for some time.

2

Finding no motive to go back into the house, he locked the door and climbed back into the saddle. Though tired and snorting, the stallion trotted down the live-oak lane to the road. From there David made his way beside the tall hedge to the Heartwood farm. The aroma of honeysuckle hung in the air and a fat rabbit jumped from the underbrush, crossing his path. A nuthatch moved up and down the trunk of a pine tree. The little house in the shade of the sprawling live oak was just as he remembered it.

He rode into the yard and to the porch and called out in the deep quiet, "Anyone home?"

Met only by silence, he called again. No one responded. Though by now his leg was aching and numb, he slipped off the horse, climbed the steps to the porch, and knocked on the familiar door. He waited for his old friend Jeremy to fling it open. The door remained shut. No one was home. All was quiet. The Heartwood farmhouse was also deserted.

As he hobbled down the steps he saw a scrap of paper nailed to a post. He was about to pass it by when a voice within told him to look at it. In the sunlight of a bright day in summer, he read several words printed in bold letters by hand: *Welcome home, my friend! We know you are tired but please ride on to my house. We shall wait for you!—O. Cooper.* He read the brief note again, looking carefully at the words in thick black ink. Though he had never seen a message from Cooper, he knew this came from him. What he didn't know was why. A breeze was coming up, the southeasterly breeze he knew quite well. He shaded his eyes and looked at the sky. It was pale blue and dappled with rows of fleecy clouds, a mackerel sky in the heat of July.

The time was four o'clock in the afternoon. He was weary and hungry and disappointed at finding no one home. His drooping horse needed rest in the shade and fodder. Cooper's estate was miles away to the northeast. He was reluctant to go there but how could he not? His own house was empty and the note, if not urgent, had an air of command. He climbed back into the saddle and rode leisurely in that direction and through the village. A sallow youth in a bowler hat gray with dust—perhaps Timothy Swope, Anna's tormentor of years gone by—put his fingers between his teeth and whistled loudly as the horseman passed. Birds scattered skyward from the trees and whirled in flight. A fat orange and white cat, prowling for mice and tracking a spoor, ran across the road. The stallion, though tired, moved faster.

The countryside was clearly more prosperous than in the past. On either side of the road were golden fields of grain, and the scent of hay was in the air. Farther off were cultivated acres with burgeoning food crops. Even the road itself, famous for its deep ruts and knotty roots that could trip a horse or break a carriage wheel, had seen improvement. He could tell that some type of heavy grader had been used to smooth the ruts and cut the roots. Farther on he passed chestnut oaks with thick green leaves standing motionless in the sunlight against a backdrop of willows.

On either side of the road the ditches were festooned with purple wild flowers.

When he came to a place called Windy Pond, the swimming hole of children in summer and known for its spring-fed water, he went to it and slaked his thirst. Then finding no one near the pond, he shed his clothes and bathed his body in the shallow water near the bank. Propriety would not allow him to go into the company of others dirty and sweaty, and so he was glad to be clean again though without soap. He dug his toes into the sandy bottom and felt them tingle. The cool water soothed and refreshed him. His thoughts were on his children who often came to this same place to frolic in the shallow water just as he was doing now. Each time he dipped his shoulders beneath the cooling water his body urged him to stay longer though his brain advised him to hurry. He found a small towel in a saddle-bag and dried off. Then he sharpened his straight razor on his boots and shaved his jaw without any lather or a mirror. His high-stepping stallion gingerly moved to the water's edge, eyed it with caution, sipped the cool and clear water with guarded satisfaction, pawed the damp ground, and whinnied.

In the saddle again, David rode through country washed with color and alive with beauty. He passed lush meadows and vibrant, undulating hedges dripping with red valerian and dog roses. A fresh breeze laden with the perfume of honeysuckle and clover touched his face. At length he saw in the distance the stately home of his friend. In flat county, the mansion with its tall Doric columns sat on a gently rising hill surrounded by oaks and pines and brightly colored shrubs. It was built of limestone and the façade had grown more beautiful with each passing year. Time in its unhurried way had colored the stone to a golden richness, adding subtle hues of gray and green. In the late afternoon a yellow sky looked down on the house, bathing it with more color. The tiles of the red roof glowed in the sun, and shadows of brown and black wavered under the eaves. Coming closer and viewing this place, David could not be sure what he would find there.

Did Cooper's note mean that a number of people would be waiting? Or would he find just the man himself and his aide? Oh well, someone would be there in that big fancy house, and maybe he would find out where his family had gone. The stallion, on turning up the lane, had slowed from a canter to a trot and was now walking. Slowly David came into the broad expanse of lawn and yard and saw a gathering of people standing on the wide verandah. His leg and buttocks were aching now and he longed for rest, but seeing good friends ready to welcome him home renewed and refreshed him. "We know you are tired," Cooper's note had read, and yet at that moment his fatigue fell away like an unwanted garment.

3

Owen Cooper had received a message from the same agents who had used their skill to help Jade Scurlock penetrate the siege of Petersburg and get David into North Carolina. He knew exactly when David would be riding home, and so he planned with his gracious wife a reception such as Blue Anchor had never seen. All the people in the village had been invite to attend the event, and most of them had accepted. That explained why even Sarah was absent from her kitchen at the Kingston house and why David passed only the lone boy on the road. He was a bit reluctant to receive so much attention from so many people but was in no position to object. Such a huge gathering in a such an elegant home was foreign to Quaker tradition and to his own personal taste. And yet, when he thought about it, this mansion once owned by Thomas Bolton and now restored to its original opulence, was larger and more spacious and certainly more comfortable than the Meeting House where most events were held.

Attendants led the horse away and Jade Scurlock, with a chuckle and sly wink, ushered David to the verandah. Before he could ascend the steps, his left hand firmly grasping the carved head of his walking stick, a beautiful woman in a flowing gray gown came flying toward him. With arms outstretched she flung herself into his arms, her supple body slamming against his own and almost knocking him down. She buried her face in his shoulder and hugged him with desperate intensity, her beauty and rapture overwhelming his senses. He could feel her breath on his cheek and her beating heart against his chest. Long pent up, her fervor was racing now even to her fingertips. He could smell a sweetness in her hair and hear her sobbing and laughing at the same time. Her heart was singing when he touched her lemon and cherry lips with a warm though fleeting kiss. Returning her embrace, he mumbled soft, hesitant, clumsy words to calm and comfort her. She laughed and wiped her eyes and drew back to look at him.

"Oh, my! How thin you are! And you look so tired! That outfit you're wearing will have to be burned! It hangs on thee like rags on a scarecrow!

And when was the last time you shaved? Oh, your cheeks are red and your face sunburnt!" He wanted to tell her he had shaved in a crude sort of way at the swimming hole and finally got a word in edgewise.

"Windy Pond? Ah, the children were there only a few days ago!"

Her words flowed fast from a full heart. She was no longer thinking. It was all feeling now and miraculous. "Well you did get sort of clean there, but oh my! You're not at all the handsome returning hero I had imagined!" The parched emotional desert she had endured longer than she ever thought possible was being turned into a green, vibrant, flowering oasis. Cool water, even cooler than the spring-fed pond, was quenching her thirst and soothing her body and spirit. The deepest recesses of her hidden heart, once gloomy and dark, were now brilliant with sunshine.

The two were clinging to each other and talking at the same time, and even as excitement and joy flooded his senses David could feel his left leg burning with pain. Rachel had always walked on his right side as they strolled together, but now she walked on his left to support him just a little as they made their way slowly across the yard. Then pausing for a moment, they forgot their commitment to Quaker doctrine and kissed each other long and hard with passion and without shame. A number of people watching from the porch delivered in unison a roar of approval. Embarrassed but looking stronger than ever in her life, Rachel walked with her husband along an even flagstone path to the wide verandah. Friends and family were standing there waiting to greet him. In a moment he was lost in the crowd, a noisy number wishing him well, but somehow he held onto Rachel who led him forward to the wide, double-door entrance and into the house.

Chapter 58

They went into the living room, the parlor as they called it, and there with the tall and open casement windows behind him David sat in a large overstuffed chair on an intricate Persian rug surrounded by a shining hardwood floor. There like a monarch of old he received his friends. It was not the custom among Quakers for children to go first, but Jesse and Anna couldn't wait. Whooping with laughter and the abundant energy of children, they bounded to their father holding little gifts for him. Shyly Jesse shook his hand, then hugged him. Anna sprang into his lap and hugged his face and neck, crying "Papa! Papa!" Matthew came to honor his father with a handshake and a cursory hug and welcomed him home. Catherine with her wide-eyed children came next and kissed him on both cheeks, her children clutching her skirts. Then Jeremy Heartwood, his old friend of many years, joked with him and shook his hand vigorously.

As David looked around to receive the next person someone called out, "Where's Sarah? Where is Sarah?"

They found her in the back of the room and brought her forward.

"Welcome home, Corporal Kingston," she said with a sly and toothsome grin. "We glad to have you back."

"Thank you, Sarah, thank you very much. Are you well? Is your life all right? I looked for you in your kitchen at home."

"Yessuh," she replied, shyly moving away into the crowd, "I jus' fine, and thank you for askin'. I done left my kitchen to be with the folks here."

Then it dawned on him that she had called him corporal.

"How did you know that?" he called to her over the laughter and chatter. She did not reply. Later he learned that everyone in the village knew about his daring exploit at Petersburg. Dispatches with all the details had reached Owen Cooper who gave them to Leo Mack to broadcast. The man went from house to house in his creaky old wagon, hoping to mend a pot or pan, but expecting also to deliver news his customers had not heard.

He was a fixture in the community, not really loved by anyone but cherished as a man of strong personality and a will to live. Generally he was taken for granted by the villagers but would have been sorely missed had he gone elsewhere to live. With a wide grin that showed his bad teeth and his one gold tooth, he stood in line to shake hands with David and wish him well. He found it hard to resist offering a bit of down-home advice.

"Now that you're out of the war and back home," he said, "don't poke no sleeping dogs and don't stir no mud."

David knew all about the dogs but was not certain he understood the meaning of mud. Before he could ask, Mack had moved on and another person was in his place. All of them came, familiar faces smiling and happy and glad to have him home again. Owen Cooper with his new wife Lucy welcomed his friend home with a fine choice of words. Just about everybody in Blue Anchor, Quaker and non-Quaker alike, had come to the mansion. Only Timothy Swope seemed to be absent and his father Calvin, wounded in battle. David's leg was throbbing with persistent pain, but he ignored it and forgot the injury and became whole again. An easterly breeze cooled his back.

He had tried hard to put down the feeling of pride when commended at Petersburg in the company of stalwart comrades. Now that same feeling was upon him with a vengeance, insistent and overwhelming.

Someone called out, "Speech, Corporal Kingston! Speech!" But all he could say was this: "Thank you, my friends, thank you for welcoming me home. Thank you for caring. Never expect me to leave you again."

Though surprised at the response, he was genuinely pleased when all his friends clapped and cheered. He was intensely proud to be associated with these people and their community, and their lives and work, and he would not deny it. Though burning with immoderate pride, foremost of the seven deadly sins, he knew his God would forgive him.

In the dining room he sat down to eat a special meal. The others too had moved into the room with its gleaming mahogany table under the crystal chandelier, but their food was different. David was hungrily eating a juicy steak and hoping God would forgive his gluttony. He ate the huge steak in the company of Rachel, Catherine, Jeremy, and Matthew, and he savored the rare treat as they chatted over a dinner of roast pork and wild game. Eileen Norwaite, well known for her culinary magic, had broiled the tender steak to perfection and had placed on another platter a buttered roll, a baked potato, green beans, sliced tomatoes, fried okra, and a helping of sweet corn. From a tall glass David drank a sparkling punch made of fresh strawberries. In a crystal dish he found his favorite dessert, ambrosia. He wondered where Cooper in hard times could have found oranges and coconuts for the dessert and a succulent, premium-cut steak for him alone. It did not occur to him to ask. He knew that Owen Cooper was a capable man.

2

Through the summer and to the end of the year, life went on as usual in Blue Anchor. Even as the war dragged on and on—even as Sherman sacked Atlanta and began his infamous march to the sea—the villagers lived their lives in rural tranquility. When summer grew old and yielded to fall, they worked to bring in copious harvests untrampled as in the past by the boots of soldiers. No one in Blue Anchor would go hungry during the winter. Their daily round of activity was increasingly affected by the war, but they went on living as people have always done in desperate times. Brandimore was no longer among them to offer sage advice, but regarding the war and the suffering it brought he would have said for all to hear, "This too shall pass."

It did indeed. The Battle of Appomattox Court House was fought on the morning of April 9, 1865. It was the final engagement of General Robert E. Lee before he surrendered to General Ulysses S. Grant. When he realized his army was greatly outnumbered and in danger of annihilation, Lee had no choice but to surrender. The signing of the official documents took place that afternoon in the parlor of a sturdy brick house owned by Wilmer McLean. General Grant had sent a message to Lee, saying he could choose the place of surrender. An aide to General Lee rejected the first suitable house as too dilapidated and settled on the McLean residence built in 1848.

McLean and his family had lived near Manassas Junction during the First Battle of Bull Run. Afterwards, they left that location and retired to Appomattox to escape the war. As destiny would have it, the war marched in their direction once again. Lee arrived at the McLean house in a gray uniform described as crisp and immaculate. Grant came later in a mud-spattered blue uniform and muddy boots. It was the first time the two men had seen each other face to face in almost two decades. Briefly they embraced as old friends, and leisurely they talked of the times when they had fought together.

In Blue Anchor, as hostilities were winding down, Catherine Kingston's children grew strong of limb and bright of mind. Quickly she became pregnant again to fulfill her dream of many children. Matthew would rejoice in daughters as well as sons, and his wife in her new house would grow in beauty year by year. Her radiance never faded into nothingness even when she had become very old. The same was true of Rachel Kingston. In the bosom of her family again, she looked younger than ever and remained a leader in the community. Happy now and knowing their worth, both women jogged along with caution as the years came and went.

3

Until the summer of 1865 the war would grind on and young men would die and Lincoln himself would suffer a violent death. The combat officially ended in the spring, but some isolated units went on fighting until mid-summer. Not until the surrender at Appomattox did Petersburg surrender. Not until then did Southerners come to grips with their emotional and economic devastation. After four long years the horrible thing committed in the land had run its ugly course. Reconstruction and restoration would soon begin. All segments of the population, including those who went against the grain and suffered retaliation, could now get on with their lives.

Until the end of their lives Colonel Cooper and Corporal Kingston were good friends. When breezes came in from the southeast and the Great Dismal Swamp smelled of moss and stagnant water but stirred with new life in the warmth of a sunny April morning, they explored the swamp in a skiff. Breathing deeply the musty spring air, they were glad to be alive. Owen Cooper remained the man of mystery even after the war, often leaving home on business and not returning for as long as a week. He walked with a cane, as did his friend, but somehow escaped growing old. In his eighties he was tall and slender and handsome, alert and quick in movement, and rugged enough to disturb the ladies. His loving wife in the early years left the village only long enough to have her babies in Raleigh.

One of several children was a bonny little girl who began to talk early and never stopped. They named her Deborah to honor their Quaker friends who admired the biblical Deborah for her sense and wisdom. Because the name seemed a bit too formal for an active child who loved the outdoors, they called her Debbie all the time she was growing up. Only Rachel Kingston, given to formal language, called her Deborah. She attended Duke University, where she met a young law student who later became her husband. In time he was elected Governor of North Carolina. And then, at the apex of his career, he served as a senator in Washington. Deborah wrote a series of children's books, and each one she read to her children even while finding time to campaign for her husband and support his career.

Jeremy Heartwood cultivated his garden to a ripe old age and gathered his own firewood in the swamp. After the Kingston family burned all the logs of Bupee's cabin and after the railroad came to Blue Anchor, he hauled in pitchy railroad ties left behind by the workers. They burned even better than the logs. Beloved by all the village children, he could often be seen spoiling them with treats at Darboy's General Store and telling them exciting yarns. "This king," he began, "wore a golden suit and wanted to ride an elephant over the mountains . . ."

A fat boy with mischief in his eyes called out, "Mr. Heartwood, Mr. Heartwood! It's the same old story you told us last Thursday!" He nodded in agreement, for the little rogue was right.

In his old chestnut suit, very durable but showing signs of wear, he sat before the fire and spoke in measured syllables of a good life well spent. For an hour or so before bedtime, his suit hanging behind a door and his long johns keeping him warm, he sat in front of the fire to study the flames in the grate. His blue-gray eyes twinkled in the firelight as the loyal old clock ticked in the corner. The lessons he learned from the dancing flames he passed on to his grandchildren.